MATHEMATICS OF ETERNITY

David M. Kelly

Mathematics of Eternity

ISBN-13: 978-0-9953294-1-6

ISBN-10: 0-9953294-1-9

First Published 2017

Nemesis Press

Wahnapitae, Ontario

www.nemesispress.com

Printed in U.S.A

Dedication

*In memory of my father, and for "average Joes" every-
where—the true heroes of the world.*

One

"Negotiations between the assembled Earth nations and Atoll representatives broke down today, with no relaxation of the restrictions on Earth-based extra-orbital operations. General Chadwick, from the combined Atoll security forces, stated there would be a vigorous response to any attempt by Earth to increase operations outside Low Earth Orbit, other than the Mars mining operation. He also said that this boycott included the starship—"

I stabbed the off-button hard enough to make the plastic click sound like a gun had gone off inside the car. The news shouldn't have bothered me, but it did. The fact that I used to work in space was part of it—the fact that I couldn't any longer was another. But mostly it was because the Atolls were right—we didn't deserve another chance.

I pulled up outside *The Kase* waiting for the traffic lights to change. The rain on the windshield distorted the garish neon and holo-projections from the bar into painful tracks that burned ghostly afterimages on my retina. I rubbed my face to ease the ache in my eyes, a two-day growth of beard rasping against my palms. *Time to polish yourself up a bit, Ballen, otherwise someone's going to think you stole this cab.* It had been *that* kind of night. The only thing keeping me going was the thought that my tour was over for another twelve hours.

The cab bucked and I grabbed the shuddering controls, wrestling the car into a level attitude. The door hissed open as someone slid in the back. The turbines whined as the stability systems fought to compensate for the shift in weight distribution and for a second I thought we were going to plummet to the ground.

I cursed loudly, my fingers only slowly releasing the death grip I had on the controls as the motions steadied, not caring if my new passenger heard. The old adage was true—there really is always one.

"You better watch yourself, chief." My cab had been almost a meter away from the Jump-Off platform—a potential disaster when you're sixty meters up at L4. "That's not a choice likely to take you to retirement."

All I could see in the mirror was a dark shadow filling the entire back seat. "I'm off duty. You'll have to call someone else."

"Two-Seven-Three Fairland Road, Ell-One. Rossmoor." The voice had a liquid rasp that didn't sound like it came from drink alone. More like the death rattle from a set of lungs drowning in a sea of flesh.

Maybe he hadn't heard. I sure didn't want a forty-kilometer detour on my own clock. "The light's out, chief—I'm off-duty. Give me a break and get out."

I nudged against the Jump-Off and re-opened the door. He didn't move, and I turned round to get my first proper look at him. Purple and red bar lights reflected on his waxy skin, and he must have weighed well over a hundred-eighty kilos. A sweat-drenched green jacket molded itself to both his torso and the seat, making his face look sickly. I couldn't remember ever seeing anyone so overweight, outside historicals. Everything about him was bloated. From the head that flowed directly into his shoulders without the benefit of an intervening neck, to the corpulent fingers gripping the worn parahyde seat as if he were scared he'd fall off the world. It was no wonder the car had struggled—he was a one-man weight-restriction violation.

Sometimes when the circuits fail, all you can do is accept it and reroute. There wasn't a chance I'd be able to get him out single-handed. It would be easier to take him where he wanted to go and hope he was sober enough to get out under his own steam.

I shrugged and hit the meter. The lights had long since gone green, so I eased the throttle forward to minimize any motion sickness. The last thing I needed was the alcoholic excess in his gut emptying in the back of the cab. Then, as if I needed anything else to make my night miserable, an asshole in a Saber cut me up from below. His streamlined tail almost clipping the front of the cab as I wrestled to keep things together in the turbulent wash from the arrest-me red sports car.

I shook my head. "Life's too short," I muttered.

"Your statement carries a paradoxical veracity that forms a Universal comedy."

I hadn't meant to be overheard and didn't generally start conversations with drunks. His quirky mannerisms singled him out from the usual fare, though. It's true you see pretty much every aspect of life while driving a cab, and after two years I'd seen them all. But I'd never had anyone using phrases like *paradoxical veracity*—not even sober.

"It was a rather discourteous maneuver. You should tag him."

My jaw tightened. Decades ago, the Saber driver would have been handled by the national sport known as "drive-by shooting." Now, with the promotion of civic thinking, we had the more humane, if less immediate, option of tagging anti-social behavior. The all-seeing Argus brain reviewed each tag and, if judged guilty, the appropriate points were added to your citizenship record. Amass enough, and you faced fines, community service, or "attitudinal re-adjustment" in severe cases. An electronic voxpop bringing peace and tranquility to the teeming streets and suburbs of the United States and Provinces.

I should have tagged the guy, but I'd never really bought into the idea. My previous life had left me used to the rough and tumble of a more anarchic environment, where you relied on personal relationships and dealt with problems by rolling up your sleeves and getting stuck in when needed. Marking someone with a coded low-energy laser felt a little unsatisfying, not to mention cowardly.

"I guess I'm not quick enough," I said. "No harm done."

My passenger's deep-set eyes seemed to darken in the RearView. "You have a good heart, sir. Most people find it easy to use that particular reflex."

"You've definitely had too much to drink." His manner and old-fashioned speech piqued my curiosity enough for me to break my own rule and attempt a conversation. "A good night, chief?"

"Good night?" He hesitated. "In the bar?"

"Sure. You were in *The Kase*, right?"

"Was that its name? I didn't really take much notice." He looked out of the window as the city lights from the buildings slipped past us. "I don't get out much."

His size made that seem likely. "You must have had a good few drinks if you don't know where you were. Was it a celebration?"

"Oh, I wasn't drinking. I've been in so many bars tonight I don't remember them all."

I was getting annoyed now. Not with my passenger, but with myself. I'd broken my no-engagement rule, and now it turned out he was simply another drunk who couldn't remember how much he'd had, or where he'd been. Besides, I should have been home. "What were you doing then? Those places only have one purpose."

"I bought a lot of people drinks. They seemed to enjoy it."

"That's pretty generous. You must be one of those eccentric millionaires I see in the trashy Solidos."

"Millionaire?" He seemed genuinely surprised and coughed wetly. "No, I'm not especially wealthy. Money doesn't matter anymore."

"It does to some of us, chief."

I followed Broadway south, passing over the bloated wetlands that stretched across the old Inner Harbor and Federal Hill. The once grand buildings footed several meters in the water lapping around their crumbling lower levels. Many were flood-thrus, but I could see faint glimmers of light creeping out of the grimy windows. Wet-foot didn't care where they lived. All they wanted was a roof over their heads. Danger and disease didn't deter them in the slightest.

"They should put those people in proper buildings." The liquid voice rolled out of the darkness of the back seat. He must have followed my gaze and guessed what I was thinking.

The Big Shake and rising sea levels had driven people inland, away from the encroaching ocean. Waterfront property no longer commanded a premium—it was a danger to be avoided. As a result, even the most precarious of condemned buildings held groups of otherwise homeless residents. Not all of them lived there illegally—as long as you stretched the definition of legal. City health ordinances were often "overlooked," and upper-level apartments in buildings that should have been torn down, or concrete-filled as sea defenses, were frequently rented out. Sometimes at ridiculous prices, but when you've lost everything, even crap is better than nothing.

We swept over the distended extremes of the Patapsco, pushing west until we hit Silver Lake, then I settled the car into Airway Six which followed the path of the old Highway One, heading southwest. I kept the car within the 100/100 'City' zoning limits as we followed the track of the highway, the ribbon of crumbling pavement lined with equally crumbling buildings that looked like splintered teeth pushing out of a jawbone of some huge leviathan.

"Housing isn't the problem," I said. "There are subdivisions past the old Beltway virtually empty, thousands of homes—but those people can't afford even subsidized rent."

"That can't be."

My passenger sounded shocked, and I wondered where he'd been hiding. The FabHome scandal had left swathes of houses built with taxpayers' money lying empty and slowly falling apart, while city officials enjoyed generous business trips. It was an old story even back when Ramses was building pyramids, but fresh enough to fill the news for the last three months. Human altruism at its finest.

We finally escaped the limiters past Larch, and I lifted the nose, bringing the cab up to 500 meters while boosting to 200 klicks. The landscape was flat, and outside the managed traffic zone I was free to use my own discretion, as long as I didn't break the general free flight regs for an AeroMobile. Of course, the cab could have managed all this on its own, but since the ICab debacle, a human driver was mandatory.

"They should let those poor unfortunates have those houses for free. Are people really that selfish and greedy?"

"Free? That's a four-letter word with a lot of people." The Pilot beeped several times, warning me of our imminent arrival. I

9

throttled back and did a slow drift, spiraling around the U-shaped apartment building as I brought the car down outside the main entranceway at L1—ground level. "Talking of which, we're here, and you owe an even fifty-five."

He didn't answer, so I turned to encourage his exit. I could hear his breathing, the wheezy inhalation of air followed by an almost spluttering exhalation. For a moment, I thought he'd fallen asleep and cursed, wondering how the hell I'd get him out. Then I noticed tears rolling down his fat cheeks.

"There's a girl."

"There usually is…" Something in his tone made me think he wasn't using the word *girl* euphemistically. "Maybe you should keep that to yourself though."

He leaned forward, and I tasted his fetid breath as it filtered through the screen. "Take care of her."

"Sure… don't worry, chief, I'll take care of it." All I wanted was to get him out of the cab so I could go home. "Now go sleep it off. Everything will look better in the morning."

"Sleep? Yes. 'What dreams may come?'" His voice sounded tiny and afraid—like something was eating him up inside. "I don't want to be alone."

"No one does. Call your girl tomorrow and apologize. It'll be fine." It was time to draw this melodrama to a close. "Look, chief, I've got a wife and kids waiting. If I don't get home soon, I'll be alone too." It was a lie, but claiming a family usually helped with drunks.

He dragged his credit chip out from a pocket and tapped it against the payment scanner. A couple of seconds later it let out a doleful beep, and the screen flashed with a red declined warning. The doors locked automatically, and the plastic security window between me and the passenger compartment shuttered tight.

"I have no money left?" His tear-streaked face swam close to the transparent barrier. "I must have spent it in the bars. I'm so terribly sorry."

It was more likely the bank had stopped his credit chip if he'd been as generous as he claimed, but my patience was exhausted. I got out and manually unfolded the back door, opening it wide. "Come on, chief. Forget the money and get out."

"I'm sorry for causing trouble, I really am." He shuffled part way through the door. The car dipped alarmingly on its landing gear, and I was glad I was dropping him off at ground level. "I have some cash in my apartment. I'll get it and return immediately."

"I may look stupid, but I'm not. I *am* tired though." I sighed. "Get out of here before I change my mind. I won't even watch what direction you go."

He struggled out, barely making it even with the door opened fully and again I wondered how he'd managed to get in at the lights. Maybe he was an acrobat under those layers of flab, but it seemed unlikely.

"Please, don't be angry." His eyes shone like two titanium bearings freshly bathed in oil. "I *will* bring you some money, I promise. This won't take very long."

My boss is pretty tight when it comes to non-payers, but I really didn't care. All I wanted was a hot shower and a cold beer—not necessarily in that order—but if agreeing would get him out of my hair then I'd play along. "Okay, you get some cash. I'll wait five minutes and if you choose not to come back, don't worry. I won't be disappointed."

He nodded profusely, tears running down his face as he waddled towards the arched entrance. I was surprised when the entry system recognized him and allowed him into the protected interior. I leaned against the car, wondering whether to cut my losses or give the guy the benefit.

The condo had that bare functionality mixed with quality workmanship typical of late-twentieth architecture, all sharp lines and black quartz walls mixed with a pinstripe steel exoskeleton. It was probably part of the growth of *designed communities* that enjoyed a brief popularity before their eco-conscious designers gave up and went back to making money. It wasn't the kind of place I'd associate with drunken non-payers, but that didn't mean anything. His claim to have real cash was intriguing. I hadn't seen any in years and wondered if I'd still recognize it.

A light flickered several floors up, outlining a pagoda style section forming the top floor corner of the *U*, and I saw an unmistakable shadow totter past thinly screened windows. A penthouse then—maybe he was genuine.

11

There was a faint smell of cooked meat in the air. It could have come from the apartments, but at that time of night, it was more likely a NeverSee in the sewer. It wasn't pleasant—maybe cat or something even worse. I pulled out my Scroll and, with a slight sense of embarrassment, called up the inappropriately-named *WorldLink News*—one of the sleaziest news-tabs. I'd be the first to admit it was mostly mindless dross, but it held a perverse fascination. I opened up the classifieds—nothing else reveals the true depths humanity can sink to any better—and scanned various enigmatic headlines.

My mind was toying with the delights of "Willy. Got the powder, you still got the meat? H.," when a sickening wet impact shattered my guilty entertainment. A heartbeat later a burning snap of *something* stabbed deep into the back of my shoulder, and I staggered forward. Time seemed suspended in the dust-heavy wind as the Scroll slipped from my fingers and clattered on the rough concrete paving.

I turned—not having to look far for the source of the sodden explosion. A lump of still-quivering gelatinous protoplasm was splashed over the pavement a few meters away. Snakes of uncoiled intestine slithered towards me as the moist, salty odor from the steam drifted into my nostrils on the cold night air.

Twin rows of burst ribs reached upwards through the green jacket, like claws from a pair of cupped hands begging for more. Remnants of a head were scattered across the sidewalk, its once precious cache discarded in a casual puddle of gray and crimson mucous.

I wasn't going to get my fare after all.

Two

It's possible some people like being grilled by the cops at four in the morning, in the same way that some people might like the asphyxiation that accompanies a p-suit tank running dry. I wouldn't add either of them to my bucket list, but here I was, getting a quick introduction to police procedure.

In my experience, there are two species of cop. One kind will give you the benefit of the doubt, even when appearances are against you. They want to understand what happened and don't jump to conclusions. It's not that they're slow or stupid, they just want to do their job properly and make sure the right people get taken off the streets. Unfortunately, like good bosses, they're about as common as snow in space.

The other is a very different animal. They see crap wherever they look, and you're another part of the pile. Everything you do or say is wrong and, if you're not guilty of whatever brought you to their microscopic attention, that only means you're guilty of something else. These guys want easy arrests so they can go back to skimming drug deals and strong-arming working girls for freebies.

Detective James Sterle was thankfully of the first type. Which was good, as no matter how hard I play dumb and innocent it never works out. He didn't look much like a typical cop—kind of slight and despite the over-sized sweater I could see the unmistakable paunch of someone who spends too much time sitting down. His eyes were bright hematite buttons that scanned everything, as if nothing could slip by without being recorded for future reference.

Right now, he was putting on a good show of being friendly.

I couldn't blame him for not being entirely successful. Getting dragged out in the middle of the night to quite literally scrape someone off the sidewalk isn't likely to put anyone in the best of moods.

"Joe Ballen?" He waved my license in front of me. "You're a cabbie? Didn't know the victim?"

"I told you. I picked him up at *The Kase* and brought him home. Then he did an ungraceful swan dive from L4." The conversation might have gone smoother if I was interested in anything other than getting home and sleeping. "That's all there is to it."

"You're all heart, Ballen. Just a fare?"

"One I didn't want." I yawned in Sterle's face, hoping he'd get the message. "He hopped in my cab after I'd finished my shift."

"But you drove him home anyway?" Sterle fingered his reedy gray mustache, mulling over what I'd said as though it was the most significant information he'd ever heard. "Most drivers would have thrown him out."

"I would have too. Except I don't keep a two-ton hoist in my pocket."

I wasn't dressed for standing outside. The chill from the damp night air was cutting into my arms and legs, and I fought to stop them trembling. A second cop shambled up, his heavy frame and scowling features absorbing the flickering blue and red lights like a piece of granite. "Got an ID on the victim. Ganz—Doctor, Hubert. Lives here. Positive bio-match on the remains and one of the neighbors with a strong stomach confirmed it too. Would you believe it? The son of a bitch left a two-centimeter dent in the sidewalk."

"Ballen, this is Detective Francis." Sterle waved his stylus at the newcomer. "Anything else?"

"Yeah, he was some kind of brain at the University. No immediate family. Everyone says he was quiet and, get this Jimmy, he was dry as a virgin's crack."

Sterle winced. "He didn't drink?" His eyes wandered over to me.

Francis shook his head. "Had some kind of condition—confirmed with MedCent—couldn't touch a drop."

I sighed. Well, that blew my story, and I tried not to let my nervousness show. I couldn't stand much poking around by the cops. If they ran *my* details through MedCent, they'd find I was missing the mandated health certifications needed to pilot a cab.

"See if you can get hold of someone from the University." Sterle tapped his DataPad. "Maybe they can throw some light on this. Did he have any debts? Relationship problems? You know the routine."

"Seriously? Come on, Jimmy..." Francis peered at me with a gray concrete stare, then leaned forward. "It's as clear as the shine on this sick bastard's skull. What was it? Were you going to clean out his apartment and panicked when he fell through the window, or did you throw him out for kicks?"

Like most people who work in space I kept my hair cropped tight—free-fall isn't the place for a mess of hair—and although I didn't work on the High-Rig anymore, I'd never gotten out of the habit. For some reason, that was enough to convict me in Francis' eyes.

"I'm a cab driver not a thief. Some people think there's not much difference, but you can blame the taxes for that. I told you what I know. He got in my cab outside *The Kase*. I dropped him here. He did a dive out the window."

"Do you Stim, Ballen?" Francis held up a skullcap, dangling it off his finger, the thin silver electrodes giving the gossamer material the iridescent shimmer of fairy wings in the harsh glint of the streetlights.

Mutual Electronic Brain Stimulation, or *Stim* for short, isn't exactly illegal. It started out as an approved treatment for mental health conditions and, in that uniquely human way, had been perverted into a pleasure toy for the loneliest night for the weak. I'm old-fashioned. Hooking my brain up to someone else's for the benefits of direct stimulation of the septal region wasn't my idea of a hot date. "You're not really my type. Maybe if you bought me flowers first..."

Francis snarled and edged closer. "You ain't so big I can't—"

Sterle caught his arm. "Okay, Dan. Go check with the University." He took the StimCap and held it up. "This was inside Dr. Ganz' apartment. The Sargent thinks you guys were into that and had a lovers' tiff. What do you think of that theory?"

I watched as Francis shuffled towards their squad car. It was a grimy old Victory, but I easily spotted the widened body-lines used to accommodate the law enforcement grade turbines. Exhaustion had set in. My shoulder throbbed, my eyes crunched every time I blinked, and my legs felt like bloody stumps that had been dipped in molten steel. "Is he always like that, or did someone feed him raw meat today?" It was a dig, but Sterle let it pass. I thought of telling him that the dead guy had mentioned a girl, but decided discretion was the better part of volunteering. "Are we finished? I need to sleep before my next shift."

Sterle chewed the end of his stylus, his jowls wrinkling like his skin didn't fit properly. "I'd prefer you to stay around until we know what we're dealing with."

"I'd prefer to hit the sack." I felt my temper rise and fought to keep it in check. Francis might be a bastard, but Sterle seemed more reasonable—at least on the surface. "You have my address. You can get me there or through the cab company if you need more."

"If you did this..." Sterle nodded in the direction of the forensic team. "It'll show on Argus."

"I won't lose any sleep over that."

I jumped in the cab, lifting off before he could change his mind. My right arm was beginning to shake uncontrollably, and I couldn't feel the yaw controls under my feet. It was all I could do to punch *home* and let the car do the work. My place was over in the sprawling low rental district north of Towson—and there was no way I could risk opening her up on manual in my condition. The Pilot would limit me to the same 100/100 limits as the City zone, but slow and alive beats quick and dead any day.

It isn't luck that the roof to my apartment has a reinforced private landing pad. It means I only have to manage a single set of stairs and I'm home. Better than dealing with temperamental elevators, plus it also insulates me from the street noise when I work shifts. There's a heavy-duty cage door at the top of the stairwell and another at the elevator, so I'm fairly secure and rarely go out on foot anyway.

Tonight I pretty much slid down the stairs, relying on my one good arm to help me stay upright. The door recognized me, opening automatically as I approached and dragged myself inside, only to collapse on the floor by the bathroom.

"Sir, my sensors detect a dangerously elevated pulse, erratic cardiograms, and high quantities of adrenaline in your biometrics. Respond in thirty seconds, or I shall call for medical assistance."

"Shove it, you brainless piece of junk." I swatted the *Don't Worry* paddle on top of the insurance-mandated Medibo and crawled one-handed across the floor into the bathroom and onto the edge of the tub.

I rattled through the small drawer by the washbasin and grabbed a hypo-nozzle, jabbing the end against the side of my neck. Almost before the discharge *hiss* finished, I felt the nerve dampening agents soothing the jangle in my patched together nervous system. It had been months since the last attack and I usually had an hour or so's warning, letting me detour back to my place to inject. Tonight, the ganglionic shock was biting hard.

Grabbing a bottle in the lounge, I poured myself a large tumbler full of whiskey then twisted and kneaded my arm to fight off the painful pins and needles—the inevitable result of the injection. As I ran my fingers over the back of my shoulder, I felt something sharp buried close to the thin scar that ran around my arm.

I shuffled wearily to the bathroom. It wasn't easy positioning a mirror to see what it was—an angry crater, dark with clotted blood and fibers from my shirt. I dipped a corner of a hand towel in my glass and dabbed at the wound until it was clean enough to probe with the tip of a thin screwdriver—the only thing I could think to use.

Whatever it was, it was buried deep enough in the muscle to resist, and I slid the screwdriver blade awkwardly down the edge to lever it out. The whole thing was getting increasingly messy when the blade slipped, stabbing deep into my shoulder, and I grunted in pain. I tried again and this time managed to hook the tip underneath the lump and twisted it out.

The hole was pretty deep and next to the boundary between live flesh and my semi-dead arm. It was an unstable part of my anatomy. The impact at that point was probably what had triggered the unexpected attack.

Picking up the gore-coated fragment from where it had fallen,

I threw it in the sink and ran warm water over it. I expected to find a piece of sidewalk, but as the blood washed away it revealed a white lump about the size of a fingertip.

A human tooth.

I felt the blood surge in my head, and my temples throbbed. I drained the whiskey, then my legs buckled under me again and I staggered over to the bed alcove. It took absolutely no effort to crumple inelegantly on the mattress.

The injection mixed with the alcohol was really kicking in, and the flesh of my legs and arm felt like they were burning off my bones. Even though I knew it wasn't the case, I checked them anyway. The only visible difference between my regen'd limbs and the rest of me was a slight color difference on either side of the scars.

I tried to sit up to take off my shirt but didn't make it. The last thing I remembered was the thud of my head as it hit the foam pillow. It made the same sound my passenger had made when he hit the concrete.

Three

Sometimes in my dreams, I see a reflection of a life that could have been, or was, but is no more. A world seen through a distorting mirror, not quite right, but not quite wrong.

I was back on the High-Rig, a common theme in my nighttime interludes. Off to the right, the evil eye of the sun hovered, its intensity baking everything to a stark contrast, lighting the station's outer skin to almost painful white and simultaneously plunging the shadows into pitch.

I was doing routine maintenance inspections on the station's thermal radiators—an array of them lifted from the main spars like sails from an ancient schooner, but magnificently bigger. I'd already checked the first two groups and was on my way to the next, passing by the space-dock where the "starship" *Ananta* was being built. It had virtually no chance of success from what I could see. The construction was patchy and from what I understood the physics behind it was questionable.

To me, it was nothing but a boondoggle, designed to distract people from the political reality that Earth had been trapped under the domination of the space-faring Atolls for over a hundred years.

I changed my vector, angling the engineering pod so I'd pass along the length of the ship. The superstructure ribbing was about all that was in place, each girder sliding past as though I was drifting alongside a giant skeleton.

The PlaSteel of the superstructure distorted and cracked, twisting into ugly blood-covered bone and the ship became a real set of ribs, writhing under the furnace-like sun. Something looked wrong, and I brought the pod to a halt, locking it in place then slipping out through the hatch. I hooked my safety line onto the superstructure and pushed inside. I'd seen the plans for the ship, and the analytical part of my subconscious sensed that something didn't match.

A movement caught my eye, and as I turned, I was knocked sideways. The mass of the pod pinned me against the heavy framework, its manipulator arms grating against the bones in my arm and legs. The serrated edges of the claws slicing through the reinforced fabric of my p-suit effortlessly. My severed right arm tumbled away, leaving a painfully graceful arc of flash-frozen blood. My heart thumped loudly, and I begged it to stop, knowing each beat would pump more blood from my body. Then my sliced-off legs floated past my field of vision, bringing my mind to a terrified halt. Seconds later my suit's environmental management system sealed the gaping holes where my limbs had been, and everything went numb.

The pod transformed into Ganz' corpse, his bloated flesh enveloping me. I should have been able to push the corpse away—he wasn't *that* heavy—but somehow the inertia was too much. His rib cage peeled open, the bones inside *cracking* as they reached to join the superstructure behind me, fusing with them and locking me there—staring into his fleshy, tear-filled face. The immense weight pressing ever tighter against me.

My body crumpled around the girder behind me, rolling around the edge with the force of the pod/corpse hitting me. I slipped away from the *Ananta,* and my safety line snapped. The whip of the line sent me spinning, rotating sideways and head over where my heels had been. I was falling in slow motion, every rotation taking me further from the High-Rig and safety.

With the dizzy spin of stars and ship my stomach churned and I fought the urge to retch. I was dead. Though it would take some time for my body to realize that. I figured I had a few minutes before the pain broke through the anesthetic injected into me by the trauma system. Then my brain would recognize what had happened and shut down. After that, I had maybe ten or fifteen minutes of air and perhaps a further three until I actually died of asphyxia. Twenty minutes max, but I didn't want to spend them suffering the indignity of trying not to breathe in my own vomit.

I sat up screaming. Incapable of moving until the vision subsided. When I could manage it, I checked my arm and legs for signs of the instability from last night and was relieved to find no obvious after-effects. The medication had done its job, and other than a slight tingling in the extremities of my fingers and toes I was whole once more. At least as whole as I get now.

The clock read ten-thirty, so there wasn't much point staying in bed. I was due back on shift at two and the shower I definitely needed, along with breakfast, would fill the time easily.

I didn't want to look in the sink but forced myself, wrapping the molar in a wad of tissue so I could flush it down the toilet. The hole in the back of my shoulder was red and swollen, but it seemed like no permanent damage had been done. I couldn't get it checked out without drawing attention I didn't want, so I hoped my erstwhile passenger was reasonably free from communicable diseases.

After boiling myself in the shower, I threw a DentiKleen pack in my mouth. The fizzing action of the Nanomites left my teeth clean and my gum-line slightly sore. I waited the prescribed two minutes then slooshed with deactivating mouthwash and went in search of breakfast and enlightenment.

The news was full of the usual garbage. The FabHomes were still locked up and empty while the great and the good argued. Some New-Hollywood plastic clown of no fixed allure was cheating on a similarly plastic clown with a third and possibly fourth. Someone was pushing yet another scheme to reclaim Seattle and Vancouver, even more improbable than the last. The ever-present news of developments on the High-Rig screamed for my attention as always, but I ignored that siren call. There was nothing there for me now.

The Atolls were demanding even more restrictions on Earth space flight and threatening military action unless we complied with their wishes. It was the same old chest thumping. What did they expect us to do? Cower on Earth until we drowned in our own squalor? Anyone could see that wasn't a viable solution—the human race needed to grow to survive, and the Atolls hadn't expanded much beyond the immediate vicinity of Earth.

What I *didn't* see was "Extremely large man tries to do impression of bird and fails. "Which meant the cops were sitting on the story. Probably there was some poor relative they hadn't been able to contact yet. Or maybe the story *had* been released, and no one gave a damn.

The last piece of low-fat-processed-vegetable-protein bacon-substitute went down with the remaining corner of low-fat but real-grain toast and I thanked the patron saint of natural food production that at least the coffee was still real, even if I had to pay a small fortune for it.

I was headed for the door when my Scroll rang. The call automatically re-routed to the large wall-screen and I saw the number prefix was off-world. There was only one person I knew who'd go to the expense of calling from the High-Rig. I briefly considered not answering, but my conscience jumped up and down inside my head. It was pointless anyway. I was sure the man on the other end would know if I ignored the call.

"Hello, Logan." I transferred the call to my Scroll and opened up the 3V. The image blossomed in front of me as I walked, a ghostly figure held at the same apparent distance regardless of my movements. "You calling to order more dancing girls?"

Logan Twofeathers had probably never looked at a dancing girl, unless it was at a native ceremony. He had proud traditions and held onto them with a quiet passion that reflected in his dark gray eyes. Two-hundred and fifty years ago his ancestors had built high-rise New York. Now he was taking that tradition out to Earth orbit.

"Only if you can find some pretty ones." His voice sounded like a slow-moving river, gurgling over smoothly worn stone. "That last batch was so bad the Great Spirit wouldn't talk to me for three months."

"When are you coming to visit again? We could stick our heads in the nearest watering hole and not come out for a week."

"You're having problems. You're drinking again." His broad jaw tightened. "I know it's not easy for you."

He'd said almost the same thing eight years earlier when he'd wandered into my office looking for work. That was pretty unusual in itself. People don't typically visit the High-Rig unannounced, and I'd received no résumé or inquiry beforehand. After all, who would take a 100,000 km trip up the Ribbon on chance?

Nevertheless, Logan sat down in front of me and said, "You're having problems—I came to help."

He had no references, and when I ran a NetCheck, it showed only the skimpiest of details—some construction and engineering experience, mostly low-grade and all on Earth. But he was right. The work was way behind schedule, and I was crumbling from trying to oversee four crews and manage the project. At the same time, I was drowning in a pile of *lack-of-progress* reports designed to appease investors who'd never seen a TiCaLam I-beam, let alone tried to use them in a construction project in geostationary orbit at the end of a paper thin carbon rail.

"Sorry, friend. I haven't got time to waste on someone who's never been Geo-S before. What makes you think you're qualified to work up here?"

He shrugged slightly. "I'm just a man, as flexible and as useful as any. The Great Spirit told me to come and help you, so I came."

It was all I could do not to laugh. All I needed was a crazy native running around on one of the most ambitious construction projects of all time. I smiled my best thanks-but-not-today grin. "I don't believe we have anything right now. If you leave your details, I'll be happy to consider—"

He stood up suddenly. Too suddenly for a low-grav environment. I expected his boots to break free and give me the amusement of watching him flap about in freefall and maybe hitting the roof. Instead, his hand shot out, and he used my desk to brake the movement perfectly. His fist closed around a sheaf of worksheets, and he walked out the door, collaring a junior framer who was passing by.

I heard him say, "Take me to the foremen." Then they vanished down the corridor.

I expected to get called to some kind of incident before the day was through. Riggers aren't the most congenial bunch and are more than happy to play rough with anyone they consider inexperienced or otherwise lacking the necessary skills. In the meantime, I concentrated on wading through the backlog of paperwork.

It didn't happen. At shift change, I saw one of the big front riggers, skulking towards the lockers like a Frost Giant as the moisture in the air condensed against his pressure suit. He was grinning like a fool on his way to blow his wages at *The Sleaze Pit* and it wasn't even Wednesday.

"What got you so happy?" The last time I'd seen Maloney smile, he'd got the news his mother-in-law had broken her collarbone.

"Hey, Boss. You sure picked a good 'un with that new guy. Man, I never knew anyone could work so hard. Where'd you find him? He knows the plans like the back of his hand. Any time there was a problem he was there, helping out. Making it work. Then Turk—you know what that crazy fool is like—called him out." Maloney chuckled. "The new guy out-lifted him. We pulled back *three* schedule hours in *one* shift."

"Three hours?" That was impossible—no one made up that much time on one shift, especially a team led by someone with no ZeeGee experience.

The worksheets said differently though. By the end of the week, we'd gained over fourteen hours, and I'd managed seven solid hours sleep per night, rather than the catnaps at my desk I'd been getting.

"You know, Logan, I couldn't get rid of you now, even if I wanted to. The men would space me—for the first time in months there's a chance they might get a productivity bonus." We were in my drab office surrounded by plans and worksheets. I reached in my drawer for a bottle, squeezed out two generous helpings of ocher whiskey into ZeeGee beakers and offered him one.

"My grandfather used to tell me this stuff was white man's poison." He took a long swallow. "But he also kept a bottle hidden under his pillow—said the Great Spirit spoke louder to those who undertook such a trial by ordeal."

Logan was with me from then on. I don't think he took a day off in seven years. And as it turned out, he was the one who dragged me inside after the accident.

*

I walked to the tiny kitchen and put the Scroll on the countertop with the display projecting where I could see it. I needed to clean my vintage moka pot before leaving for work.

"How's the spook business?"

Logan grinned. "Don't say that. I'm only a consultant. Besides, they're probably monitoring this transmission."

After my accident had grounded me, Logan worked his way up to chief engineer. He'd also picked up several contracts with government security services as an off-Earth specialist. He joked that he couldn't tell me what he did for them because then he'd have to ask his ancestors to kill mine. With the clashes between Earth and the Atolls though, it seemed a sure bet he was working on projects aimed at breaking the Atolls' grip on space traffic.

"Those guys seem to need a lot of training." I swilled the lower coffee chamber. "You've been at it for over six months."

"ZeeGee takes time. You know that."

I did know it. Some people never acclimatize in fact. That was what made people like us so special, or people like Logan at least. I wasn't part of that elite group anymore.

"It doesn't have to be that way, Joe."

Damn Logan, I never could hide anything from him.

The smile I flashed towards his image was meant to be reassuring, but I doubted Logan was fooled. He always knew far more about me than was comfortable. "I'm not drinking anymore. A few beers, that's it. Anything else causes rejection problems, you know that."

"That's what you've always told me, but there was a time when you didn't seem to know it. Perhaps that's what you wanted." Logan looked down, his eyes darkening. "Should I have left you, Joe?"

How many times had I wished that he had? Dozens? Hundreds? "You did what you thought was right. I know that."

"You're a warrior, Joe. It's hard on a man when he can't be that anymore. But you still have a life, and a lot to do. You should come back to the Rig."

"And do what exactly?" I slapped the metal coffeepot down so hard Logan's image flickered. I used to be at the top of my line—a five-star High-Rigger. There were only a few dozen of us in the world. No one knew more about orbital construction than I did. Maybe crazy Atoll engineers perhaps, but they didn't count. What they did was more of a crystalline growth process than construction. "I don't think they have many openings for cripples, do they?"

"You're not a cripple. You could teach. They need experienced guys to bring these young kids up to speed. You know how ZeeGee can catch you out if you're not paying attention."

His words stung. "Thanks, I really appreciate that."

"I didn't mean your accident." Logan sighed. "I still don't understand what happened. You tied off. Locked the pod down. How the hell did it get loose?"

"Hey. I'm a working man, and it's time for my next shift." I forced another smile as I rinsed the rest of the coffee pot and put it on the drainer. "I'm okay. Had a bad night. That's all."

"You still piloting those flying rickshaws?"

"It's a living." I leaned back from the display.

"You shouldn't be doing it. It's dangerous, and you know it."

"What isn't these days?" I saw a slight scowl form on Logan's face and held up my hand in apology. "Look, I'm doing okay. I've never had any problems. Really."

Logan's eyes seemed to burn in the projected image, as if he could read everything that happened the previous night just by looking at me. Who knows, maybe he could.

"Who're you trying to convince?" Logan's face grew serious. "I'll see you back up here, Joe. I know it. Stay off the booze."

I nodded and cut the call off before I could say anything stupid. Logan was probably the most honorable and selfless friend I'd ever had. It wasn't fair to blame him for what had happened. But somehow I did. Not for the accident itself—a maintenance pod incorrectly locked-down had come loose at exactly the wrong time. I didn't want to admit it, but I blamed Logan for not letting me die out there.

Four

On a good day, when the customers haven't been too difficult, driving the cab can lift me out of the daily grind. Sometimes it feels like it could lift me so high that I'd almost feel like a spaceman again. A whole person. Not the smashed and broken remnant of what used to be a man. On those days, I head out of controlled space and point the cab up at the maximum climb rate, hoping beyond hope that I'll escape the atmosphere and tiresome gravity and feel free once more.

Of course, the car's safety systems don't allow that and force me to level off before the air gets too thin, and either I suffocate, or the engines die, and we plunge down to good old Mother Earth.

Sometimes I wish the engineering wasn't quite that good.

Today I let the cab sniff its way back to the Taxi Hub on East 33rd. While the Pilot was driving, I did a more thorough search of the news items on my Scroll. Nothing. No story of anyone jumping so much as a red light, let alone from a building. Either last night's passenger was so unimportant that even the most news-starved media in history couldn't be bothered, or something else was going on.

My only theory was that the guy had been something big somewhere, rather than the bloated drunk he appeared. In that case, the cops would probably sit on the story until they knew exactly what they were dealing with. It also meant I could expect another interview from the boys with the badges at any time.

Maybe Logan was right. A training job on the High-Rig was probably better than what I was doing now. And things only get worse when cops start sniffing around. One MedCent check would put an end to my current job and probably any opportunities on the 'Rig too.

The excitable cop said the jumper worked at the University, so finding something out about him shouldn't be too hard. A search for "Ganz" or "Gants," limited to educational references, brought back a bunch of results. I opened a couple of entries that looked most likely and soon had the guy's credentials laid out before me.

My investigations were interesting, but only in a *what was so important about this guy?* kind of way. He had a completely uninspiring career record, no family connections of importance, and his list of published papers didn't really help. *Diachronic Analysis of Stochastic Quantum Irregularities* meant about as much to me as real-time digitally-enhanced immersive VoyPorn would to the ancient Greeks.

I'd only been reading a few minutes when the Hub loomed up in front of me—taking up two floors halfway up a cylindrical monolith that stabbed into the sky like a giant finger. The cab slid into the cradle and swung around so I could get out while the AutoDrones did the daily diagnostic and service.

The Taxi Hub was in one of the tower blocks in the new downtown section of Baltimore. The building was originally meant to house an emergency response facility and had all the cradles and docking ports set up. Then the powers-that-be decided centralization was once again the way to go, at least until the next election. After that, they'll no doubt reverse themselves again. Either way, it was the perfect location for Dollie's Cabs, without the usual expense of custom construction.

I hurried through the spacious customer area with my eyes down, skirting the single customer waiting in one of the lounge chairs and similarly ignoring the blast of newsfeeds from the array of displays lining the walls. Dotted between the displays were vivid splashes of color from Dollie's vintage pinup art collection. Add to that the daylight pouring through the glass walls and the whole effect was enough to give anyone a headache if they lingered too long.

The operators' lounge was altogether calmer, with its washed-out beige walls that an interior designer would optimistically call *sand*. Right now it was almost empty. Not unusual for mid-afternoon. For a cab driver, if it's daylight and you're in the lounge then you're more than likely about to cash in your last pay check.

Charlie Anderson was by the coffeepot as always, refilling his liter-sized travel mug and taking his time about it. I didn't know how old Charlie was exactly, but his face looked like it had been carved from granite sometime around the Cretaceous. He'd mentioned once remembering the first ocean lift as a boy. Not the one that breached most of the East Coast's sea defenses, but the one before, which had to make him well over a hundred. The only hair on his head was a flamboyant mustache of pure white, except for where it was stained brown by coffee.

I raised my hand. "How's it going, Charlie?"

He grinned, his mustache lifting like a hairy worm. "I did it, Joe. I got the old bird going again. You should'ha heard her. Purring like a kitten she was, and just as eager to please. Not a minute too soon either." His voice lowered. "The Fundies are getting stronger. They're waiting. Making everyone think they've gone away and all, but they're gittin' ready to strike and then... well, watch out."

"Which old bird is it this time?" Charlie helped around the place, fixing stuff and keeping the AutoDrones in line. At one time he'd been a driver, and I guess he didn't want to leave it all behind, though Dollie didn't let him do regular runs anymore. It seemed every time I spoke to him he was tinkering with some unlikely piece of junk and worrying over when the Fundamentalists were going to rise up and strike again. That the Fundie movement effectively died with the secession of the old United States seemed to have missed him completely. Anyone with those kinds of ideas was on the other side of the border that cut across the continent from Richmond, VA to just below Vegas—in the self-declared MusCat Alliance.

"The old Broadsword. Once I cleaned up the core, she fired up right away. D-Flek worked 'n everything." He looked over his shoulder. "Did you hear about the blackouts in Denver? The Fundies were doing a test run—gonna fritz the whole grid. Then where will we be? How long can we last without power, eh? Once they're ready, that'll be it—everything will be taken out, just like that."

"There are always power problems, Charlie. It's not terrorists, the power companies just don't know how to manage their resources very well. Have you really got a Broadsword?"

"Sure. I told you that. Don't you remember? Won it from old Bruerge six months ago. Raised him four of a kind when he was trying to bluff with two pairs. The old bastard finally paid what he owed." Charlie looked at me, shaking his head in slow arcs. "I *did* tell you, didn't I, Joe? Sure I did. I remember clear as yesterday."

Broadswords were early assault craft used by the military, and I don't think one had flown since before I was born. They had none of the safeties and regulators mandatory on current vehicles and little in the way of intelligent avionics. Those things would stay upright—if you were lucky. The rest was down to the pilot's skills or lack thereof. Charlie hadn't mentioned it before, but it didn't really matter.

"Sure, Charlie." I shrugged. "Guess I must be getting old."

"Well, sure glad it's you, not me." His laugh was like a donkey braying, then he leaned in close. "You should watch yourself—get prepared. Smart guy like you should get hisself something disconnected. What'll you do when the Fundies bring down the traffic net? Huh? I could find you something. Still got a few good contacts."

I slapped his shoulder. His concern was touching, even though the Fundamentalists he fretted over no longer existed. "Don't worry about me. I'm good."

He tapped the side of his nose. "Don't say no more. Good to know you're covered. More people need to get smart like you and me. Those Fundies, they don't care. Not about nothing and no—"

"Chaos! Where the hell are you, you senile old goat?"

A shadow washed over Charlie's face. He hated that nickname, but like many people he was intimidated by the owner of this peculiar voice. A voice that mixed a sweet contralto with a decidedly gruff masculine baritone during antagonistic moments.

"Gotta go." Charlie glanced down the corridor towards the front desk and shook his head. "Beats me how any woman could be so hard-hearted. Watch her, Joe. She's in a nasty mood today."

"Keep your head down, Charlie. I'll distract her."

Charlie nodded. "Thanks, Joe. You're a true friend." He shuffled into the back rooms, no doubt intent on staying well out of the way. I watched him disappear then grabbed my coffee and headed in the opposite direction, feeling more of a resigned fatality than bravado.

Like a lot of Geness she/he was staggeringly beautiful. After all, who'd spend the kind of money needed for gene ReSeeq to become a genuine biological hermaphrodite only to look bad? In Dollie Buntin's case, she had the face of an angel, long and oval with a perfect butterfly pout. Today her hair was as black as a raven's soul, framing her almond-white face. Each could change at will through the miracles of nano-aesthetics, though one thing that never changed was her lithe and decidedly pneumatic body.

With some Geness, they wanted a combination of visual looks—breasts with beards as Dollie would say. But with my boss, nothing detracted from her perfectly feminine form—until she took her clothes off to reveal she was *gifted* in more than one way.

Dollie had told me once, in a moment of way too much intimacy, that she never tired of the thrill when a new quarry, freshly caught in the throes of amorous besot, was first exposed, face to face as it were, with the last thing they expected. The girls would giggle at first, at least until fascination took over. With the guys, it was often a loathing and horror that their new conquest wasn't quite what *she* appeared to be. Although more than a few stayed around to sample her forbidden fruit from what she'd said.

She was unwrapping a large package by the main desk and held up two bright prints of vintage pinups. "One Vargas, one Evgren. I was going to put them by the entrance. What do you think?"

"Take it easy on Chaos, would you?" I strolled up, trying not to look at the steamy artwork. "You've got him spooked six ways from Sunday."

"You've been busy, Joe. I don't like it when one of my boys attracts attention." Dollie's eyes flashed icily, despite the warmth of her voice. "Two sets of visitors. One official, the other not." She nodded towards the cubicles at the back of the office that passed for private rooms.

"It's tough out there. I was mugged by a little old lady on my way home yesterday." Dollie couldn't know what kind of trouble I was facing, but official attention was something most ReSeeq patients were wary of. Although completely legal here in the United States and Provinces, Geneering was strictly controlled and sometimes outlawed to a greater or lesser extent in other regions. In Pan-Asia, Geneered were automatically enslaved, owned by their creator, while the MusCat Alliance had an open season allowing them to be killed at will. It wasn't an accident that the USP had the world's largest Geneered population. Many were refugees.

I looked at the cubicle doors, identical down to the random spots of discoloration on the composite panels. The rooms were small private areas usually used to corral drunken or otherwise belligerent clients. I sighed. "Which is which?"

Dollie's perfectly sculptured nose wrinkled mischievously. "Your choice, Soldier. The lady or the tiger."

Dollie had a habit of nicknaming people based on her assessment of their personality or background. Sometimes the names made sense, sometimes they were humorous, and some were more the product of fantasy. Charlie hated the nickname she'd given him, but I wasn't really bothered by mine—I'd been called much worse. She'd seen the scars on my shoulder and combined that with my reluctance to talk about my past, deciding I'd been *something in the military*. This was usually accompanied by the suggestion that she'd like to see me in uniform—briefly.

"I thought you liked me?"

"Oh, I do, Joe. I do. But you wouldn't deny a girl a little fun, would you?"

Dollie's idea of fun generally involved liberal exchanges of bodily fluids and a complete lack of inhibition, which wasn't really a scenario I wanted to revisit. I found it hard enough figuring out if I should treat her as a she/he/boss/friend without complicating things with that kind of a relationship.

"Is there anything you can do to help?" I said.

"That depends." She leaned close, her breath warm on my ear.

"Are you going to make it worth my while?"

The way she husked the words was enough to set off alarm bells inside my head. She was certainly attractive and lively company, but my prejudices got in the way.

"Coffee and a pastry?' Her jaw tightened almost imperceptibly, and I guessed I needed to up the stakes. "Hot dog and a ball game?"

Dollie still didn't say anything, but she moved away and perched on her chair.

"Dinner at *Disrespected*?" Still nothing. This was going to be an expensive night. "And a show?"

Dollie tapped the screen in front of her to bring up the optics from the private rooms. "Mama will watch over you, Soldier."

I moved round so I could see too. "Put the audio on."

Dollie pressed a button and voices sounded quietly. The two cops from the previous night sat at a battered metal card table.

"...see that babe outside. I wouldn't mind showing her my Shock-Wand. How 'bout you, Jimmy?"

"Try and keep it professional, Dan. These are taxpayers. You know, the nice people who pay us every month." Sterle sounded exasperated, and from my earlier encounter with his partner, I could understand why.

'No law against using my imagination. You know?" Francis pantomimed a sexual act as he sat.

"That talk will get you into trouble one of these days."

"Who's to know?" Francis stopped to consider. "You might be right though. The trim this morning was a better bet. What was her name? Tana? Like a fine piece of chocolate. She looked like she could take it hard."

"Knock it off, Dan. I'm tired."

"Easier going for the vulnerable ones, don't you think? Maybe I should interview her again, do a thorough *follow-up...*"

"That asshole probably looks in the mirror while he's jerking," Dollie whispered. "I've half a mind to tell him a thing or two."

I missed the next couple of lines as Dollie talked over Francis. Then Sterle spoke up again.

"How's Millie?"

"Cold as an icebox, and just as empty. Still bitching about the time I put in, same every day for the last three years."

"You *do* remember you're married though?"

"Bitch won't let me forget. A man's gotta take any opportunity that comes up though." Francis made a pumping motion with one fist. "I got needs."

Sterle shook his head. "Don't mess up this investigation, and keep it cool with this Ballen guy. Something's going on, and I want to know what."

"He's a StimBoy. Let's arrest him so we can dump the paperwork."

"Despite how he plays it, he isn't dumb."

"The other?" I asked.

Dollie flipped a switch, and the view changed. A woman stood at the far end of the room, peering through the narrow slit window. I didn't recognize her.

"I better get in there."

Dollie muted the chatter from the cops. "Don't get me into trouble, Joe. I've got my license to think of."

I nodded and shuffled toward the two doors, still no wiser as to who was in which. I grabbed the handle on the right.

"Joe?"

I looked back. Dollie was grinning mischievously behind her desk. "You had me at the pastry."

That pretty much summed up the luck I was having. I shrugged. "If I'm not back in a few days, send out search parties."

"Go get 'em, Soldier." Dollie gave me a mock salute.

Five

The woman I'd seen on the screen stood with her back to me, still staring out of the window. She looked like she was gazing across the Promised Land rather than the gray-blue concrete blocks that turned downtown Baltimore into an immense Giants Causeway of geometric caverns.

Her general appearance provided little information. Her clothes were all earthen hues of brown and gray—no doubt of good manufacture. But unless fashions had changed dramatically over-night, they weren't the sort of thing women generally chose to wear, other than for outside chores.

"Excuse me, Miss." I kept my voice low. As if breaking her reverie would be some kind of criminal act. "You're looking for me?"

She turned, her skin looking almost ashen under the artificial lights. There was something about her face, a slight asymmetry to her nose perhaps, a hint of heaviness to her jaw—nothing that truly stood out, but enough to describe her as plain. With the wide availability of Geneering these days, both pre-natal and post, that was rare enough to be noticeable. Even the new world order couldn't subdue the tendency to admire surface perfection, regardless of how superficial it was.

"You're... Bannen?" She looked at me like I was something that had escaped from a specimen jar.

"Ballen. Joe Ballen." I held out my hand, then withdrew it when there was no reciprocal gesture. "And you are?"

"He kept telling me something was going to happen. I thought it was the stress from his work. He was worried they'd cut his funding. Then I realized he was scared he was going to die. You can't keep that sort of thing hidden from someone when you st..." The hesitation was barely noticeable. "When you work closely with someone."

I scratched my ear. "I must have missed something. Are you looking to go somewhere?"

"You get used to hearing it in the news. No one seems valuable these days. But you'd expect to be safe with a licensed cab."

Her nostrils flared, a look of disgust distorting her face. "Did you kill him for money? Or are you the kind of sick animal that gets a kick out of hurting people?"

My fingers sent the signal that the coffee was burning my fingers, so I set the cup on the table and sat. This was sounding painfully familiar. The dead guy had mentioned a girl, and my guess was that this was the one. She didn't appear to need much looking after though.

"There must be a shortage in the suspect market. Seems like everyone wants to accuse me of murder." Her eyes pinned me to the chair for several long moments. "So who do *you* think I've killed? Any proof? A motive?"

"The police visited the lab this morning. They said Dr. Ganz was dead, probably murdered." Her malachite eyes fixed on me as if I were already tried and convicted. "Tana Radebaugh. I'm a Research Graduate. He was my Professor. I worked for him."

"What's that got to do with me?" This must be who Francis was talking about in such a complimentary fashion a few minutes ago.

"The younger policeman said they had a good suspect lined up." There was a glint in her eyes—a mixture of fear and hatred that burned brightly. "He told me a cab driver called Bannen or Ballon was involved."

I stood up. Angry at the police, her, myself, and the world. I'd have kicked the whole thing to the curb at that moment and gone to live on a beach somewhere. Except there weren't many beaches left and the remaining ones were strictly controlled by the rich and feckless.

"Do you want to go to the police now? It's very easy if you do. They're waiting for me next door. In fact, I'm sure they'd love to hear your accusations." I snapped the words through gritted teeth and took her wrist. "Come on. I'll walk right in there with you."

"They're here?" She pulled back. "Let go of me, you idiot."

I released her, and she darted into the far corner, as if wanting to be as far away from me as possible. My ego told me it was more to do with her not wanting to get involved with the police than a reflection on me personally, but I could have been wrong.

Opening the door wide, I gestured for her to go through, somewhat relieved when she made no move to do so. Once they started to dig into my personal record, my license would be revoked quicker than a politician can make a U-turn.

"Do they know I'm here?" Her voice had lost its angry defiance. She looked as if she had swallowed something she thought was ice cream, only to find it was waste machine oil.

"Wait here."

"No, don't. Please."

She fell quiet as I put my finger to my lips and left the office. Dollie's gleaming eyes tracked me like a laser cutting guide as I walked over to her desk.

"Do they know about her?"

Dollie raised an eyebrow to form a perfect arch, her fingers casually manipulating the nail-colorizer that she pretended to be occupied with. "Not yet. Should they?" She held up her fingers. "Do you like Angelwing?"

Her fingernails displayed a honey-golden mottled effect that shimmered in the light as she turned her hand.

"Not bold enough." I pointed to the second office. "How about them?"

"Oh, I'm sure they'd like it. That younger one was kind of cute—before I heard him talking like that anyway." She pouted. "Some people actually like me you know."

Why is it conversations with women are always so damn complicated? It seems to be a common characteristic regardless of their original chromosome makeup.

"Have I ever said I didn't like you?" From her expression, my question hadn't soothed anything. "You make me kind of nervous."

Her face softened, and she reached out to touch my hand. "Did I frighten you that much, Soldier?" She spoke in the little girl squeak I'd only heard her use when she was thoroughly happy. "We really need to work on that. Why don't you stop by this evening? I'm having a few people round. A nice intimate get together. You'd enjoy it."

Her emphasis on the word "intimate" was enough to tell me she wasn't talking about a quiet dinner for two.

"Maybe. It depends what happens in there." I jerked my head towards the offices. "What do they know?"

"You know what my problem is?" Her pout deepened. "I trust too easily. They don't know anything. They arrived before she did."

"Thanks, Dollie, you're the best."

"I keep telling you that—problem is you never listen." Her perfectly sculpted brow furrowed. "Watch yourself, Joe. These plain girls have got a lot of pent-up frustrations that need letting out. I know—I used to be one."

"You could persuade me of almost anything." I patted her arm in what I hoped was a fraternal way. "But don't ever tell me you were plain."

Dollie's face lit up with a smile. "Aww Joe, you *do* like me after all."

The girl looked up as I entered, her face momentarily full of fear. She was younger and smaller than I'd thought. Her eyes were red and her cheeks puffy, completely devoid of makeup.

"The police don't know you're here. Maybe we can keep it that way." I watched the relief creep over her face. "I've no reason to do that though."

She jerked as if she'd been slapped. "What do you mean?"

"I've played straight with the cops so far, and I'm not about to change that without a reason. You've not given me one that would make it worth me doing that."

Her eyes opened wider. "You want to be paid?"

"Money helps. Enough money can help pretty much anything. But I'm not a complete mercenary."

The roar of the traffic outside seemed to get louder as she silently considered what I'd said, then finally her head sank, and she shrugged.

"I don't have much money. They shouldn't have told me about you. The older one said so and told me not to do anything... anything stupid. He said I could be arrested if I did."

"Fine. They can arrest you instead of me."

Her head snapped up and her eyes locked with mine again, the anger burning through. "I have the final review for my Doctorate in three months. I've worked for over seven years to get to this point. A scandal would destroy my chances."

There's a feeling you get when you know you're being lied to, but you're not sure which part is the lie. I was getting it all the way down to my boots. A Doctorate is important and hard to get with so much competition from Pan-Asia and United Africa, but I wasn't convinced by what she said.

At the same time, I couldn't see myself handing her over to Sterle, or more particularly, Francis. That she'd tracked me down to accuse me of murder meant she was pretty messed up, but she didn't deserve getting tossed into the jaws of that particular wolf.

"I'll accept that." I heard her breathe, loud in the stillness of the room. "For now."

It was time to face the Tiger.

Six

I nodded to Dollie as I moved to the other door and opened it firmly, with far more bravado than I felt.

The cops were waiting for me like a pair of terriers looking for a fight—one cautious, looking for any opening, the other far too eager and excitable, though both with a potentially deadly bite.

"Hello again, Joe." Sterle bared his teeth in what I guessed was supposed to be a smile. "Sorry to bother you again, especially at work. Have a seat why don't you?"

"Yeah, have a seat." Francis barely held back the insult. "We're all friends."

I slipped into one of the chairs by the card table in the middle of the room, and Francis sidled behind me, deliberately positioning himself between me and the door. I'd rather have wrestled a medium-sized Kodiak bear than sit down with these two, but I didn't have much choice.

"I'm surprised you find me so fascinating." I leaned back in the chair, not wanting to display the weakness tingling through my legs. Like all predators, cops can smell fear. "Seems to me a suicide wouldn't be *this* interesting. Is Detective Francis still searching for a date? Or you think I had something to do with it?"

"You're such a smart guy, Ballen." Francis leaned in close to my ear. "I like smart guys—they have so much fun when we lock 'em up. Ain't that right, Jimmy?"

"You could try to be a little more cooperative, Joe." Sterle gave a slight nod to his partner that I probably wasn't meant to see. "It looks like we're dealing with a murder."

The news wasn't exactly earth shattering. What I couldn't understand was why the police were lining me up in their sights.

"I was by my cab when the fat guy decided to step outside without the benefit of a building. Shouldn't take you longer than thirty minutes to check Argus. Don't they teach the basics in police school anymore, or did you guys not graduate?"

"You're well-informed, Ballen." Francis moved up behind me, his breath hot and damp on the back of my neck. "How'd *you* like to take a ride out the window?"

"Keep trying to stick your tongue in my ear, and you might persuade me to jump without any help." I kept my eyes firmly on Sterle, knowing I probably shouldn't goad a cop, but blusterers like Francis bring out,the worst in me. "You need to get your buddy a leash or buy him some breath mints."

The chair hinged backward, and the next thing I knew my head cracked against the floor, the rubberized coating providing virtually no cushioning to the blow. Francis loomed over me, his snarling features blurred as my eyes tried to refocus after the impact.

"That's enough, Dan." Sterle's voice pushed through the mush of my thoughts only vaguely, as if I were hearing him while wearing a p-suit. His words were followed by a series of muffled noises I couldn't identify, then I felt hands tugging on the arm that had taken the brunt of the damage last night.

I yelled, lashing out with my good arm and feeling a soft, but satisfying thud as I connected with something fleshy. In the condition I was in, it probably did as much damage as a bug hitting the front of my cab, but at least I'd fulfilled my obligation as a warrior. I was sure Logan would have approved.

"—filing a complaint. You can't come in here and abuse my staff for no reason."

I recognized Dollie's voice, but my vision refocused slowly.

"There's no need to take that kind of attitude, Miss. It was an accident. Mr. Ballen got a little agitated and fell off his chair."

Francis' voice was full of mock-soothing, nauseating in its sliminess. I'd have been happy to introduce him to a falling chair, if I'd been able to do anything more than groan in pain.

I levered myself up from the floor, hooking the elbow of my

good arm over the edge of the table to pull myself up, slumping heavily into the chair. Not missing the irony that someone had set *it* back on its feet while leaving me to flop helplessly on the ground.

"Dollie, make a copy of the security records, please. I wouldn't want the evidence of my *fall* to get lost."

"You okay, Joe?" The concern in Dollie's voice wasn't just because the office had no built-in recording system. "I'm not sure I—"

"Just do it." My voice was a more of a rasp than an order. "I'll be fine."

Dollie's eyes tracked from Sterle to Francis like a laser cutter. "Don't touch him again."

She'd used the trick she had of dropping her voice register down an entire octave, and the words came out as if she'd spoken from the depths of Sheol. Both men stepped back as she stalked out, bringing a slight smile to my lips.

"She won't bite—unless I ask her to. Do you want to leave now or would you like to rough me up some more for the cameras?"

"I'm genuinely sorry about that, Joe." Sterle looked over at his partner. "It won't happen again, I assure you."

"And I'm supposed to trust you?" I rubbed my thoroughly abused arm, trying to knead some sensation into it that wasn't simply pain.

Francis peered around the room like a day-blind hound, his jowly features lending physical substance to the impression. "I don't see any cameras."

"I'm sure someone with your *professional* qualifications knows how easy it is to hide optical pick-ups."

Sterle pulled his chair back to the table and sat down. "Funny. That's pretty much what brings us here, Joe." His fingers teased the ends of his wiry mustache. "See. We checked the Argus records and guess what we found?"

The way my luck was playing I could half guess, but wasn't going to admit it. "Footage of your partner beating a suspect with a rubber hose?"

I heard Francis move, but Sterle waved him back. "The interesting thing is that the records don't show anything for half a dozen blocks around the Ganz apartment. Nothing at all."

"For exactly seventeen minutes, Argus didn't see *anything* in that area. There are one hundred and twenty-three cameras there, Joe, and not one of them recorded anything. Any idea how unusual that is?"

Officially known as the Argus Project, the system used a saturation of cheap optical pickups linked to some of the most powerful computer systems ever built. With the advent of cheap quantum processors and partitioned nanocore storage, the system recorded every movement made by everyone and everything. Orwell didn't get it quite right. Big Brother wasn't just watching— he remembered everything too.

This torrent of data was stored and, with the right authority, could be retrieved--providing a completely three-dimensional real-time display of what people had done in any given area. It was the implementation of this technology that brought crime under control after the Big Shake and was used daily to resolve the millions of "tags" people recorded against each other.

Without it, society would slip back into chaos. The system was sealed, redundant, and self-healing. It was inconceivable it would fail, and if it did, the failure would be headline news for at least a week.

Sterle waited patiently while the implications sank in. "There's something else, Joe. Guess when the data recording stopped?"

I didn't have time to respond before Francis spoke up. "The recording cut out the exact time your cab entered that zone. How d'ya explain that, *Mr.* StimBoy?"

The chances of that happening were virtually zero, but I certainly hadn't shut it down. I could think of a couple of ways it might be done, but only theoretically. It felt like I'd been thrown in a pit and a large stone slab was being lowered on top of me.

"Do you know how many violent crimes there were in Baltimore before Argus?" Sterle leaned towards me. "Over thirty thousand. Within three years of its introduction, that number dropped to less than ten thousand, and now we're talking hundreds—most of them domestic incidents.

"The city was dying, like a lot of places. Sinking under the weight of its own filth and scum. But we pulled it back, we made it a place where it was safe to be normal again." Sterle jabbed a finger at me. "Safe to raise a family and have a job. That's what Argus gives us. Knowledge is power. The power to record crimes and punish those who commit them."

I'd heard it a million times. It was a story that had the dust blown off it whenever any makeshift libertarians raised protests against the ongoing total surveillance. If you're innocent, you have nothing to hide. There was even talk of bringing internal building security under the Argus umbrella, so actions inside private buildings would be recorded. But to me, freedom was an excessive price to pay in the name of ersatz security.

"If Argus failed, then you got nothing on me." I stretched my arm, trying to ease the painful stabs. "So arrest me or let me get on with my job."

Francis' voice drifted over from where he leaned against the wall. "You wouldn't mind if we checked over that buggy of yours, would you, Ballen?"

"Check anything you like. Make sure you clear it with Ms. Buntin before you start tearing up her property."

"She was quick to rush in here." Francis snorted. "You involved with her, Ballen? Why she'd want anything to do with an insect like you, I can't imagine."

I turned to look at Francis for the first time since I'd recovered. Something in his voice told me he wasn't asking purely for the sake of his investigation. "If you're interested let the lady know, but most guys find she's quite a handful."

"A woman needs a real man to take care of her." Francis sneered. "Not a StimBoy who can't get it up without a bunch of wires."

"Drop the insults, Dan." Sterle sounded as if he felt the same way about his partner as I did. "We're here on business."

"Sure. Sure. Where's your cab now?"

"In the hands of the AutoDrones, getting its mandated daily service." I gave them a broad smile. "You better be quick—they clean the cars pretty thoroughly."

"What?" Francis jerked upright like he was wired to the mains and someone had pulled the switch. He bolted through the door without another word.

I looked back at Sterle, disgust etched on his lined, brown face. "I almost believed you until this."

"Ever heard of coincidence, Sterle?"

He squeezed his face between his stubby fingers and shook his head. "Coincidence only means you haven't figured out the real cause yet."

Sterle marched out, following in Francis' tracks so quickly that I felt like a piece of unwanted gristle left on the plate. Whatever they thought they might find wasn't going to be in my cab—not after the drones had finished. I guessed their next step would be to impound the cleaning waste and work through it. Which should at least give me some breathing room.

Like Sterle, I didn't trust coincidence. I couldn't figure how Argus could be out of action right at the moment I was dropping off Ganz. The idea that a section of one of the most efficient security monitoring systems ever invented would go offline at the exact moment that a violent incident was taking place didn't hold up. But either I was guilty and didn't know it, or that's exactly what happened.

One thing was certain. If they really wanted to, they'd find a way of dragging me in for a long interrogation. The kind that ends with people confessing regardless of their guilt.

Dollie looked up as I came out of the office.

"Ballen," she hissed. "What the hell are you up to? I don't like this one tiny little bit..."

"Hold on, Dollie." I spoke fast—the cops would be back as soon as they realized everything from the cab was in the garbage dump. "My last fare of the night jumped from a building, and the cops think I'm involved."

Dollie's forehead wrinkled. "But that's impossible. Surely Argus shows—"

Watching Dollie chewing her lip in thought has to be one of the more stimulating experiences you can have. Those perfect lips made it more of a seductive moment than some dates I'd had, but right now I needed action.

"I don't have time to explain." I nodded towards the office with the girl. "She knew the guy. Worked with him. I need to get her out of here."

"I don't know, Joe." The little girl pout was back. "Gee, if only you showed a girl some appreciation sometime."

"I'll make it up to you, Dollie, I—"

Sterle walked back into the lobby with Francis scrambling behind him like a gun dog looking for a piece of wounded game. He didn't look pleased, and I could guess why.

"Your drones empty everything into a collective garbage chute servicing this entire building," he said.

"Twenty-six floors of garbage collected in one spot, ready to be compacted and taken away." Francis leaned towards me. "That was almost a neat trick you pulled there, StimBoy."

"Did you know that, Joe?" Sterle's face darkened further. "Any idea how long it's going to take to sift through three and a half tons of garbage?"

"Long enough for Detective Francis to find his balls?"

I tried to block the punch, but my arm had no strength to counter the blow. Francis' fist stabbed deep into my stomach making me retch and sink to my knees.

"That's enough!" Sterle's voice bounced around the lobby as he dragged Francis back.

"I'm calling the police." Dollie's voice was ice.

"We *are* the police. You've seen our ID." Sterle pressed Francis against the wall.

"I'm calling the *real* police."

The last thing I needed was more of these official clowns, and I struggled to my feet, ignoring the pain burning in the pit of my stomach.

"It's okay, Dollie. I'm fine. Detective Francis doesn't punch any better than he thinks."

"Knock off the insults, Joe," Sterle growled. "Let's keep this professional. Okay?"

"Tell that to your pet Neanderthal."

"Joe, are you sure you don't..." Dollie twisted her hands together.

"I'm going to talk a little longer with these *officers* and then they're going to leave. Isn't that right, Detective Sterle?"

Sterle looked as miserable as I felt, despite the fact that it was me playing punch-bag for his fist-happy partner.

"Sure thing, Joe," he said, releasing Francis, but staying close to him.

"Take care of things for me out here, Dollie." Her eyes held with mine briefly. "This'll be straightened out in a few minutes."

I re-entered the room and grabbed my coffee from the table. I stood with my back to the window while Sterle and his buddy closed the door and sat down. I might look stupid, but I wasn't about to let Francis get behind me again.

"Okay. If you guys want to switch on your Argus recorder, go ahead. Presumably one of you was smart enough to bring a True-Or-False, so you might as well switch that on too." Sterle didn't move, but there was a not so surreptitious wriggling from his partner.

"I drive cabs for a living. It's not much, but that's what I do, and it ends there.

"Last night I picked up a fare outside *The Kase*. I'd officially clocked off for the night, but maybe he didn't see my light was out or didn't care. He seemed kind of lost, which normally wouldn't matter much to me. He was way too big to deal with on my own, so I decided the easiest way to get rid of him was to take him where he wanted to go." This wasn't the time for more games, and I was telling it straight.

"When we arrived at his address he had no money and said he'd go get some cash. I figured it was a scam. Who has cash? But I waited in case. I don't like non-payers and my boss"—I pointed at the door to the lobby—"makes us pay for any losses. Next thing I knew, he made a hole in the pavement big enough to park in.

"I never saw the guy before last night. I've no connection with him and I know nothing about him other than what I've told you and seen in the news. End of story."

Sterle and Francis didn't move for several minutes, and I thought that maybe the True-Or-False had picked something up. You can only pack so much intelligence into something the size of a pen after all, especially when it contains a short-range brain wave scanner.

Then Francis let out a disgusted sigh and stalked out of the office, leaving Sterle staring at me like I was some new species he didn't quite know what to do with.

"You know something? As much as this new technology helps us, it's not infallible. I still believe in good old-fashioned detective work."

He gave a short laugh, his face wrinkling like faded leather. "My superiors don't like it when I say things like that—they're always pushing for more Enforcement Tech. The more tech you use, the bigger the budget you can claim. That never seemed right to me. People are what's important. You can't measure someone's value, or what drives them, with a machine."

He walked part way to the door, stopped and turned back towards me. "At the moment, you look clean. This thing smells though, and we're going to check every lead. You better pray you *are* clean. If not, I'll take great pleasure in sending you down."

"One thing, Sterle?"

"What's that?"

"Did he have my fifty-five bucks on him?"

Sterle shook his head. "Just hope we don't need to see you again. You wouldn't want that."

The muscles around my chest relaxed as soon as he left. Breathing is such a simple part of life that you don't really notice how good it is until it's restricted. At that moment the gentle draught of air filling my lungs combined with the low hiss of traffic outside, producing a feeling of curious tranquility. It also felt like the heavy calm you feel ahead of a building storm.

Dollie was at her desk when I limped out. I was battered, bruised, and generally messed up. My body simply couldn't take the kind of pounding it had over the last twenty-four hours. A few years ago I'd have taken the punishment and got back up with a smile on my face, but now I was a pile of fractured parts held together with string and tape.

"Those cops didn't look happy, Joe." Dollie frowned as I approached. "Don't worry, Charlie got your girlfriend out of here."

"I swear I'm innocent on all counts." I groaned. "I never met her before and hope I never do again."

Dollie's only response was to arch an eyebrow. "Are you going to see me later, Soldier? I promise you a wild ride. Won't even cost you a coffee."

Under the warm, breathy words ran a current of pure liquid

nitrogen that triggered warning lights in my mind as if I'd lost a stabilizing thruster.

"I'll do what I can." I hoped I sounded non-committal, but Dollie's smile told me I probably didn't succeed. "I'm down on time today. I better do some catch-up."

I hurried to my car before Dollie thought up a more personal way of me *catching up*.

Seven

The second half of my day was uninterrupted routine, which for once I was more than grateful for. By the time I dropped the cab on the landing pad above my apartment, the strains of the morning were a lingering ache carried along the nerve cells in my shoulder and legs. I'd swallowed a nerve-tranq late in the afternoon to boost the effects of last night's shot, and it saw me through the ubiquitous four-till-eight rush until my knock-off time at midnight.

The Medibo fretted over me as soon as I was home, the sensors waving like stalks from its cylindrical body. But it lost interest when its sniffers couldn't detect much wrong. That electro-mechanical spy was supposedly there for my own good, but I was ready to kick its intrusive ass into the nearest recycler and pay them for the trouble.

I checked the news again, but the streams were hot over a clash by some of the 'Belt teams. The Atolls had claimed ownership over several more of the compact asteroid fields and posted defense buoys around them. With the restrictions already in place, Earth Belt mining teams were a declining group, but their frustration was understandable. Imagine traveling a couple of AUs, only to find signs saying *Private—Keep out!* It was a petty gesture, deliberately provocative, but not exactly unexpected behavior from the Atolls.

A hundred and fifty years ago the world changed. The seas rose, the land shook, and life on Earth became a rougher deal for everyone except those living in space.

They formed artificial communities, called Atolls, from the brightest and the best, and left the rest of us to fight over the crumbling ashes of a half-destroyed world. Old nations died and new alliances formed, but none rivaled the technological advances of the Atolls. They controlled us, isolated us, and trapped us here.

We had no escape. Virtually all space travel beyond Earth/Luna was at their discretion. They allowed the space elevators to continue, mostly to provide them with the Earthside delicacies they wanted, and to provide resources for the Lunar colonies they wanted no part of. Beyond that we had nothing. Earth's *fleet* consisted of a few ore carriers that shuttled minerals from the shared mining operations on Mars, and attempts by any Earth nation to change that were robustly discouraged.

I hated their casual bigotry at an almost instinctual level, while at the same time finding it all too easy to understand. The population of Earth had lost its drive decades ago, with technical ambition being largely replaced by instant gratification *experiences* that were anything but. Sure, not everyone had given up, but the ones who hadn't were too few and powerless. The world as a whole was as crippled as I was. The Atolls were trying to lay that corpse to rest.

Finally, I found what I was looking for. My friend from last night callously banished to a low-interest link in the minor news section. I was surprised given the interest shown by Sterle and Francis, but when I read it, I realized why.

"Respected scientist dies."

The detail was sketchy, to say the least—*unexpected* didn't seem the correct term for someone throwing themselves off the top of a building. They were playing it as a suicide. As always, he was going to be sorely missed by his colleagues... Death transforms even the most heartless into martyrs who were the only thing that kept the world spinning. There was no mention of the Argus failure, or the possibility of murder. Maybe the cops were still waist-deep in garbage looking for clues, but I doubted they'd forgotten about me.

The prickly tingle from the hot shower worked wonders in easing the remaining muscle pain, though it didn't do anything to diminish the swollen, angry lines of scar tissue around my arm and legs. But by the time I'd stepped out and swallowed two fingers of *Wild Cougar*, I'd mellowed to the point where I was considering heading out to Dollie's place. Company might be nice for a change.

The phone screen flashed an incoming call warning, and I half expected it to be Dollie checking to see where I was. Rather more to my surprise, it turned out to be another call from on high.

"Two calls in a week? Did I forget your birthday?" I poured myself another half-tumbler and slumped in front of the main pickup.

Logan chuckled, the laugh creases around his eyes deepening into fissures. "Actually, I think it's yours."

There was something in his manner that I hadn't seen since the last time we'd gotten drunk together. That was at his family's ranch several years back. We'd met up with several of his relatives, including his uncle, Dan. After a few drinks I was feeling relaxed, and both Logan and Dan encouraged me to give bull riding a try. Logan had the same look of mischief and self-satisfaction on his face now as when I'd hit the ground barely a minute after climbing on the creature's back.

"What do you want, Joe? More than anything else."

"That's a wide-open question if ever I heard one. How about a no-holds-barred date with the CherryBerry triplets, my own starship, and a lifetime subscription to *Honey House* re-runs?"

Logan frowned. "Be serious for a minute."

"You dialed rent-a-schmuck by mistake, I'm sorry if our humor offends. Please stay on the line for a specialist operator." I couldn't be serious because then I'd have to admit what I really wanted, and they don't regrow arms and legs properly yet. I had the best they could do, and they weren't good enough.

Logan's mischievous smile beamed again. "You want to space again. Don't you?"

Does a bee buzz in summer? Does a bird soar through the skies on currents of air? Does a fish love to feel oxygen-rich water sliding through its gills? "I'm a cripple. No good for that kind of work anymore."

"You don't have trauma-induced neural inhibition, Joe. That's psych-babble. Like Uncle Dan told you—you need to get back on the horse."

"It was a bull, not a horse." My fingers tightened around the glass in my hand. "That's why they can't cure me. The problem's with my brain, not my legs and arm."

Logan shook his head. "What's the difference between flying cabs and flying a Hopper or EMU?"

"Gravity. LowGee triggers an uncontrolled emotional response, causing intense muscular spasms. You read the report."

"That was over two years ago." He dismissed my comment with a derisive snort. "I found you a job."

"That's a crock. No one would take me with my record."

"Maybe, maybe not." He held up his hand. "I know what you keep telling me and what the report said. I'm not arguing. There's a job for you. You've heard the Atolls are shutting down the Main Belt clusters? I was talking to some guys at the refectory. One was a SecOps type. He was real unhappy. They're putting together an operation to annex some territory for Earth use only. The thing is, they need people with brains and experience to manage the operation. I told him about you, and he's interested if you are."

I gulped on the whiskey, feeling it burn as it went down. "I'm not a soldier and couldn't fight even if I was dumb enough to let you persuade me otherwise."

His eyes flicked to the glass in my hand. "That's the beauty of it, Joe. You wouldn't be on active duty. You'd be a consultant adviser. All you do is get ferried around and stop those idiots running into an asteroid."

Logan can be a persuasive man, as I knew all too well. But I couldn't see how he could talk some SecOps big gun into using a crippled ex-construction worker as an adviser for a military operation. Much as I wanted it to be true, I knew it couldn't be and expressed my doubt in blunt terms.

"Have I ever lied to you?" He looked hurt. "They're going crazy with this Atoll fiasco and can't afford to make mistakes. You know what kind of mischief the Freeworld disciples will make if they don't do something. They need people with space experience. They'd sign up a monkey if he turned up with his own p-suit."

My laugh was sharp. "You really know how to make a guy feel better."

Logan's eyes narrowed, his crag-like eyebrows looming out of the screen towards me. "I know you better than anyone and how much you want to hide away from everything, but you can't, Joe.

No matter how deep you bury yourself. Life finds a way of sneaking up and biting you on the ass when you're not ready for it."

"Know what? You'd make a killing in the fortune cookie market." Before he could answer, the door alert flashed. "Someone's here, I have to go."

There was no image on the door display, but I could guess who was there. The police might be slow of foot, but they're annoyingly persistent at times. Despite a slight edge of panic, I was almost grateful for the excuse to end the conversation with Logan. I didn't want to embarrass him or myself further.

"Who is it?" Logan was immediately suspicious. He knew the high price I placed on my privacy, and how few people knew my address. "Are you expecting someone?"

I shrugged, trying not to think about how Sterle and his partner had behaved last time I saw them. "No idea. I guess the optic is busted."

"I don't like it, Joe." Logan's eyes tightened into polished carbon slits. "You're not telling me everything."

The screen flashed as my visitor hit the announcer again. Whoever it was, they didn't have a lot of patience. "I appreciate the call, Logan, believe me. But I better go."

"Think about it. Okay?" I saw him reach for the disconnect. "Second chances don't come along very often."

With that, he was gone. It didn't matter how annoyed he made me, and he certainly had his moments, but in the end, I always ended up realizing he was right. Logan is such a straight person and usually has a hugely calming influence that defies rational explanation. But this time I felt strangely troubled when he left.

I switched on the door intercom and waited silently for the other person to speak. Bad manners perhaps, but under the circumstances, I was looking for any edge I could get.

"Mr. Ballen?"

I didn't recognize the voice, other than that it was female. I relaxed. I didn't really care that the person knew who I was. All that mattered was that it wasn't Sterle and his pet bulldog. "What d'ya want?"

I tried to make my voice as unappealing as possible. Making casual friends isn't my style, and I was looking forward to a hot date with oblivion with the help of my Cougar buddy.

"Can I come in? I don't feel very safe out here."

The second time of hearing I realized it was the girl from the taxi office. Though how she'd found me was a mystery. "I don't take house calls, and I'm off-duty. Call the office. 8118-Dollies-Cabs. Discretion guaranteed."

Where I live isn't the nicest part of town, but it had full Argus coverage, so she had no real reason to feel vulnerable. But then, her boss's place had been covered too.

"I don't want a cab. I came to see you." There was an almost imperceptible hesitation. "I think someone might be following me."

If she was being tracked that was even more reason not to get involved. The smart move would be to leave her out there until she got tired and left. Some days I guess I'm just not smart enough. I thumbed the door release, hearing the door clunk open in the distance, followed a few seconds later by the rattle of the elevator.

She was waiting at the ancient cage door when I went out. Despite what she'd said, she didn't look especially disturbed as I palmed the lock and opened the bars.

"It looks like the prisons you see on old shows." She hunched her shoulders as if cold.

I swung the gate closed and re-activated the locks. I didn't miss the slight rise of her eyebrows as I did. "If you're worried about my intentions, feel free to leave."

She shook her head—a tight movement that clearly betrayed her discomfort, but that was her problem. I led her into my apartment, and she perched on the edge of the couch, a silhouette against the faded salmon furnishing. She was dressed in gray now, her rich brown skin seeming to absorb the colorlessness of her clothing.

"I'm sorry for bothering you so late." Her voice was low and hesitant. "It's been a hard day."

"Interesting." I poured myself another drink and looked around for a clean glass to offer her one, then gave up on the idea. "Don't think I've heard a woman apologize before. Especially to a stranger."

She drew her arms closer. "Are you always so chauvinistic?"

"Only with women that lie badly to me." I tipped my glass at her. "Tell me why you're here. If you like, you can pretend to tell the truth, and I'll pretend to care. But make it quick, you're hampering my social life."

"Please don't be like the others." She stood up and walked around the couch, placing it between us.

"I ran out of sympathy last week and haven't been to the store yet." I had no reason to be nice, and maybe if I was unpleasant enough, she'd leave. "Presumably you don't think I killed your teacher now."

"He wasn't my 'teacher.' I did research for him."

"Which brings up an interesting question. How did you find out where I lived?"

"The man who took me to the University..."

I held up my hand. Charlie was a turkey-necked old fool who didn't know when to keep his mouth shut. The damage was done though. "I don't know what you came here for, but I can't tell you anything I haven't already told the police."

"I need your help."

I snorted into my drink. Was I supposed to feel flattered or something? I wasn't much of a knight errant, and she didn't look like a maiden in distress. Maybe some other time I might have reacted better, but that was long ago and part of a different world.

"You have me confused with someone who gives a damn." The whiskey burned as I swallowed a mouthful. "I don't even know you."

"Tana Radebaugh. I told you earlier."

She held out her hand. She'd refused my handshake earlier, now I returned the favor. Women rarely shake hands, and when they do, it's usually limp as if they're saying hello to a snake. After a few moments, she pulled back and looked away.

"I need to go to Dr. Ganz' apartment." Her voice was harsh, as if she didn't want to talk to me, but had no choice. "There are some important files I need to get—research notes—I need them for my work."

"Fine. Go to the cops and ask for them."

She shook her head. "I already asked, but everything in the apartment is part of a crime scene. They can't release them until their investigation is finished."

"Then you'll have to wait."

"That might be months. I don't have that long to complete my studies." Her knuckles whitened as she clenched her hands.

"Appearances can deceive. I only look dumb." My glass was empty, and I refilled it, enjoying the look of disapproval on her face. "I'm sure as hell not invading a crime scene for someone I barely know. Find yourself another hero, Ms. Radebaugh."

"Call me Tana, please." Her smile showed definite signs of being forced. Then she looked away. "Have you ever been to a zoo, Mr. Ballen? There are the chimps, the bigger ones picking on the small... the lions all proud and thoroughly lazy... the hippos wallowing and consuming everything they can, and the peacocks strutting about like lords of creation. It's exactly the same at a university. They're nothing more than animal houses for people with delusions of intelligence."

"Nice picture. Now, if you're done..."

She continued as if I hadn't spoken. "My parents went through hell to put me through school. They thought, like most Americans, that *our* universities were easily as good as any upstart African or Asian institutions. How could they not be? Anything lost in technological excellence was sure to be compensated for by the heritage and high standards of a domestic education.

"But memories of past glories don't attract grants or offers for high-profile collaborations." Tana shrugged. "Yaoundé, Kansong, and New Hong Kong receive millions from industry, but here, JHU struggles to fund programs costing a few thousand."

There was nothing new in what she was saying, and I yawned deliberately. Decades ago, while the "developed world" invested billions in feeding their people to death, and then billions more teaching them how to cure the self-taught obesity, developing nations poured their resources into education. The movement was led by the then Chinese and Indian governments, but later spread to the newly formed United African Democracies. The results were entirely predictable—like dropping a five-kilogram weight in a one-g gravity frame and hearing it crash to the floor.

When the Atolls broke away from terrestrial control, it simply completed the process of removing a large part of the collective intelligence and vitality from cultures drowning in the morass of their own short-sightedness and lack of discipline. As with the sea-level rise, the West was worst hit, but everyone suffered.

"We all have problems." Mine seemed to be growing by the second and I wasn't about to add hers to the pile.

"It's a hard place to survive. Everyone competes with everyone else." She smiled, but I could see the pain behind her eyes. "The slightest mistake is exploited by a malicious rumor mill. The most innocuous of activities can be misinterpreted and put you on a sponsor's black list. And you never know if it's down to ostracism, prejudice, or whether you simply weren't good enough."

Her story had more holes in it than a chunk of AeroFoam. "So, what's the deal? I'm sure the University can get them for you. I doubt the police would refuse a direct request."

For a moment I almost felt sorry for her. She was probably a good kid, far too naive for the crappy world she found herself in, but I had myself to think about. The cops were trying to tie me up in knots over this and even being with her would add to their suspicion.

"I hoped we could help each other." She glared at me. "But it seems I was wrong."

Eight

Before I could answer, the door announcer warbled for attention. "Do you think I won a popularity contest and they forgot to tell me?"

I leaned toward the pickup and activated the door speaker again.

"Mr. Ballen? Detective Coyan. I've been sent to bring you in for further questioning."

I cursed silently before speaking. "Welcome to the party, Detective. I hope you brought enough men. I'm a desperate criminal you know."

"There's only me, sir. Please open the door before I have to call for an override."

Swiping the door latch I spun towards the girl. "Can you fly an AeroMobile?"

It was a dumb idea. The cops would presumably have the building surrounded and under observation, but if I could get rid of Tana, there was a small chance I could avoid digging myself a deeper hole. It didn't take much imagination to figure out what they'd think if they caught us together.

That slim hope disappeared with the barest shake of her head. I imagined several different scenarios to try to explain things—each one more fantastic and implausible than the last, but the elevator click came too soon for me to put anything coherent together. I walked over and unlocked the gate.

"Ballen?" Coyan flashed his ID, the holographic badge clearly visible over his picture. He was enveloped in a bulky dark blue suit, but I got the impression his appearance was due to muscle rather than too much pasta like many of his colleagues.

He turned his wide face to Tana, more than casually interested. "Ms. Radebaugh?"

Tana jerked, her broad face wearing an expression I couldn't quite place—surprise, shock, or maybe something else. She opened her mouth as if to say something, but nothing came out.

"Whatever you're thinking, this isn't it. I'm happy to go to the precinct with you though." Maybe I could persuade him to ignore Tana. "My friend was just leaving."

Coyan shook his head slowly, squeezing through the door to the living room. "I'm afraid that's impossible. I have orders to bring in both of you. You see we found *this*."

This was a black and silver gadget about the size of an old-fashioned cigarette lighter. He brandished it like a vampire hunter in a cheesy horror flick might wave his silver cross.

"I'm sure you recognize it." His face was stony.

"I'd guess it was the gift wrap they packaged Detective Francis' brains in, except it seems too big."

Coyan fought back a smile. "It's a narrow-band EM Disruptor—enough power to knock out Argus pickups within a three or four block radius. Very expensive and difficult to get hold of. Where do you think we found it?"

"*Spy Gear Trader?*" I said.

Coyan snorted. "Try again."

"The way my luck is running, probably inside the hem of my pajamas."

"In the garbage cleaned out of your cab." Coyan lifted his thumb. "Get whatever you need and let's go. I don't have all night."

I put my glass in the sink and grabbed my jacket. When I turned back, Coyan was playing with something on my counter-top.

"You seen these things?" He let out a laugh. "They're crazy-ass funny."

On the counter was a small purple gorilla about two centimeters high that Coyan must have brought with him. It was doing what looked like an old-fashioned soft-shoe dance, complete with miniature cane, bow tie, and top hat. As it danced, it sang in a squeaky whistle.

"… the old lady was doing a broken-down conga in twenty-five. We hoofed it 'till we couldn't take it any longer and had to jive…"

It was the kind of toy given away with candy for kids, but Coyan seemed entranced. He curled his thick fist around it, scooping it up from the counter and pushing it deep in his pocket.

"Is your car outside?" I asked.

Tana looked uneasy and edged away from Coyan. "Ballen. I don't think—"

"Quiet," barked Coyan. I wasn't even slightly surprised to see the broad muzzle of a pistol emerge from inside his jacket.

"There's no need for that. I already said we'd go with you."

"He's not—" Tana stopped as Coyan swung the pistol towards her.

"Whatever you were gonna say, don't."

I took a half-step forward. "Tell us what you want us to do. We're not going to be any trouble."

He swung the gun back to me and gestured upwards with a flick of the muzzle. "Your cab is upstairs. Let's go."

We clambered up to the roof platform, our feet clanking on the metal stairs. Coyan sent me first, with Tana between us. A few minutes later I strapped in and told the cab to lift and merge into the traffic stream. The slick chill of the pistol pressed against my temple.

"Ganz' apartment and don't worry about the speed limits."

Tana's voice wavered from the back seat, "Don't do it, Ballen. He'll kill us even if you do what he says."

"I thought I told you to shut up." The gun ground harder against my head. "Tell your girlfriend to keep quiet, Ballen, or else."

The "or else" wasn't specified, but the rasp in his voice was enough to make me want to avoid it. I got the impression he wouldn't be disappointed if I put up a struggle and gave him an excuse to kill me. I wasn't going to do that if at all possible.

The cab swept to maximum speed, and I leaned back slightly, moving slowly so as not to panic Coyan. "You're not going to shoot me. You said someone ordered you to fetch us, and at this speed, you'd crash before you could untangle my body from the controls.

"So why don't we all play nice and get this game over with. Whatever it is, we'll cooperate. Then we can go on our way."

"You're smart, Ballen, I'll give you that. How 'bout I shoot *her* instead?" He pointed the gun at Tana and chuckled. "Would you prefer that?"

Tana whimpered. I could see in the RearView that she was rigid in the seat.

"This thing won't move any quicker. We'll be there in three minutes. Even if you shoot us both, you won't get there any sooner."

"Sounds like your boyfriend doesn't really care. Maybe I should—"

The cab rocked as Tana grabbed his arm, swinging it hard against the headrest. I heard his shoulder pop and the gun snapped from his fingers. Coyan scrambled to reach into the back of the cab, but Tana got there first and pushed the gun in his face.

"That's enough." Her voice wavered. She sounded on the edge of panic, and I hoped she'd hold it together long enough for me to set down. "I don't want to have to use this."

Incredibly, Coyan started laughing. At first a soft giggle, but it grew into a loud belly laugh as he massaged his shoulder, almost as if he enjoyed the pain. "Go ahead," he finally spluttered. "Do your worst."

Tana looked puzzled, then checked the gun before throwing it to the other side of the cab. "Fingerprint Lock." She spat.

"Do I look stupid?" Coyan was still giggling. "Ya should have seen the look on your face. So funny, wish I had a picture."

His hand disappeared and came back with another pistol, smaller than the first, but equally deadly. "Always carry a spare."

"You learn that at 'Thugs-R-Us?'" I was getting close to breaking point and fought to clamp down on my emotions. "Ganz' apartment coming up. What should I do?"

"Landing pad round back. Put her down there." The gun swung towards my face. "And keep it professional."

Nine

According to the adage, a criminal always returns to the scene of the crime. I'm not convinced crooks are really that dumb, but in this case, I wasn't the criminal, and I don't think being forced to return really counts.

Ganz' apartment wasn't the stereotypical dust and print-book mess beloved of so many Solido shows. The room was sparsely decorated, but the furniture was old and expensive looking. The couch and chairs looked as if they'd been placed with laser precision and there wasn't a hint of a well-thumbed journal among the pale walls and ruddy wooden highlights. The lights came on automatically as we entered, the warm glow from the cream walls providing an almost dreamlike effect as satin drapes billowed in the air currents. Ganz enjoyed his comfort, even if the style was a little dated.

Coyan directed us to stand by a small tree growing in the middle of the room. I wasn't sure what it was, possibly Cherry, but I'm no botanist. Around the tree was a perfectly manicured indoor lawn. They'd been popular maybe fifty years ago, but weren't common anymore. Hardly surprising, as the setup must have cost several months of my salary to install and I couldn't even guess the maintenance cost.

"He sure knew how to live." Coyan whistled. "Wouldn't think a whale from a university would pull in that kind of money."

To my relief, Tana managed to control her feelings and said nothing.

I pointed to the grass patch. "If you needed somebody to water the lawn, you could have just asked."

I should have followed Tana's lead and stayed silent, because a moment later Coyan's gun slammed into my kidney and I staggered to my knees, my hands clawing at the perfect lawn.

"Shaddap. You're here to answer, not ask."

This time I kept quiet. The way he'd hit me told me he was the kind of person that enjoyed pain, especially other people's. Not someone you want to provoke.

"On the floor, cross-legged. And sit on your hands." Coyan stepped back a little, but the gun stayed on us. "Don't make me wait."

Tana sat down immediately, but I struggled to fold my legs beneath me. The lawn felt surprisingly clean, but after the everyday grime of city living anything natural would.

Tana's eyes darted about the room as if searching for something, but I had no idea what. She shivered, not as though she were cold, more the involuntary muscle spasms provoked by the desire to escape. All I could do was hope she wouldn't do anything to get her, or me, into more trouble.

Coyan wandered over to the side of the room, pulling out the purple gorilla we'd seen earlier and setting it on the mantle where it started dancing a frenetic bop.

He laughed immediately. Maybe it was funny to him, but I couldn't quite get into the spirit. Having guns pointed at me always takes away my light-hearted, easy-going demeanor—can't think why.

I sensed rather than saw movement around me, as a series of shadows slipped through the darkened room on both sides. One of the "shadows" rippled and thickened in substance, forming an armored figure pointing the heavy barrel of a military QuenchGun directly at my chest. The visor on his helmet reflected a distorted view of the room as more shadows coalesced into people.

Tana leapt from the grass.

"Stay where you are." The voice was deliberately harsh and metallic through the helmet.

Tana stopped but didn't lower herself back down. The figure cuffed her with the back of his armored gauntlet, the crack bouncing around the wide room. Coyan moved closer too, and my muscles tightened as I pressed down against the grass despite my weakness.

"Move, and you will be shot," the figure commanded.

It's difficult to argue with that kind of logic, and I didn't try. As Logan would have said—when cornered by a grizzly, be polite and hope he isn't hungry.

"That's enough." A new shadow distilled into solidity, with a slighter build than the others. It moved towards Tana with the grace of a panther stalking its prey, despite the bulk of the armored suit.

The figure reached down and tousled Tana's hair, before lifting a hand and cracking the seal on their combat visor. The faceplate lifted to reveal an almond-shaped face with two of the deepest brown eyes I'd ever seen and a pair of luscious dark red lips that rivaled Dollie's.

"There was a body outside." Her voice was emotionless—she could have been talking about a discarded newspaper.

"Building Supervisor," one of the men muttered, but I didn't catch which.

"I said no one was to be hurt." There was a scrape of uneasy foot shuffling. "That isn't how we do things, and you should know that. Who did it?"

I watched as she stalked in front of the men, dragging the muzzle of her gun across each one in turn. Finally, she reached the thug who'd hit Tana and wedged the muzzle firmly against his crotch. His shoulders dropped slightly, and he nodded.

"It was a mistake." The man's voice was penitent. "It won't happen again."

"You're right, Schanning. It *was* a mistake. Go back to the vehicle."

"But... that is, I'm still..." Schanning moved away, hesitating at the door. "I can still be useful to—"

"Leave. Immediately. Before I forget I'm a lady."

She waited until Schanning lumbered out of the room then turned back to us with a radiant smile. Dentamite companies would have shed blood to have that look promoting their products.

Though her shaved head was slightly at odds with that image.

"I'm so sorry about that. You've no idea how hard it is to get reliable help these days." She stood in front of us, holding her gun casually.

"Creating your own death squad sure ain't what it used to be," I muttered.

"Oh, these were the best I could find. Although Jarheads have good stamina in the bedroom, intelligence isn't among their strong points."

"Why do you need them?" Tana pulled back. "What could you possibly want with us?"

"Oh, I don't really need them, though sometimes men do have their uses—despite their obvious limitations." She gestured to the men to step back and circled the lawn, examining it intently. "Nutrient deficiency. Somebody should feed this, or it will die."

"We'll take care of that," I said. "After you leave."

"Please, stand up. There's no need for this. My name is Gabriella Faulk, and my sole purpose here is to recover some information. If we can do that, my interest ends and everyone can be on their way. You, and the lawn, can live."

I struggled to my feet, trying to place her accent. There were traces that sounded British, but interwoven with hints suggesting she'd spent time in more exotic places.

"So we give you what you're looking for, we can go?" I brushed at my clothing, trying to sound as dumb as possible.

She moved close, her eyes glistening as she looked up at me, hands behind her back in an oh-so-demure-but-willing pose that I didn't believe for one second.

"I wouldn't want to hurt a man like you." She sighed. "You're too charming for me to want to *waste*."

"I'm always willing to help a lady. What're you looking for?"

Tana shuffled uncomfortably next to me. "Ballen? What are you doing? We know this creature's name." She sniffed. "She's not going to let us walk out of here."

While there are numerous rumors to the contrary, I'm not actually stupid. I knew how much danger we were in, but surrounded by a goon squad packing high-powered assault weapons and combat armor, I figured I'd let *Gabriella* talk as long as she wanted.

"I'm a business person. I get paid to deliver what my clients want, in the best possible fashion. If they paid me for a bloodbath, I'd happily provide one." She laughed lightly. "In this instance, they're a little squeamish. They only want the professor's documents."

Tana took half a step back. "His research papers are in the central University repository. Go to any public library terminal and log into GARNET. None of this is necessary."

"You know you're so right." Gabriella reached up and stroked Tana's thick hair again. "Your hair is very pretty, I'm almost envious. Though it would be a handicap in my position.

"My sponsors have checked the legitimate routes and what they want isn't there. We live in a sad world. It gets me angry when I find that people don't want to share. Perhaps they cling to the quaint idea of producing something unique all by themselves, or possibly they're just selfish."

Gabriella spat the last word, pulling Tana's hair and forcing her head back until the tendons in her neck were clearly visible. "Give me Ganz' private research papers and the key to his personal GARNET account."

Tana bent backwards in an attempt to relieve the pressure on her neck. In desperation, her elbow shot out and caught Gabriella in the midriff, but it had no effect.

"I don't have either of those things. I only did research for him."

"Oh come now. Don't sell yourself short." Gabriella let out a soft giggle and pulled Tana's head back further. "You and Ganz were Stimmers. I'm sure he shared everything in those tender moments of post-orgasmic mutual pleasure—give a man sexual relief, and he's a grateful puppy drooling at the mouth."

I wasn't sure if Tana tried to answer. All I heard was a sickening sound gurgling out of her throat.

"Let her go. I can give you what you're looking for."

Gabriella smiled at me but didn't release her hold. "That's very sweet. Stupid, but sweet nevertheless."

She twisted Tana around by the hair as she turned to me. "Joe Ballen. Male, thirty-seven. Ex-construction worker specializing in

LEO projects. Grounded after losing an arm and both legs in an industrial accident. Now driving cabs illegally." She waved her gun towards my legs. "The ReGen therapy worked well."

"So you know a lot about me. Now let her go."

"You *are* rather handsome and undoubtedly very charming, but what could you possibly have that I would be interested in?" She gave an earthy laugh. "Other than what's inside your pants…"

"The girl came to me for help. She gave me Ganz' files and his access code. Let her go, and I'll turn them over to you."

"Ballen…" Tana groaned, but nothing else was understandable.

"Oh, Joe, you've lied to me. What am I to do with you now?"

What she did was shoot me in the leg.

Limb ReGen has some curious aspects. One is the problem of fine motor control. Although medical technologists can connect the major nerve bundles, a lot of the smaller ones either refuse to connect, or the pathways get jumbled. This produces a kind of neural noise, which is why I sometimes get hit by the shakes and take medication to dampen the rogue signals.

A side-effect of this is that any pain becomes magnified, and even under moderately high load conditions the neural relays simply shut down, leaving me a mass of quivering flesh. My leg folded under me and the next thing I knew my face was slapping the grass.

"You see what happens when people are unreasonable?" Gabriella jerked Tana upright with a strength I had to guess was a result of Geneering, and spoke into Tana's ear. "Give me what I want, and this will be over."

Tana struggled but said nothing.

"My powers of persuasion seem to be failing. Perhaps I need help from these men after all." She pushed the gun down between Tana's legs. "They like to take turns, and their urges are far too primitive to be satisfied by *Stimming*."

Tana sagged as if her skeleton had disintegrated. "I *can't*. I don't have what you want."

I fumbled in my pocket for some nerve-tranq to deaden the searing stump of pain my leg had become. Three or four of the tiny pills would deaden the agony at least to the point where I might be able to function again.

"Whatever you're thinking" —Coyan loomed over me, pinning my arm to the floor with his boot— "You're not going to make it."

The pressure on my arm increased as he ground his foot down harder, making me grunt in pain. My sight faded, and I fought not to pass out, but it seemed like I wasn't going to have any option.

Everything began to white out, the contrast disappearing from the people and room. I might have heard several shots, but even my hearing seemed remote and disconnected. Then I seemed to surface briefly, as if a pressure had been lifted. Instead of blacking out, my vision dissolved with clouds of grit. Like watching an old restored movie. I reached for the pills, my hand trembling and swallowed a fistful, not stopping to count them, hoping they would kick in fast.

Coyan was no longer standing over me, and I heard a tumult of wild cries, punctuated by the high-pitched zing of guns firing. I felt a tug on my arm. Tana had dragged me off the grass toward the door, a large pistol now in her hand. I saw Coyan lying on the floor, his nose a flattened blood-streamed mess. One of the other men was down too, his arm twisted at an unnatural angle.

Tana lifted the gun again, firing another volley. A shot caught one of Gabriella's men as he dived for cover, the high-velocity needles from the QuenchGun ricocheting off the armor in a splash of sparks.

"Put down the weapon," Gabriella bellowed. "No one will hurt you, you have my word."

Tana wasn't convinced and pulled me to my feet. Slipping my arm over her shoulders, she half carried me to the entrance hall.

We staggered forward, the walls and floor around us rippling like a drug-inspired phantasm as the volley of needles shredded the short hallway. Gabriella's men were firing blindly, and we weren't hit, but it was something of a miracle.

"Cease fire," Gabriella shouted, and silence fell. "Joe… you really shouldn't leave the party without the rest of us."

We were at the main door, and I couldn't resist glancing back as we crossed the threshold. Gabriella held a short tube in her hand, pointed towards us. I couldn't make out what it was, but it looked a little like a metal flashlight.

There was a slight flash, and a blur of tendrils shot towards us. One caught Tana on the arm and stuck to her, holding her in place. She held the gun close to her arm and fired, the muzzle flash melting the sticky tendril and burning her skin. The filaments snapped back and stuck to the inner door frame, forming what looked like a monstrous spider's web that cut Gabriella off from any easy pursuit.

The frame exploded as another furious barrage of needles hit the oak surface, covering us with a blast of splinters that bit deep.

We turned to find Schanning blocking the entrance.

"Far enough."

I'll say this for Tana. There wasn't the slightest hesitation. She dived forward, curling into a ball and barreling into him with a force that hardly seemed possible. They went down in a tangled pile, and I staggered towards them as quickly as I could. I ripped open Schanning's visor, punching his heavy jaw until he stopped moving.

Tana grabbed the QuenchGun Schanning had dropped and hauled me through the door, the agony of moving almost more than I could deal with. It felt like we crawled up the small flight of stairs before finally stumbling into the dank night air.

I dropped into the driver's seat of the cab, grateful for the relief of sitting. The pills were kicking in and easing the pain, making movement easier. With a few quick stabs on the controls, I warmed up the engine, ready to jump as soon as Tana got in.

The cab shivered as a burst of needles slammed into the side of the car, tearing gouges in the vehicle's composite skin and splintering the toughened glass canopy. Either Gabriella had found a way around the web, or Schanning had recovered.

Tana jumped in the back seat. "Go!"

Ten

I pulled back on the controls, overriding the safeties and hit full throttle. The cab leapt up, the dashboard flashing every warning and violation message it was capable of as I broke every safety limit in the book, climbing at twice the permitted rate.

As we passed the lip of the building, I cut the turbines so we'd plummet towards the ground. Hoping to drop us out of a direct line of fire from anyone following. We were slammed against the safety belts as the emergency systems triggered the thrusters to prevent our impact. Wheeling the cab around hard I punched maximum boost to put as much distance as I could between us and Gabriella.

"You know how to use that thing?" I gestured at the gun cradled on Tana's lap.

"Yes. It doesn't have the fingerprint lock." She glared at me, then glanced over her shoulder. "Do you think they'll come after us?"

"They must have transport, and they won't let us get away that easily."

Tana gripped the gun. "We should call the police."

"You do that. Tell them to send a coroner's team, they'll need one."

A flicker on the RearView caught my eye. Something was behind us though I couldn't see anything clearly. Without thinking I jammed the controls over, dragging the cab in the tightest arc I could. The back quarter-panel shattered as a burst of gunfire sliced the composite body to thin slivers.

"They're on us." I scanned the RearView. "Do you see them?"

Tana was hunkered down, her eyes barely peeping over the seat. "Nothing visible."

They must have been using a ShimmerField equipped vehicle, virtually invisible unless you caught it right, which meant there was some serious money behind Gabriella and her team. Technology like that wasn't cheap.

"Why haven't the police responded to the Argus feeds?"

"Coyan had a disrupter. Even if someone's monitoring this area, all they'll see is another sensor failure."

I felt something snap at the rear of the cab as if we'd been kicked by a giant boot. Instead of fighting it I let us spin, using the momentum to kick around a corner between two low rows of disused concrete buildings. Tana must have seen something because she opened up with the QuenchGun, blowing out the side window as the inside of the cab filled with screams from the ultra-velocity rounds.

"I think I hit them," she said, her breath short and fast. "But I don't think this is powerful enough to do any damage."

"Today is definitely a good news day." I swung the cab in a high arc, the vectoring nozzles creaking noisily against their stops as I pushed the maneuver as tight to the buildings as possible. "I'd appreciate a little more optimism in future."

Tana let off another stream of shots. "That was a definite hit. No effect."

I pushed down, and we shot underneath a large AdSurf, the glowing billboard temporarily filling the interior with intense purple and orange. Tana gasped, and I pulled up to avoid clipping the building parapet. A second later the screen behind us exploded in a shower of plastic, glass, and mica, revealing the bulky toad-like shape of an Arroyo heavy lifter.

"We haven't got a chance against that thing." I dropped the cab below rooftop level. "If they get close enough they can easily push us out of the air."

The voltage from the billboard must have affected the Arroyo's ShimmerField. The vehicle cut in and out of existence as I watched the RearView, the flickering apparition somehow more intimidating than the invisibility had been.

Even at this time of night, the traffic grew heavier as we approached downtown, forcing me to swing the cab to avoid several vehicles. We were smaller than the Arroyo and in theory, should have had an edge, but we were driving a sedan—not a sports car.

Originally I'd been heading towards the city center above old Highway 95, but at some point I'd zigged when maybe I should have zagged, and we were now coming in parallel to Columbia Pike. I dragged us southeast then back above the 95.

"Do you have a plan or are we flying at random?" Tana shouted, as another blast caught us from behind.

"If you have any suggestions feel free to contact our main office on 555-6162." I swerved to avoid a commuter transport, slamming bone-crunchingly hard into the side of a transporter in the process.

I felt the cold muzzle against my head. I didn't need to turn around to know what was happening.

"Head for the nearest police station." Tana's voice was almost a squeak. "We need help."

I felt the gun shake. Like many people, Tana had a simplistic faith that some vague authority figure would always be there to help. Trouble is, the authorities can sometimes be as bad as what you're running from.

"Sorry, I've already used up my daily quota of being shot at."

I flipped the cab up and slid to the right as the Arroyo lunged forward to ram us. For a while we ran side by side along the crowded skyways. Then I banked hard, throwing Tana against the canopy, the g-force pinning the gun against the wall.

"City regulations dictate that passengers should be securely belted up at all times," I said.

"Ballen, this is crazy." She gasped loudly against the acceleration.

I swung the cab the other way, avoiding another vehicle as we veered through the onrushing traffic. "Crazy? You're the one threatening to shoot the driver."

The Arroyo slammed into the back of us, sending us into a spiral. Every stabilizer screamed as they fought to catch the uncontrolled plunge. Worse, the safety restraints deployed, making me as much of a passenger as Tana as the nose of the cab arced through an apartment's picture window.

As the storm of glass particles cleared, I noticed the inside of the apartment was decorated with a sky and cloud pattern and the room was filled with the sleek lines of a bright red rocket-plane, like the ones used in the SkyRacer league. I had no idea how anyone had managed to squeeze that into an apartment at L6. It looked like you'd have to crouch to cross from one side of the room to the other and what they did with the plane was impossible to guess. The cab had smashed through one of the upturned wingtips—the owner wasn't going to be happy we'd paid them a visit.

I managed to move my hand enough to override the restraints and pulled the cab out of the window hole. The turbines whined in protest and the cab moved with a distinct list. Almost immediately I saw blue and red lights flashing in the RearView.

"Hooray for the cavalry," I murmured.

The police car came up behind me quickly, dogging my tail like a case of bad breath. I was still weaving, trying to see any sign of the gunmen, but they'd vanished with the arrival of the cops.

Our speed dropped as if we'd flown into a mass of floating marshmallows. The cops had triggered a hold on my car and the engines were throttling back to hover mode. I reached over to punch the emergency button and override the hold, but they were alongside before I could.

"Vehicle DD0724," the communicator squawked. "This is the police. You are in violation of Air-Traffic Safety Regulations. Prepare to follow us to the nearest precinct for processing."

"Tell me something I don't know." I reached under the console, flipped a couple of switches that weren't supposed to be there, and the turbines whined back up to full power.

"Ballen, I think you should do wh—"

The Arroyo reappeared, slamming into the police car so hard that it smashed into the side of my car in turn. I twisted the controls, but part of the mangled bodywork locked us together, and all I did was drag the cops through the air.

I craned my neck to follow the Arroyo as it moved away and then vanished again. The cops were yelling at us through their windshield, but nothing was coming through the communicator.

Whether they weren't broadcasting or the system was damaged, I had no idea, but it wasn't hard to guess what they were shouting.

Looking around I saw the Arroyo making another dive and hit the throttle. I barely managed to push both cars out of the way as the heavy truck completed the demolition job we'd started on the window, doing further damage to the beautiful rocket-plane.

"We need to lose our penalty weight," I growled, more to myself than anyone. "Or we aren't going to make it."

I signaled to the cops through the window, trying to convey the idea of them pulling backwards while I went the other way. Maybe we'd have a chance if we could unhook the two vehicles.

They nodded in silent agreement. I opened the throttles wide and pulled the cab hard right. The car shuddered as the turbines spluttered and coughed, making our movements a drunken lurch rather than a strong tug.

"Ballen..."

I didn't need Tana to finish her sentence to know the Arroyo was closing in again. I yanked on the controls, but they were soggy and unresponsive, barely changing our movement.

An explosion hit the base of my spine as they speared us full-on, sandwiching us between the Arroyo and the cop car. The engines and stabilizing systems quit, turning us into two and a half tons of expensive composite scrap with all the aerodynamic properties of a flying pig—minus its wings.

I glimpsed the half-demolished police car flail into the water below us, then the swollen fingers of the muddy Patapsco filled the view through the windshield. For one second I thought we might be lucky enough to enter the water cleanly, but at the last moment we clipped a wave hard and the world dissolved to watery blackness.

Eleven

I was floating in solid blackness, with no external stimuli beyond the voice I heard. It was peaceful. I could have stayed there a long time.

"This one's dead, Bea."

Half of me wished I was the subject of the whispered conversation and maybe I was, except I don't believe in an afterlife. The fact I heard, or even imagined, voices was a clue. Then, when the pain started to tear at my nerves and a stream of brackish liquid sucked into my nostrils, I rolled over. The coughing fits wracked my chest as I tried to clear my breathing, proving I was still among the living even if I didn't feel much like it.

"Not dead, Bea! Not dead."

A flicker of orange light tumbled through the darkness, dimly lighting the area around me. The glinting highlights provided some guidance as to where the surface of the water was. My feet caught something solid, and I staggered to hold myself upright. I was surrounded by what appeared to be the largest pile of flotsam known to humanity, which meant I was either in the mid-Atlantic or somewhere along the extended flood areas of Chesapeake Bay.

A pair of strong hands slid under my armpits and pulled me backwards, dragging my feet through the sub-surface mud behind me. Rough splinters dug painfully into my back as I was hauled out of the water onto a ramshackle wooden walkway, and I did my best impersonation of a drowned rat.

I shook my head to clear my sight, and a face appeared above me, the grim features lined both by time and prolonged water exposure. One large ear stuck out at an odd angle from the rough sacking wrapped around his head, and a grin split his face.

"Definitely alive. Definitely." He let out a whistle. "Two in one night eh, Bea? Shoulda set the dinner table."

Rolling onto my side produced more pain in my ribs which I'd have happily done without. But as it was a pre-requisite for further movement, I didn't have much choice unless I wanted to become one with the piles of floating garbage.

A rough platform rambled into the dank shoreline fog. The early spring air was damp and clamped around my chest as I breathed, chilling me through to my bones. I thought I saw a distant light submerged in the mist, but whether it was from the city or something else I wasn't sure.

"Have you seen a girl?" My throat was raw from the cocktail of putrescent water I'd swallowed and the wet fog. "She was with me when I..."

"He's a talker, Bea. Gotta like a talker. Eh?" He edged closer, one foot rasping along the wooden docking as he moved. "This way, Talker. This way."

Wet-foot aren't known for their hospitality. They're more likely to accost regular citizens than act as Samaritans, so I was cautious about following him. The overhead whoosh of an AeroMobile reminded me that our pursuers were not too far behind us, so my choice was either to follow him or jump back in the water and I wasn't at that point—yet.

The rough boardwalk ran into the deeper blackness of the shoreline. Some of it looked like deliberate construction, while other sections were made from rough wooden pallets wired haphazardly to barrels and other makeshift supports. My wet-foot acquaintance shuffled along with familiarity, moving fast despite his broken gait. His wet rags slithered across the wooden slats, hissing like a demonic sea-serpent as he led me to a destination only he knew.

I saw a flicker of yellow-orange light and felt something brush against my face. A hand reached up to pull my head down. I was forced to squirm forward in a crouch as I pushed through several layers of tarpaulin before blinking my way into a smoke-filled glare.

I could only see one room but had no sense of whether it was part of a bigger building or not. Every corner was filled with heaps of what appeared to be garbage, but as my eyes accommodated the smoky light, I realized it was salvage. A tower of food cans dominated one area, while a pile of mildewed blankets filled another. One wall was taken up by the filthiest bed I'd ever seen occupied by an unmoving prone figure. The ache in my ribs eased a little when I recognized Tana's sprawled shape.

"Thanks for helping us," I said.

The wet-foot poked through the piles of junk around me.

"He *appreciates* it, Bea. What do you think of that?" Torn rags of paper and cloth sailed into the air as he dug furiously into a pile like a dog retrieving a long-lost bone. "Don't appreciate you when you need help, eh? Only when *they* need it."

"Who's Bea?" I couldn't see who he was talking to.

"Who's Bea? Who's Bea, he asks?" His words became a cackle. "Who's Bea? Who's Bea?"

The wet-foot had clearly left a stable orbit years ago. I had no idea how long he'd been living in these conditions, but no one in their right mind would stay in such filth. Even if you were broke, there were drier spots further inland.

"You don't want us hanging around. People will be looking for us. Unpleasant people." That had to be the understatement of the year. "If you show me the way out, I'll take my friend and leave you in peace."

His digging subsided, and a pair of grimy overalls sailed through the air, wrapping themselves around my arm. I guessed they were meant as an alternative to my soaked clothing, but the stink of the rotten material told me I was better off keeping the clothes I had, despite their condition.

The wet-foot shuffled over to Tana and brushed his fingers across her cheek. I thought for a moment he was crying, then realized that the high-pitched ululation was some kind of song.

"She's so sweet, my little reet petite. My angel with a smile, lay with me a while. God knows how I miss, your everlasting kiss. The sunsets aren't the same, now I call your name. Beatrice, my one and only Beatrice."

Tears glistened down his cheeks in the bronze light, trails that ran along the crevices in his stubbled, blackened face. I felt a sudden sense of complete loss and anger at a world that could bring this kind of lament to people's lives. No matter what his history, no one deserved to live like this.

"Where's Bea?" I said quietly, reluctant to intrude.

"Went away. Couldn't take it no more. Kept telling me she couldn't take it, she did, but I didn't listen. Can't take it, Pa. Just can't take it." He cradled Tana's head and sniffed. "She went away."

"We need to leave too."

He stroked Tana's cheek again. "So pretty. Pretty like Bea."

It was difficult keeping track of where the wet-foot's thoughts were. He seemed to switch from the present into his dreams and memories repeatedly, his thoughts drifting like the smoke from the yellowed candles filling the room.

Tana stirred, groaning slightly as she recovered. Her eyes flashed open, and she bolted upright on the cot, hunching back against the wall.

"Joe?"

It was the first time she'd used my name and I wondered if that was some kind of promotion. "Here." I kept my voice low. Situations involving people are like engineering problems in a lot of ways—the less energy you put in, the easier it is to control, and the less likely it is to blow up in your face. "This fine gentleman rescued us from the water."

"Th-th-thank you," she said, her back still pinned against the wall. I could see she was trying to stay calm, but her instincts were clear from the tension in her body and her darting eyes.

"So pretty, eh, Bea?" The wet-foot flopped down to sit on a pile of boxes near to Tana. He leaned close and inhaled deeply. "Smells pretty too."

Tana's eyes sought mine. She was trembling, and I didn't think it was from the cold. There was a bright spark of fear inside her that threatened to erupt at any moment. The wet-foot *seemed* harmless, but that didn't mean anything.

"I'm Joe. This is Tana." I heard some soft skittering noises that were probably rats.

The wet-foot looked from Tana to me and back again. He seemed to struggle, as though personal introductions were something long gone from his world. "Walt," he finally mouthed, his grizzled lips moving as if the name was unfamiliar. "But not Disney! No, no, no! Not Disney! Ehh, Bea?"

"Pleased to meet you, Walt." Tana slowly held out her hand.

Walt gazed at it for a few moments, then reached out with both fabric-wrapped hands to clasp hers. "So pretty. Skin so soft and young. Like Bea."

"Was Bea your wife?" Tana's nose wrinkled as though the fetid locker room smell had finally hit her.

While she was talking, I looked for any sign of a way out other than the one we'd used coming in. My eyes were slowly adapting to the feeble, inconsistent light from the candles, but I didn't want to brave the ice-cold waters again if I could help it.

"Wife? No, no." Walt shuddered, drawing in deep breaths. "My girl. My sweet, beautiful little girl."

It wasn't difficult to guess his story. After the Big Shake, the flood waters came several times, until the time they came and didn't leave. Anyone who could escape the low-lying buildings did, but many had nowhere else to go. As usual, the authorities were too pre-occupied with saving their own skins to be overly concerned with people who didn't vote, people who had neither friends in high places or money to buy such friends. The lucky ones survived by clinging on to life however they could. Many were swept away by the coursing diseases and malnutrition that followed the deadly tides. Even now, decades later, we were still dealing with the aftermath.

"I'm sure she got away fine. She's probably safe and warm somewhere." Tana was trying to be sympathetic, though her voice wavered. Whether from the damp air or her own fears, I couldn't tell.

"Poor Bea. Bea. Bea." Walt's voice cracked. "We ate the dogs, and then the cats. Finally, we ate the rats." He wandered over to a small tarpaulin-covered pile, his sobs bouncing around the thick air as his hand dragged against the rough material. "So pretty. Don't leave."

The tarp slid down and what was left of a little girl stared blindly at us. The long-blackened skin and empty-socketed head accused us, as if we were the ones that had wound the heavy-duty wire around the wrists and feet, binding them to the chair she died on. There was the sound of low creaking, probably some of the tie-ropes on the dock outside, but right then it sounded like a little girl weeping.

Tana choked incoherently, and I waved her over to me.

"We're leaving, Walt. Don't try and stop us."

"No, stay."

I edged towards the entrance, but Tana pulled the other way. I'd been ready to head out the way we'd come in—even the water was better than staying with the crazed wet-foot—but maybe she'd spotted something I hadn't.

Tana looked away from the shriveled remains on the chair as she led me to the far corner. I could feel her hand quivering in mine as we edged past the debris. I pushed through the heavy blanket to find a concealed exit, the dim light revealing a broken series of steps leading upwards.

Tana shrieked, and I looked back. Walt had his rag-covered hands locked around her arm. She shouldered him out of the way and rushed past me up the steps.

"Bea! Don't leave me again… please don't." Walt sounded like a tortured soul from the depths of hell. Maybe he was.

Tana's hand gripped mine so tight the blood was squeezed from my fingers. We picked our way carefully up the stairs, kicking up what seemed years of dust that swirled around us in gray clouds. Moments later we scrambled through a roughly boarded entrance, coughing and choking our way onto the light-less alleys that formed a buffer between the flooded habitations and the neon streets of Baltimore.

Twelve

After staggering away from the hovel I hesitated. I wasn't sure where we were, though we couldn't have traveled too far from where we'd crashed. There was a good chance Gabriella's team was still in the area, unless they thought we'd died in the wreckage. Which was all too nearly true.

Tana was shaking so violently she could barely move, her skin looking greasy under what few lights there were. She was mumbling to herself, but I couldn't catch what she was saying clearly. I thought I heard her say "dad" a few times though.

I aimed generally northward, knowing we'd end up in civilization eventually. I pulled my Scroll out from my pocket and pressed the connect button. The screen lit up which was a surprise, given the impact and the water, but I had no service—the comms company probably didn't have too many wet-foot customers.

Fifteen minutes later I felt the Scroll buzz in my hand. It had hooked up although the signal strength was minimal. I could see streetlights in the distance and was wary of going too close. Lights would be accompanied by Argus pickups, and I had a feeling we'd be better off staying clear of any kind of monitoring.

Using my Scroll was a calculated risk. The cops could be scanning for my phone signal, but I had to balance that with the necessity of getting off the streets as soon as possible. With facial and ergonomic pattern matching algorithms as good as they were, once we were back under the eyes of Argus it would only be a matter of minutes before the police would be able to track us in quasi-real-time.

I guided Tana over to the wall of a half-collapsed building for some support and urged her to stay there while I made the call. She was cold, and her skin waxy which I guessed was more related to shock than temperature.

"Soldier! Are you finally coming to see me? I've been real lonely here without you."

I heard faint giggles in the background, which told me Dollie hadn't been *entirely* inconsolable. "Have you got someone with you?"

"No one I won't send home for you." Dollie almost purred. "Don't be jealous."

"Sure, Dollie. Look I had a..." I hesitated only briefly. "...some trouble, could you send a car to pick me up?"

"Sure, honey." She looked away, checking where I was and reached off screen. "Dispatching to your location."

"Can you send a Husher?"

"Awww, Joe, are you afraid people will find out?"

Some of the more upmarket cab companies, like Dollie's, have a few cars equipped with privacy screens and no active Argus pickups. Mostly they're used to transport VIPs or corporate execs not wanting to be targeted by every radical in the USP. Right now, my reasons were much more practical—they were one of the few classes of AeroMobile allowed to self-drive.

"I guess I'm a little shy."

Dollie licked her lips, making them shine in the subdued light of her apartment. "I'll soon cure you of that. You'll see."

I ended the call, feeling bad. I had no intention of going to Dollie's and dragging her into this mess, but I was short on options. Visibility wasn't a desirable characteristic for us, so our public movements had to be limited.

I turned back to Tana. "A Husher will let us move around without being tracked, too much, but we need somewhere to go. My apartment isn't safe, that's for sure."

She didn't really seem to follow what I was saying. "Did you see? Those eyes..."

"Tana..."

I squeezed her shoulder, and she stiffened. It wasn't the reaction of someone startled, more like the idea of being touched was repugnant to her. I tried not to be offended but failed. I'd been dragged into this mess despite trying not to be, but it wasn't mine.

"Sorry, Ballen." She took several deep breaths. "I... what do we do now?"

In the Solidos the hero always comes up with a brilliant, but difficult, way of clearing himself from whatever he's faced with. Usually sealing the bad guy's fate at the same time. Unfortunately, this wasn't a 3V show, and I was better at driving cabs than playing the hero. I'd been trying to figure out a plan since we left the wet-foot, but hadn't come up with anything—brilliant or otherwise.

"The cab will be here soon. That gets us off the streets temporarily. Maybe gives us time to figure out what to do next. But beyond that I'm stuck."

Tana still wasn't listening. "When I was a girl, my dad used to..." Her eyes were wide, the distant street lights reflecting in them. "He did things... after Mom left."

Now I felt even more useless. How do you respond to something like that? If I lived a million lifetimes, I probably wouldn't find the answer.

"He wasn't a bad man. He didn't know how to cope with things and lost his way. That girl..." She breathed sharply, the air hissing through her teeth. "Down there... she was so..."

It didn't take much to understand why Tana had lost it. I wanted to say something but failed. Then the cab arrived, saving me from my awkward embarrassment. Tana jumped in the passenger side, and I slid painfully behind the controls, the blood from my injured leg smearing messily over the seats. Dollie wasn't going to like this.

Tana seemed to see my wound for the first time. "You're shot."

"It feels like it." I punched the controls. The driver-less car lifted ponderously, then we were drifting sedately above the streets. One of the things that limits the use of Hushers is their government-mandated programming. Their range is extremely limited, and they're ultra-cautious. Slow might be reassuring from a passenger safety perspective but wasn't good business—which is why cab companies charge them out at premium rates. Lucky for me, I wasn't paying.

"How did you manage to walk?"

"I'm tough." There didn't seem any point discussing the details of my previous injuries or the odd effects of my medication. "Anyway, if it wasn't for you, we'd both be dead, not simply injured."

"We need a hospital."

I programmed the cab to fly around in a lazy wide circle so we wouldn't attract too much interest from traffic control. "If I walk into a hospital with a gunshot, they'll call the police. Then we'll have no chance of figuring this out."

"The wound needs to be cleaned, sterilized. Who knows what infection you might have picked up from that water." She sounded like a scientist again, all business and matter-of-fact.

"Check the glove box. But really that's not the priority right now. This has to be connected to Ganz' work." I fought not to let my irritation show—hard when you're nursing a gunshot wound and trying to find out why someone's trying to kill you. Even with the cab doing most of the work it was difficult to concentrate. "Tana, what was he working on?"

She was rummaging through the contents of the glove box and not really listening to me. I could feel my pulse throbbing in my temple.

"You did work for him, didn't you?"

"I do... did... I was one of his research assistants."

"Okay, so what was he researching?"

"His main area was quantum cosmology—statistical analysis of heptaquark shifts and their origins." She pulled out a white box marked with the universal first-aid symbol. "Got it."

"I'm only a cab driver." The polished trim of the arm-rest was cold against my arm, and I shivered. "Quantum stuff is out of my league."

Tana pursed her lips. "There should be a field theory—one equation—that describes everything in the eleven-dimensional Universe." She tore open a bunch of small sachets. "This is going to sting."

I felt something against my leg and winced as the antiseptic bit deep into the muscle. I didn't look down. Tana carried on talking, as though treating a gunshot wound was an everyday occurrence.

"Due to fluctuations at a quantum level, the Universe must exist in all dimensions in a sort of probability cloud, and we live in the Universe that is the most likely. No one has ever been able to determine that equation though."

I more or less followed what she was saying. Despite what I'd said, even an engineer has to have a basic grasp of the theory, and I knew that uncertainty played a large part in it. "That doesn't sound like a motive for murder. Was there more to it?"

"Lift your leg."

I moved up in the seat awkwardly, and Tana slid something under me. She pulled it around and I realized she was wrapping a dressing over the wound.

"That will have to do for now." She chewed her lip. "We still need to go to a hospital. You need professional care."

"People have been telling me that for years." My leg throbbed mercilessly, even after Tana's efforts and with the benefit of the drugs. "Anything else on Ganz' work?"

"There are minor variances in heptaquark distributions throughout the Universe. Dr. Ganz felt that sufficient analysis of those might pinpoint the overall field and show us the scaffolding that holds everything together."

Scientists are odd creatures. While most of us go around more or less ignorant of the greater Universe, they worry about minute details we wouldn't care about even if we knew they existed. Even I wasn't interested in what makes things tick at that level, and space was my chosen working environment—or would be if I wasn't a broken-down cripple.

"He called it his *Mathematics of Eternity*." Tana sighed. "I never really saw the whole picture. My work was collecting and cleaning the data streams. I'm not even sure the other professors understood it all."

"Ganz worked with other people? I thought he was a loner."

This could be the breakthrough I needed. If Ganz collaborated with others, there was a chance one of them might know what happened and why. Which could help me with the cops. I felt my Scroll buzz in my pocket but ignored it. I knew who was calling.

"Socially yes, but no one works alone. If we did, the Eastern institutes would completely march over what little science we have left here. It's the only way to make progress."

"Okay. So you must know who they are."

Tana's brow furrowed slightly. "Only from dealing with his messages occasionally. He didn't involve us at those levels." She paused. "There was Dr. Black at the institute here and a couple of others I'm not entirely sure of. And there was Paresh, of course, but he's an assistant like me."

I suppose I should have been able to instantly pick out the prime suspect from that shortlist. But it was nothing but a bunch of meaningless names.

"Where would we find this Paresh?" If he was an assistant, I figured he might be more approachable than the highbrow types. "Maybe he can throw some light on things."

Tana twisted her hands and looked toward the distant skyscrapers. As we slipped into skyway eleven, I saw another car slide into the lane behind us, the blue and white police livery clearly visible. *Just a coincidence, Joe, Take it easy.* They had no reason to follow us, but my stomach tightened nevertheless.

"Is there some reason not to see him?"

She grimaced. "He's hard to take, that's all. Have you ever met anyone from Pan-Asia?"

"Only the occasional passenger in my cab." I dropped to a lower lane, and the bastard followed me. He was probably nosing around to catch a glimpse of who was in the Husher. I held the controls lightly and reached out ready to flick the autopilot off.

"They're unbearable." Tana almost spat the words.

"Damn." My attention was fully on the RearView. "Cops."

She turned to look at the cop car. "We could turn ourselves into them. That would be sensible."

"I didn't think Pan-Asians came here to get an education." There was a turn up ahead, and I edged the car towards it.

Everyone blamed the near death of science and technology in North America on the after-effects of the Big Shake, but there'd been systematic underfunding and political interference in those fields for decades. So it was a mystery why this Paresh character would be studying over here.

The Pan-Asians acted like they were superior because the Atolls still traded with them for resources. Who knows? Maybe they're right. Combine that with a historical, cultural misogynism, and Tana's venom was understandable.

"They don't usually." Tana shrugged. "But Paresh is here and worked with Dr. Ganz closer than I did."

If I was reading between the lines correctly it didn't seem likely *anyone* would have been closer to Ganz than Tana, so I was a little surprised. I guess my doubt showed because her eyes hardened.

"Whatever you think you know about me and Dr. Ganz, you're wrong."

"Listen. All I want to do is figure out what the hell is going on before the cops throw me in a very small, very dark, cell. Anything else is none of my business."

Tana sniffed, her eyes straight ahead. "Paresh is probably at the lab right now. He doesn't like mornings and usually works late—Advanced Theory Center, Dumbarton Road Campus."

I set the Pilot, and the cab slid us tentatively into the local traffic stream. "Thank goodness we don't have to deal with a morning grouch then. That would be too hard."

Tana's glare drilled into the side of my head, but I ignored her. Dealing with another surly student didn't place high on my "list of things to worry about" right then. The cop car continued on its original path and slid out of sight. I took a deep breath and sank back in the seat.

Thirteen

The lab complex looked much like any other university built more than half a century ago, a sprawling set of brick and glass buildings terminated at one end by what would once have been an elegant gray concrete auditorium. Now it was an unwelcoming greenish-tinged drum that looked like it had spent several years at sea.

I set the Husher down in a designated parking area closest to the building. Even with the patching Tana had done, I didn't think I'd get very far with my leg. As with all modern buildings, the internal lights had dimmed automatically to save power, and the gloomy illumination gave everything a slightly foreboding appearance.

It was a calculated risk visiting the University—the police would certainly check for leads there—but given how late it was, I was gambling on them having been here and moved on.

Tana led me inside, my injured leg dragging slightly and rasping against the concrete. The noise mixed with the quiet echoes of our footsteps reverberating in the stillness.

"Where's the lab?" I asked quietly.

"Floor five, room three. The elevators will be off at this time of night. Can you manage the stairs?" In contrast to mine, Tana's voice was loud and confident. She was familiar with the University and relaxed now we were here.

"Sure. I haven't completed my altitude training this week." I did my best to speak normally and winced as the echo seemed to shout in my ear.

Have you ever been through Limb Regen, been shot in the leg, hopped yourself up on nerve-tranq, survived a car wreck, been dragged out of the Patapsco, and then tried to climb five flights of stairs? I have one word of advice. Don't.

I did, and without a lot of help from Tana, I wouldn't have made it beyond the first two flights. As it was, by the time we reached the fourth floor my leg was a solid lump of brain-jangling pain and covered in a sheen of blood that started mid-thigh.

Tana propped me against the balcony wall on the floating stairway. "This isn't going to work."

"I can make it," I grunted, my breathing tight in my chest. There was a soft buzz and flickering from some of the subdued lighting. Combined with the bitter smell of my blood, it gave the journey a nightmarish quality.

"I mean seeing Paresh while you're in this state. He'll probably call security, not answer questions."

"I'm a practical kind of guy. I'm open to suggestions." Especially when I was having difficulty staying conscious.

"My room is close. In the student quarters. I have some medical supplies there."

"Close?" I wasn't sure I could make it more than a few meters in my condition. "Downstairs?"

"Yes, we'd have to go back down." Tana glanced back down the stairs and bit her lip. "You really need some help."

I was about to give her the benefit of my thoughts on that plan when suddenly I couldn't stand up anymore. I grabbed at the railing, felt my hand smack against it ineffectually, then the ground lunged up and hit me hard.

When I woke I was lying down, the lights around me dimmed to a soft glow. My leg felt tight, with pain working at it like dull needles, but better than earlier. My head was groggy from the nerve-tranq, and for a while I lay there unmoving, fighting to do something more than stare at the dim ceiling above me.

I caught a vague scent, flowers and freshly cut grass mixed with a more general slightly fusty odor. Then I realized I wasn't alone. Tana was curled up beside me in a semi-fetal position, her arm partially around me almost as if in protection.

Her skin smelled nice, and I thought of telling her that, but it didn't seem like a good way to start a... Was it a new day, in fact? I really wasn't sure. I had a sense of time passing at a subconscious level, but no real idea of how long.

For a while, I watched her breathing, the soft intakes of breath almost inaudible as the light glowed against her skin. It was almost hypnotic, and at that point, all I wanted to do was stay there forever—or at least some rough approximation of that. After several minutes I thought to check my leg. The bloody hole was gone and in its place was a blister of artificial flesh where a wound patch had been applied. The deadness of the muscle around it told me that the analgesic gels were working.

Tana rolled away from me slightly and her eyes opened.

"I didn't mean to fall asleep. Sorry," she murmured, still drowsy.

This was the second time she'd saved me, and I didn't like the feeling. It carried obligations that I wasn't ready to deal with. "What happened?"

She stretched a little. "We're safe. You collapsed, and I brought you here."

"You carried me back down?" It didn't seem possible.

She shook her head briefly and sat up, moving to the edge of the bed. "This is Dr. Ganz' campus study. It was a lot closer and easier to get you here."

We were on a heavily padded lounger, almost the size of a bed, which made sense remembering how large Ganz was. I could dimly pick out shelves of old style data disks around the walls. "Does anyone know about this place?"

"Of course, it's not a secret. Most of the professors have an office like this on campus. It's useful if you're working late. International projects across time zones, that sort of thing."

That meant it wasn't "safe" by any rational assessment. Gabriella would undoubtedly know of it or find it quickly enough, which made me want to get the hell out of there as soon as we could.

"Gabriella mentioned Dr. Ganz' files. Would he have kept them here?"

"Here?" Tana seemed puzzled by my question. "That's stupid." She slipped off the lounger, looking a little self-conscious. "Everything is in his GARNET account. This isn't the stone age."

I must have looked confused, and Tana sighed.

"That idea of secret notes and documents is straight out of an unintelligent thriller. Everyone is so anxious about priority and proper attribution that *everything* is held in GARNET—a fifty-year patent could hang in the balance. All Ganz' notes would be there." She waved her finger at a console across the room. "And available across the world."

I felt more than a little dumb—I'd imagined dusty volumes and old-fashioned filing cabinets. The Global Academic Research Network had been only partially developed back in my student days, but was now presumably everywhere. "They need his personal access codes to get into that?"

Tana nodded. "It's secured against disputes. Though I suppose with the right skills it could be broken. Most things can be."

She was right. Even with DNA-encoded access protection and retina scan seals, there was no shortage of news stories about systems being compromised either through faulty design or accident. No one's yet figured out how to build a completely infallible network.

"What about private files? Notes? I mean, there could be something... personal." I broke eye contact. "Or embarrassing..."

"GARNET has public and private areas, but no one uses the private one much. The point of the system is to publish and establish what you've done before someone else. The only things in there would be theories or notes that were completely speculative. If it's not there, then it only existed in Hubert's head."

"Can you access his account?" I had a wild half-formed idea—one that might be the reason behind what was happening.

Tana hesitated, her eyes dropping from mine. "Only Ganz could—"

"What's this, Tana?" A figure stood in the doorway, eyes as black as midnight pinning us to the bed. "Do you specialize in sleeping with broken-down old men?"

"Paresh? What are you doing here? This is Dr. Ganz' private room."

"That would be precisely my question too." Paresh strode through the door, his humorless olive-skinned face turning in all directions. "I know you and Ganz had your 'special relationship', but the good Doctor is dead. I don't imagine the police would be happy to see you entertaining in his quarters. The poor man is barely in his grave."

I'd only been in the same room as this guy for two minutes, but I already didn't like him. His voice and face held a sneering disregard for others that as far as I was concerned had no room in polite conversation. I also knew it wouldn't take too many more minutes before I'd be ready to "entertain" *him*.

"I'm with the cab company." I creaked my way over to him, offering my hand. "I was dropping the lady off when I was taken ill—"

"My, my, Tana. This one is a step *up* for you." Paresh brushed his long raven hair back and stalked around us, examining me like a scientific curiosity. "Not only does he talk, but he actually attempts to put a deception together to protect you."

Tana was breathing heavily. "Paresh. Stop it. There's no reason for this."

"But there is." Paresh's eyes darted across to her then back to me, and he smiled, his lips thinning to a line. "You're with the cab company that's true, but your name is Joe Ballen. Wanted in connection with killing Doctor Ganz and several police officers, I believe."

My teeth were grinding, and I was getting very close to hitting someone tall, with a decidedly supercilious attitude. Violence isn't generally a successful strategy, but it can be highly satisfying. Fortunately for Paresh, my weakness prevented me from indulging my immediate desire for "satisfied stupidity."

He stepped towards Tana, his height making her appear child-like next to him. "Why don't you explain it to me?"

Tana was several centimeters shorter than him but tilted her head disdainfully. "Why are you obsessed with me? You don't even like me. This has nothing to do with you, so leave."

For a moment I thought Paresh was going to hit Tana and I edged sideways, hoping to get close enough to try and stop him. Instead, he shivered slightly and took half a step backwards.

"That you speak to me in such a manner shows you have a diseased mind and demonstrates how unworthy of me you are. That you, a farmer's girl, should insult me in such a fashion, it is un—"

"You never wanted me, Paresh. You wanted me to jump into bed with you out of gratitude, because you were *gracious* enough to offer such a favor to someone as low-bred and unattractive as me. I'm supposed to chase after you and provide convenient no-strings sex when your *pretty* girlfriends are busy or otherwise unavailable."

Tana's breathing was deep and sharp. "What I'm doing here is none of your business. What I choose to do with this or any other man is none of your business. You don't own me—I owe you nothing."

"I will leave, chudakkad. You should know too, I have informed the appropriate people of your presence."

Tana's hand lashed out like a power-hammer. Paresh's only response was the *thud* he made as he hit the floor. I shuffled across and checked him over. She'd caught him perfectly on his jutting chin.

"Out cold." I glanced at Tana. "Remind me never to get on your bad side."

For several seconds I thought she was going to hit me too. Finally, she gave a derisory snort and marched to the other side of the room.

"Can't say I blame you. You realized he had no useful information before you hit him presumably...?" Tana didn't react. "What did he do for Ganz?"

"Paresh specializes in statistical analysis. He did regression analysis on the data because Doctor Ganz thought there were patterns to the fluctuations."

"Statistical? I don't see the connection."

"You wouldn't." Tana sniffed. "Lots of fields in science cross over. When Newton learned how to solve binomial equations they were useful in countless fields. It's the same with many ideas.

"Doctor Ganz was trying to map the structural evolution of the Universe by tracking quantum fluctuations. He believed this would finally give us a true picture of why the Universe developed the way it did." Tana chewed her lip. "I didn't like to tell him, but it always seemed a pointless exercise. Even if there were such patterns, randomness in quantum phenomena would remove all traces of them. I think many of the other professors thought the same."

Most of what she said made sense—even a "dirt under the fingernails" engineer knows the basics. Any quantum effect is random by default, and you can't create information out of nothing. That would be like trying to figure out "which came first," without having either chicken or egg.

"If his work was no good, how come they let him carry on?"

"You don't understand universities, do you? Ganz had tenure. It would be almost impossible to remove him unless he was proved to be incompetent, refused his duties, or found guilty of..." Her head lowered. "...moral turpitude."

That sounded kind of fun to me, but I knew better than to make a joke about it.

"Would any of the people Ganz worked with want him out of the way?" She stared at me as if I were insane. "You said it's important to get recognition for scientific work—what if he discovered something new and someone else wanted to take the credit?"

"People at the University?" She looked like she'd bitten into an apple and found a worm. "No one would think of such a thing."

Maybe that was true, but scientists are still people and have the same crazy ideas as the rest of us—at least sometimes. If a discovery was so important, wouldn't even the best of them break down and "do the unthinkable?"

Tana moved to a large electronic board that almost filled one wall and picked up a thick stylus. She rubbed out some of the numbers on an impressive looking graph then added more data points and redrew the curve. She looked back at me, fidgeting with the stylus. "The data was wrong."

I wasn't sure how a scientist would have the finances or political muscle to organize the kill team we'd faced in Ganz' apartment. Judging from what Tana had told me, scientists preferred to stay isolated in their ivory towers. It seemed unlikely one of them would have those kinds of connections, even if well-motivated.

I kicked Paresh in the ribs sharply, but he didn't respond. Tana had really done a number on him. He was blocking the exit, so I dragged him over to the lounger with Tana's half-hearted help.

"What about the Disruptor planted in my cab? It's a specialized piece of equipment. Hard to get hold of. Would any of Ganz' collaborators have access to that kind of technology?"

Tana thought for several seconds, as if considering a new hypothesis, then shook her head. "Well, there's Mac, but he wouldn't do anything to hurt Hubert. I mean Doctor Ganz."

"Mac?"

"Dr. Mackenzie Black. He's in Applied Physics. They always have lots of electronics and gadgets about—he'd have access to that kind of technology if he wanted."

"And he worked with Ganz?"

Tana nodded seriously. "But that's not a motive. They've been friends for many years."

I thought about it. Black might have been able to get hold of such a device, but that didn't mean he'd done anything. If guilt rested purely on opportunity, we'd all need locking up. Something was nagging at me though.

"So, what does he actually do?" I asked.

"Aside from teaching, he's probably the greatest authority on self-organizing nano-technology outside of the Atolls." Tana raised an eyebrow. "Haven't you heard of him?"

"There are a lot of scientists in the world. Should I have?"

"Mac is the person who almost single-handedly designed the hull of the *Ananta*."

Once the connection was made, I knew immediately who she was talking about. In fact, I knew more about it than most. The *Ananta* starship was under construction in LEO on the High-Rig and had cost me three limbs. It was the new Great Hope that would challenge the space superiority of the Atolls, with the potential to provide freedom for the entire world—if successful. If it failed, we'd be stuck on a diseased and decaying Earth, while the smug Atolls continued their dominance.

"Where would we find him?"

Tana checked the old-fashioned clock on the wall. "At this time? He's undoubtedly at home asleep."

Exactly where I should be. "Do you know where he lives?"

Tana shook her head. "He'll be listed in the faculty directory though." She activated the console and searched.

"You should stay here. The police don't suspect you of being involved in any of this."

"Try to keep me out of it, and I'll call the police myself." Tana faced me head on, and her chin lifted. "From what that Gabriella woman said, I'm already involved."

I pointed to the console. "Could you use that to download a copy of Ganz' files into my Scroll? Including the private ones?"

Tana pinched her lower lip. "They'll be locked, I can't—"

"Tana... we need them. And I think you can get them." She hesitated for so long I thought she was going to refuse, but then she nodded and took my Pad.

"Black's address is 1202 West Liberty."

I sighed. Dragging myself across town again was only slightly more appealing than the idea of crawling over broken glass while being flogged by two dozen sadists.

"A copied file is only limited evidence." Tana worked on the console for a few minutes and then held out my Scroll. "There's no guarantee a copy hasn't been tampered with."

I looked down at the immobile form of Paresh. He'd certainly messed with the wrong woman, and I admired the way Tana had laid him out, but we weren't going to get anything useful out of him now. We needed to leave and quickly. If he *had* contacted the police, they were probably on their way. And I didn't like the kind of "moral turpitude" they served in jail.

Fourteen

There have been times in the past when people have accused me of being smart, and sometimes I believe them. But heading out to rouse a scientist from his bed in the early hours of the morning, while keeping one eye open for the cops and another for a bunch of armed killers, didn't lend support to that theory.

Doctor Mackenzie's house was in a brownstone neighborhood that had undoubtedly been exclusive and fashionable eighty or ninety years ago. As we dropped down, the signs of neglect became all too apparent, the sidewalks and streets filled with a tangle of ramshackle shelters made from cardboard and other makeshift building materials. NeverSees—Non-Economically Viable Refugee Citizens- to give them their official designation—were people who had lost it all and never recovered.

Baltimore, like everywhere on the East Coast, was flooded not only with water but with refugees. People without jobs, homes, prospects, or the initiative to change things. Most lived illegally in the streets despite complaints and being periodically rousted by the cops. When you've nothing to lose, zoning laws and residential committees aren't at the top of your priority list.

"I didn't realize there were so many," Tana whispered as if those in the cardboard city below might hear. "Are they always here?"

"Some have spots staked out where they've lived for years. The cops move them along now and then, but they always come back. You should be grateful you live at the University. At least they manage the homeless reasonably well."

Tana's eyes were fixed on the shacks below.

"There's 1202." Unfortunately, the crude shelters were more densely packed there, almost entirely jamming the street. "I'll have to set down and make my way through. You better stay in the car—NeverSees aren't known for their hospitality."

"You're hardly in any state to confront them on your own." Tana pointed at my wounded leg. "Besides, I know Mac, you don't. He might not listen to you."

She had a point. Black was a scientist. Conversation with a blood-soaked cab driver about murders and assassins was more likely to result in him calling the cops or hospital authorities than anything. He'd listen to Tana in a way that he'd never do with me.

The aeropad perched on the top of the house was already occupied with what was presumably Mackenzie's own car. Safety regs prevented me from putting the cab on hover and leaving it unattended. Otherwise, it would have been easy. Instead, I dropped us into the clearest area I could, double checking the controls were locked before getting out. The last thing I needed was some juiced up NeverSee spotting my cab and deciding to take a longer trip.

The street was quiet, and a cold breeze provided the only sound as it scattered leaves and litter between the boxes and clutter. Tana still had the QuenchGun she'd snatched from Coyan. I gestured for her to pass it to me and wait.

I crept to the nearest box and listened carefully. A smell like damp cloth or wet leaves stuck in my nostrils, and my mouth was dry as I edged forward, peeking around the top to look inside. After checking several others, I went back to Tana and gave her the gun back.

"Is something wrong?" she hissed.

"Empty."

"Good. NeverSees scare me." She swallowed twice. "Kind of silly I suppose, since by definition you almost never see them. Where do you think they are?"

I shrugged. Who could understand the behavior of people forced to live like animals. "What worries me more is why aren't they here?" Some of the NeverSees would be out foraging, but all of them gone at the same time? Unlikely, unless they were all at the annual NeverSee ball.

We skirted wide around the first few boxes, but as we got closer to the house the hovels became more tightly packed, and it was increasingly difficult to keep away from them.

NeverSees were part of the reason why cities that survived the Big Shake had built increasingly upward. Away from the dirt and stench of the ground level streets. Away from the water and damp. Away from danger. "Going up in the world" took on a whole new meaning when ninety percent of cities close to coastal waters had been flooded out.

The gate separating Black's yard from the street looked functional enough and effective at keeping the NeverSees at bay. It was equipped with all the modern tricks necessary for survival in the suburbs—microwave heat projectors, dedicated Eye-feeds, nano-coated non-grip surfaces, and a big lock that was no doubt encrypted and secured in multiple ways.

The lock was also very melted. There were long runs of metal tracking down from blackened burns on the mechanism.

The gate swung open silently when I pushed it. Then I noticed a large plastic barrel mounted on the wall alongside. There was a line operated hopper system attached to it that came from inside the gate. That explained why the NeverSees had clustered around Black's house—he'd been feeding them.

We picked our way through the garden, walking on the grass instead of the gravel paths to deaden our footsteps. As we drew nearer, I saw the doorway was open. A dark gaping mouth of a giant skull building.

"Mac would never leave his house open like this." Tana's whisper made me jump.

"We should leave." I'd already seen enough.

I'd heard of people leaving their doors unlocked, even open sometimes, but that was the stuff of history—from before millions were forced to live in the streets. It belonged to the time before crime statistics became classified information, and made the public more than willing to embrace the Argus Eye and trade freedom for security.

Sure the police solved more crimes than ever—Argus virtually guaranteed that. It was also true that more crimes were being committed. Argus ensured that the authorities knew who to send for psych-adjustment, but "treatment" rather than prevention didn't change the outcome for the unfortunate victim.

I always wondered how the counselors explained to the teary-eyed survivors that punishment was an outdated concept that did nothing to deter the "socially mal-adjusted." How do you sell the idea that behavioral analysis and modification programs are a better way to manage the psycho who'd butchered your nearest-and-dearest? Maybe in the interests of fairness, they simply modified the victims *and* perpetrators equally. No harm, no foul—as they used to say.

"What if he needs help?" Tana moved toward the door and twisted away from me when I tried to stop her. "You need this more than I do." She held out the pistol.

"Tana..." I was going to refuse, but my objection was automatic and illogical, driven by a foolish romantic heroism even I didn't think I possessed.

"You're wounded, and you're handicapped." She pushed the gun into my hand. "I'm not blind or stupid. I've seen your scars. I even remember seeing the accident in the news, though I wouldn't have recognized your face. I can look after myself."

That had been apparent several times. I drummed up the rationalization that I had the best judgment as to when and if to use the gun. Which was pure nonsense, even if it was comforting. I wasn't trained in combat any more than she was. "Stay behind me then."

She ignored me and we stepped into the darkness side by side. The first thing I saw when my eyes adapted was an overturned table. Smashed pottery littered the floor around it, the broken shards glinting like knife edges in the dim light.

I gestured for Tana to wait and strained my ears for the slightest sound, but all I could hear was the soft breath of chilly air through the front door. Even if there had been a noise, it would have been drowned out by the hammer of my own pulse. The house smelled clean, antiseptically so, and I wondered if Mackenzie was one of those health nuts who sterilized everything. I caught a trace of ozone. It could have been a health device or part of the climate control. Or it could be a sign of an energy weapon discharge.

"What's that?" Tana whispered as we moved forward.

Something warm and rancid. A salty tang of cooked meat that triggered memories of seared flesh and bone. I gulped nausea down several times before I could answer. "Tana, I really think it would be better if you stay here. I'm not just being pro—"

Tana strode forward, and I sighed. One time. Back on the High-Rig, one of the crew had dropped his Zero-G wrench. Now these cost a couple of thousand with "shipping," and company policy was that if you lost one, you paid for it. This wasn't the usual company penny-pinching—a lost fastener could cause hundreds of thousands in damage if it impacted something in orbit.

This guy had instinctively scrabbled for the wrench. And put himself right in front of a laser torch. 6000 degrees centigrade sliced through him and his suit as if he wasn't even there. He was frozen before they discovered him, but his remains started to defrost as soon as they were brought in, giving off a sweet and sour metallic tang that caught in your throat. That's what I smelled now.

A broad flight of oak stairs led upstairs, and the air seemed somehow thicker. A black canister lay on the floor in a circle of scorched carpet. It looked threatening even though I had no idea what it was. I hoped the burnt area meant it was used and no longer dangerous, but I skirted it with a wide margin and moved along the balcony.

Up ahead a blue-white light flickered through a partly open door, bouncing from the painted door surround and casting shadows through the railings on the left. Light patterns on the wall danced like evil ghosts laughing in the semi-darkness.

I edged closer and flinched as Tana's moist hand slipped into mine. Her earlier confidence had slipped away as we went further inside, even though we'd encountered nothing so far.

"Let's call the police," she hissed.

Normally I'd have been happy to do that. I knew my limitations and was reminded of them daily. But now I was a suspect in the death of Ganz as well as one, possibly two, cops. Under those circumstances, the police would be almost as dangerous as Gabriella's death squad. Cops take an extreme dislike to people they think have hurt one of their own and often don't bother to check too closely when they catch the suspect.

Tana dragged my hand back as I moved forward, but she followed me despite her resistance. I paused at the door. I still couldn't hear anything above a slight hiss that told me nothing, but seemed to waver in time with the flickering pale blue light. The smell was stronger here, and I took a shallow breath before stepping through.

The head on the floor looked up at me with lifeless black eyes, staring at me as though in accusation. On the bed the torso still dripped, blood oozing to join the thick inky pool that covered the floor. The flickering 3V screen rendered everything almost colorless, even the multiple burn holes in the skull. More than enough to end the life of the owner. Decapitation had been a meaningless act of brutality. An act of destruction from a psychotic mind.

Tana's fingers snapped tight around mine, making me grimace.

"Black?" I asked, fighting to keep my voice level and emotionless. As if speaking angrily would somehow add to the already over-whelming scene of desecration.

Tana nodded and walked back to the balcony. Her voice blurred with tears.

"Monsters... why would anyone do this?"

The reflected light flickered in Mackenzie's dead eyes as if he were asking the same question.

"What's wrong with the 3V?" I muttered.

"Someone's been murdered, and you're worried about what shows you're missing?" Tana spat the words out coldly.

"It doesn't appear damaged..." I pulled out my Scroll and tried to bring up a channel, but there was only static.

A soft beep cut through the hiss from the 3V, barely noticeable, but annoying my ears like an insect hovering ready to bite. I closed my eyes and tried to let my mind lock on to the source, following where my ears drew me. Kneeling down I ignored the feeling of revulsion as I lifted the soiled linen. The beep was louder, pulling my attention forward. There it was, something under the bed. It could have been a shoe box.

Except shoe boxes don't beep and don't come with red flashing lights.

"We have to go. Now!"

I pushed Tana towards the stairs as the room behind us filled with a scorching orange flash. I jumped forward, wrapping my arms around her and felt the blast tear through my clothes. The next few seconds were confused as we tumbled down the stairs, slamming to a halt in a mess of arms and legs. I looked back as flames streamed along the roof and walls, jumping from surface to surface like Satan's breath.

"Come on!" I struggled to get to my feet, then Tana hit me waist high and knocked me almost effortlessly on to my stomach. A second later she was kneeling over me and thumping my back as if she wanted to kill me. "What the h—"

"You're on fire, Ballen."

I realized she was trying to pat the flames out with her coat, and then I felt the first barbs of pain. Tana grabbed my arm. She lifted me and dragged me towards the front door as pieces of burning roof tumbled around us in a shower of embers.

Once outside the true scale of the fire became clear. The entire upper floor was burning and in danger of spreading to neighboring houses. Bright sparks vaulted high into the black night, only to fall back as dull red embers. To the left a cardboard home suddenly burst into yellow flames, the wind pushing the fire to nearby boxes as we watched.

Charred particles rained down as we hobbled to the Husher, the denser pieces zinging off the pavement into the night. Tana shuddered occasionally as the pieces hit her, and I tried to hold myself up more. The cab beckoned to us across the sea of flaming cardboard. Ten meters and a thousand light years away. Tana pulled harder, almost lifting me off the ground and we moved forward again.

A scream erupted, and a blazing figure shot across our path to the left, flames streaking behind them as they vanished in to the night. Whether it was a man or woman was impossible to tell.

We thumped into the side of the car. I opened the doors, and we dived in. The car's skin rattled with hissing pellets from the house, but we were relatively safe.

Temporarily. Sirens were already dopplering towards us in the distance. And where fire trucks went, the police would surely be close behind.

I flipped a dozen switches in two swipes and pulled the nose of the Husher up to clear us from the ground as quickly as possible. The fire outside filled the interior of the cab with a golden bouncing glow that turned the shadows blood red.

"Lean forward," Tana said.

I winced as Tana tore the remnants of my shirt open, the melted fabric tugging at my skin. She swore under her breath.

"Where's the medical kit?" I jammed the throttle fully open. "There might be some burn cream."

"You need a hospital. Those are more than..." Tana moved back, and I heard her sobbing, then the noise of tearing paper. "Why, Ballen? That was a stupid thing to do."

The sting of antiseptic made my hands clench on the controls and the cab bucked. It felt like Tana was pouring acid over my raw skin—far more painful than the burn had felt, though I knew that was because adrenaline had stopped me from feeling the initial damage.

"I tripped when the bomb went off," I hissed through clenched teeth.

"Don't lie to me."

Perhaps it was because I believed in the idea of "women and children first" and that men were supposed to protect women. Maybe it was because she'd saved my life and I felt I owed her. It was the kind of old-fashioned ideology I knew I'd never be able to explain properly. But I was glad I'd done it, despite the pain.

"I was clumsy even as a child. Hell, you should see me try to dance."

Something cool froze my spine as Tana wiped some sort of anesthetic against me, the burning dissolving almost to nothing at the touch.

"Who else was on the list of Ganz' collaborators?" I eased off on the controls as the cab hit four thousand, leveling off in the high cruising band for local traffic.

"It can't be connected."

"Maybe Ganz committed suicide, but at the same time the killers were looking for his work? Then they try to kill you. Now Mackenzie has been murdered. That's not coincidence. There has to be a reason."

Tana accessed Ganz' files and looked at me. She frowned. "Dr. Katarin Acevado is listed in his primary research group. She's listed as 916 Elm Ridge, over in Beechfield."

I spun the cab around to head west, bringing my speed up to maximum.

"Ballen?" Tana was almost too quiet to hear. "Will they know about Dr. Acevado too?"

I wondered that too and didn't want another run-in with Gabriella's killers, but I wasn't sure we had another choice. "We can't let her get murdered without trying."

"The police?" Tana didn't sound anymore convinced by her suggestion than I was.

"You know that wouldn't work."

"What if we called her?" Tana waved her Scroll at me. "We could warn her."

If we made a call and the wrong people picked it up, we could be dead. That said, after what they'd done to Mackenzie, I wasn't going to object. I nodded to Tana, and she tapped the number into the Scroll.

I heard the faint buzz of a ring tone and then a voice, although I couldn't make out the words.

"She's not there, Ballen. She's at the lab." Tana checked the information on the Scroll. "The Advanced Theory Center over in Reisterstown."

I did another highly illegal banked turn and pointed the cab almost due north. Thirty seconds later the console pinged several times.

"What's that?" Tana's voice was filled with alarm.

I laughed. "I got a ticket."

Fifteen

"There's no answer." Tana ended the connection with a stab of a finger.

"What would Acevado be doing there this early?" It was three in the morning and the night sky was a dark, cloudy dome with not a star showing. Lights from the buildings below crawled past as if we were floating in a hot air balloon rather than moving at two hundred kilometers per hour. As we arrowed above the city, I copied Ganz' files into my technical journals account on remote storage. Multiple redundancy was an engineering habit—in my experience being too careful always paid off.

"She's probably been there all night," Tana said. "It's not uncommon—when you get wrapped up in your work you don't want to lose focus."

When they dedicate their lives to unscrewing the inscrutable, scientists seem to lose connection with the rest of us. That's undoubtedly what's behind their infamous communication problems. They spend so much time peering through telescopes and microscopes that the rest of us end up as nothing more than specimens to be dissected and categorized.

"Why can't scientists be like ordinary people and answer phones?" I couldn't hustle the limo any faster. Even if I overrode the safeties, any speed limit infractions would be detected and quickly acted upon, either by fines or police cruisers being dispatched. The fines didn't worry me, but the attention from the cops did.

Tana threw her Scroll on the dash and turned to face me. "What do you have against scientists?"

It wasn't rational, but the Atolls were initially founded by scientists, and I saw that same smug egotism in the ones still trapped on Earth. If it wasn't for the embargo, they'd be up in space with their Atoll cousins. I'd have happily walked away from this mess and left them to their chances if I didn't need them to prove my innocence.

"Call again," I said, trying to will the car faster.

"I just did." Tana grabbed her Scroll like she was trying to choke it. "And don't growl at me. It's not my fault she doesn't answer."

I checked the navigation system for what seemed like the thousandth time. We were fifteen kilometers from the lab and closing quickly. I throttled back, letting us coast towards the buildings as the air-resistance bled off our speed. We had no idea what we'd find there. If we were lucky Gabriella would be waiting for Acevado to return home. I wasn't counting on it though—there was an old guy called Murphy whose DNA liberally peppered my own genome.

"Do you know her personally?" I dropped the car into the local traffic zone, braking to comply with the limits.

Tana shook her head. The instruments reflected on her face, giving it the appearance of a bizarre death mask. "I saw her at a few official functions, or occasionally when she met with Hubert. She wasn't in my field."

"What was she working on for Ganz?"

"She didn't work *for* him." Tana leaned forward to look out of the window. "She had her own research. I'm not sure what she actually did with Hubert. Sometimes professors collaborate because they want an unbiased check on their work."

That made sense, though it wasn't exactly helpful. An idea came to me. "Call Acevado again. On her home number."

"Why?" Tana frowned. "We know she's not there."

"I like watching you dial the number." My comment drew a bewildered glare. "Humor me."

Tana tapped in the number and waited.

"Hello? Dr. Acevado?" She paused, and I heard a muted voice on the other end. "You don't really know me. I worked…"

Tana's voice tailed off, and I felt a chill in the small of my back at the click of the Scroll disconnecting.

"It was her. Ballen, it was *her*... That woman." Tana turned towards me. "You knew, didn't you? That she'd be there."

"Not exactly. It seemed like a good guess though."

"Then why?"

"If they think we're focused on Acevado's home they might not think to check her messages. It's a long shot, but might buy us some time if they don't know she's working at the lab."

Tana was quiet for several seconds. "That was good thinking. I approve."

I wasn't sure how to answer that and concentrated on the instruments. We skimmed over the soft undulating landscape that had barely a visible feature in the night, but I knew where we were even without checking. In the distance, a low sprawling complex became visible—an island in an oasis of pale floodlights that flickered as wind-blown trees obscured them temporarily.

Tana's Scroll trilled, and she gasped when she looked at it. It didn't take much to guess who the caller was.

"I'll swing around the buildings. Look for anything suspicious."

I brought the cab in a gentle arc to the right, curving over the complex and around the opposite side. Tana said nothing. I couldn't see anything either and brought the car lower.

The floodlights had the silvery gleam of high-efficiency lamps that were efficient in a power-consumption sense, but produced local pools of light rather than illuminating the area. They left countless shadows that could conceal an army and the vehicles to transport it if necessary.

"Hang on," I called to Tana before moving the cab into a spiraling curve, orbiting the building with the cab's headlights pointed inward to better illuminate the dark areas.

"I still don't see anything," Tana said. "But anyone inside must be wondering what's going on."

"We'll tell them we're doing a survey for nocturnal wildlife."

Tense for any sign of trouble, I brought the nose down until we landed in the parking area by the main entrance. Minutes later Tana's University pass allowed us access through the double glass doors.

At this time of day, the reception area was empty, but someone had handily left a thin jacket hung over the chair. The cold outside

115

had brought blood rushing to the surface of my skin and with it came more pain. The jacket had a badge on the chest saying *Security* and fit me like socks on a flea, but I felt no guilt and swore I'd return it to its owner fully cleaned. I paused, straining to hear any kind of sound, cupping my ear to indicate to Tana what I was doing. There was the vaguest low-level humming that seemed a natural part of the environment, but other than that I couldn't hear anything. She shook her head when I raised an eyebrow in her direction, and together we crept into the undecorated corridors.

It was entirely unlike the gloomy environment we'd found at Mackenzie's. The darkness there seemed to almost presage the Doctor's fate. Here the pervasive white plastic and cold glow panels threw up a barrier against unpleasantness—as if brightness on its own could forestall death.

"Where do we find Acevado?"

Tana shrugged. "I've only been here a few times."

We were at the foot of a stairwell leading to the upper floor, and I pointed upwards. "Should we split up?"

Tana shivered. "I don't think that's a good idea. We'll be more convincing together. And what if one of us got lost?"

There was an optical pickup for the security system at the base of the stairwell. Nothing unusual in that, but this one caught my eye. The telltale power light was out. It could have been a malfunctioning unit, but on the other hand...

"Don't move."

I hurried back to the entrance and glanced behind the barrier of the reception desk, checking the security screens. They were full of turbulent static. There was a small box half hidden under the overhang of the desk, and I scooped it up. It was a Disruptor like the one Coyan had shown us—maybe I could use it as evidence. Returning to Tana, I whirled a finger in the air. "They're here."

She seemed to shrink, her shoulders trembling as she wrapped her arms around herself. "We should leave. We can't help her now."

I lifted the gun and checked it was primed. "I can't do that, but you can wait in the car if you want. I'll be as quick as possible."

Tana hesitated. "Let's start on this floor."

We made our way slowly down the corridor. Banks of lockers

lined the passage and could easily hide a full grown person. We had to be cautious, and our progress slowed to something resembling a glacial flow. We checked each room as we came to them, but most were darkened, punctuated only occasionally by the star-fleck of ubiquitous computer consoles. One room held a giant sphere, its smooth surface roiling with glowing trails of light that flickered and twisted like plasma streams. I had no idea what it was, but the sign on the door said *Cybernetic Research*.

"Geek nightclub," I said, shaking my head.

I heard a faint noise and stopped, trying to understand where it was coming from. It danced on the edge of perception, like an annoying mosquito of sound. There, but not quite there.

Tana pointed up and forward. Her hearing must have been a lot more sensitive than mine—chalk up another "benefit" of a lifetime of cycling through pressure locks—hearing degradation was an occupational hazard on the High-Rig.

The noise grew louder, until it became clear someone was moving on the upper floor. They passed overhead, moving towards the front of the building. I tightened my grip on the gun. Once there, they'd see the cab and know they weren't alone. Either it was too late, or we didn't have much time to find Acevado.

I leaned over to Tana and whispered, "We should head back befo—"

The lights darkened as if a shutter had dropped, replaced by a garish red that flicked on and off in stroboscopic flashes. At the same time, the air filled with a pulsating sound like the collective tortured death screams of a thousand electronic geese.

A shadow darted out of the room next to us, and something heavy and metallic slammed into my chest. The impact punched the wind out of me, and I collapsed on the floor gasping for breath. The red flickering made it impossible to see as Tana merged with the shadows. A second later a dark object slammed into the wall, sliding down to reveal a slim, brown-haired woman. I didn't need to be the great Sherlock to deduce we'd found Dr. Acevado.

Tana knelt down next to me, shouting through the noise. "Are you okay?" She pointed at the red cylinder on the floor. "She hit you with a fire extinguisher."

"We could have used that earlier." My breath was still ragged. "Acevado?"

"She's stunned. Nothing serious."

"You seem very sure of yourself." Again I was surprised by Tana's physical strength and speed.

"I learned to take care of myself when I was younger." She looked across to Acevado. "We need to move."

I pushed myself up off the floor. My ribs hurt like I'd played tag with a RockRhino, but I couldn't feel any obvious damage—a blessing considering what I'd dealt with over the last twenty-four hours. Tana moved back to Acevado, leaning over to make herself heard. Acevado nodded a couple of times, then Tana helped her up.

"This way," I shouted over the alarm, pointing back the way we'd come. "It's our only chance."

We picked our way back toward the front entrance, the flashing red lights dancing off every surface, making it almost impossible to focus. Tana had her arm around Acevado, almost carrying the other woman despite her being almost the same size. As we moved, Tana talked to Acevado and relayed some of it to me.

"She pulled the plug on the simulation processor back there. It needs to be super-cooled. Triggered the alarm."

I didn't really care what had triggered it. I only hoped the gunmen were headed in a different direction. The noise made it impossible to get any idea of where they were. We passed the room where we'd seen the glowing ball earlier. It was dark now, and I guessed it must be the processor Tana had mentioned.

"Ballen!"

Tana's voice barely reached me through the clamor, her fear unmistakable despite the masking effect of the alarm. The gleam of a laser targeting system scanned across the cabinet in front of me. I dropped instinctively as the corner of the cabinet evaporated in a hail of whining sparks, ricochets swarming around us like molten steel wasps.

I fired several rounds into the darkness behind us more or less at random, not really expecting to hit anyone. If I was lucky, I might be able to keep their heads down and slow them down. But as usual, the Seven Lucky Gods were on vacation, and the entire corridor erupted with a mass volley of ricochets, forcing me to drop down again. I curled up as small as I could, hoping nothing would hit me, though the density of the barrage made it almost inevitable.

Somehow when the shooting stopped, I was unharmed. The shots had triggered the fire system, filling the corridor with billowing clouds that turned the darkness into Stygian pools. I looked around to check on Tana and Acevado. They were by the wall on the other side of the corridor.

Tana was holding the older woman close. There was a bloody gash on Acevado's face where a round had sliced across the side of her skull, splitting the skin wide. Tana's hand was pressed over a wound in Acevado's chest, trying to stem the heavy spurts of thick blood.

Tana was covered in blood and looked like a demon from a show. I couldn't tell if she'd been injured or not. It could have been Acevado's blood, her own, or a mixture.

"I'm okay." She answered my unspoken question. "Get her out of here."

"I'm not going to le—"

"We don't have time for a debate." She held out her hand. "Give me the gun and take her."

I could see Tana's shoulders jerking. I wasn't sure if it was fear, anger, or both, but she was clearly fighting it. This girl was a bewildering mixture of emotions, and every time I thought I'd figured her out something else surprised me. I handed her the gun, and she vanished into the inky blackness. I had no idea what she was planning, but I wouldn't want to be one of the men behind us.

I slipped my arm under Acevado and dragged her towards the entrance. Each step was agony and seemed to last longer than a lunar night as we stumbled on. I imagined the tracking laser dancing on my neck and the back of my head tingled. The primitive part of my brain screamed at me to turn and look for the killers, but one misstep would be fatal, and I fought the urge.

At the reception desk, the monitoring station still showed the security system was offline. I'd been hoping that the alarms might have attracted the authorities—at that moment even the cops would have been a welcome sight. I heaved again, pulling Acevado's almost lifeless body through the doors and into the dank night air. A wet gurgle came from her mouth and what remained of her strength gave way. She fell forward like a blood-soaked mannequin, pulling me with her.

I tried to get back up, but exhaustion made it impossible. I crawled a painful meter over to Acevedo and checked her pulse. I couldn't find it, but that must have been my clumsiness because her eyes flickered open. Despite the overwhelming smell of blood, I could still catch the sweet scent of her perfume.

"Who're you?" The words came through pale cracked lips.

"Friends of Dr. Ganz."

"Hubert?" Her voice was a rasp. "He's dead."

"It was the same people who did this to you." I stroked her hair with one hand as the hole in her chest pumped hot blood around the useless fingers of my other, each spurt weaker than the last.

"It's... in the files..."

Acevado's head went limp, and the gleam in her eyes died.

"Joe..."

I looked up as Tana limped out of the building using a military style rifle to prop herself up. Her eyes were black in the pale light and blood ran down her face. She looked even more terrifying than the last time I'd seen her. Blood dripped from the hand clenched around the QuenchGun, leaving a speckled trail behind her.

"She's dead, Tana."

"Damn it!" Tana's scream echoed around the parking lot, bouncing off the concrete buildings. "This can't be happening. We don't live like this. What has this to do with any of us? We're scientists, that's all."

I dragged myself up on shaky legs and went to her. She dropped the rifle and pushed herself into my arms as she ranted incoherently for several minutes. Finally, she looked up at me, her blood and tear stained face like something straight from hell.

"Joe?" She winced as if she had a stitch in her side, then her full weight pressed against me. "I'm shot."

She folded and dropped to the ground as I struggled to break her fall.

Sixteen

"Dollie, it's Ballen," I croaked into the announcer pickup, the rough wall cold as I leaned against it for support. We were at the secured street-level entrance and the apartment block rose up into the darkness like a concrete Titan.

"What time is it?" Dollie sounded like she'd been asleep. "I'd given up on you. You ordered the Husher over five hours ago."

"It's a long story. Can we come up?"

"We?" Dollie hesitated. "Did you bring me a gift?"

"Not exactly. I need some help. I can't carry her."

"Carry *her*? I'll be right down. But Ballen..." There was a distinct frost in her voice. "This better be good."

A few minutes later the gate opened and Dollie emerged, dressed in an extremely sheer red silk negligee. She sniffed loudly when she saw us, but that didn't stop her helping maneuver Tana into the elevator up to her L12 apartment.

Dollie's living room is a diverse mixture of styles, some might say eccentric. A sunken central area surrounds a real infra-red fire-pit that spreads a warm glow to the circular couch around it. The decoration reminded me of a cross between an African tribal jungle scene and Scheherazade's bedroom. Around the walls are various reproductions of paintings and statues that I didn't really understand, but all shared a peculiar eroticism.

Dollie pointed to the badge on my jacket. "You moonlighting?" She pulled out a SootheStick, sucking deep on it before sending out a long plume of pink-tinted smoke. "Jesus, you look like crap."

"You should see me before I've had my coffee."

121

Dollie spread a blanket on the couch, and I laid Tana down.

"We probably have about two minutes before the police arrive," she said. "They'll track you all the way to my door. Hushers aren't completely anonymous you know."

I was trying to clean Tana's wounds with a bunch of small wipes—an operation comprised of equal parts blood and frustration. I wanted to assess how badly she was hurt before attempting any treatment.

"We weren't tracked." I held up the Disruptor. "I got this from our erstwhile killers."

"I don't want to know what that is, Ballen." She ground the half-smoked SootheStick into a receptacle on the low table. "Knowing you, I'm sure it's illegal. Any idea what will happen if you're caught here? The cops will pull my license. They could shut me down permanently. Why? Because you wanted to play kidnapper with this little girl?"

I held up my blood-caked hands in a futile attempt to ward off her fury. "I can explain. I haven't done anything, I swear. Listen—"

"No, you listen, Ballen. Listen real good. I saw this two hours ago. When I still thought you wanted to see me."

Dollie hit a button and a concealed screen opened on the other side of the room and lit up. It was tuned to the local news station. Headlines scrolled along the bottom, and after a few seconds, she pulled one into full-screen.

"Police search for the killer of two police officers in the Rossmoor area continues. A spokesman for the BPD stated that at around 9.30 PM, Officers Mitchell Boven and Thea Campese were forced into the Patapsco while attempting to apprehend a driver for multiple traffic violations. Both officers died from their injuries.

"No motive for the killings has been established, though the events are apparently connected to the earlier suicide of a scientist and subsequent murder of the Building Supervisor at the scientist's former residence. Joseph Ballen, a local cab driver and Tana Radebaugh, one of Dr. Ganz' students have been named as persons of interest in the case. Anonymous information provided to us at BKNC News suggests Radebaugh may have been in a relationship with Dr. Ganz and this sparked—"

I hit the controls and killed the broadcast.

"That's not true, Dollie." I turned to face her. "None of the important parts. I'm sure Ganz was murdered, but—"

"And *I'm* sure I don't want to hear this right now." She stood up. "Is there any reason I shouldn't call the police myself?"

Sure Dollie liked me, and we'd shared a few lonely nights together. But she didn't owe me anything. We worked together, and she was one of the few people I genuinely liked. "Because you're my friend. And right now I really need one."

Dollie stalked off without a word. She might have gone to call the cops for all I knew. I felt powerless, as if she was somehow rejecting me and making decisions about me that I had no control over. Though given the circumstances, I could hardly blame her.

I looked at Tana and wondered what had gone on between her and Ganz. It certainly wasn't a simple teacher/student relationship. For some reason that bothered me, even though I knew it was none of my business. It was also hard to imagine it happening. Tana seemed to have such a negative response to any form of intimacy, no matter how slight.

Dollie reappeared and scooped Tana up from the couch. "That rug is over two-hundred years old. I can't let someone bleed to death on it."

I followed her to a room at the back of the apartment I'd never seen before. It was dimly lit and unlike the rest of her place had no decoration at all, which was surprising. Even more surprising was the full-body Treatment Unit that dominated the center of the room like a high-tech sarcophagus nestling in a tangle of tendril-like data cables.

"Did the previous owners leave this behind when you got the place?" I moved closer to examine the machine as Dollie slid Tana's unconscious body into the unit and removed the girl's clothes. I could only guess what Tana's response would have been if she'd been awake—nothing pretty, that was for sure.

"Genetic manipulation has its downsides." Dollie arranged Tana inside the treatment chamber, her gaze deliberately avoiding mine. "It's not something we talk about."

"But—" I gestured vaguely at the Treatment Unit.

"ReSeeq sometimes involves deliberately suppressing the immune system. That can lead to all kinds of side-effects, many of them cancerous to some extent. It's cheaper to rent your own unit than repeat visits to a clinic, and I don't like being dependent on others."

Dollie ran her fingers over the control panel, deftly manipulating the controls as the scan head moved back and forth. Each pass revealing a more detailed view of Tana on the diagnostic screen.

"Multiple minor lacerations, they're simple enough. A dislocated wrist, again not a worry." Dollie paused. "Burn hole through her right shoulder. Probably from an energy weapon. It's sliced, not clean."

"Can you fix it?"

"Maybe. I think so. It's going to take some time though."

"One more thing." Dollie manipulated the controls and the diagnostic outline of Tana changed to a pulsing mass of minute glowing trails. "That's a display of any DNA showing polymorphic sequences."

"Dollie, let's pretend I don't have a clue what you're talking about for a few minutes."

"Jesus, Ballen. That's large-scale genetic manipulation. Your girlfriend has been through ReSeeq. She's Geneered."

That didn't make sense. ReSeeq was typically used for medical or cosmetic reasons. Neither situation seemed to fit in Tana's case. It explained some things though, like her speed and strength, but why would someone implement such widespread changes and *not* select optimum aesthetics?

Dollie locked the treatment controls. "There's nothing more we can do here. I have a portable dermal regenerator that you could make good use of."

I followed her into the living room, sat down on the couch and eased the jacket off. Dollie had only seen the scrapes on my hands and face, and I heard her gasp when she caught sight of my back. A moment later the tingle of the regenerator soothed my skin, and the gentle heat relaxed my mind. I started to drift until I wasn't sure if I was awake or asleep.

Dollie seemed to float away, as if carried on the flickering golden glow from the fire-pit. I walked up to the Treatment Unit and opened it. Tana sat upright and smiled at me. I moved to hold her and suddenly it wasn't Tana, it was Dollie, and we were tangled in the sheets of her bed. Then it was Tana again, and I held her close. She whispered in my ear. It was Acevado's voice though.

"It's in the files, Joe. It's in the files."

The dream shifted once more. Now I was holding on to Gabriella. She pushed the barrel of a pistol into my throat, the cool metal tip tickling my skin.

"I like pretty boys, Ballen. They're good for one's ego. But I do tire of them. Now, give me the code to access Ganz' files. I really don't want to make a mess on Dollie's rug. She wouldn't like that."

My vocal cords were locked tight as I fought to say something. Anything. Gabriella laughed maniacally, then she leaned over and kissed me. Her lips were fiery against mine and opened as the kiss deepened. I felt the gun tighten against my Adam's apple as she squeezed the trigger and shot me through the throat.

I tried to scream. Move. Twist. Sit. Anything to avoid dealing with my death.

"Joe?"

It was Dollie's voice. I sensed that she'd called me several times and when I opened my eyes her face was full of worry.

"You were squealing." Her hand was pressed against my chest.

"Squealing?" I ran my hand over my damp scalp, the bristles from my hair grating against my palm.

"It sounded like you were trying to talk. Maybe."

"I was having a nightmare. Sorry, I didn't mean to wake you."

Dollie sat upright and lit a SootheStick, drawing deep on the gently intoxicating narcotic vapors before offering it to me. I shook my head, though I appreciated the offer. Right now I needed to keep my mind clear so I could think straight. Or as straight as I was capable of, which wasn't looking good these days.

"You're a damn mess, Ballen." She looked me up and down like a side of beef.

She was right. Despite the treatment, my back was a mass of red sores mixed with skin that had an all too crunchy feel to it. Dermal regenerators had limits and were only designed to deal with small cuts and wounds. Something—I couldn't even remember what—had caught my cheek, making it swell and force my eye half-shut. Not only that, but my leg was still raw and scarred from where I'd been shot earlier.

"If I was a horse they'd put me out of my misery," I muttered.

"When did you last see a horse? Outside of an old TooDee I mean?"

"A few years ago. I visited a friend's ranch. His family still breeds them. I actually rode one."

Logan's family was about as traditional as you could get in the late Twenty-Second. They grew crops, bred and hunted animals and occasionally even ate them. Geneered meat and fish never found a place on their tables. Logan's dad said he'd rather starve than eat "that shit."

"You rode one? How was it?" Dollie stubbed out the 'Stick.

"Lumpy. Like driving a cab with a bad turbine—never knew quite which direction it was going to go."

"I don't think I'd like that." She moved closer, her slim fingers tracing across my chest. "I like to be in charge."

"I've been through a lot." I felt a moment of panic.

"Don't worry. Dollie will do all the work." Her hand moved lower.

"I really am beat up. I need to rest."

"Sure, sure. I guess we'll let it slip this time." Dollie released her hold. "But don't forget we have some unfinished business, and you owe me."

Dollie was right, I did owe her, not only for taking us in when she had absolutely no need to, but for many other things. Including my job. If only she weren't so damned confusing.

She stood there, her curves clearly visible as the dim firelight shone through her sheer nightgown. Part of me regretted my reluctance and I wondered if it was too late to change my mind. Maybe I was too much of a coward.

"I'm going to get some more sleep." She yawned. "The bed is far more comfortable than the couch. Coming?"

"Dollie? Why didn't you run a MedCent check on me?"

"What makes you think I didn't?"

I couldn't think of a suitable reply. If she'd done that, she knew about my injuries and flight status. She held out her hand, and I took it, letting her lead me to the bedroom.

Seventeen

Despite feeling as if I'd been at the wrong end of a train wreck, I woke with less pain than the last couple of days. Thankfully, the bad dreams hadn't returned. Dollie was already out of bed, and I felt an odd mixture of relief and disappointment, wondering if she'd risen early to save my modesty.

The shower blasted me from all sides with scalding water, then scalding air, and finally warm air—an energy efficient process that always left me feeling clean, but in an uncomfortable freshly-boiled-lobster sort of way. It only took a minute and in that time someone, presumably Dollie, had placed a full casual outfit on the bed. I wondered briefly about its previous owner, then spotted a receipt from a twenty-four hour instant clothes retailer.

I found Dollie in the kitchen, munching on a piece of toast. The table was laid for three with plates, cutlery, and coffee cups. The coffee smelled especially inviting, even if it wasn't my usual blend, and I almost drooled in Pavlovian response. She was scanning several news feeds, her eyes flicking from one to another like an orbital tracking system scanning for potential collisions.

"Toast there. Cereal there. Newsfeeds here." She nodded at the screen. "Krystal Blyss is coming to town—she's scheduled for three nights next week. That's one lady whose pants I'd like to get inside. Want to take me to the show, Soldier? We could sneak backstage—who knows, we might both get lucky."

Dollie never hid her carnal desires, but looking at Krystal gyrating her famously pneumatic torso on the screen, I wouldn't turn the singer out of my bed on a cold night either. Krystal's managers claimed she was one hundred percent natural, but instinct told me no one achieved that level of perfection without *some* Geneering. I took out my Scroll and was about to log into some of my favorite news sources, but Dollie shook her head.

"That would be a really bad move."

"Huh?"

Dollie snatched the Scroll out of my hand before I could say anything and tossed it in the oven. Thirty seconds of random flashes and unpleasant smells later, she pulled out the steaming pile of melted plastic, rubber and graphene with a pair of kitchen tongs and dropped it in the waste chute.

"Even the base signal could be a problem, Ballen." She shook her head at my stunned silence. "It seems you're dead."

"I know I'm slow in the mornings, but there's no need to get insulting. Coffee fixes *everything*." I felt stupid. Of course they'd have a watch set on my account, ready to pinpoint my location as soon as I used the Scroll. I was relieved to know that copies of Ganz' files were still safely hidden in my technical journals, though I hadn't expected to need the extra backup as protection against an overzealous Dollie.

She expanded one of the news channels to fill the screen. There were images of a burnt-out shell of a half-flooded building. As the camera zoomed in I recognized the wet-foot hovel we'd crashed near the night before. When we'd left, the building had been flooded and probably a danger to sanitary health, but the images showed it had been virtually destroyed. Not a single piece of framework above the water surface was intact, and the remnants looked like they'd had an unfortunate encounter with a flame thrower. Dollie turned the sound up.

"...attempting to flee followed by several undercover Detectives. In the ensuing pursuit the driver, identified as Joseph Ballen, lost control of his vehicle and crashed into an unofficial flood-through residence. Investigators say the fuel cell ruptured, causing a fire that consumed the building and could easily have spread to nearby properties if it hadn't been for quick action by local fire-fighting teams.

"Authorities say several bodies *have* been recovered, but the intensity of the blaze means that full identification will be forensic in nature and take time. In the meantime, Police have released the following Argus footage."

A 3D reconstruction came up on the screen, allowing a full Six Degrees of Freedom. The cab veered wildly across the screen, yawing and pitching furiously, chased by a very obvious police undercover vehicle. Suddenly, the cab rolled upside down in a lunatic movement, before pitching head first into the wet-foot slum.

"That's impossible. It never happened."

"Of course it didn't, Soldier. Otherwise I'd have had a corpse in my bed last night, and necrophilia really isn't my style."

"Dollie, did you..."

I didn't think she could have arranged anything like this, but she never ceased to surprise me. Whatever her background was, she had resources and skills far beyond those you'd normally associate with the owner of a cab company.

"I know I'm good, but not that good." She ran the 3D again, spinning the image around to see it from all sides. "Whoever did this had a lot of pull, or a lot of money. Probably both. The quality is incredible. By the way, you owe me a cab."

I was still trying to come up with a suitable response when we were interrupted.

"They think we're dead?" Tana stood in the kitchen doorway wearing a vivid pink silk gown that was very obviously not her style. She looked haggard, her eyes living in sunken hollows and her features drawn and sharp.

"That's what the news feeds are saying, though they didn't mention you specifically. How do you feel?" I slid out a chair so she could join us.

"Battered. Sore. My shoulder doesn't work properly."

"You shouldn't even be out of the Treatment Unit yet," said Dollie. She moved around to examine Tana, who flinched and pulled away.

Dollie looked across at me, and I shrugged. Tana seemed to have some kind of touch taboo that was beyond anything I'd ever seen. Whatever her personal feelings though, she needed medical help.

"Let's get you back into the unit and make sure nothing bad is going to happen. Okay?" Tana took her time following me into the treatment room, but once there she clambered into the unit and lay down. She moved awkwardly as she struggled to keep the gown wrapped tightly around her. I had no idea how to operate the damned thing and had to wait until Dollie joined us. I could follow the basic displays, but that was as far as it went. Scanning beams whirled around, rippling over Tana's body and the display soon filled with the ghostly green image of her internals.

"Hmmmmm..." Dollie chewed her lip and flicked through several alternative views.

"What's wrong?" Tana's skin had darkened. I couldn't tell if it was from embarrassment or anger.

"Nothing." Dollie glanced at me and pointed out several areas on the display. "You're doing fine."

I had a rudimentary knowledge of trauma and care—that's part of basic training when you work Spaceside. From what I could see, the scans showed all of Tana's major injuries were healing well. That in itself wasn't a surprise—the unusual thing was the apparent speed. It was happening much faster than normal, even allowing for the acceleration from the Treatment Unit.

Dollie raised her eyebrows. Rapid healing supported her idea that Tana had been through ReSeeq therapy at some point. Boosting tissue regeneration capacity is as tricky as matching velocities in space by eye. Done badly it can lead to explosive cancer growth, which added to my assessment that someone had spent a *lot* of money on Tana's ReSeeq.

I could tell Dollie wanted me to ask Tana about her treatment. She always said there was a special bond between the Geneered, but I wasn't sure if that was true. Maybe that was just the ones she'd met. Either way, it wasn't my business. Although Dollie didn't mind discussing such things it didn't mean everyone else was comfortable with it.

"I hope they *do* think we're dead." Tana's sharp voice broke into my thoughts. "That way we can get on with our lives."

It was hard to understand how she could be so smart and yet so out of touch with how the world really worked. Tana was undoubtedly very intelligent, but she was clearly one of those academics who distanced themselves from the real world—frustrating for the rest of us who have to live in it.

"That broadcast was faked. For one thing, there are no Argus pickups in that part of town." I limped around to face Tana. "It could be the police trying to throw the killers off track and lure us out into the open. Or it could be the killers trying to throw the police off our scent, so they have a clear shot at us. Think about it. They know we didn't die, and I doubt the police would have torched anybody—even a wet-foot—to put on a show. Either way, doesn't look good for us."

"If you step in front of an Eye the system will recognize you in minutes. Same if you try using a net-enabled device." Dollie stared at Tana. "Do you have a Scroll? We need to destroy it—otherwise, they'll trace it."

Tana shook her head and I felt uneasy. I'd seen her with a Scroll several times. "Tana…"

"I don't, Ballen." She breathed heavily. "I had… did have… I mean I lost it. When I fought those men…"

Suddenly the tears flooded out. Tana slid out of the unit and threw herself against me. After a few awkward moments, I put my arms around her shoulders ineffectually. I could almost feel Dollie's eyes drilling into me. "Take it easy. It's not important."

I nodded to Dollie to leave. I knew what she was thinking as clearly as if I were telepathic. *Don't trust her, Ballen. Don't trust her.*

"We could still contact the police. They can't arrest us for being innocent." Tana wiped the tears from her eyes. She seemed relieved that Dollie had left.

Her naivety was bewildering. "Haven't you heard? Everyone in the Readjustment Centers is innocent. Just ask them."

"Don't make fun of me. I know everyone *claims* they haven't done anything, but the police don't bother people for no reason."

"Yeah, and the Atolls *love* people from Earth. What about the poor bastards who happened to be in the wrong place at the wrong time? Like us." I stepped back. "Cops can be as wrong or biased as anyone else. But they get really dangerous when their own have been hurt. If they think you're responsible, they don't look any further."

"But—"

I called out through the door. "Dollie? Do you have a NullScroll?"

A NullScroll scrambles location information and has no personal ID tagged to it so it can't be easily traced. Like the Husher they're not common, but have their uses.

Dollie appeared at the door, a large old fashioned Scroll in hand. "You're an ass, Joe. Do you know how much these things cost?"

"Add it to my bill." The problem with NullScrolls is that they can only be used a few times. After that their ability to mask themselves declines as the system logs every activation.

Tana grabbed her clothes from a table near the Treatment Unit and indicated for me to turn around. I dialed the number for Sterle, grateful when his face appeared on the small display at the third ring.

"Joe?" His eyes widened. "Now I have to add network identity nullification to the list. He reached off screen, probably to trigger a trace. "You killed two cops, Joe. Why?"

"You know that's not the case."

"And the Super at Ganz' building? Not to mention Ganz. That's quite a list." He glanced to one side again. "Were you anywhere near the Advanced Theory Center in Reisterstown recently? I've got reports of another dead scientist from there."

"Well, well. If it ain't StimBoy." Francis cut in on the call, the display splitting to show both of them. "How 'bout we get together? I've got an old style revolver and haven't played Russian roulette in a while."

"Someone killed them. But it wasn't me. In fact, they've been trying to kill me too."

"Well, why didn't you say that earlier, StimBoy?" Francis muttered something away from the pickup. "And I suppose you're going to tell us why."

"It has to do with Ganz and his work. That's all I know."

"Don't play me for a fool, Joe," Sterle said. "The first thing anyone who's guilty does is claim they're a victim."

"I'm telling you the truth."

"Got anyone to corroborate that, Stimmer?" Francis sniggered when I didn't answer. "Didn't think so."

Tana pointed at herself, and I dismissed her with a quick shake of my head. The police didn't know there was any definite connection between us yet, and it was safer it stayed that way. When it comes to the authorities, it's better to keep them in as much ignorance as possible.

"Okay, Joe. Let's say for one minute I believe you." Sterle leaned closer to the pickup. "I'm assuming you don't mind telling us where you are? Or for that matter coming into the department so we can question you some more."

"And I'll be free to leave afterward?" I knew the answer but decided to play along.

"In due course, perhaps." Sterle looked at something to his left. "After we finish our investigation."

The signal from Francis cut off, and Sterle's face expanded to fill the screen. I had a good idea why he'd vanished. "Should I start running? Presumably, your pet bulldog is on his way to pick me up."

"That's up to you." Sterle's gray stubble formed a fuzzy halo around his dark face. "Whatever you do though, I guarantee we'll track you down."

I disconnected and turned the phone off.

"They're coming here?" Tana looked worried again. "If I'm arrested I'll..."

"Whatever trace they got, it wasn't this one. At best they got a signal location from a random point in the city."

Tana only seemed slightly relieved. "What now?"

That was a good question. The only plan I had was the one we'd already tried. Find one of Ganz' acquaintances who could explain why he and the others had been killed. The trick was getting to them first.

"Think, Tana. There must be somebody else. A friend maybe?"

Tana's brow furrowed. "No. I already told you Hubert didn't socialize much. He didn't see many people apart from m—"

The announcer chime sounded. Someone was outside the door.

Before I could react, Dollie's voice came through concealed speakers.

"What the hell did you do, Ballen? The police are here. Stay where you are. I'll try to get rid of them."

They couldn't have traced the NullScroll let alone got here so quickly. Not after a single use. Neither Tana or me had our Scrolls anymore. Which ruled out that possibility. The Husher was parked in the basement, but that couldn't be traced to me and was a regular part of Dollie's fleet. Despite that, the cops were outside. I looked around. There was only one entrance to the room and as far as I knew only one way out of the apartment. Other than the Treatment Unit the room was bare.

"Ballen?" Tana looked puzzled.

"Can you see any other way out?"

The only opening, if you could call it that, was a narrow window overlooking the city. Two strides and I was there, pressing my face to the cool glass to look outside. The angle wasn't good. There was nothing visible but smooth concrete and steel, and if I remembered correctly all the Jump-Offs were on the North and South faces of the building, the window was facing East. Not to mention that the glass was sealed and I'd need to figure out a way of smashing it—with the cops in the next room.

"Maybe we should go with them." Tana looked at the door. "We could explain. I'm sure that they'd listen if I told them—"

I thought about trying to shoot through the window. The glass was undoubtedly reinforced, but it might work. Of course, the shots would alert the cops... Then I remembered I'd left the gun on the table in the bedroom.

"Told them what?" I turned back to face Tana. "Is there something I should know about?"

"What? No, of course not." Tana looked down, her hand smoothing the front of her shirt unnecessarily. Her clothes were torn and dirty, but nothing in Dollie's wardrobe would have fit.

I knew she was lying to me again, but about what I had no idea. And there wasn't much I could do about it, especially with the cops in the other room. Maybe if they left...

Several minutes had passed since Dollie had answered the

door and when I stopped to listen, I could hear nothing. No movement outside the room, no voices in the distance. Nothing. The soundproofing was good in her apartment, but not up to that level.

Once again I cursed myself for leaving the pistol in the other room. I wasn't used to thinking like a fugitive, and it had left me defenseless. The logical part of my brain said it was an understandable oversight, but the proud-to-be-smart half was silently cursing and spitting.

I moved to the door, bringing my ear close to the surface. I still couldn't hear anything.

"Ballen? What's—"

I held up my hand to hush Tana. Sometimes her yammering got on my nerves. Now was one of those moments. I reached out, my hand hesitating on the cool surface of the door, then I pushed it open. Barely enough to form a gap a couple of centimeters wide.

I waited. Sunlight from the window opposite picked out dust motes in the air, creating a glowing pillar that angled towards me. But it wasn't the kind of enlightenment I was looking for.

I nudged the door open wider.

"You can come out of there, Ballen."

That wasn't Dollie. The voice was distinctly male, with a nasal quality to it. It sounded familiar, though I couldn't immediately place it.

"Come out, or this bitch gets it in the neck."

I waved Tana to wait and slid the door open, stepping through the short corridor into the main living room. One guy was on the far right, his gun targeted directly on me. Someone else was near the door with an arm locked around Dollie's chest and a large pistol pointed at her neck. It was Coyan.

"Lift the hands and turn around slowly." He flicked the gun towards me momentarily. His voice was harsh, and his heavily bandaged nose did little to cover the swelling on his face. "Now."

I did as he'd ordered and turned around, letting him see I had no weapons.

"Check him, Tervo," Coyan ordered. "And don't be gentle."

The man in the far corner edged up, his gun never leaving my chest. His face was hard, despite the large, heavily-bearded jowls. He had musical notes tattooed under his eyes, but whether they were meant to be whimsical or threatening, I couldn't tell.

He patted his hands over my waist and chest then moved behind me to repeat the process.

I felt rather than saw movement. A dark figure crouched low crossing the space behind us faster than I'd have thought possible. Tervo speared into the back of me, and we both went down in a tumble. At almost the same time I heard a shriek, then an explosion filled the room. My ears nearly burst at the concussion wave from the shot.

I squirmed, trying to get away. Tervo grabbed me and wrenched my head back, almost breaking my spine as he jammed a knee into it for leverage. I had a brief glimpse of Dollie struggling with Coyan then fell back, my neck feeling like it was going to snap.

"Stop."

It was Tana. I couldn't see her, and Tervo ignored her. The cords in my neck bulged as he pulled backwards and my sight dimmed.

"Stop!" Tana yelled this time.

I felt the vertebrae in my neck crunch. It was probably internal, but the noise seemed to rumble around the room like the blast from a mining charge.

I heard an oily click so low it almost seemed it was from outside. Then another explosion went off. My ears popped, and Tervo yanked my head back even harder.

The next thing I remembered was opening my eyes, a swarm of fuzzy shapes dancing the samba inside my eyeballs. All I could hear was a soft sobbing as my vision slowly returned to normal. I looked cautiously over my shoulder, the muscles in my neck feeling like my head would drop off if I moved too fast.

Tervo was on his back, blood pooling on the marble-pattern tile floor. Tana was kneeling a few meters away, her head hung low. Her breathing was hoarse, coming in tight shudders, and in her hands was Tervo's gun.

I remembered Dollie and spun around. I nearly blacked out at the pain burning through my neck. She was sitting on Coyan with his gun in her hand. The dressing on his face was flatter than earlier, and dark rivulets of fresh blood oozed from underneath it.

"Nice of you to help." Dollie stood and kicked Coyan in the ribs harshly. "This one is out for a while. Him?"

She pointed to Tervo, and I shook my head slightly, moving as little as possible to avoid more pain.

"Thank God I can't afford real marble," she said. "Rags and cleaning supplies in the kitchen under the sink. Hurry up before he stains my damn rug."

I felt like I was being dismissed. Dollie looked pointedly over to Tana. "Make yourself useful, Ballen."

I took my time collecting the supplies. When I returned, Dollie and Tana had vanished, and a pistol had appeared on a side table near the kitchen door. I tucked it inside my belt then went over to Coyan. Along with the cleaning supplies, I'd grabbed some heavy-duty cord and quickly hog-tied his hands and feet. It was rough and ready, but should make it awkward for him if he woke up. Then I mopped up the blood under his head and left some rags to soak up any more leaks.

Dollie had done a real number on his nose from what I could tell. Even worse than Tana had done a few hours earlier. His face was so badly impacted I wasn't sure he'd survive, and part of me hoped he wouldn't.

Then I turned to the much more distasteful job of cleaning up Tervo.

Rolling him over, I slid some black bags under him to catch any more blood and sprayed the wound in his back with a layer of expanding pipe sealant to stem the flow. Tana had shot him at close range with his own pistol—a large caliber StubGun designed to cause maximum damage and not over-penetrate. Lucky for me, or she could easily have shot us both.

Once he was on the bags, I wrapped several more around him and sealed them with tape, then dragged him into the bathroom before returning to mop up the tiles.

Dollie came in as I was finishing up. "I gave her a 'Tranq to calm her down."

"You've got more dead meat here than the local Bozo's Burgers,"

I said. "I've no idea how the hell they traced us here."

"Probably covering all bases." Dollie leaned over the still unconscious Coyan. "This guy is seriously ugly."

"No kidding." I tapped my nose. "Looks like you finished what Tana started earlier."

"I didn't invite him." Dollie went into the kitchen briefly. When she came back, she was slightly pale and carrying some heavy-duty cable ties. "This is a mess, Joe."

I nodded and took the cable ties from her. Kneeling next to Coyan, I reinforced my improvised cord with several of the plastic straps until I was convinced he was secure. He was a resilient son-of-a-slitch for sure and was still breathing, albeit with a rasp. I wondered if he was Geneered, but even if he was he'd have a hard time breaking out of these straps.

When I looked back up, Dollie was shaking a little. "You okay?"

She took a deep breath. "You know me. I'm tough."

I wondered how much I really did know about her. Sure we were friends, kind of, but how much does anyone really know about another person? I'd never seen her break down, and she didn't now, despite the chaos I'd brought into her life.

"We have to leave."

Dollie folded her arms around her shoulders and shrugged. "And go where?"

She had a point. But it wouldn't be long before the real police checked out Dollie's place, and when Coyan and Tervo failed to report back or return it was a safe bet Gabriella would show up in force.

I pointed at Coyan. "Let's see if we can get some answers first."

Eighteen

I went to check on Tana, but when I poked my head in the guest room, I heard the shower running.

"I'll fight you for the next turn," called Dollie from the living room.

"You take it. I'll check if our prisoner is still breathing."

With the StubGun tight in my fist, I went back to Coyan who was still flopped by the door. I pushed him with my toe, not being particularly gentle, and his eyes flickered a little, but didn't open.

"Good. You're awake." I nudged him with the gun. "I've got some questions, and you look like someone who likes to talk."

He opened his eyes. "I get outta this, you're dead." He croaked even more than earlier as he struggled to breathe in-between his words.

"You can always join your buddy in a bag in the kitchen."

Coyan sneered. "You ain't that tough."

"Maybe, but I'm on a learning curve." I reached down and pulled him up.

His ankles were still tied, and he wobbled for a minute. "Undo my legs. How'm I supposed to move?"

"Slowly and carefully." I prodded him harder with the StubGun. "In the corner."

Coyan shuffled forward, moving a centimeter or so at a time as his legs tugged at the ties. "This is stupid. You know what I'm gonna do when I—"

"Shut up."

I pushed him to a chair in the corner of the room facing the wall. Not that he didn't know who we all were, but I felt that psychologically it would add some extra pressure if he couldn't see exactly what was going on.

Dollie disappeared momentarily and came back holding a thin-bladed utility knife. "He isn't dead yet? Okay, there's still time."

"Screw you, bitch," Coyan muttered. "I'm so gonna hurt you when I get my hands on you."

"That worked out so well for you last time." Dollie looked at me. "Why are you keeping him around?"

I wasn't cut out for cold-blooded murder and didn't think Dollie was either, but the tone of her voice said otherwise. "Maybe we can get some information out of him," I said.

Coyan laughed and coughed. "Fat chance, fancy-boy."

I hadn't noticed Tana come into the room. The first I knew she was there was when she spoke. "Give me the gun. I'll kill him."

Tana stood there stiffly, completely expressionless. It would have been easy to pass the StubGun over, but I'd already reached my daily limit for cleaning up corpses. "Why would you want to do that?"

"He killed Hubert. Or one of them did at least."

"Ya got the wrong guy," Coyan rasped. "I ain't done nothing."

"Do you often pretend to be the police and threaten people for no reason?" Tana said.

Coyan shrugged slightly. "Blow me."

Tana rushed forward, but I caught her mid-stride. She could probably have gone straight through me but managed to control herself. Her nostrils flared as she drew in deep breaths.

"He's not worth it," Dollie said. She guided Tana back towards the dark plush couch. "Some people are born scum."

"You can shut it too, Mafadite."

Dollie's jaw tightened, and I saw her tremble, but she stayed with Tana on the couch. "Kill him, Joe, and have done. I'm sick of listening to him."

Dollie brought up a thumping 3V of Krystal Bliss's *Rebop Zazuhzana*, turning the volume up loud enough to rattle the ribcage on an elephant.

"You're not a very popular guy around here." I moved up behind him and pressed the StubGun lightly against Coyan's neck. "It looks like I'm out-voted."

Coyan glanced at me out of the corner of his eyes. "What's with the crazy music?"

Krystal was shaking it and screeching how "It don't mean a thing, Zuzah Zuzaling."

"We could change the music I guess. Any last requests?" I asked.

"Man... I'm quaking here."

Despite his bravado, he was sweating. "Of course, if you want to cooperate, I might be able to persuade the ladies to let you live."

Krystal's lithe torso jiggled and bounced in the corner of my eye. "He's so smoky, he love strokey-strokey. Rebop, rebop, Zazuhzana."

"I don't know anything." He cringed and tried to look backward, but I'd tied him too well. "Don't matter what you do to me. That ain't gonna change. Jesus, turn that shit off."

"Why was Ganz killed?"

He ignored me, and I chopped the gun into the back of his head. The crack of the metal against his skull was jarring even against the background of thudding music. "Why?"

Coyan grunted, and a trail of blood trickled from his busted nose. "Never heard of him."

"You're not very smart." I moved so he could see the gun in my hand. "Are they really paying you enough for this?"

"Screw you."

I had a problem here. I wasn't a heavy and would happily avoid violence if possible. That limited how much I could lean on him.

Krystal was yelling louder. "I'm goin' south, water in my mouth. I want the heat, Rebob the meat. Zazu Zazah." Then the volume dropped slightly.

"Let me cut him, Joe," Dollie called out. "I'd enjoy that."

"Keep that crazy maffa away from me."

"I don't think she likes that word."

Coyan strained against the ties. "Don't give a shit what *it* likes. Keep it away."

Dollie moved up behind Coyan and breathed next his ear. "Do I scare you?"

143

Krystal was screeching like a banshee as she writhed on the 3V and the hairs on the back of my neck bristled.

"Get away from me, bitch."

"You know how much I like knives, Joe." Dollie winked at me. "This one could use a bit of sharpening, but it should be okay as long as I saw."

Dollie sang along with Krystal. "Rebop, rebop, Zazuhzana."

The sweat was dripping into Coyan's eyes now, making him squint. Dollie sounded far too convincing.

"Where are you going to start?" I said.

"Well, he's a real man. So I think I'll maybe rebop *his* meat then work outwards."

Coyan swallowed heavily. "You guys ain't scaring me. You ain't got the balls..."

He trailed off as Dollie rasped the knife over the back of his neck. "Mmmm... We *could* force-feed him his own testicles."

"He might enjoy that," I said. "Then again, big guy like this might choke."

Tana suddenly stood up. "I can't watch this. Call me when you're done." She disappeared into the bedroom.

"Weak stomach," Dollie said. She dragged the knife across Coyan's neck again, the tiny serrations leaving long scratches. "What about you?"

"Look, I don't know anything," Coyan yelped as the knife bit deeper into his skin. "Will you turn that goddamn music off?"

"You're not a fan?" The pounding beat was starting to get to me, so I could imagine how Coyan was feeling. "Why was Ganz killed?"

"You can keep someone alive for weeks after their skin's removed, you know," Dollie cooed. "I'll need some food wrap to stop him bleeding out."

"There's probably some in the kitchen." I stepped away. "Don't start without me."

"Rebop, rebop, Zazuhzana." Again Dollie sang along.

"Wait! Don't leave me alone with it... her..." Coyan twisted sharply in the chair, trying to break the ties.

I stopped, but didn't walk back to them. "Why was he killed?"

"I don't know. I swear. We were told to get his papers and stop people from finding out what was in them."

"He's full of it, Joe. I'm going to slice him up."

I took a step closer, raising my voice. "What was in the papers?"

Dollie reached around and pressed the blade between Coyan's legs. "Left or right first, Zazuhzana?"

The music was thumping louder as it got close to the end of the track, the tempo picking up until it was almost painful.

"I don't know anything!" Coyan almost screamed out the words. "They said to get his papers and clear up anyone connected with them. That's all I can tell you."

"Who are 'they'?"

"Dunno." He shook his head. "The boss lady deals with all that."

"Should I cut his eyes out, or let him watch?" Dollie pressed the knife against his cheek, just under his right eye.

"Jesus!" Coyan was sucking in one huge lungful of air after the other. "I can't tell you what I don't know."

"Maybe that's enough," I said, turning the music off. "Leave him, Dollie, we can take him to the cops."

"Sure, you do that." Coyan relaxed slightly. "But I ain't talking to no cops."

"You already did." I pulled out the NullScroll and switched off the record function.

I backed away from him, taking Dollie with me, then whispered to her, "That confession might not hold up in court, but should be enough to clear us and get the cops looking for the real killers."

Dollie frowned. "Sounds like a long shot."

"Best I've got."

I retreated to the guest room and dialed the number for Sterle.

"I figured it must be you." Sterle glanced at the screen. It looked like he was driving and had a mouthful of hamburger. "I don't get many anonymous calls, and I'm on lunch."

"I have a witness," I said pointedly.

"To what?"

"Stop playing games. One of the killers—name of Coyan—him and his buddy tried to kill me this morning." I deliberately didn't mention Dollie or Tana.

"You said *witness* singular. Where's the other guy?"

"Decomposing."

Sterle frowned. "That doesn't sound good, Joe. Could be some guys you picked up off the street."

"I've got a recorded confession."

The picture wobbled, and I realized he'd set his AeroMobile down. "Okay, I'm listening. What do you want to do?"

"I'll turn Coyan over as a witness. No tricks. You get him and get off my back."

Sterle looked skeptical. "What if I play along and grab you anyway? Then I'll have you both."

"I don't really care as long as you start looking for the real killers." I paused. "These people killed those cops. I think you're probably far more interested in them than me."

"Okay. Are you going to bring him into the main precinct?"

"Under the circumstances, I'd prefer somewhere neutral. Let's make it my apartment. Thirty minutes."

"You better play it straight this time, Joe. Or I'm going to be very unhappy."

"That's the idea." I was already reaching for the door. "One thing, Sterle. Keep your pet Rottweiler out of this. I'm in no mood to bang heads with him again."

Sterle nodded and signed off. I went back into the other room and looked at Dollie. "I'll need help getting him in the car."

Dropping down on my rooftop pad was a challenge. The pad wasn't large, and the Husher was a different configuration to my regular cab. I brought the car in steadily and lined it up, concentrating on the landing system display more intently than normal. When we finally dropped the last couple of centimeters, I unlocked the stabilizers and waited until the creaking stopped and I was sure the car wasn't going to tip.

I half dragged Coyan out, and we moved down through the secured gates with him shuffling and swearing. I'd watched the traffic carefully on the way in, looking for cops, but so far it seemed like Sterle was doing the right thing. We had ten minutes until the designated time, and I pushed Coyan down on a stool in the middle of my living room while I stood by the door announcer, gun in hand.

"You're dead. No matter what happens." He gestured vaguely. "One way or another."

He'd said the same thing several times on the way over. I wasn't worried. He was heading to jail for a long time—if the cops let him get that far. "Your mama should have taught you not to make promises you can't keep."

The door signal triggered, and I opened the ID display. Sterle was in front of the pickup and seemed to be on his own.

A few minutes later the elevator rattled to a stop, and I released the locks. Sterle followed me into the apartment and gave my prisoner the once over, moving Coyan's face from side to side as he looked at the bandage-wrapped damage. "The other one?"

"In the trunk of my car." There was no pointing trying to hide it.

Sterle's eyebrows lifted, but he turned back to my prisoner. "Eddy Coyan?" he asked, holding up his badge. "I checked. There are a lot of people who'd like to get hold of you. You should have stayed in the army."

Coyan pulled his head back. "Screw you, old man."

Sterle shrugged. "But the military want you too, don't they? Unfortunately for you, I'm the one who's got you. The families of those officers you killed will—"

I heard the elevator rattle again. It would have returned to the ground level automatically, but I hadn't locked the upper gate. A second later I heard an all too familiar voice.

"What's this? StimBoy and friends." Francis held a heavy looking pistol in one hand and a door security override key in the other. He was grinning like he'd caught the biggest fish of his life. "I figured if I watched this place long enough you'd show up."

"Better check if he's armed, Dan." Sterle drew his own pistol, pointing it at me.

"Sure. But what the hell's going on here, Jimmy? I thought we were partners."

"Ballen arranged a meet. Said he didn't want you around, so I played along."

Francis shuffled his bulk forward, his gun still pointed at me. "That ain't what partners are about."

"You're right, Dan. Sorry."

Sterle turned slightly and before anyone could react he pulled the trigger. Francis jerked. The bullet had hit him square in the chest. He looked as surprised as I felt, but didn't go down. "Jimmy? Christ... What'll I tell Millie?"

Sterle fired again, hitting Francis in the throat and shutting him up forever. "Millie'll get a nice pension. Don't worry."

It all happened so fast I had no chance to move. I stood there stupidly, unable to put words together.

Sterle twisted towards me and lifted his gun. "You know how it is, Joe. Gets to a time when a man has to look after himself. I always wanted to retire to Luna Free State, but that wasn't about to happen on a police pension. They say the low gravity can add up to forty years to your life."

I finally found my voice. "So you betrayed your own partner?"

Sterle shook his head. "I didn't tell him to come. Poor Dan, he wasn't much of a cop. Even at the end." He aimed his gun directly at my head. "Are you armed, Joe? My friends will be here in a minute. I don't want any surprises for them."

The elevator started up again. "I'm unarmed."

Sterle looked doubtful. "Still, maybe I should check that."

The elevator creaked as it slid open and out of the corner of my eye, I saw Gabriella approaching. She lifted her hand, raising a large caliber pistol. "Thank you, Detective Sterle."

She pointed the gun at Sterle and fired. He reeled, and his gun exploded, the shot blowing a chunk out of the roof. I dived forward and tackled him through the doorway into a pile with Gabriella and two of her men. Sterle grunted in pain. There was a bloody hole in his shoulder. I clubbed my hands together and smashed them into his face, hoping to keep him down for a while, then grabbed his gun.

Coyan lurched out of the living room, breathing heavily. He'd managed to work the ties off his legs and was clutching Francis' service pistol in his still tied hands.

"You're fucken dead, Ballen. I swear."

I scrambled to my feet, keeping Sterle and the tangle of bodies between us. "I'm very nervous right now, so I suggest nobody move."

I edged toward the stairs to the roof, dragging Sterle with me. His breathing was short and fast, but he seemed in shock and didn't try to fight.

When I reached the upper door, I kicked it open and was through in a second. Sterle snagged against the door frame, and Coyan's gun flashed once. Sterle went momentarily rigid, then became a dead weight in my arms. I pushed him down the steps into the scrambling pile of people below and locked the door behind me, hoping it would hold them for at least a few minutes.

I sprinted to the Husher and started the warm-sequence on the turbines. I was only part way through when the rooftop door exploded in a barrage of heavy gunfire.

Another explosion and a second later the door flew open. I pulled back on the stick, and the Husher hopped. The turbines weren't at full speed and the car tipped wildly. I tried to correct as the nose dropped below the parapet ledge of the apartment block, pointing at the pavement forty meters below. A police AeroMobile was parked outside the building entrance along with the Arroyo I'd seen before. Even if I took off, my troubles wouldn't be over.

I felt something hit the Husher and it bucked like a bee-stung horse, the nose dropping even further. I pushed harder on the throttles to try and control it, but felt the car sliding away from me. It was going down.

I let out a scream of pure adrenaline and cut the turbines completely. The Husher careened over the edge of the building, plummeting with all the aerodynamic grace of a brick as I jerked on the controls. I was trying to aim the Husher at the cop car, hoping it might absorb some of the impact.

The nose of the Husher crumpled as we hit the cop car. The whole front end of the car jammed backwards almost in slow motion. The windshield buckled and twisted until it popped, sending a storm of glass pellets into the car, and for a second I wondered if I was going to lose more body parts. Everything went white as the inflatable restraints ballooned, cocooning me as the Husher squashed the cop car like a plastic composite and aluminum bug.

When everything stopped moving, I tried to open the door. It was stuck. The frame buckled crazily, and I kicked at it several times with both legs. I mustn't have been as feeble as I thought and after the third or fourth try it sprang open, sending me sprawling unceremoniously onto the sidewalk.

Pulling myself up I hobbled towards the Arroyo, jumped in the driver's seat and started the turbines. They responded faster than the sedate units on the Husher and were at fifty percent when I saw the first of Gabriella's men emerge from the front door.

"Ballen, you are seriously crazy," I said to myself.

A series of explosions rattled the car, and I thumped on the dashboard, willing the engines to turn faster. The thrust gauge edged towards the green flight zone. Almost there.

Another burst of gunshots shuddered into the Arroyo and I pulled back on the stick. Coyan ran towards the car and jumped on the front, only to slide off as I punched the car into the air.

Nineteen

I parked the Arroyo outside Dollie's place. There was no reason to think the vehicle would be on any hunting list. Presumably Gabriella's mob would take steps to ensure their own anonymity, so I didn't think it was too much of a chance.

Dollie and Tana looked up as I half fell through the door into the living room.

"What happened?" said Tana.

Dollie jumped out of her seat. "Jesus, Joe, you look like you tried to screw a roll of razor wire."

The cuts on my face and arms from the glass shards were stinging, and my ribcage felt like someone had pounded me with an industrial press. I collapsed all-too-willingly into a chair. "Drink."

Dollie knew I didn't mean water and returned with a large tumbler half full of Bourbon. I gulped at it.

"Coyan?" Dollie asked.

I shook my head and took another gulp. "That bastard Sterle sold me out."

"The policeman?" Tana asked wide-eyed.

"Yeah, the wonderful police officers you wanted to trust."

I swallowed the rest of the drink, my head swimming from a mixture of alcohol, adrenaline, and exhaustion. "I need rest. Wake me in an hour."

I dragged myself into Dollie's bedroom and collapsed on the overstuffed king bed. I felt like a fly that had been swatted, and swallowed a couple of painkillers. They mixed with the alcohol in no time and sent me into a deep, but restless sleep.

I woke to screaming. At first, I thought it was part of a nightmare, but realized it was coming from the living room. When I walked in Tana and Dollie were shouting at each other, but I couldn't tell what they were arguing about. Finally, Dollie stopped trying to make her point and vanished into her bedroom. Tana quietened and after several minutes turned away. I waited for her to speak. Eventually she looked back at me.

"Ballen. Is she...?" Tana paused, her face screwing up as if she'd bitten into something distasteful. "Is she really one of those *things*?"

There was something incredibly ugly in her tone that turned her words into the worst form of poison. People always manage to surprise me somehow. The world was crumbling around us, still struggling to find its feet after the Big Shake. The Muslim-Catholic Alliance had split the once mighty USA, leaving behind the United States and Provinces—what was left of Canada and the moderate US states, while the Atolls blocked most of Earth from getting into space. Yet despite this, there were still people with the time and energy to get in a hootie over someone because they were different.

"Dollie took us in when we needed help. That makes her a good person in my book. Do you decide who's worthwhile based on whether they conform to your ideas of gender?"

"That's not fair. I don't make that kind of judgment." She turned away. "It's just..."

"The news said you were having an affair with Ganz. Is that true?"

Tana snapped her head back to face me, her scowl turning her face into a dark mask. "That's none of your business." Her hands clenched then opened. "What about you and *it*? You slept with it last night, didn't you?"

"That's not *your* business. And stop calling Dollie *it*."

Tana pointed at me. "You don't like having your personal life as a topic for open discussion then? Well, neither do I."

"My relationship with Dollie isn't a potential motive for murder."

The silence became stifling around us until I thought my head would explode if no one spoke. When I eventually looked back at Tana, her eyes were lowered, and she was shaking. Perhaps she was hurt by my words, or perhaps she'd only now realized she was in as much danger as I was.

"You've lied to me about everything. You didn't need any research papers from Ganz' apartment. And you hid your relationship with him." I wanted to shake her, break her out of her silence, but that would have been stupid. "Are you trying to find the papers too? Like Gabriella? Is that what this is about?"

Tana walked across the room, her back stiff as she looked through the window at the flitting rush hour traffic. "You don't really understand scientists do you?"

I've usually found people share the same motivations, needs, and ambitions, but had to admit that scientists were a confusing bunch. The ones attracted to space science on the High-Rig? They were crazy by definition—who'd want to study something they could never get closer to than the Atolls allowed?

"Let me guess. You're better than the rest of us."

"Some might think that." Tana snorted. "But that's not what I meant. What's the most important thing to a scientist? What keeps them up at night? What drives them to jealousy and fear and hate?"

"That they don't get invited to the really fun parties?"

"Stop it, Joe." Tana turned away from the wall and sank into an armchair, her eyes still not connecting with mine. "You're not really that snippy."

"Okay. The most important thing? Probably that they get to work at the right facilities. Everyone knows the Pan-Asians have the best and ours don't measure up. Hell, even United Africa competes favorably with us now."

"Location doesn't really matter. It's scientific priority. Establishing it clearly is so hard. Ideas often seem to float around the community almost at random." Tana grimaced. "Then suddenly several people will have very similar insights at the same time. And some people censor themselves, thinking it has no value. Later someone else comes up with the same concept, and they lose out."

She was struggling to hold her temper in check and lectured me almost like a child. "Tana, I don't see—"

"This is *everything*, Ballen. That's the point. There's massive competition throughout the sciences, especially with the domination of the Eastern communities. Priority has to be determined. Losing a single insight or scribbled note could mean the loss of thousands in research credits, not to mention a place in the history books. That's what science is about, what scientists are about."

Her nostrils flared, and she breathed in deeply. "So to safeguard that—and to promote collaboration—the community built GARNET. It acts as a global repository of research and knowledge, so nothing is ever lost. It also provides us with security. Once something is entered there, it ensures Priority."

What Tana said made a kind of crazy sense—if you accepted the "monomaniac recognition seeker" idea she ascribed to academics. I knew that research facilities in the USP were always calling for more cash and resources and condemning the amount of work sent overseas. Exporting *brain work* might not be as deranged as exporting your industry, but it no doubt had the same effects.

I rubbed my shoulder near the scar tissue and felt a twinge of pain. "How is this relevant to Ganz and his work?"

"When someone dies, their workplace has to check their private GARNET area in case there's anything of possible scientific interest. Normally everything is flagged as 'provisional' and gets released into the public archives—storage costs almost nothing."

"And Ganz' files?"

"Not released yet. I wanted to check them first to make sure anything valuable would get accredited to him properly."

I had to think about this. Possible? Sure. Plausible? Maybe. It certainly explained her interest in his notes but not the need for secrecy.

"They could be waiting until this is cleared up." I made a circle in the air with my finger. "Most organizations wouldn't be too happy about this kind of attention. I don't imagine the University is any different."

"It could be that..."

"But you don't think so?" Why couldn't it be simple? Just once.

"I think Hubert was killed because of his work and the others because they were associated with him. We're being hunted because someone thinks we know something about his research. So regardless of who's behind this, it must be important."

Logically it made sense, but still didn't prove the moon was made of green cheese. "But who?"

"Professor Idell. He's the head of the ATC. I know that he and Hubert argued several times." Tana's cheeks reddened. "When you Stim, sometimes things leak through that aren't supposed to. It only happens occasionally and only when a person has strong feelings about a subject."

"Do you know what they argued about?"

"No. But there was fear inside Hubert. Anger and fear."

Dollie glided into the room and I started.

"Easy, Soldier. Only me."

"Anything new?"

"Nothing except you now owe me a taxi *and* a Husher. The expenses are piling up."

"Thanks, Dollie, I..." I looked pointedly over at Tana. "We, owe you a lot."

"I know." Dollie's lips curved into a mischievous smile. "I have a good memory for such things."

Tana deliberately avoided making eye contact with Dollie. "Could we order some food?"

My stomach was grumbling too, but stopping for lunch didn't seem like a smart move at that point. We needed a plan. "Let's go back to Professor Idell."

"Who?" Dollie asked.

I quickly explained about Idell and Ganz, skimming lightly over the subject of scientific priority—which I wasn't convinced of myself.

"So, the question is... how do we get to speak to him? I don't imagine he'd agree to meet a couple of supposedly dead murder suspects."

"Actually, you're the only one who's dead, Soldier." Dollie looked directly at Tana. "The reports haven't mentioned her."

"I don't think that helps in any way. He doesn't know me." Tana folded her arms across her chest. "And I don't want to meet him."

"He may be the only way to find out what happened to Ganz."

My words sounded hollow, but we needed Tana's help. "Don't you owe him that much?"

Tana pulled her wiry hair. "Even if I do,I can't say I want to talk to him because I think he was involved in Hubert's death."

"From what you've said, all you need to do is call him and say you have some of Ganz' private files that you want to ensure get the right priority. Once he hears that he'll be more than happy to talk to you."

"I can't, Joe." Tana's eyes glistened. "I can't do it."

"Of course she can't, Ballen. How could you think that?"

Dollie smiled sympathetically at Tana, who looked surprised but grateful for the unexpected support.

"I don't mean Tana should go alone. I'd be with her."

"Neither of you can go wandering around in public. You'd be identified by the Eye in seconds."

The Eye can be programmed to distinguish people by combined biometrics, anthropometrics, and gait analysis. Sure, it takes longer than identification based on facial recognition, but even in disguise, we'd probably be picked up within ninety minutes.

"We could change some things to make it harder." Dollie pointed her thumb over her shoulder. "The Treatment Unit has a fully functional cosmetic processing module."

I should have guessed that, but appearance was only part of the problem. "Would that be enough to fool the biometrics?"

"Those systems are pathetic." Tana reddened and looked flustered. "Sorry, this is something I know about professionally. The biometrics look for patterns in movement and key limb length proportions, but the mathematical models are easily fooled. 'Stones in your shoes' will throw off your walk enough to defy any kind of analysis."

"It's still risky."

"Would you rather wait till they find us here?" Dollie said.

I looked at Tana. Her features were set like frozen obsidian, but she didn't object.

While Dollie set up the Treatment Unit, I scanned the news feeds again, looking for further information on the story of my supposed demise. News stories have a half-life shorter than

Mendelevium-257 though, and the coverage was already slowing. Reporters were more interested in "regular folks'" response to the Atoll announcements than a dead cab driver lost below the muddy surface of the Patapsco. Even the deaths of Sterle and Francis hadn't made the news yet.

Dollie appeared in the doorway and nodded. I took a deep breath. "Okay, let's get this done."

The unit was in standby mode. I peeled off my clothes and edged onto the cold plastic surface of the treatment bed, uncomfortable at the thought of being surgically changed. My face isn't the most handsome, but I'd kind of gotten used to it over the years.

Dollie moved to the controls, and I tensed up, knowing it was going to hurt. "Someone is behind all this, and we still have no idea who or why." The hairs on my body stood on end as the treatment beams hit me. "We need more information."

"But how?" Tana had turned away when I'd stripped and was hunched up in a chair next to the unit. "We don't have the resources."

"Maybe we do. I'll need to make a call." I said, after a couple of minutes of thought. Then I gasped as the beams started to slice. "Once I'm through being butchered."

"Joe?" Logan's frown seemed to fill not only the small Scroll's screen, but the entire one-hundred kilometer void between us. "Is that really you?" His doubt was understandable as I'd called him with the NullScroll and no longer looked much like I did when we last talked.

"It's me. I have the scars to prove it." My body was still sore from the surgery. "Want me to demonstrate?"

"Not in front of the ladies." His smile broadened. "Are those the dancing girls? They look a lot better than last time."

"I'll get Tana started," Dollie said, walking back into the treatment room.

Tana looked scared but followed Dollie when I nodded.

"Logan, I need a favor. From some of those... errr... friends of yours."

The screen image twisted and for a second the optical pickup didn't seem to know which was Logan's back and which was his front, but after a few seconds it stabilized.

"That will make sure we aren't listened to." Logan moved closer to the pickup. "At least for a little while. What is it you want?"

"Intelligence."

"That's something you've needed for a long time, Joe. Tell me everything..."

Twenty

Have you ever been distorted? It's definitely near the top of my "weird'" list. Dollie had remodeled us, using a combination of local anesthetic, temporary internal pads, and sutures along with chemical color adjustment. Looking in the mirror was disturbing. The face looking back might have passed for a relative, but it definitely wasn't me.

Dollie had also done better than the "rocks in the shoes" idea and applied various tightening and temporary pinning procedures to my feet, legs, and arms. Nothing drastic, but enough to make me move differently and in ways that felt slightly unnatural.

Tana looked at me unhappily. Where my alterations had been relatively subtle, Dollie had transformed Tana completely. Her usual scraped back hair had been recolored and fluffed into a wild black mane. Her eyes were now gray-blue, and her skin color had been lightened by at least two full tones, so that she looked like she had a deep tan. Along with that, Dollie had dressed her to emphasize her breasts and hips and minimize her waist. While none of it really looked like Tana, it was the kind of thing common to fashionable women I'd ferried in my cab.

"I look like a prostitute," Tana said through clenched teeth.

"Of course you don't." I tried not to smile, partly because it was uncomfortable, but also because I didn't want to provoke a reaction from her. "You look good. Different."

"What do you know? You're a man." Tana pulled at the hem of her short dress as if the pink gauze material was infectious. "You probably think I look better like this."

The truth was that she did look better, although in a somewhat superficial manner. It was as if someone had taken the Tana I was acquainted with and forced her through one of those bizarre make-over 3V shows. The only problem was that regardless of the outward appearance, the real Tana was still underneath. Just as smart, just as naive, and possibly even angrier than before. Again I wondered how someone could pay for ReSeeq and forget about appearance. I'm a personality first guy and wasn't even cute in my baby pictures, but no matter how much you to try to deny it—looks make a difference to the vast majority of the world. So, if you're Geneering your child, why not make the most of it?

I tried again. "Think of it as playing a part, like in a school play."

"I'm a lousy actor." She tugged at the bottom of her blouse as if she could pull it hard enough to cover her semi-bare midriff.

"Everyone ready?"

I turned. Dollie stood in the door looking stunning in an almost skin tight SkinSuit that seemed to be almost equal parts shiny black ParaHyde, tightly bound strapping, and flesh-revealing slits. At least, I assumed it was ParaHyde—I don't think she could afford a real leather outfit. She was brandishing a Shock-Wand. I didn't want to try and guess what she usually used *that* for.

I tried to let out a low whistle, but my face was still too frozen, and I drooled instead. "You look like you could kill someone by staring hard."

"You sure say all the right things, Soldier." She pursed her now black-lined lips and blew me a kiss.

Tana made a face. "Please. If you'd keep your biological urges in check, I'd really appreciate it."

"Maybe you should try it someday." Dollie's tongue brushed over her lips suggestively. "You might find you like it. Besides, you look pretty now."

Tana turned away, but couldn't hide the anger on her face. "Let's go."

The Arroyo was still in the parking lot, and we clambered in. Dollie took the controls and pulled us into the traffic stream in a tight spiral, barely staying within the legal limits of Managed Airspace. Entering the maximum City zone, she took her hands off the controls, leaving the car to pilot itself.

"I don't like this, Joe. It's not a good place to go."

Logan had directed us to a contact called Sigurd on the other side of town and said he'd arrange a meeting. So far the plan was limited to getting more information. The police had more resources but were unlikely to share, so we needed an alternative. Sigurd was apparently number one in illicit monitoring, at least outside of the government.

"I know it's not ideal, but I'm all out of options."

Dollie stayed silent, but she'd been unhappy since she first saw the contact details.

Roxbury, in northern Baltimore, hadn't been an attractive area since well before the Big Shake. Not since the city had been selected as the USP capital in fact. There were arguments that the capital should have been Toronto in Old Canada, since that was the largest population center left more or less intact. But Toronto was the USP financial center which made it too politically sensitive to have as both—especially to people who still basked in memories of the former U.S. glory days.

More recently, Roxbury's movement had been increasingly in the downward direction. Once splendid homes had crumbled, to be replaced by a muddle of cheap tenements and the ubiquitous festering *temporary* shelters, until it was a rat's maze of danger.

"We shouldn't go there." Dollie didn't let her drivers pick up or drop off in Roxbury anymore. Too many cabs didn't come back.

"I understand, but the person we're meeting is there." I shrugged. "They probably don't make house calls."

Dollie turned back to the controls, looking out through the windshield. "It scares me."

"You could have stayed behind."

I was upset by Dollie's attitude. Even if Roxbury were a bad place, we'd be there for a minimum amount of time. I'd offered to do the journey myself, but Dollie wouldn't allow it. And when I suggested to Tana that she stay behind, she'd had an almost childish fit. So here we all were.

"How can this person help us?" Tana sounded petulant. In fact, she'd been decidedly antagonistic since the argument at Dollie's.

It felt like we were cramped inside an econobus, even though the inside of the Arroyo was almost as spacious as the Husher and upholstered only slightly less comfortably.

"We need information. Professor Idell might be involved, but we've got no evidence. Certainly nothing we could go to the police with now. Both the police and Gabriella have access to live Argus data. If we can turn that around—watch *them*, then maybe we can find out what's going on and have a chance to fight back."

"I really don't like this." Dollie twitched the Shock-Wand in her palm. "You can't trust Sigurd."

"Do you know something about him?" I wouldn't have been too surprised. Dollie knew a wide variety of people.

She shook her head curtly. "I've heard things... rumors. I—"

Dollie isn't usually the sort to keep quiet, and I wanted to find out what she knew and what she wasn't telling, but she said no more.

Tana fidgeted in the back seat. "This won't work. Argus isn't some children's toy."

"What do you mean?" I asked, somewhat annoyed at the interruption and Tana's apparent insensitivity to Dollie's feelings. We were risking a lot, and part of that was based on her assessment. "I thought you said it was easy to fool it?"

"Argus isn't only a collection of cameras, it's a sophisticated monitoring system. It can retrieve data from almost any 3V, video, audio, motion or other type of environmental detection sensor. Half of the pickups it uses aren't even owned by the authorities, they're private monitoring points it makes use of.

"It knows where all these sensors are and combines that information with biographical ID processing so it can match one source dataset to another in quasi-real-time. The system is highly protected—it has to be—if it wasn't, privacy would essentially end. Fooling it is one thing, but hacking it is a different thing."

"You seem to know a lot all of a sudden," Dollie said suspiciously.

"Paresh." Tana glanced at me then looked away. "Someone I know from the University. One of his interests is security and quantum encryption. He analyzed Argus as part of his studies, looking for flaws. He said it was virtually impenetrable."

"We better hope he's wrong." I hoped I sounded confident, but think I missed it by a few hundred kilometers.

Dollie set us down in a clear area that wasn't overlooked by any large buildings and I clambered out, my skin tight and my movements awkward with the fresh cosmetic alterations. Tana followed me. I didn't really want her with me, but she refused to stay in the Arroyo.

"Circle until we come out again," I shouted over the whine of the turbines. "We might need to get out of here quickly."

"I'm on it." Dollie scanned the buildings around us uneasily. "Make sure you come back."

I was going to reassure her, but the Arroyo roared into the sky before I had the chance. Suddenly the weight of the StubGun tucked inside my belt gave me no comfort at all.

Twenty-One

We worked our way through the jumble of buildings down gray alleys with stained concrete walls and garbage-encrusted pavement. It was getting late, though not late enough to justify the emptiness we encountered and I had the feeling we were being watched by countless eyes from the dark shadows thrown by the scant lighting.

Turning left at the remnants of a crumbling church, we entered a narrow alley barely wide enough for the both of us. Someone had piled stacks of garbage on either side, forcing us to walk single file most of the way.

"I don't like this," Tana whispered. She was shivering, and I didn't think it was from the cold wind.

I could hear scratching from the piles of garbage. I hoped it was only rats. "I don't either, but we don't have any choice."

My nose wrinkled at the smells in the smoky air. Mixed in with the acrid stench of urine, vomit and some kind of burning oil was something that reminded me of cheap hot-dogs, but I doubted it was anything so palatable. The floor beneath us squished as we moved and I really didn't want to look too closely to see what we were stepping in.

Above us, the gaps between buildings were connected haphazardly by makeshift raised walkways, as if the residents were trying to create their own version of the more luxurious elevated corridors downtown. Though here the packing case and plastic structures looked barely able to hold the weight of even a single person.

The rusting steel door at the end of the alley was thick enough to act as an airlock. The pitted surface made it looked disused, but there were signs of fresh oil on the heavy hinges. I lifted my hand to bang on the door, but as I did, it opened a few centimeters. A voice sounded from inside.

"Ballen?"

"Yes. Logan sent me."

"Prove it." The voice sounded unnatural and metallic. "What tribe is he?"

Thankfully I'd heard that from him at least a thousand times, how his tribe had originally lived North of Vancouver, but after the second coming of the great Thunderbird they'd been forced to move east like so many.

"Logan is Coast Salish."

"Which coast?"

"West, of course."

"Wrong! There is no West Coast anymore." There was a harsh metallic laugh. "But you're right. You can come in."

I stepped up to the door, and Tana closed in behind me.

"*You* can come in. Logan's invite is only good for one person."

I looked back at Tana and saw the fear in her eyes. "I can't leave her out here. Who knows what might happen?"

"It's your dime, bub. I don't care either way." The door started to close.

"It's dangerous. You know that," I said.

"Life always is. She ain't coming in. She'll be safe if she stays by the door. No one will touch her on my ground."

Tana drew herself up. "Go on. I'll be okay."

I pulled out the StubGun and handed it to her. "Just in case."

"I'm making you personally responsible," I said to the guy behind the door.

"Everyone is. But some people are too dumb to realize it."

I turned back and nodded at Tana, then the door closed and I was in complete darkness. It was like a sensory deprivation chamber. My eyes strained to see even the slightest detail, and my brain created fictitious monsters from innocent moiré patterns. When the lights came on they burnt my eyes with their intensity. After a few seconds, my vision adapted so I could see my contact. Not that there was much to see. He wore a pure white outfit tight enough to be a second skin, and his face was entirely obscured by the mirror shine of a full-face immersion alt-reality mask. It made him look more like an old-fashioned idea of a future spaceman than anything human.

"Are you Sigurd?"

"Want me to sing some opera to prove it?"

I shook my head, and he laughed raucously. On second glance I could have the wrong gender completely. There didn't seem to be any telltale "bulge" in the appropriate place for a man. That said, there were no signs of swelling in the chest area to make it clear it was a woman either. I decided I'd treat him as "male" until proved otherwise.

Alt-reals don't have too much to do with the rest of us. They like to stay in their own world, tailored to whatever peculiarities they have and often their ideas of the real world are significantly disconnected from the one the rest of us inhabit. When you can choose your own idealized perfect environment, why would you want to include the crappy mess the rest of us are forced to live in?

We walked along a corridor as white as his outfit, into a room that smelled clean almost to the point of being antiseptic. I guessed Sigurd was allowing my physical presence to intrude into his Alt-world as minimally as possible. To him, I'd be a ghostly overlay to be digitally processed and incorporated with as little disruption as possible. For all I knew he might see me as a medieval beggar soliciting alms for the poor. Or maybe a unicorn looking for a navel piercing.

"Our tribal friend outlined what you're looking for. He has a lot of confidence in me, but what you want is impossible."

My temper spiked, thinking about Tana stuck outside facing who knew what. We'd risked our lives for this. "Logan said—"

"Logan doesn't define my capabilities. In this instance, it's impossible even for someone with my resources and knowledge."

I started to turn. "So you're a fraud. Thanks for nothing."

"Don't get me angry. I can remove you without any problem, be assured of that."

In the corners of the room and corridor, I'd spotted a series of sensors. Perhaps they were motion trackers supporting Sigurd's virtual environment, but they could also have been a sophisticated targeting system. I also noticed that his voice had changed. Earlier his speech had sounded coarse. Now there was a trace of refinement and education.

"Without the right kind of influence—of a political nature—access to Argus simply isn't possible. If I were foolish enough to work on the problem for three-hundred and sixty-five days, all I'd achieve would be the waste of a year."

I heard a faint tapping noise, like someone knocking on a piece of metal. I wondered if it was the air-conditioning or something more sophisticated. "So *you* can't do it. Is there anyone who can?"

"Ballen..." Sigurd sounded offended. "I'm sure Logan explained my standing in the community. There's no one higher. Not accessible to you at least. Tell me, did you kill those people?"

He made the question sound like *would you like some tea?*—a triviality for idle chatter.

"I didn't kill Ganz. Or anyone else."

Sigurd let out a disappointed sigh. "That's a shame. I could have worked that into my Alt-world. It's based on pirate warriors, the kind that roamed the seas several hundred years ago. Extremely interesting, wouldn't you agree? I'm a collector, Ballen. Anything related to the military or weapons—items, experiences, or technical material. Come, let me show you."

I wanted to tell him where to shove it, but there was still a slim hope he could provide us with something useful, so I kept my mouth shut. He guided me into a side chamber, our feet scuffing softly on the bare concrete floor. As we entered, the room lit up. It seemed entirely empty, not as though it held a collection of anything.

"This is an early twenty-first power skeleton. The forerunner of the modern day military powered armor."

One of the wall panels slid aside with a quiet hiss, revealing the bulk of an exoskeleton. I didn't see how it could possibly be of practical use. It was too bulky and appeared to offer almost zero protection for the added clumsiness. It was a similar setup to the rigger suits we'd used in orbital work, but they were much more sophisticated. I'd seen historicals about the early designs and the number of design flaws that resulted in many of the testers suffering serious or even fatal accidents.

Sigurd made a grandiose gesture to the left. "This is Clyde. He represents one of the high points of nano-technology. A replica of a wasp, fully capable of independent flight and targeting, and armed with a toxic stinger."

Another panel slid open, showing a magnified view of a mechanical insect surrounded by several design documents. I moved a little closer. That was something even I hadn't seen before.

"Ingenious don't you think? It's a pity they didn't realize that nature had done it all before. So much easier to Geneer what we want in an actual creature than build from scratch.

"Talking of which, this is Jane, one of the first truly successful Geneered products. Isn't she beautiful?"

Another panel opened to reveal a naked partial woman's body. The majority of the torso was there, but the legs and arms terminated before the knee and elbow joints. I also couldn't help noticing there was a perfect set of genitalia. It had a head too, but instead of eyes, there were two featureless hollows that couldn't possibly have left space for actual eyeballs. A large nose and exaggerated large-lipped mouth completed the face. It repulsed me just looking at it, and I felt a shiver in the small of my back.

As I watched, the head moved and the lips pursed into a grotesque imitation of a kiss, and I realized what Jane was almost before Sigurd could make his breathless announcement.

"Jane was designed as a military comforter. Useful when the local *talent* was either unavailable or considered too risky for political or security reasons. She spawned a whole industry that catered for those rich enough to afford her and her sisters." Sigurd snorted. "They must have been pretty loathsome if their money couldn't buy them a regular date."

"She does have some advantages over a real woman though—no talking back, never says no, no alimony payments. Some would say," Sigurd laughed harshly again, "The perfect woman."

The lips moved again, and my stomach knotted. For the first time I was glad that he'd left Tana outside.

"Is it alive?"

"Technically. Though the design mostly called for extended functionality with little degradation and a high degree of resistance to disease. Which is why this one looks so good. I keep her in cold storage to extend the lifespan as much as possible. The higher brain functions were disposed of, naturally. The only intact neural responses are those associated with sexual stimulation. Beyond that, it's really just a hunk of meat. Sadly for the soldier boys, they were too expensive. Would you like to touch her? She responds to all the usual stimulation, her nipples are especially sensitive."

"Could we get back to the point?" I turned away, fighting the response to gag. "If you can't help me, I'll leave."

Sigurd sighed. "You Lifers. Always in a hurry to get to the wrong place. I didn't say I couldn't help you, just that I couldn't get you access to Argus. You need to think a little wider."

"Sorry, Sigurd, I'm an engineer— they don't teach us original thinking."

"Ha! A sense of humor." Again the metallic laugh. "If you can't get into Argus, you need to create your own."

The panel closed over Jane and the light in the collection room mercifully switched off as we left. He was starting to annoy me with his affected mannerisms and obscure hints. His "collection" made my skin crawl, and I was rapidly getting to the point where I'd leave regardless of anything he said. Create my own Argus? Ridiculous. Not only were the resources needed practically infinite from a solitary person's perspective, but it would take years.

Sigurd seemed to sense my confusion and laughed raucously, his upper body rocking. "You need to monitor people, with both sight and sound. Over distance and without them knowing. Correct?"

That seemed to cover it, but I still didn't understand what he meant. He reached over to a shelf and pulled out a tiny box, flipping open the lid to reveal three cobweb-like circles.

"Nowadays, tracking a target through Argus is done through pattern recognition within the system itself. Perfect for the system operators because it puts control in their hands—control access to Argus and you control the ability to track people. Early iterations of the system were designed more as simple monitoring systems though—they weren't powerful enough to manage that kind of tracking. So they had to tag people specifically. Pickups were equipped with sensors that could read a tag's unique pattern and send back the appropriate feeds. But there are two main drawbacks. Make that three. Or maybe four."

I waited for him to stop counting.

"This isn't perfect, but it's better than what you have." He pointed to the box. "First, plant the target tracker on the person you want to surveil. That's such a delicious word, don't you think? Second, you need to access the data feed tied to the active tracker. I can give you a feed pickup box. The problem is that not all the sensors can key on the trackers, so the results might be patchy. Another drawback is that the tracking information is visible to anyone with access to Argus—a security scan will detect the surveillance—so you probably won't be able to monitor for long."

That seemed like more than four, but it didn't really matter—I was already convinced the idea was doomed. "Anything else?"

Sigurd hesitated. "Yes. A security scan will detect the location of the pickup box."

The list sounded more like fatal design flaws than drawbacks, but I wasn't in a position to argue. "How much?"

"The going price is a hundred and seventy-five thousand credits. A bargain considering the development costs were over one million and the fact that it's essentially a unique system."

I whistled softly. "That's a good deal for sure. But I don't have that kind of money."

Sigurd stepped back. "What do you have?"

"Ten thousand." Even that was Dollie's money. My account was useless.

Sigurd laughed derisively, the sound grating through the facemask. I turned to leave, but he caught my arm and pulled me back. "That's the price to anyone else. For a friend of Logan, the cost is..." He gave a wistful sigh. "Nothing."

"Huh?"

"There's no charge. And you don't know how much that pains me."

"So why?"

"That's between me and Logan. But tell him this is the final payment." His gleaming silver mask pushed closer to my face, a bloated reflection of my own face staring back at me. "Make sure you tell him that, Ballen."

"I will." I took the box and the remote viewer and turned to leave. As I did, a caterwaul of alarms filled the room, and I jumped like someone had jacked a high frequency cable into my p-suit.

Sigurd reached over and silenced the alarm. "Don't worry, it's your friend outside. She received a call, and it set off some of my sensors."

"Tana got a call?" I felt a weight in the pit of my stomach.

"It's not unusual these days you know. Universal communication has been with us for at least a century and a half."

Sigurd led me back to the entrance. The door opened, and the lingering stench assailed my nostrils. I stepped through the heavy doorway and Tana spun away from me, but not before I spotted the Scroll in her hand. When she turned back her hands were empty, her face as dark as the inside of a black hole.

"I'll take the gun and the Scroll." I held out my hand.

"I'm not sure what you mean."

"Don't insult me." I was so angry my hand was trembling.

Tana pulled back. "It's not what you think, Ballen."

"You said you lost it. You know they can trace us through a Scroll." I strode forward, my hand still outstretched. She handed me the gun, but nothing else.

"It's not registered to me. It's a ghost given to me by Hubert." She turned away. "So we could keep in touch privately."

"And you didn't think to mention it when Dollie asked?"

Tana shook her head. "It's none of *its* business, or yours for that matter."

Regardless of the current circumstances, there was something else about Tana's behavior that I couldn't quite place. Her fingers clenched and unclenched as if she were stressed, but I got the impression it wasn't from being caught with the Scroll.

"Who was the call from?" I asked.

"It... it was nothing..."

It was darker now, the shadows deepening around us, and I didn't want to linger. "Damn it. It's not *nothing* when you put us all in danger."

"It was Paresh. If you really must know." Tana spat the words out.

"Paresh? Why would he call you on a Scroll given to you by Ganz?"

"Because, Ballen, I once stupidly gave him the number. Because once, I was stupid enough to try Stimming with him. Because once, I actually thought there might be more than one decent person in the world."

Tana slammed her fist into a wooden pallet leaning against the wall. "But Paresh saw it as foreplay to the real thing. Amusing. Titillating. Nothing but a warm up exercise. And since then he's been trying to sort out what he calls unfinished business."

"Sorry, Tana, I didn't mean to—"

"Are you happy now?' She glared at me. "Do you feel better knowing how stupid I can be?"

I shook my head. "I don't make those kinds of judgments. The only person who can make you a fool is yourself."

The look on Tana's face told me she didn't believe me. Maybe she'd been so hurt in her life that she couldn't believe anyone now, especially after losing Ganz. Nothing in the world ever seems straightforward. Not unless you're one of those people who cruises through life without a single moment of self-doubt. I sometimes wished I could be like that.

I tucked the gun into my belt. "We should go. I have the gear and Dollie will be waiting."

"I want to keep the Scroll, Joe." Tana looked down. "It's all I have left to remind me of him."

I'd have thought that was reason to get rid of it, but I knew feminine logic didn't work the way I thought it should. "Okay, but no more calls. Turn the damn thing off. At least until we're out of this mess."

Tana nodded. "Please don't tell Dollie. I'm not sure she'd understand."

I couldn't imagine Dollie being concerned either way. Though she'd probably think I was stupid for trusting Tana again. Maybe I was. When I looked at Tana, I saw the torso of *Jane*. Some things, and some people, seem to exist simply to be used—I didn't want

Tana to be one of them.

I sighed, and we hurried back along the route we'd come in. The walls around us looked almost monochrome as we made our way towards the landing area. The shadows could have concealed an army. As we approached the clearing the Arroyo dropped out of the sky, the landing lights switching on with a blaze that illuminated the area around us. The doors opened as the landing gear touched the ground and Tana scrabbled inside. As she did, three people rippled into view around us. I wouldn't have thought the average Roxbury resident would have access to refractive camouflage suits, but it looked like I was wrong again.

"If the car tries to take off, we'll kill you," the closest one said, his voice distorted by the digital amplifier in his face mask.

"All I want is the Geness. You and the girl can leave." Even with the distortion, I recognized Sigurd's voice.

Before the situation had time to develop, I whipped out the StubGun and pointed it directly at Sigurd's helmet. "If you didn't want to let me have the gear, why agree to meet?"

The men with Sigurd stepped forward, and I waved the pistol in a wide arc, pointing it at each one in turn. "The next one who moves gets to play catch with a bullet."

"That thing won't stop all of us," one of the figures to Sigurd's left growled.

"So take that step, tough guy."

I thought he was about to call my bluff when they suddenly crumpled to the ground, except Sigurd who tucked some kind of control unit back inside a pocket.

"They were a mistake." He looked down at the bodies. "I was desperate. I don't care about the equipment, Ballen. Let me have Dollie."

Something was seriously messed up here. What kind of connection was there between Dollie and an underworld black-ops supplier? Yet another missing jigsaw piece. I didn't lower the gun though.

"Stay away from me, Sigurd," Dollie shouted from the car.

"Please come back." Sigurd moved forward, stopping at a wave of my gun. "It'll be different, I promise."

"I really don't want to have to shoot you." I put the gun muzzle against his reflective visor.

Sigurd didn't say anything, but turned on his heels and vanished into the concrete backdrop. I waited several long seconds before jumping through the open car door and slamming it shut.

I could feel the sweat inside my shirt despite the cool air outside. "Hit it, Dollie. Before he changes his mind."

The Arroyo shot upwards, pinning me to the seat as we climbed.

"Are you okay, Joe?" Dollie asked.

"Nothing a pile of honesty wouldn't fix. What's between you and him?"

"Her." Dollie's voice was completely devoid of emotion.

"Her?"

Though Sigurd had never been visible to me, I'd thought I was dealing with a man. Now I was even more confused. And there was some kind of relationship between the two of them that I couldn't even begin to guess at. On the back of Tana's dishonesty over the Scroll, the fact that Dollie had also endangered us was too much to take. I slammed my fist against the door frame.

Dollie kept her eyes fixed straight ahead. "Where to?"

"The Interstellar," I snapped, holding up the equipment Sigurd had given me. "We better figure out how to use this stuff."

Twenty-Two

Here's a little tip from a one-time space engineer turned cab driver. If you're looking for anonymity and a place to hide it's hard to beat automation. For over seventy years Interstellar FH have provided clean and secure rooms for travelers, cheaters, people on-the-run, and businessmen with their secretaries.

The chain boasts of being one hundred percent automated, though I don't believe that's strictly true. There has to be some staff involved, but you'd never guess that from the service. Supplies are replenished automatically, the kitchen is thoroughly robotized, and all linen is delivered and changed by housekeeping units similar to the Medibo I have at home. All you need is a credit chip, and you can stay as long you want. Without seeing anyone, unless you choose to. Or your credit runs out.

They also have fully automated parking complete with direct access to your room. Making it perfect for us. The nearest Interstellar was in Lochearn on the old Parkway to the east, a short thirty-kilometer hop, but one that happily kept us out of the busier and more heavily monitored city sections closer to the downtown areas.

I used Dollie's chip to check into the hotel, booking a large suite for the three of us. It was a calculated risk, but undoubtedly safer than using my own credit. After settling the Arroyo onto the aeropad we made our way inside. Despite my mood, I couldn't resist trying out a floating chair, one of the trademark features of the spaceship interior design.

Checking into a room with two women would rate five stars

on many guys' fantasy list, but after recent experiences, I'd have much rather settled down on my own with a large bottle. I'd have been happy to float into whiskey-buoyed oblivion right then, but Tana's frown reminded me we needed to focus on why we were there.

Some people claim restrictions breed creativity, that when your options are limited the human mind rebels and finds ways around those limits. But if that were true, it was sure passing me by. I spread the tracking components on the floating coffee table between us, Dollie and Tana listening intently while I explained the shortcomings of the system.

"So, first we need to physically plant the tracker?" Dollie picked up the small box containing the gossamer-like webs. It was pretty much the first thing she'd said since the incident with Sigurd.

I opted for an all-business approach. My feelings would have to take a back seat for now. I opened my hands wide. "Yeah, I know. We can't exactly walk up to Idell and ask to shake his hand."

I hoped that either Tana or Dollie might have the spark of brilliance that was eluding me, but they seemed as lost as I was. I'm usually an ideas guy, and it made me feel even more desperate that all I could do at this time was grind my gears.

"I'm sure I could seduce Idell if it were necessary," Dollie volunteered, then pulled a face. "You'd have to make it incredibly more important to me than it is right now though—he looks pretty loathsome."

"I wouldn't have thought that bothered someone like *you*," Tana hissed.

Dollie's hand came up in a flash, aimed at Tana's face. I jumped forward to stop her—so much for keeping things business-like—but Tana was as quick and blocked the slap. Somehow I managed to interject myself between the blow and counter-blow and the simultaneous slaps rang around the sparsely decorated living room. My face burned on both sides, and I dropped back, tripping over the armchair and flopping down into it.

Both women were breathing heavily and looked ready to tackle a bull with bare hands. I rubbed my jaw and grimaced.

"If you want to fight go ahead. Give me a minute to check room service— see if they have a good supply of jello. Women's wrestling just ain't the same without it."

"Sorry, Joe." Tana half choked the words out and sat down as far away from Dollie as she could.

"Sorry, Soldier."

Dollie didn't sound any more convincing than Tana and I slid my chair back out of the potential line of fire. If they were going to come to blows again, they were going to have to deal with it alone.

"So, after that fun interlude... Does anyone have any other suggestions?" I asked. "Beyond attempted seduction, which nobody seems to be volunteering for."

"Maybe you should try it, Joe." Dollie winked at me. "I could dress you up real pretty."

I heard a metallic clunk. The hotel was well sound-proofed, so anything that loud must be close. I held up a hand to warn the others, and the white interior of the room fell silent other than the soft hiss from the ventilation system.

I moved to the door and cracked it open, barely wide enough to see through. There was nothing immediately visible, so I opened the door wider and tried to glimpse in the other direction.

The aeropads covered the hotel's beehive-like exterior like some kind of bizarre fungus. At the next pad over I saw the boxy outlines of a Luxus Caravanaire. It was more of a general-purpose run-about, not the kind of vehicle typically used by the police, but that didn't mean anything. I heard a distant shriek. A moment later a couple moved toward the car, pulled out some heavily stuffed luggage and started back to their room. Then I noticed white streamers tied to the back of the vehicle and closed the door again.

"Newlyweds," I said in answer to the questioning looks from Tana and Dollie. "They'll be having more fun than we will tonight."

"Doesn't have to be that way," Dollie husked.

"Please..." Tana cringed in her chair and brought up the newsfeeds on the large screen.

The space access talks had broken down yet again after the Atolls had refused to hear any of the petitions for increased Earth operations. It wasn't much of a surprise, but people were still infuriated by the ongoing refusal to consider the proposals. I wanted to throw something at the screen when I saw the jeering crowds. The Atolls won, we lost. That was the end of it.

The announcer continued, "In related news, this week's Aero-Space Expo will showcase the largest display of Earth space technology and developments, demonstrating clearly how much we have to contribute. Presentations in the main hall will be hosted by Professor Lawson Idell and will include a speech by Devan Rohloff, whose prototype starship is in the last stages of—"

Tana muted the sound, jumping up from her seat. "The Expo? Would that be a good enough opportunity?"

"He must have a talent for fake plaudits." I was still thinking about the ridiculous protesters.

Tana stared at me coldly. "At the end of each session, there's an opportunity to meet the presenters. Lots of handshaking and back patting."

I looked at Dollie, but she shrugged. I could see it might work, though it would be risky going to a crowded conference, undoubtedly saturated with security people. I didn't have any alternatives to suggest though. "Maybe. If there's time."

Tana's laugh was hollow. "Don't underestimate the size of the average professor's ego. They bask in the limelight as long as they can."

"Idell would take a cab there, wouldn't he?" Dollie leaned forward.

Tana frowned. "They usually use limousines to ferry the important guests around. These events are all about fanning their egos."

"A limo? That's even better. Leave it to me. I'll pick him up and plant the tracker as he leaves the car." Dollie grinned. "Maybe I should seduce him as well—to prove a point."

Dollie's suggestion seemed workable, though I was worried about her continued involvement. If anyone could plant the Tracker on Idell and get away with it, she was probably the best equipped. Most guys turn to goo when she switches on the charm, so I doubted some aging professor would be able to resist. Even knowing that though, my engineer's mind was still looking for the "belt and braces" approach.

"Okay. But we'll go as general visitors too." I waggled my finger between me and Tana. "In case something comes up."

Tana left to go to bed, and I waited a couple of minutes. "Dollie?"

"Don't." She started to walk away too. "It's none of your business."

"It's my business when you let me walk into a situation where my ass is on the line."

Dollie's smile flickered briefly. "I thought your ass was already *on the line* because of Tana."

Although that was true, she was using it as a diversion. "If you already knew Sigurd, why didn't you say so?"

"It was a long time ago." Dollie sighed. "We all have a right to a private life, Joe. Even if you don't like it."

She was right. She was my boss and also my friend. I cared what happened to her, but that didn't give me the right to demand answers. "Okay. I won't push it."

"Get some rest too, Joe." She squeezed my hand, then swept away to her room.

I slumped on the couch wondering what to make of it. On one side I had Tana making surreptitious calls on an untraceable phone. Then on the other, I had Dollie involved with a person who'd tried to kill us to get to her. It seemed everyone had secrets—playing a game with their own set of cards and I didn't know if we were playing Poker, Blackjack, or Tiddlywinks.

I must have drifted asleep. When I woke, the warm golden lighting had automatically dimmed to a deeply shadowed brown. I felt someone next to me on the couch and was momentarily disoriented. There was a head pressed into my lap and a slim arm wrapped around me.

"Hold me, Joe." Dollie's voice was a haunted whisper. "Please."

I wrapped my arms around her, cradling her close to me. She was trembling slightly even though the room wasn't cold, and I realized that she was crying almost too quietly to be heard.

"I used to get treatments through her that I needed. Things I couldn't afford legally."

"Shhh... You don't have to tell me."

"At first it was just a business deal. Then it became... more." Dollie sniffed. "I thought it was part of the *cost*, but she..."

I stroked Dollie's hair, soothing and calming her. I'd wanted to know more about her relationship with Sigurd, but hadn't bargained for this.

"...she became more involved than I realized. I tried to break it off, go back to our original arrangement. But she wouldn't accept that. When I went to collect my things she..." Dollie shuddered. "She threatened to sell me. She has contacts in the MusCat Alliance. Geneered are illegal there, but some of them will pay a lot for a special plaything."

I'll never understand why some people feel they can treat others like property. Everyone should be able to follow their own path, as long as they're not hurting others. Everyone has the right to make their own choices—good or bad. Forcing your ideals on someone else is the ultimate in egotistic selfishness.

I cradled Dollie in my arms, holding her until she relaxed into sleep.

You know that expression about the "calm before the storm?" This wasn't it. It was the calm between storms. We'd already had plenty of them over the last couple of days, and I'd have happily avoided anymore.

Dollie spent most of the morning on the phone arranging to pick up Idell the following day. The contract for the job would have been set up months in advance, so I could only guess what favors she was calling in to line up the job. Twice she came out of her bedroom and shook her head disparagingly.

"People in this town have short memories," she growled, refreshing her coffee before vanishing again.

I couldn't accept what Tana had told me about the Scroll and Paresh without question. She'd had an unsuccessful Stim relationship with him, so why would she speak to him again? On the other hand, after Tana had punched out his lights, why would he contact her again? I was playing along, but that didn't mean I'd checked in my brain at the entrance to the show.

Why couldn't things be simple for a change? All I wanted was a world that made sense, but outside engineering it seemed as complex as ever. Logan had told me many times that the world has its own existence—it isn't obliged to pay lip service to what we want it to be—and he was right.

Smells wafting from the kitchen area made my mouth water, and I realized it was a long time since breakfast. When I joined them, Tana and Dollie were already eating, while a stream of news feeds splashed over the large screen on the far wall.

"Tell me there's been a surprising police breakthrough, and they've caught the real killers." My joke was as flat as a carbon mono-film.

Dollie passed me a heavily loaded plate of bagels, cream cheese, and salmon and I dug in.

"You're now wanted for the death of Sergeant Dan Francis and Thomas Jeggson." Dollie paused to nibble on her bagel. "Also the attempted murder of Detective James Sterle."

"Who the hell is Jeggson?" I grunted around a mouthful of bagel.

"One of your neighbors. Caught in the crossfire apparently."

I pushed the plate away.

"One interesting thing," said Dollie. "Devan Rohloff *is* going to appear at the Expo. No one thought he would—you know how much of a hermit he is."

"He's not a recluse..."

There was an urban myth that Rohloff was a hermit of some sort, but it had about as much truth to it as the MusCat Philosophy of Harmonious Union. He was building a starship and the only place to do that was in Low Earth Orbit. So it wasn't surprising that he spent most of his time there. Communications from the High-Rig were expensive. The press didn't have the free access they enjoyed with EarthSide celebrities, so they made up "news." Rohloff was a common sight on the High-Rig and had always been more than willing to talk about his great project—sometimes to the point of exhaustion. "I'm glad I'm not picking up the bill for that transmission."

"He's on Earth," Tana mumbled.

Dollie swallowed the last piece of her bagel, threw her plate in the Recycler, and pulled on a peak cap.

"Time for me to go to work. Think I'll pass?" She gave a mock salute. She'd made use of the hotel ordering system to change her black outfit for a sharp gray chauffeur costume reminiscent of something from the pre-Shake days of automobiles. I say *reminiscent* because it was tailored to maximize the display of her quasi-natural assets in a way that would probably have got her arrested a hundred years ago.

"You look... good, Dollie," Tana said, but her eyes shifted over to me.

"Tana's right, you do. Good enough to drive a limo, or perform a seduction." I reached out and held her hand briefly. "Don't let anything happen to you."

"Easy, Soldier. You'll make my makeup run." She sniffed theatrically. "I'm doing my regular job. You two will be in more danger, especially if Argus picks you up."

In some ways she was right. Although we were the backup plan, in this case, our part was far riskier. Especially with the ever increasing pile of charges leveled against me.

Dollie headed out in the limo she'd arranged through her calls, leaving us with the Arroyo still parked on the aeropad. That left us with thirty anxious minutes before we had to leave.

Twenty-Three

I set the car to take me and Tana to the Expo, but even as we curved through the skyways, I was hoping we'd hear that Dollie had been successful and we'd be able to turn back. That might sound cowardly, and maybe it was, but after being shot at so many times, I'd have been happy to get out of this mess without ever seeing another gun.

We had a hiccup at the ticket booth when I insisted on paying cash. My credit account was useless now, undoubtedly frozen and monitored by the police. I also didn't want to use the business account Dollie had given me access to, and once again she'd come to the rescue by supplying a small roll of notes. Despite our current plans, I was still hoping I could keep her at arm's length from the chaos.

The ticket booth whined and beeped multiple times when I inserted the notes, sounding like a miserable electronic rodent trapped in a cage. Finally, it deigned to redirect us to a special operator—a bored looking guy who didn't even look up as he snapped my picture for "security purposes." The price for being so subversive as to use actual money. After signing a couple of pointless forms and wasting ten minutes, the tickets were reluctantly issued, and we were allowed to enter.

Tana took the eFlimsy guide, sifting through the various presentations and exhibitions with her fingertips for directions. We pushed through the crowds as she guided our turns, based on the lights on the translucent map sheet. "He's part of the *Ananta* discussions in the *Hall of Visionaries*. Along here and left."

The main corridor formed a pretentious display of curved latticework, white beams, and purple-shaded glass. The design an obvious imitation of Atoll architecture—which was what the self-declared intelligentsia insisted was "good art," despite the on-going embargo. It was only a concrete and glass facsimile though—Atoll crystalline construction was one of their closely guarded secrets.

The concourse was lined with food and drink vendors and almost solidly packed with people, and it took several minutes to work our way through. When we finally arrived the introductory statements had started, and we slipped into seats at the back to attract as little attention as possible. The room was quietly buzzing with the collected whispers of the audience, while the podium was filled with an array of nondescript political types, but the face magnified on the huge screen behind them was immediately identifiable—Devan Rohloff. The designer and chief architect of the experimental starship *Ananta*, the man who was going to take us not only back into space, but to the stars themselves. He was sitting behind the main group of tables, with an optical pickup trained on him. I was surprised he was there in person. It must have been difficult adapting to full Earth gravity after so many years in ZeeGee, especially at his age. Presumably though, the personal touch was much more effective when it came to attracting funding.

"Which one is Idell?" I whispered.

Tana pointed to a stocky, bearded man on the right of the podium. He didn't look like I'd expected the university head to look, though I wasn't sure what I had in mind exactly. A studious, bookworm type I suppose—someone who stammered a lot and forgot your name seven point five seconds after being introduced.

This guy looked entirely unlike that. His suit would have cost me a month's pay, his hair and beard were perfectly trimmed, and he seemed entirely too at ease with himself and those around him. He looked like he should have been a game show host, or maybe one of those old style preachers that still existed in the MusCat Alliance. Whatever his background, it was a safe bet he'd never suffered a day of discomfort in his life.

The person speaking sat down and was replaced by a thin,

greasy guy whose clothes and demeanor shouted "government pimp." In a 3V conspiracy thriller, he'd have been cast as the not-immediately-obvious bad guy. Which meant he was probably a nice guy in real life. At least as far as bean-counters go.

He waved his hands over the dais until the crowd quietened. "Delegates and spectators. For decades we on Earth have been oppressed by our cousins who dominate space. Not by law, not by treaty, not by merit, but simply because they were there first. They have treated us as second class citizens, insulted our achievements, and tried to convince us that our world and technology was at best second-rate and at worse, worthless."

The crowd booed, and he waved them quiet again. "We know that isn't true, ladies and gentlemen, and so it gives me great pleasure to introduce the man who puts shame to the Atoll lies. The man who will single-handedly carve out a path to end this oppression. The man responsible for giving the entire Earth hope for the future once more. Devon Rohloff!"

I'd heard it all before. But political rhetoric doesn't work so well when most of the engineering and scientific brains had emigrated to the Atolls en-mass a hundred and fifty years earlier. Some facts are hard to swallow, and no amount of window dressing changes that.

I had good reason to hate the *Ananta*, even if it was our one hope left. After the Treeby cult vanished from Earth, everyone wanted the secret they'd taken with them. So far, no one had figured it out, and Rohloff didn't strike me as the guy to do the job either. Despite my cynicism, I *wanted* him to succeed. For the sake of the whole stinking mess of humanity who'd been trapped by the Atolls for decades. But my gut told me otherwise, and it's usually right.

Rohloff stood up unsteadily, and the giant six-meter high screen flickered several times as it tracked him. For a moment Rohloff's gray-bearded face was clear, the lines in his skin like crevices in the Earth itself. Then the image flickered, and he was replaced by a new face, almost as recognizable. Anthony Anthonio, the self-described *Last of the Fat Kids*, was broadcasting from his secret location in the depths of the USP bread-basket, Manitoba.

"We demand the right to be whatever bodyweight we choose," he screamed, in-between stuffing fistfuls of syrup-dripping pie into his mouth. "We demand an end to persecution by an obesophobic society."

Anthonio wasn't fat of course. He'd never been fat and literally couldn't be. He wasn't the *last* of the fat kids, so much as the *first* of the Geneered can't-get-fat kids. After the obesity epidemic had laid waste to two generations, the government decided children's dietary health was too important to leave in the over-indulgent hands of parents. So children were modified, in vitro, to be biochemically incapable of overeating.

"We are the subjects of illegal experimentation that is against all moral and international laws. We demand this is reversed, so we can develop naturally. We have the right to be fat. We have the right to eat whatever"—he stuffed a huge slice of sticky chocolate cream pie into his face—"we like."

"Fat people everywhere unite! You have nothing to lose, but your genetic chains..."

Anthony's face screwed up in agony, his features turning ghostlike as the anti-obesic mechanisms in his body kicked in. A fraction later the screen dissolved in a wave of vomit, as he ended the broadcast in his traditional style.

The audience reaction was predictable as the great and the good turned their heads to avoid the sight. There were loud voices from the podium as technicians tried desperately to re-establish the picture of Rohloff.

"Please, ladies and gentlemen. Please." The government official lifted his voice over the roar of the crowd. "That was obviously *not* our intended speaker. I'm sure that we will correct our... *technical difficulty* shortly." He clasped a hand to his ear, listening to some direct prompt. "Yes. Yes. I understand. Right. Now... ladies and gentlemen. Please. Devon Rohloff."

Finally, Rohloff's face appeared on screen once more. He looked like Moses staring across the sea of the audience, his dark leathery skin framed in a halo of grizzled white hair. And the similarity wasn't in appearance alone. When he spoke, he *sounded* like Moses, and told us he would take us to the Promised Land.

"I'd like to apologize for that, delegates." Rohloff pointed over his shoulder with his thumb. "I'd like to, but I can't. That young man has a hatred that drives him to do these things, and I can't apologize for that. I can, however, sympathize with his feelings. When I think about how the Atolls have subjugated Earth, their very own antecedents, I *share* that level of hatred. Anthony, regardless of what we think of his misguided ideals, is one of us. He's an Earth citizen. He deserves better than the terrible price he and his generation was forced to pay through enforced genetic health because we're confined to this world.

"I do not deserve the plaudits in my introduction by Minister Sarnelli. He speaks for the government of the United States and Provinces, whereas I speak as a man. One that has lived and"— Rohloff stabbed his finger at the audience—"like all of you, seethed under this oppression for far too long. I do not take offense at the Junior Minister's words, even though I can't accept them. But I do have to make a special point."

Rohloff peered over the top of his glasses. "The *Ananta* project has involved over five thousand individuals through the years. I am merely one of that vast army. We have all shared one goal—to end Atoll tyranny and take humanity back to the stars."

The crowd exploded in a thunderous roar of cheers and whistles. Rohloff waved and waited until the tumult had died down.

I knew the story. The *Ananta* was designed to make use of zero-point fields, powered by the Casimir effect. In theory, it could create boundless energy from nothing and short-cut space-time itself. We'd known for decades of potentially hospitable exo-planets, but the problem was always the same: *how do you get there from here?* The technology looked like so much hand-waving to me. Even the static tests had been inconclusive.

"Even the mighty Atolls, as good as their technology is, have only probed to the edges of our solar system. Even *they* know it is foolish to attempt to go further with their existing ships. *Ananta* will overtake them in one giant leap, echoing the words of the very first space explorers."

The crowd rose en masse, applause rolling around the room like an artillery barrage. Everyone believed in Rohloff—except

189

maybe me. Everyone needed to believe Earth could rise up and return to the stars once more.

"If this wonderful audience doesn't object..." Rohloff smiled, and it seemed like the whole room smiled with him. "I'd like to take the opportunity to walk you through *Ananta*'s systems and demonstrate some of our latest simulations."

A 3V simulation of the ship accelerating from Earth filled the space immediately above our heads, its graceful lines looking like they'd been sculpted in the heart of a particle accelerator. Who knows, maybe they had. Rohloff continued to prattle about the design and capabilities, but it was only noise to me.

The NullScroll buzzed in my hand, and I lifted it to my ear, cupping the back to cut down the noise in the high-vaulted room.

"Ballen?" Dollie's voice was metallic through the tiny speaker. "I failed."

Damn that guy, Murphy. Why couldn't something go right, just once. "You're fired."

"I got him with the Tracker. That guy's a pushover. But keep it from his wife, of course." Dollie sounded annoyed. "But when I checked the feed nothing came through. No acknowledgment, no signal."

The whole thing was starting to feel like a funeral without a corpse. Could we even trust Sigurd's tech to work? Activate it and plant it on the target. Supposedly it was that simple, but non-functional is even simpler.

"No point you hanging around here," I said. "Head back to the hotel, and we'll see what we can do."

Tana seemed strangely unworried when I told her. "What did you expect? That kind of tracking is old and useless. Who knows how long that equipment's been gathering dust? Failures were to be expected."

Her dismissive attitude grated on me. We should have had a contingency—Dollie could have taken two trackers perhaps. Then I remembered *we* were the back-up and stopped my internal bitching.

"We only have three chances." It felt like having an unreliable techno-genie. One who wanted to play games rather than do what it was asked. "You know what we have to do now."

Tana's face distorted in fear and her voice lowered. "You mean me?"

"You have the background to talk to him. He'd see through me immediately."

"Don't make me do this. Please."

Tana was incredibly confusing. In some ways she was intelligent and confident—anything related to science or her work seemed effortless to her, even though most would find it incredibly hard. But when it came to interpersonal interactions she fell apart.

"Have you met Idell before?"

Tana shook her head. "No. A couple of times in group meetings perhaps, but not what you would call direct one-to-one communication."

"All I want you to do is talk to him. Scientific chit-chat." I felt slightly stupid. What *do* scientists talk about? "Whatever you'd normally discuss if you bumped into him at a conference."

She glanced nervously at the stage. "I'd never… approach him like that. You do it, Joe. Please?"

"I'd sound like a klutz, no matter what I said. I'd make him suspicious."

"I can't." Tana clutched at her blouse. "Especially looking like this."

Dollie had dressed her in clothes that were designed to be professional, but a little flirty. "Tana, we've already discussed this. You look good. Idell will think so too. And that's the point."

"But what if he had Hubert killed?"

"You want justice for Ganz, don't you?"

"Yes… But what do I say?" One of the people in the throng banged into her, and she jumped.

"You're a scientist, talk science to him. Tell him you've admired him for a long time." I was laying it on thick. "Guys like hearing that sort of thing. It doesn't have to be true."

"I'm not sure…"

I struggled against the impulse to shake her. "It's our only chance."

Tana's jaw tensed. "I'll try."

The presentation ended, and the hall filled with wild cheering and rhythmic foot-stamping. It seemed that everyone in the conference room was convinced Rohloff was mankind's Savior, or a close facsimile at the very least.

The lights brightened as the delegates gathered at the front of the hall to take informal questions and be feted by the rowdy mob. Tana wobbled forward on the heels Dollie had forced her into. She stopped to talk to one of the panelists. Whatever she said must have been successful judging by the laughter. Then she moved on and made conversation with someone else.

I wondered what she was playing at. Tana didn't even try to approach Idell. But after a few minutes of further conversation, her new friend ushered her across to him and introduced her. I felt embarrassed I'd doubted her. Despite her reluctance and fear she was often a lot smarter than I gave her credit for.

Idell greeted them both enthusiastically. I couldn't tell what they were saying, but everyone seemed to be smiling and convivial. Sarnelli, the bean-counter type, tried to interrupt the discussion several times, only to be brushed off with a dismissive wave from Idell. Tana surprised me by throwing herself into the role—joking with Idell almost flirtatiously. After her earlier protests, I'd expected her to be awkward and would have been happy if she'd only got close enough to plant the tracker.

The Professor leaned over and whispered something to her. Tana laughed and put her arms around him in an apparently friendly hug. She moved back and made a sly *OK* sign in my direction.

I could see Tana trying to get away, but Idell had other ideas. Each time she tried to leave, he'd physically pull her back into the conversation. Even from where I was standing I could see something hungry in his expression—he must have thought he had it made. I wondered if I should try and create some kind of diversion, then the NullScroll buzzed in my hand.

"Soldier, the carrier signal is coming in loud and clear." Dollie sounded almost excited. "You've done it."

"It worked?" After the initial failure, I'd lost faith in the antiquated technology. "That's great, but Tana is still with Idell."

"Don't worry. She had some tips from me, she'll be fine."

"What do you mean?"

"Girl talk, don't ask. Get out of there."

I looked around. Idell had vanished and Tana as well. I edged forward, scanning the crowd around the stage, suddenly aware of the smell of warm bodies around me. I'd let myself get distracted by the call, but I couldn't believe Tana would leave with Idell after everything she'd said.

"Joe?"

I looked over to my left. Tana was partly hidden behind a display advertising Luna City vacations, and I pushed my way through the people, feeling relieved. I still owed her for saving my life, and I hated the thought that I'd thrown her in with someone like Idell.

"What happened?"

Tana made a face. "Idell started getting personal. I thought I should encourage it."

"You did?" The idea seemed entirely unlike her.

"I imagined it was an Alt-real game, then planted the Tracker while he was leering down my cleavage. He wanted me to go to his hotel room, and I pretended to agree, then ducked into the restroom as soon as I could. Did the tracker work?"

"Dollie said it did." I winked at her. "Not bad for something old and useless."

We headed to the parking area, but as we rounded the corner, I spotted a cop car in the middle of the exit lane and a couple of cops looking around the parked Arroyo. The news reports hadn't mentioned the car, but Sterle knew about it.

I grabbed Tana's wrist and pulled her back, edging towards the elevators as I called Dollie. "We've got problems. The cops are nosing around the car."

Dollie barely hesitated. "I'll be on the roof in fifteen."

I didn't press the button for the elevator. Elevators are confined and can be stopped by remote. Instead, we headed through the door to the emergency stairwell. "This way. We have time."

Tana looked puzzled but didn't object. The roof was six stories above us on L11, so it wasn't a short climb. Tana moved like a goat, climbing each step with determined resilience. Certainly no expense had been spared on her physical Geneering from what I could see. My messed up legs on the other hand, felt more and more like unsupported jelly with each flight.

Although the stairs were safer than the elevator, we couldn't afford to linger. Few people used them, and we'd stand out like a supernova if anyone checked the security cameras. The problem was that I got slower on each step.

"Here." Tana put her arm around my waist and slid my arm over her shoulder, taking a significant part of my weight.

Tana kicked off her heels and hauled me up the stairs one by one, the steps and levels blending into one as my legs turned into stumps of pure pain. We stopped a couple of times briefly so I could rest, but starting to move again after each pause was almost worse than keeping moving.

We burst onto the roof and looked around the dimly lit area. The limo was already waiting, and Tana dragged me towards it. I fell through the door with a grunt.

Twenty-Four

I don't know if anyone spotted us as we tumbled into the cavernous backseat of the limo and to be honest didn't really care. They could make of it what they wanted. Dollie hit the thrusters, forcing us into the plush seats and in less than a minute we were weaving steadily through the swarms of local traffic. It seemed like the Expo had brought everyone out for the night and the skyways were crowded beyond normal commuter levels.

Dollie handed the tracker unit over her shoulder, her eyes widening when she saw me. "You look like shit."

I reached down to massage my legs, wincing at the pain. "I like you too."

"I'm going to have to stay on the controls." Dollie hit the horn as a dark gray Firestar cut across the lanes inches from us, a gaggle of orange-tanned children peering out the back window.

"We need to keep moving." Tana didn't look up. She was already working on the tracker pickup. "If we stay in one zone they'll be able to trace us more easily."

"Dollie, try to hit every part of the city possible," I grunted through the waves of pain coming from my legs.

She nodded, and a few seconds later we cut right, heading to one of the orbital corridors. She tossed a box of painkillers into the back, and I swallowed a handful without counting them.

Tana hunched over a portable screen on her lap. I leaned over to get a better look. The display was filled with a swirling geometric mess of lines and colors that looked more like an abstract painting than an image. "The video isn't working?"

195

"It's working," Tana snapped. "It's supposed to be self-configuring, but it's not locking in the filter settings properly."

I looked back at the kaleidoscope on the screen, hoping we hadn't gone through all that for nothing. Tana adjusted the feed controls, and the roiling patterns solidified. A few more tweaks and the image clarified into a view of a wide office dominated by a dark slab of a desk. To one side, next to a tall set of shelves full of awards were several heavily padded seats arranged around a low coffee table. Sarnelli sat more or less facing the pickup, while Idell stood gazing out of a large picture window behind him. Moments later the audio came on, both Tana and me leaning in to hear better.

"That went well." Idell was as loud as his smile was broad.

"I suppose so." Sarnelli straightened his anachronistic necktie.

"Did you scare off that young post-grad?" Idell frowned, his jowly features trembling slightly. "She was interested. And like all of the students trying to qualify, she'd have been eager and discreet."

Idell sounded more oily through the pickup than he had over the conference's PA system. I noticed Tana wiping her hands on her skirt. Obviously he didn't have any fans inside the limo.

"More discreet than you, I'm sure."

"Does that bother you, Sarnelli?" Idell's laugh was mocking. "As a university senior administrator I have access to opportunities ordinary people don't."

Sarnelli shook his head. "So it seems."

"The students need a good recommendation. Without that, they're lucky to get menial work in some third-rate food lab. That's the way the world is now. It's only natural to make use of the circumstances. They all do it. It's expected."

The drugs were starting to kick in, and I didn't ache so much when the cab lurched. Glancing over at Tana, she looked in more pain than I was. Her lips carved a thin line across her face, almost like a knife cut. Perhaps Idell thought that kind of behavior was *expected*, but Tana's expression told me she'd be willing to debate the point with him. Violently.

"Not everyone uses sex to further their career." Her features hardened into pure titanium. "And not everyone abuses their position."

I was thinking of Ganz' relationship with Tana, and she probably was too. *Button it, Joe.*

"Did you double check the Ganz files?" Sarnelli asked.

"Of course. I already told you—there's nothing there." Idell poured drinks from the decanter on the table then settled behind the polished mahogany desk, straightening a picture cube containing images of an older woman and two girls, presumably his wife and children. "That raises a concern, in fact. The University Committee is asking awkward questions. Like why Ganz' papers haven't been released yet. Is there something scandalous in them? They think we're hiding something."

"Which we are." Sarnelli pulled out a small Scroll and made a note. "Let's make no mistake about that."

I have to admit I was wondering what they were drinking. The decanter gave no real clues, but I guessed from the color it was brandy. I could have done with a quick drink myself right about then. There was a mini-bar in the back of the seat in front of me, and I popped it open, my lips wetting in anticipation. It was empty.

"Sorry, Joe," said Dollie.

On the tracker screen, a display on Idell's wall flashed at an incoming signal, and he pressed the accept button on his desk. The screen lit up, and a figure appeared. The angle made it awkward to identify the person, but it was easy to recognize Rohloff's warm voice.

"Have you sorted out that little *problem* yet? You said it would be cleared up days ago, but I haven't had any confirmation. It's vital we keep *Ananta's* coverage positive, or we could lose public faith. The mob is very fickle. They can change sides in a few hours. I've seen it before. When I first looked for sponsorship for *Ananta* the government was very generous, but then—"

"Dr. Rohloff, believe me, I'm well aware of the shoals and reefs of public opinion."

Sarnelli picked at a bowl of Chi-z-o's on the table, and I wondered what Idell was doing serving such cheap snacks—though no doubt Anthony Anthonio would have approved.

"Which is why it's important we manage things the right way," Sarnelli continued.

"No one wants *Ananta* to be more of a success than I do." Rohloff puffed his chest out. "This is my masterpiece, my opus majorus. It is my legacy and will set humanity free."

"We all want that, Devan." Idell gestured expansively. "A gift to the world."

Despite the care Dollie was giving the controls, the limo swerved occasionally in response to the volume of traffic. It seemed as heavy as ever, despite it being late evening.

"Were the invitations sent to the Pan-Asian and MusCat representatives? I haven't received any response and it's vital they have access to this technology." Rohloff dabbed at his forehead with a handkerchief. "Sometimes it feels like things are being kept from me. Or maybe I forget things. I didn't used to forget things. But there are so many details to keep track of. It's very difficult."

"They were sent." Sarnelli chopped out the words. "Getting a response from them is always problematic. You know that."

"Yes, yes. That's true." Rohloff nodded. "Once I've proved my designs, there will be no more doubters. The *Ananta* technology will be freely available on GARNET for everyone to use. It will be a revolution. Humanity will finally take its rightful place as a species of the stars."

"That's it, Devan." Idell lifted his drink in a toast. "Your legacy and name will be secure in history, along with Newton, Einstein, and Majorana."

"Yes, without Majorana's insights, the zero-point drive would have been impossible." Rohloff's eyes narrowed, and his skin darkened. "But what of our other friend? We still don't know what his plans are. I'm telling you, nothing can be allowed to go wrong. If we fail in this, we fail all the people of Earth."

"Don't worry so, Devan." Idell smiled, but his expression looked pasted on. "His only channel was through Ganz, and that's gone now. Unless you're still contacting him? Remember what we agreed?"

"I cut off all communication. It's been months since we spoke. His access to the project has been blocked entirely. I was the one who originally suggested that, if you remember. Sarnelli wanted to wait. I said we should isolate him. I was right. Wasn't I?"

"We had to make sure we weren't acting prematurely." Sarnelli seemed about to say more then closed his mouth with a snap.

"Well, it's done now." Rohloff sounded satisfied. "This would have been so much easier if you'd listened to me from the beginning. When you have as much experience as I have, these things become easy to spot ahead of time."

Idell rolled his glass in his hand. "Quite right, Devan. But there's nothing to worry about now."

"I have work to do. Even as we enter the final phase of the project, there are numerous details that only I can handle." Rohloff hesitated, leaning back from the pickup. "Keep me informed of any progress. Nobody must be allowed to interfere with our plans. Nobody."

The screen in Idell's office darkened. I realized my breathing had been shallow throughout their conversation, almost as if I was worried they might hear. I tried to relax and breathe normally, but my chest was still tight.

Idell and Sarnelli were quiet for several moments after Rohloff ended the call, wrapped up in their own thoughts. The light had faded as they talked, and Idell stood up to switch on two corner lamps that filled the space with a subdued yellow lighting.

Our screen flickered several times, a buzz coming from the pickup unit as it filled with static and random noise. Tana twirled the controls. "We changed areas. Need to re-tune."

The screen buzzed more, the image flickering in and out.

"...worries me. He's more unstable every time we talk with him." Sarnelli dipped into the snacks again, reminding me of a vulture picking the prize entrails from a corpse. "We can't let him damage our plans—anymore than Ganz, or anyone else."

"But we need Devan to finish the *Ananta*. We can't get rid of him." Idell sounded concerned, though I got the feeling it wasn't about Rohloff's health.

"I've had people shadowing him for some time. We could finish the work without him now, if necessary. We're finally in control."

"You didn't tell me that." Idell frowned, his arms locking together. "But Devan's no threat. He lives for that damn ship."

"He's an idealist, and they're always dangerous. The government won't allow technical details of the *Ananta* to be published. And it won't allow anything to come out that threatens the ship's launch."

Tana gasped. Stopping publication was obviously a bigger deal to her than it seemed to me.

"But how can you prevent him?" Idell scampered back to his chair, suddenly looking frightened. "It's every scientist's right— guaranteed under USP and international law."

"Tell that to Ganz," I muttered.

"Laws can change in times of emergency." Sarnelli leaned forward. "We need a new wave of space flight to escape the prison the Atolls have made of Earth. Who would *you* rather see colonizing new worlds? People with the same standards and beliefs you have? Or would you rather see them overrun by the religious zealots of the Muslim-Catholic Alliance? Or perhaps you'd prefer the soulless robots of the Pan-Asian Confederation? Call me a bigot, call me a Nationalist, but I want *my* descendants occupying the stars, not someone else's. Is that wrong?"

"But... I have a responsibility to the scientific community." Idell tucked his hands into his lap. "I can't suppress a discovery of this magnitude for political reasons."

"And Ganz?" Sarnelli's expression reminded me of a snake.

Idell gulped the remnants of his drink. "That was different."

"Remember the last girl you had an affair with?" Sarnelli drained the rest of his drink. "I own her and have complete footage of your... *liaisons*. I'm sure it would be a hit on the public media channels— your wife and children would no doubt especially enjoy them."

The color drained from Idell's face. "But that... that's blackmail."

"Yes, it is. Though when someone is as foolish as you, it might be better called *poetic justice*. But let's not be timid here—we can add extortion and bribery to the charges as well. University funds will be cut by seventy-five percent if you don't do exactly what I tell you. But if you go along with our plans, we'll increase them by twenty-five percent."

The car weaved, and I looked up. Dollie glanced over her shoulder. "Cops."

"But how?" said Tana. "We can't have been tracked so quickly."

"Dammit. I thought you knew how to drive well enough not to draw attention." I risked a look through the darkened back window. The cop car was hanging about thirty meters behind us. The limo was as private as a Husher, so shouldn't have drawn attention—but there they were.

"If you don't like my driving, feel free to step out of the car." Dollie's voice was pure ice. She banked the car deliberately so I could see all the way down the canyon-like buildings to the ground. "Could be routine."

We lifted into a higher lane and turned. Checking my bearings, I realized Dollie was putting us on a path that could easily take us to the airport. Smart thinking—a limo was likely to be headed there at any time of day. "Sorry."

She grunted but didn't respond immediately. "Still following."

We traveled south for a few minutes, then Dollie moved the cab into the express lane, picking up speed until we were at the limit.

I looked behind, but there was no sign of the cop car. "Where'd they go?"

"They didn't follow the last move." Dollie took a breath. "Just nosy."

I looked back at the screen. Idell was slumped forward, a sullen frown on his face. "The extra funding... would there be any restrictions on how it's spent?"

"None at all. New facilities, extra support for poorly funded programs or..." Sarnelli had all the cards and clearly knew it. "...salary increases."

Idell smiled weakly. "Given the circumstances, I think it would be a mistake to let any of Dr. Ganz' *preliminary* findings become public." He leaned back in his chair. "It's far too soon. I'm sure I can convince the Committee of that."

"I'm sure you'll be suitably persuasive."

Idell swallowed. "What's the latest from your team?"

"Let's find out." Sarnelli tapped out a comm link, and the office screen lit up again. The image wasn't clear, but we didn't have to wait long for identification.

"Gabriella, the situation has changed. We'll have to deal with

Rohloff after all. I assume you can make the necessary *arrangements?*"

Gabriella nodded. "I'll take care of it personally."

"Good. Do you have an update on your other activities?"

"We made a positive identification on the Radebaugh girl. She's definitely involved. Given the circumstances though, we made no move to apprehend her."

"What?" Idell snapped. "What use are you if you're too—"

"Professor..." Sarnelli picked up the decanter and poured himself another. "Please explain."

"The girl made an unexpected appearance at today's Symposium. After the speeches, she approached Professor Idell and engaged him in conversation. The Professor seemed interested in her, and my operatives report he attempted to arrange a liaison. The girl had the good sense, and taste, to make a departure as soon as she was able."

"That was her?" Idell almost choked on his words.

"Superficially changed. Enough to fool normal Argus processing routines, but not the more thorough scans we targeted around Minister Sarnelli. Probability was over ninety-three percent."

"*Junior* Minister, please." Sarnelli smiled despite his words. "Let's not allow ambition to run too far ahead of reality."

"I stand corrected." Gabriella laughed lightly. "Though I'm sure it's only a matter of time before reality matches the ambition."

"So, the girl was at the presentation. I told her nothing." Idell's face was dark red. "There's no real harm done. Unless she has Ganz' papers and tries to publish them, she's a useless distraction."

Tana stiffened next to me. It's not often people get to hear the unadulterated truth of what people think of them, and she was taking a crash course.

"The real question is why was she there?" Gabriella's voice grew serious. "And why she made such an effort to contact Professor Idell when doing so was hardly in her best interests."

Tana slumped, muting the tracker and dropping it on the seat. She looked over at me, her voice weak when she spoke. "They know I talked to him?"

"Don't worry. They don't know why," I said, with more confidence than I felt.

"But now they know for sure, I'll be a target too." Tana seemed to shrink into the padded car seat. "They're going to kill me. Don't you understand? They'll kill me like everyone else. You have to do something."

"You were already a target," Dollie said from up front. "*You* dragged Joe into this, not the other way around. Or did you think someone suddenly decided there was a surplus of cab drivers in the world?"

"But now they *know*."

Tana's reaction didn't make any sense. She'd been a target since the first. I was a bystander pulled into all of this. It changed nothing. We still needed to find out what was in Ganz' work that they wanted to hide and clear our names. I grabbed the screen and turned the volume back up.

"…run a number of simulations, and there's a high probability that Radebaugh knew of the antagonism between Professor Idell and Dr. Ganz." Gabriella's voice was as hard-edged as a diamond-tipped saw. "It's highly likely that she's working with the cab driver. We didn't detect him at the symposium, but there was an unusual cash transaction that could have been him."

After a long pause, Sarnelli leaned towards the screen. "What is it, Gabriella? It's not like you to hold back."

"I'm not sure further discussion is appropriate given the situation."

"What does that mean?" Idell slammed his glass down. "I'm completely loyal to the cause, and you know—"

Sarnelli waved his hand. "Professor, please..."

Even through the transmitter, it was clear Sarnelli didn't really believe that.

"Of course, Professor. I meant no criticism of you." Gabriella's words were as believable as a laser range finder with a bad return sensor. I had a strong hunch that the Professor would be "retiring" approximately five minutes after Rohloff and any other witnesses were out of the way. It wasn't much of a comfort.

"Well, good. I'm glad I'm not being doubted. It was me who alerted you to the Ganz problem in the first place." Idell shuffled over to the table, refilled his glass and swallowed it all.

"The police are no longer a problem," Gabriella continued.

"Detective Sterle was *very* cooperative."

"Thank you, Gabriella." Sarnelli combed his fingers through his thinning hair. "Do you have anything else to report?"

"Just one item." Gabriella sounded like a Persian kitten that had inherited an entire creamery. "The chauffeur for your limousine trip this morning was *Dollie Buntin*, a Geness with a checkered past."

"Is that supposed to be of interest?" Idell snapped.

"Buntin is the owner-operator of *Buntin's Classic Cabs*. Current employer of Joe Ballen. I'd say it's almost certain she has knowledge of what he's doing and undoubtedly involved."

Sarnelli sighed. "This is getting out of hand. Add her to the list."

"I already did," Gabriella said.

"Find them and shut them up quickly." Sarnelli's voice was completely devoid of emotion. "And permanently."

"They can't do that." Tana looked like she was going to hurl the portable screen out of the window. "We have rights under the Charter."

I understood how she felt. How could Sarnelli casually order the death of three people like that? Whatever the supposed justification, taking a life shouldn't be so easy. I wasn't sure how exactly, but I promised myself that one day I'd explain it to him.

"Rights are like justice—only good when you don't need it," Dollie growled.

Gabriella ended the call, and the screen in Idell's office darkened. Idell opened his mouth several times, but nothing came out.

"You want to say something?" Sarnelli steepled his fingers.

"No. That is... well, I wondered if you're *sure*..."

Sarnelli's thin face seemed to harden, his tanned skin furrowing around his mouth. "Most people are uncomfortable when confronted with strong opinions and strong actions. *Inclusive Civility* has bred a society of conformity that challenges nothing and asks no questions. Fortunately, some of us understand that the future is determined by those with the courage to act."

"Switch that crap off." Dollie was still maneuvering through the traffic. "I've heard enough."

Tana glanced at me and switched the feed off when I nodded.

"I hope someone has an idea because I'm all out," I said. All of us were known to our enemies, so returning to any of our usual locations would likely be fatal.

"Back to the hotel?" Tana looked puzzled.

"It was paid for with Dollie's credit chip. It's only a matter of time before they track it down." I shrugged. "If they haven't already."

"The Geneium?" Dollie said.

Tana looked at Dollie, then at me. I got the feeling she'd rather Dollie had suggested a trip to hell, but her personal bigotry was going to have to take a back seat. We needed a bolt-hole and didn't have many options.

"How would we get there? If they know who we are, won't they track us?" Tana's jaw was almost rigid.

"We have this." I held up the Disruptor.

"That's like a flashlight in a dark room," Dollie mused. "If you activate it people will know something's happening at that location, even if they're temporarily blinded. It would give them a trail—even if not very precise."

Sometimes I hate Dollie for being so damn logical, especially when she's right.

"I might be able to change that." Tana took the Disruptor and popped the cover off it. In a few minutes, she'd stripped out the power terminals and had a couple of exposed leads.

"Can we connect this to the car's main power?"

Dollie raised her eyebrows, lowering the car until she was safely in the Local zone and could hover. She reached under the dash and with a jerk, ripped out a power cable, then passed the line to us through the open privacy window. "There goes the audiotronics."

"I wasn't planning on dancing." I pulled the cable through and handed it to Tana. There was enough juice in it to deliver a nasty shock. "I hope you know what you're doing."

Tana's brow furrowed as she worked on the wires. "So do I."

A few minutes later Tana nodded to Dollie. Dollie stabbed the audio power button, and the inside of the cab lit up like we were at ground-zero of a small nuclear test. The smell of flames and the sour taste of melting plastic caught in my lungs, and I coughed heavily. Several seconds passed before my sight recovered. I hoped Dollie didn't hit the controls accidentally and throw us into a building.

The Disruptor was shooting sparks like a mini firework display, molten splatters from the unit burning through the ParaHyde seat covering, which was already blackened from the initial explosion. The Disruptor itself looked like a fried electronic insect, the neat packaging burst into a mess of burnt circuitry and plastics

"That should disrupt pickups across half of Baltimore." Tana slid her window open to let the smoke escape, coughing into her cupped hand.

Dollie gunned the turbines, and the limo lifted back into the regular traffic lanes, rising swiftly through the skyways until we were in the fast city level. Circling around she aimed the car northwest. "This is coming out of your wages, Soldier. It's not my limo."

After the earlier loss of the cab, I winced at how much this was going to end up costing me.

Twenty-Five

The Geneium didn't make ordinary people welcome. Unless you're one of the fifteen or so percent who have had significant genetic work done, stay away. Want to find out what makes the Geneered tick? Stay away. Interested in becoming a genetic engineer? Find a university program. Have some kind of crazy obsession with the Geneered? Stay the hell away, Mac.

I'd never been to the Geneium, not even dropping off or picking up a fare. I'd seen it many times when I'd cabbed out that way, but that was it. The building dominated the old Reservoir Hill skyline as a shining chrome, glass, and steel celebration of genetic engineering. It sat in the center of what had once been the grassy meadows of Druid Hill Park, heavily fenced and patrolled by twenty-four-hour security to prevent ground-based intrusions. Each glassed level was rumored to be dedicated to one step in research on the transformation process from fertilization to embryo, with the upper ten floors dedicated to advanced Geneering.

We circled the stylized X-chromosome building to the entry door at the cross in the X. As we approached, the oval doors slid apart. I'd heard there was no ground level entrance, but that seemed a stretch and put far too much faith in AeroMobiles. Dollie let go of the controls as the Geneium's traffic system took over and brought the car into one of the inside cradles. There would be no surprise visitors here, that was certain.

Once the car cradled and the turbines wound down, the doors unlocked. Tana hesitated, but Dollie leapt out. She trotted over to the unoccupied front desk and placed her hand inside the scanner.

After a moment the indicator flashed green.

"Someone will be here in a moment." Dollie turned back to us, her face serious. "I don't come here often. None of us do. It's a place you come when... well, when you need help."

We certainly qualified on that front, though not in the Geneering sense. We were more like guests of a family member. I hoped they were as friendly as Dollie seemed to think they would be.

There was an elevator on the other side of the wide lobby, though I guessed it would be useless to anyone without the right clearance. The room itself was surrounded by darkened glass walls and large screens showing animations of Geneering processes that I probably wouldn't understand even if I studied them. I hadn't known what to expect—almost no one ever saw inside—but apart from the screens, it looked very much like a regular hotel lobby. There was a slight hum that I couldn't place, like a swarm of honeybees singing happily to each other.

"Dollie," a voice boomed from the far side of the room. "What a divine pleasure. You bring summer with you whenever you visit."

Dollie ran to the newcomer and literally jumped on him, wrapping her legs around his waist and spinning him around. The guy was white-haired, with stick arms poking out from the wide openings in his robe-like garment. He looked like he should have been crushed, but somehow withstood Dollie's clinches.

"Are you trying to kill an old man? Get down, before my heart gives way." His smile was wide.

"You're strong enough for three, Roel. As always."

Despite her words, Dollie swung her legs to the floor and turned to us. "This is Principal Geneticist, Roel Kinsella. He made me what I am."

Kinsella made a sharp bow, at an angle precise enough to calibrate a protractor, while his white fringed head bobbed up and down almost comically. "Greetings, fine people. Welcome."

"Roel, these are my friends, Joe and Tana."

Kinsella frowned. "This is most unusual. You know we don't usually allow—"

"We need a place to stay, just for a while." Dollie took Kinsella's hands in hers and squeezed, almost as if she were begging him.

"We're in trouble."

"You're always trouble, Dollie." Kinsella smiled like a proud parent welcoming the return of the prodigal child. His glance fell on me briefly, then lingered over Tana. "Your friends are not entirely unknown."

"You've seen the news?" I glanced back at the limo nervously. In a lot of ways the Geneium was separate from the rest of the city, but they lived under the same laws. A couple of supposed murderers could be more danger than they wanted.

"Anything affecting our Sib is, of course, of great interest to us." He patted Dollie's arm, but he was looking at me when he spoke. "Don't worry, we have a long history of discretion. Privacy for the Geneered is our prime concern."

Kinsella nodded all around, and his attention fixed on Tana for several moments before he turned back to Dollie. "You must fill me in on your news, my dear. We'll get your friends settled where they can relax a little. How are your Sequences holding up? Mitosis still running true?"

Kinsella wrapped Dollie's hand in his, leading her towards the elevator. I looked at Tana, and she gave a vague shrug before following them. Her previous intolerance must have been infectious because I was starting to feel we'd intruded somewhere we shouldn't.

My allocated room was large enough to be a small family unit. It had all the facilities you'd imagine and several I didn't recognize, including a Treatment Unit similar to the one at Dollie's. I could have happily married the spacious glass shower unit, especially after savoring the luxurious three-hundred and sixty degree massage program. My body still ached from the modifications and with the recent abuse I'd taken, I felt like I'd been through a high-g rocket launch. I spent a good thirty minutes letting the warm water and steam pulses ease the pain and only climbed out when I felt my skin start to shrivel. The fluffy towels on the rack were large enough to hide a corpse. I wrapped one around my waist, then wandered back into the main room.

Among the abstract pictures of nucleosome scans decorating the pastel-green walls was a display screen, the controller conveniently stashed in a holder next to it. I switched it on, searching for any news related to us, but found nothing. The channels were flooded with the same story—the Atolls had blockaded the main approaches to the Deimos mining station and proclaimed an exclusion zone for the Earth fleet.

When a disaster occurs, the news services dissolve into an endless stream of non-information. Meager facts are stretched into meaninglessness as each channel invents more "news" out of nothing. They use a formula consisting of fifty percent wild conjecture, fifty percent empty headed yammering by so-called experts, and fifty percent repeating exactly what was said before in endless variations. And yeah, I know that doesn't add up—neither does the news.

This time, the facts were sketchier than usual. There was no actual conflict known, but the last Earth ship had been sent back without a cargo, along with instructions that the mining station was now the sole property of the Atolls. Earth's "fleet" consisted of less than ten low-speed ore carriers that ferried our share of the joint Mars mining operation back to Earth orbit—as big a threat as a mosquito to a jet fighter.

This message hadn't gotten back to Earth quickly enough to prevent the ore carrier *My Weigh* from launching. While it crawled towards Mars, the Atolls launched missiles and obliterated both the ship and its five crew. The official declaration of war was almost redundant.

It's one thing to hear both sides rattling their sabers, but very different when confronted with the reality of the first space war. I wondered how we could have let things get to this point, but that was sadly easy to see—the road to hell is paved not with good intentions but the refusal to compromise. I shivered. If I'd taken the job Logan had arranged, I'd have been in the middle of all that.

I poured a whiskey from the room bar and swallowed the contents in one gulp, wondering what the hell we'd do now. The concept of *race* had long been disproved on Earth and a couple of hundred years of Atoll separation didn't change that. Earth and the Atolls were inextricably linked by genetic birthright and shared history, but I didn't think it would be possible to find a way forward now. The Atolls wouldn't back down and Earth, especially the USP and Pan-Asians, relied on the minerals from Mars and the Belt to support essential technologies.

The door slid open. I turned to see Dollie just inside the room, her face colorless. She was trembling, and I couldn't figure out if it was fear, anger, or both.

"Looks like the big boys are beating their drums." I gestured at the screen and muted the sound.

"We can't be at war." Dollie's words were almost a whisper.

Her reaction was understandable. Earth feared the Atolls with good reason. As well as their technological lead, they had the benefit of tactical position. Earth would basically be fighting from the bottom of a very steep hill, while the Atolls sat at the top, ready to pick off our orbital stations. With almost nothing to stop them from laying waste to the whole planet if they wanted.

Dollie rushed forward, and I put my arms around her. Her hair smelled fresh, and her perfume was warm and spicy in my nostrils. Somehow she seemed smaller and more vulnerable than I'd ever imagined she could be.

Dollie sniffed. "Why do you like her, Ballen?"

I felt the carpet yank from under me at the sudden change of direction. While she may have had mixed up biology, in some ways Dollie was all woman and as mercurial as Cleopatra.

"The Earth? I guess she's the only home I have now."

Dollie looked up at me. Her eyes seemed a little moist, but there were no tears. "Don't act so stupid. Tana—I can tell. I don't understand why though. She's not like us."

She was right. Tana's world was filled with logic, debates, and egalitarianism. It seemed like academics didn't really work—they played at work—compared to the rest of us anyway. Even with the competition for university places it sure wasn't the same dog-eat-dog world I'd grown up in, and I guessed Dollie had a similar background. Could that be part of it? The age-old idea of *opposites attract?*

In any case, I wasn't sure I was attracted to Tana the way Dollie meant. I felt an obligation to her—she'd saved my life several times. I also felt sympathy for her as a person. She'd been through a lot and in many ways seemed defenseless—a sheep living among a

211

pack of wolves.

"Not every altruistic act is linked to sex. I owe her—"

Dollie cut me off with a short expletive. "We both know that's crap. Everyone acts out of self-interest. If they help others, it's because it serves their interests better and it's extremely temporary. So what if you owe her? She owes you too. She'd be dead if it hadn't been for you. Responsibility has a statute of limitations, just like anything else—otherwise, we'd spend our lives paying for things done before we were even born."

"You're a complete cynic, Dollie. You don't even live by your own advice. Who put their ass on the line and gave me a job? Who helped me with the police?"

"Those were purely selfish motives." Dollie flashed a slight grin. "I just want to get inside your pants."

"You want to get in everyone's pants."

"True. But yours are special."

"So special that you regularly bed anyone you feel like." Even as I said it, I felt guilty. It wasn't my place to criticize Dollie's behavior or anyone else's for that matter.

"Ballen? Are you... jealous?"

I took a couple of steps back. Dollie often scared me, but I didn't want to think there was any truth to her accusation, no matter how slight.

I shook my head. "Tana's basically a good person. Even if she doesn't have the same ideas as us. That doesn't make her *bad*. Hell, it doesn't even make her wrong—just different. You of all people should appreciate that."

"You're trying to make me feel guilty. That kind of logic doesn't hold up." Dollie folded her arms. "Just because something is different and good doesn't mean everything that's different is good. I'm not even saying she's bad."

I sighed. "What are you saying?"

If you're a man and have ever tried to hold a logical conversation with a woman, you'll understand my advice when I say *don't*. It's not that women don't understand logic—in fact, the female of the species is typically more logical than the male. But their brand of logic is different and operates at a level that tears male reasoning into indefensible shreds. Which is why they're also deadlier.

Dollie scowled and raked her hair back. "For people to get along, *really* get along, for a long period of time, physical attraction isn't the key—look around you, and you'll see that everywhere. You don't need to be a male model to have a good relationship."

"The implication of that is deeply hurtful."

"Why don't you try listening for once?" Dollie pulled out a chair and straddled it. "There are three things vital to any relationship: mutual respect, political alignment, and physical attraction. And the last is the least."

"What happened to *love?*"

"You can get that on any street corner..." She made a crude gesture. "Fifty bucks a pop, with a course of antibiotics thrown in."

"You're such a romantic."

"No, I'm not. But you are. That's why you need protection. Before you make mistakes you can't sweet talk your way out of."

I didn't know what to say. I knew Dollie liked me, but always assumed it was at a friend/employee level. Anything else was just a side-benefit, fleeting episodes of sweaty, mutual gratification and something she seemed to share liberally with others.

When she talked about being different that definitely included herself—hell, she was deliberately engineered to be as distinctive as possible. But can you separate attractiveness from gender-specificity? I could concede the possibility, but I'd always been boringly straight in such matters. And how could that idea work on someone who is biologically both? Dollie was beautiful by anyone's standards—did a duplicity of sexual organs change that? And by her argument, even if I thought she was attractive, it wasn't important anyway. I felt dizzy just from trying to think about it.

Dollie seemed to guess my confusion. "Does the way I am still bother you, Joe?"

My thoughts squirmed away from that. For a second a question flashed through my head as I wondered if Dollie could impregnate herself or not. I didn't ask though. It was my engineer's brain trying to change the subject, and I didn't think she'd welcome an intrusion into *The Secret Life of Dollie Buntin* at that moment.

I took a breath and waited for my head to stop spinning. "I'm not doing anything stupid. I feel sorry for the girl, okay? She's been through a lot."

"Sure, she's helpless, fragile, and doesn't have a gaggle of guys chasing her. Hell, she'd probably be downright grateful if you *looked* in her direction now and then. Is that it, Joe? An easy score?"

"Is that any of your business?" Dollie didn't control me anymore than I did her.

"We've known each other almost two years. She's been around a few days, and you're defending her to me." Dollie stood and moved closer. "Why?"

"Now who sounds jealous?" She looked hurt, and neither of us said anything for a few minutes. I decided a change of subject was needed and pointed to the screen. "With all that going on, do you think they might forget about us? We're hardly big news compared to an open war between Earth and the Atolls."

Dollie didn't reply immediately. "The Police might have forgotten about you for now. And maybe with the attack, it'll take a while before they get back on your trail. But Gabriella won't be distracted. This confusion will probably help her."

Dollie was right. The only way out of this mess was to get proof of what happened to Ganz and the other scientists. Maybe then we could take it to someone and have a chance of coming out alive. If we could find someone outside the cops who'd listen.

"Joe? Did you hear—"

Tana walked in, stopping when she saw me with Dollie. She stared at me, and I realized I was still only dressed in a towel.

"Sorry, I didn't mean to interrupt."

There was something in her voice—a tinge of disappointment perhaps? Like so many aspects of her I wasn't sure.

"We've been discussing the news. Have a seat."

Tana moved as far away from Dollie as she could.

I'd been distracted and decided I better get dressed. When I came back Dollie and Tana were still ignoring each other from opposite ends of the room, and the 3V was back on, though there was no further information. I took the control from Dollie and muted it again.

"I don't like it here." Tana had her arms folded around her. "It's creepy."

"Creepy?" Dollie flared up immediately. "Why would *you* find it creepy?"

"I'm not used to..." Tana's eyes flickered to Dollie. "...hiding out like a criminal."

"It's safe. Which is what we need right now." I looked at Dollie. "Tell her."

"She's not interested in anything *I* say. Everything is filtered through her bigotry."

"Bigotry? I'm the one who suffers from prejudice, not you." Tana jumped to her feet. "What do *you* know about being despised for how they look? Or being pitied—which is even worse. What do you know about walking into a room, knowing everyone is trying not to look at you because you don't match up to their standards of what's pretty?"

Dollie stood too, stabbing her finger towards Tana. "But you look down on people like me because we don't fit into your neat little world. You're anti-Geneer."

"This really isn't helping." I was done playing peacemaker between these two. We had more important things to think about.

"That's ridiculous," Tana snapped. "And insulting."

"You know what makes it so ridiculous? The fact that *you're* one of *us*. You've been Geneered. We both know it. Roel confirmed it just now, when he recognized you.

"Why do you hate yourself so much?" Dollie smiled at Tana with a mixture of sweetness and anger. "Maybe *that's* why you can't find a proper relationship."

Tana lunged forward, and I blocked her path, barely able to check her movement. "Tana, that won't help."

"Let go of her," Dollie hissed. "I'll enjoy slapping her around."

I wasn't sure Dollie would be able to handle her. Tana's ReSeeq therapy certainly hadn't lacked physical enhancement, and Dollie might just get a shock or two if they tangled.

I pushed them apart. "We aren't going through this again. Dollie, sit down so we can discuss things."

Dollie was breathing heavily, but after a minute or so she backed off. I waited until she settled in a chair.

"One day I'd be happy to sit back and watch you two ladies fight, but we need to figure out what to do next." I rubbed my hand through the stubble on my head, feeling the hair bristling.

Dollie glared from Tana to me and back. "She—"

"It was done when I was little. I don't remember much. I was sick a lot. Always tired." Tana's words came out in fits. "I didn't realize it back then, but it took me longer to understand things than other children. Mom and Dad argued a lot, but I didn't understand what it was about. They just always seemed unhappy."

Tana looked down. "For a long time, I thought they were arguing about me. It seemed like they hated me because I was so weak and sickly. My Mom left before I had the treatment. Maybe it was that. Maybe it was other things. Then it was just me and my dad.

"After he died I found out he was paying off a multi-generation mortgage—paying for a house his grandparents had bought. He borrowed against it to pay for my treatments. I've no idea how he persuaded the bank to give him the loans—it must have been a poor risk.

"Afterward? Well, everything was different." Tana swallowed. "I could run and play. I went swimming for the first time in my life, can you imagine that? I never felt sick again and even the most complicated schoolwork became easy. In fact, it was *too* easy. I was switched into the accelerated learning streams and still found the lessons tediously slow."

Dollie looked away, and I saw the pulse beating in her neck.

"Dad was worried I'd be picked on if people knew, so he made me swear never to tell anyone." Tana looked up at us. "It became so ingrained that I accepted it as normal and didn't think of myself as anything different."

"Later when I was on my own, I found out my Mom had arranged an educational fund for me. It wasn't much, but it was enough to take me to a domestic university. Certainly nowhere near enough to go to one of the leading Pan-Asian schools, but it got me into JHU."

"Is there a point to all this?" I looked over at Dollie, but she was staring at the silent newscast.

216

"It was there that I started to notice how plain I was. Everyone was so superficial. My treatments made me healthy and smart, but I imagine my father couldn't afford cosmetic enhancements along with everything else."

"Sounds like your parents did the best they could," Dollie said. So she *had* been listening. "Nothing in that sob-story explains your hatred of other Geneered though."

Tana's reply was as cold as the surface of Pluto. "You've never been ugly."

"You don't know anything about me and you never will." Dollie tapped her fingers against her leg. "He made you healthy, and your mother did her best to get you an education. That's more than a lot of people have going for them."

Tana's looked infinitely sad, her eyes falling once more. "My father helped me, yes. Then spent the next few years abusing me. When he died, I actually cheered."

Dollie gasped, and her eyes sought mine. I'd heard some of this before, but it was the first time Tana had mentioned it while Dollie was around.

Tana didn't wait for a response. Now she'd started, it seemed she wanted to tell the whole story.

"I didn't even realize at first. It was *so* well hidden, like my Geneering. I thought it was what fathers and daughters did, and there was no one around to tell me any different. It wasn't until I started high school that I noticed other girls didn't have the same kind of relationship with their fathers.

"I asked him about it." Tana wiped her palms against her pants. "He said we were *special.* That made sense to me. I knew I was different from how people looked at me. You don't forget those side-long looks when they happen every day."

"Even if that's true"—Dollie had a slight emphasis on the word *if*—"That doesn't define you now. You're not in that situation anymore. You've made a life for yourself, through your own efforts. No one is perfect. We're all trying to make the best of things. Sometimes it's crappy, but it's all we have."

I stepped into the bathroom and drank three large glasses of cold water in succession. Just hearing what had happened to Tana made me feel nauseous, and a headache was forming behind my eyes. I never knew my parents, so I could only imagine the betrayal she felt. The cold water eased my head after a couple of minutes. I took a deep breath, then rejoined Tana and Dollie.

Twenty-Six

They were still at opposite ends of the room—the confession clearly not enough to sway Dollie. From things she'd said she'd had her own tough times and knew that you only escape them on your own. Although I understood her position, I found it hard to be as indifferent as she appeared.

"We still need to find a way out of this," I said quietly. "There are people trying to kill us."

"We should stay here, where they can't get us." Dollie drew a circle in the air with her elegant finger. "I don't think that bitch and her killers could compromise the Geneium's security."

"Anything is vulnerable given the time, inclination, and money." Sitting it out and hoping for the best was tempting, but even if Gabriella couldn't get to us in the Geneium, the police could. "That might work if there was help coming, but I don't see that happening. Do you?"

Dollie's face was grim.

"We can't stay buried here," said Tana. "We need proof of Idell and Sarnelli's crimes. If we find that, we'll be safe."

"First off, where do we find proof?" I ticked off the points on my fingers. "The only witnesses left alive are in this room, and I doubt we'll get very far now we're labeled as cop killers. Secondly, who do we go to? The police won't believe us, even if we bypass Sterle, and Gabriella will kill us any chance she gets."

"What about your friend, Logan?" Dollie lit a SootheStick and sucked deeply on it. "Would he know anyone who could help?" Dollie brandished the 'Stick like a baton. "You said he had

219

connections. Maybe he could find us a safety line while we stay hidden. Once everything is lined up, they can reel us in."

I never really knew the extent of Logan's influence in such things. It always seemed better not to ask, but he might be able to help through his SecOps connections. "I'm not sure. Maybe. But without something solid to back up our claims it would be pointless."

"Who could stand up to Sarnelli and the police?" Tana wrinkled her nose as the smoke from Dollie's 'Stick drifted over. "And even if there was someone, we'd still need proof."

"This isn't an academic exercise." Dollie pursed her lips then looked back at me. "We don't stand a chance out there, Ballen. You know that, don't you?"

I felt trapped and resentful. Both their ideas had holes big enough to launch a rocket through, but they were expecting me to decide and I knew whatever I did would be interpreted as choosing sides.

Tana wafted the smoke away. "What about Rohloff?"

"He's one of them," Dollie grunted. "How does he help?"

Tana seemed to ignore her. "He knows what's happening. If we can persuade him to talk it would prove we're innocent."

"You think he's going to switch sides because you ask nicely?" Dollie snapped. "He'd be putting his own neck in the noose."

"Rohloff is a scientist. He doesn't understand this kind of plotting. Once we explain what Idell and Sarnelli are up to he'll realize what's going on, I'm sure of it."

"That's stupid." Dollie stared at me. "He'll turn us over to the killers."

Dollie was almost certainly right—Rohloff would probably hand us over to Sarnelli given the chance. But Rohloff could be a witness, and more importantly he was big enough to be listened to by people in power. If we could persuade him, it might be enough to present the case, and if Logan could pull some strings, it might work. There were a hell of a lot of "mights" in the idea though.

"We go after Rohloff," I said. "We need proof, and he's our only chance."

Dollie jumped up and glared at me. "You're choosing her?"

"That has nothing to do with it. I make my own decisions." I moved to cut Dollie off as she marched toward the door. "I'm also going to contact Logan. See if he can pull any strings. That way we have both—"

Dollie bounced me out of the way with a twist of her shoulder, and I sprawled on my ass. I shook my head to clear it and looked around, only to see the door close behind her. I scrabbled to my feet and rushed after her, but she'd already vanished.

The old maxim says you can please some people some of the time, but not everyone all the time. The corollary to that is that sometimes you can't please anyone at all.

Tana was still there, but her face was ashen. "I didn't mean to upset... Dollie, that way, but I'm sure Rohloff isn't involved in this. Despite how it seems, it's not in his personality—he's a scientist."

"She'll calm down." I didn't buy into Tana's defense of Rohloff. "I hope you're right. I'd be more than happy for something to go our way for a change."

"I hate fights," Tana almost whispered. "I need some water."

She disappeared into the bathroom and returned a moment later with a glass. I felt the same way, but water wasn't going to cut it. I poured myself another scotch and swallowed half of it.

"Joe? I need to tell you something." Tana hesitated.

"You're really working for Gabriella?" I was joking, but with my luck, it almost wouldn't be a surprise.

Tana took a big swallow of water as if it would bolster her courage. "The night Hubert died. I didn't believe you—or the police—because I didn't accept he was out visiting bars."

"I know. He didn't drink. The police said so."

"That's not it." Tana's was quiet, almost as if she didn't dare speak. "The time that Hubert was supposed to be in those bars drinking, he was with me. That is, we were... Stimming."

The room seemed to twist around me, and I sat down on the bed heavily. That didn't make any sense. "You were together?"

She shook her head. "We were remoting. I was at the residence. He was at home."

"That can't be. There were witnesses and Argus tracks of him touring the bars downtown. Not to mention that I picked him up down there."

"I know. I know." Tana's cheeks were streaked with silver tears. "That's why I didn't say anything. But he was with me."

"You sure it wasn't..." I wasn't sure how to ask the obvious. "...well, someone else?"

Tana glared at me. "That's offensive in so many ways. Do you think I wouldn't be able to tell? Or that I'm so cheap or desperate that I'd do it with anyone?"

"That's not what I meant. I can't figure out how. He couldn't be in both places at once."

The door chime sounded. I swiped my hand over the signal patch expecting to see Dollie, but Kinsella entered. He looked serious and even more wrinkled than earlier. I wondered how old he actually was. My initial guess would have been anything from sixty upwards, but it could have been two hundred and fifty just as easily.

"My apologies for intruding, but you must leave immediately."

"I know Dollie's upset, but she wouldn't want us thrown out." Would she? I couldn't imagine Dollie acting like that, no matter how angry she was.

"Dollie made no such request." Kinsella nodded his head several times. "We have rules. Non-Geneered are only allowed when accompanied by a Geneered registered with us."

The pulse in my temple throbbed, and I swallowed the remains of the whiskey. "Where did she go?"

Kinsella drew himself up. "Sib Buntin is no longer within the Geneium. I presume they would have informed you if they wanted you to be aware of their movements. And now you must leave too. I'm sorry if that seems inhospitable, but those are the rules."

I rubbed my head with my thumbs. Where the hell had Dollie gone? She was in as much danger as we were—she'd said as much only half an hour earlier. I couldn't believe she'd simply walk away, no matter how hurt she was.

"Thank you for taking us in." I tried to mimic Kinsella's bow. "May I ask a favor before we leave? I need to make an urgent call."

"Of course. There is nothing personal in this. The rules are in place to protect our Sib. Please make whatever calls you need to."

Kinsella bowed again then vanished silently through the door.

"And you trust these people, Ballen?" Tana said. "Who are you calling?"

"Logan, as I said."

The call took several minutes to connect, and I wondered if Kinsella would have agreed so easily if he'd known it would involve the cost of an Earth/LEO connection. Working on the principle of it being easier to ask for forgiveness than seek permission, I made the call anyway.

Logan's face filled the screen, his eyes darting around as they took everything in. I recognized the familiar bulkhead patterns behind him and guessed he was in one of the administration offices on the High-Rig, but there was something different. Almost any office you see has some level of personalization, whether it's wall art, pictures from home, or work schedules. Here the walls were blank, undecorated gray—no doubt deep in the heart of *spook central*.

"Joe? The caller ID said —"

"Logan, I need some more help. I may be digging myself an even deeper hole here, and you might be my only hope of getting back out again."

I updated Logan on what had happened since our last call and told him of the plan to visit Rohloff. He was completely quiet as I spoke, his eyes half closed as he absorbed every word. "What can I do?"

Some people would have made excuses. Many would have been skeptical, but Logan accepted what I said, and I could have kissed him for it. "Talk to some of those people you know. I need a line to someone trustworthy here on Earth. Someone who'll listen to us and has some pull to make sure we don't get buried."

"I can't think of anyone." Logan's forehead wrinkled. "The only person who could deal with someone like Sarnelli would be the First Minister."

I grimaced. "Not much chance of him talking to us."

"Maybe... I'll do the best I can."

I thanked him and ended the call. Knowing Logan, his best would be closer to being a miracle, and we certainly needed one.

I grabbed the little gear I had, while Tana used the terminal to do a quick search. Rohloff was staying at the *New Hilton* and returning to the High-Rig Shipyard the following morning. We'd need to move quickly if we were going to catch him.

When we stepped out of the elevator, I was glad to see the limo cradled in the Geneium's docking bay, but it made me worry about Dollie even more. She'd either left on foot or called a cab. I wasn't sure how we'd have made it if she *had* taken the car—we'd have been targeted within minutes of trying to use any other transport.

I climbed in, and Tana clambered in next to me. She took a deep breath as I started up the engines.

"Joe… There's something else I need to tell you."

"Are we playing truth or dare?" I asked, not sure I really wanted to know what else she'd been hiding.

"Those calls I said were from Paresh." Her jaw tightened. "They were from Hubert."

My hands slid from the controls, and I shook my head. "That's impossible. I was there... I saw it. Saw *him*."

Tana held herself rigidly. She looked close to tears again but held them back. "I know. I saw his body too. But he's been calling me. Paresh doesn't know that number, only Hubert does. What's happening, Joe?"

I wasn't ready to believe seven impossible things before breakfast, but everything I came up with was ridiculous or crazy. Was Tana delusional? She could be imagining things because she couldn't face what had happened. What did I really know about her anyway? Nothing she said seemed to be real.

The cradle rattled as it moved us towards the exit and seconds later we burst out, leaving the Geneium behind.

Twenty-Seven

As soon as I unlocked the controls the Geneium's traffic control boosted the car into the local skyway staging lane. My stomach flip-flopped. The lack of manual control made me feel helpless— never a good sensation on take-off. Besides, we were leaving the closest thing to sanctuary we'd had since this whole mess started.

The car turned, picking up airspeed, and the instruments flashed as control was turned over to me. I reached out to program our destination, but the car lurched, throwing me against the restraints. The windows blacked out, leaving me blind. I jammed the elevation control to maximum and forced the control column hard left. I wasn't thinking, just reacting, trying to get us out of harm's way. Our assailants must have been waiting outside the Geneium, ready to pounce. I wondered if Kinsella had turned us over to Gabriella, or maybe the police. His loyalty to Dollie might have been above question, but me and Tana were nothing to him.

Tana screeched next to me and at that moment whatever was blocking the glass shredded, and I could see out again. There were proximity alerts flashing on all sides, and I moved us into a more controlled circle, letting the automatics take care of any avoidances needed.

We were surrounded by more air-traffic than I could ever remember seeing, forming a dense cloud of AeroMobile madness stretching into the distance. It looked like a giant cloud of hornets swarming over the city, searching for whatever had kicked over their nest. The closer vehicles were either covered with, or trailing, large improvised banners, their messages clear.

225

"Free Space!"

"Everyone Deserves Space!"

"Atoll Shame!"

"Die Toller Scum!"

The traffic control system must have dumped us in line with one of these banners and it had wrapped itself around the limo. It was pure luck we hadn't hit anything. I sympathized with the crowd's reaction, but the only thing this would achieve was a spike in the AeroMobile death statistics.

Two Zeniths shot towards us, a banner tied between them like a pair of fishing boats trawling for unsuspecting dolphin. How they'd manage to get off the ground in one piece and keep everything together, I couldn't imagine. I lifted the limo higher, shaking my head as they slid underneath.

"Has everyone gone mad?" Tana craned forward as a swarm of vehicles flashed by from random directions.

"You're the one claiming to be getting calls from dead people."

Tana glowered at me. "But this is pure insanity. We have no claim to space."

"Neither do the Atolls."

In a way Tana was right. The people who invented most of their space technology had left Earth long ago and created the Atolls. They were the true children of space. The few thousand from Earth who worked there were strictly part-timers, even if you included the corporate habitats and manufacturing plants. The Atolls had technology, experience, and territory on their side, while Earth had little by comparison, other than population. With the Atolls actively working against us, we had as much chance of enlarging our space activities as we had of holding a snowball fight on the surface of the Sun. But that didn't make them right. The only ace we had was the one everyone celebrated—Devan Rohloff and the *Ananta*—but for how long? If Sarnelli didn't need him anymore, Rohloff's lifespan was probably limited.

I flew the limo out of the local traffic streams into the city skyways and set the Pilot to take us to the hotel in Elkridge. The higher lanes were mostly free from the flying chaos choking the lower airspace, and I hoped it would get quieter as we moved away from the downtown areas.

A flash bloomed among the cloud of vehicles below us, followed by an orange gout of flame that swirled lazily in the air stream. There'd been a collision. I couldn't guess how many were involved and didn't wait to find out.

"They look like demons," Tana whispered. "Fighting over a dying planet."

The sun was setting over the city, rendering the sky a deep orange and lighting up the towering buildings with blood-soaked shadows, making it look like a medieval rendition of hell. It wasn't hard to imagine the AeroMobiles were swooping Devils, picking over the bones. The image sent a chill down my spine. At our best, humanity is the height of Earth's evolutionary development—at our worst, we're monsters barely rising above the slime.

Like many businesses, the *Hilton* had moved inland as the sea-level rose and now formed part of the urban sprawl that covered the highlands east of the city center. The buildings had risen like giant concrete and glass barnacles, overwhelming what had once been a green, tree-filled paradise. I landed the car in the drop-off/pickup parking spot on the roof and called the front desk on the communicator.

The concierge was a real life, genuine, flesh and blood person who sniffed audibly through the screen at me. I don't imagine I looked much like his usual customers, but that didn't matter—wealth cures everything.

He smiled. A trained reflex rather than a welcoming gesture. "Can I help you in some way... sir?"

I didn't let the delay before the word *sir* bother me and broke open my widest grin. What we needed was a distraction to stop him from thinking too much.

"I'm Ms. Blyss' chauffeur. You have a reservation for her under the name of Buntin—the *Dashiell Hammett Suite*."

I rolled down the privacy window halfway. It wouldn't be enough for him to see any details, but he'd be able to make out a woman in the back. If you want to impress someone, make it big.

"Ms. Blyss? The *Hammett*?" His eyes bulged as if he were undergoing explosive decompression. "Krystal Blyss. Right here? I don't see a record of..."

I waited until he'd recovered a little self-control. "We'll be staying for the entire month. Naturally, Ms. Blyss expects complete privacy."

His eyes were on the screens in front of him but flicked up, and his pupils dilated when I mentioned the length of the booking. I'd dropped enough people off at the hotel to know the *Hammett* was their most expensive suite and took up the whole of the thirtieth floor. I figured the possibility of earning well over ten thousand credits, not to mention the cachet of hosting one of the world's biggest entertainers, might soften his attitude.

"Ahhh, yes, Mr. Buntin, I have your reservation. One month in the *Hammett Suite*. You have a credit chip for the advance of course?"

I inserted the chip Dollie had given me into the console. I couldn't help myself from holding my breath as the system verified the account. I had no idea how many credits Dollie had made available, and even if it authorized the payment, I could be bankrupting her. The console flashed green, showing the transaction was good and I let out a slow breath.

"Thank you. I've encoded the suite to your ID. The elevator will take you to the thirtieth floor. You have full access to all VIP features, of course. Is there anything else I can do for you today?"

I shook my head and shut down the communicator, sliding out of the car and moving around to the rear door to open it. Tana needed to act the part—she was a "star" and that guaranteed every available hotel security system would be trained on her.

"Put my jacket over your head and take my hand."

Tana frowned. "Don't be ridiculous."

"Look, you're Krystal Bliss." I leaned in through the door of the limo. "Act like you're famous."

"Who?"

"You never heard *Pump it. Pump it, Baby? The 'Seven Succubi' tour?* Or *Love Wet Loving?*"

Her eyebrows pinched together. "I don't think I want to."

This was taking too long. "Act like you don't want to be seen."

"I don't," she said.

Once she was covered, I guided her to the waiting elevator. As promised, it was keyed to take us to the thirtieth floor.

"You have a disconcerting talent for lying." There was a strange tone in Tana's voice, but I couldn't work out what it meant.

"We can't simply ask Rohloff to meet us."

Less than a minute later we stepped out to ivory-edged gold walls and lush burgundy drapes framing the windows. And this was only the vestibule—two wide doors led to the left and right.

"Ballen? This is..." Tana seemed in shock. "We should leave before we're caught."

It was like trespassing in Xanadu. I'd expected opulence, but this was far beyond that. I felt the same urge as Tana, as if the great Khan himself might catch us at any moment.

The elevator chimed, and I spun around, wondering who it was. I ushered a wide-mouthed Tana through the doors on the left. This room was bigger and more opulent than the entrance and yet still only a "sitting room." I turned on the 3V. It only took seconds to find a Krystal Blyss stream and turn it up until the room was pumping with the music.

I motioned for Tana to stay where she was, then went back to the entrance area and hit the button to allow the elevator to open. As soon as I did, the Concierge bustled inside, trailed closely by two of his staff.

"A small sign of appreciation for Ms. Blyss. To thank her for selecting our humble establishment." He spoke loudly to be heard over the music, even though the soundproofing mostly contained it in the other room.

The first assistant set down a vase containing what must have been at least three dozen mixed roses in an arrangement fringed with white lace trimmings and colorful lilies. They must have been frozen. I couldn't believe they could order some that quickly.

At the same time, the second assistant set down an ornate silver ice-bucket complete with a magnum of vintage champagne. I almost laughed at the offerings—it's truly amazing what "fame" gets you.

"I'll be sure Ms. Blyss receives them," I yelled. "I'm afraid she's busy refreshing herself right now though."

I swiped both assistants' credit chips, giving them extremely generous tips and herded them back into the elevator. I didn't give the Concierge anything though. He'd made a blatant attempt to breach the privacy of a famous guest and should know better.

I returned to Tana and shouted "off" at the 3V. I had to wait a few minutes while my abused hearing recovered from the tortured screams. Krystal Blyss was easy enough on the eyes, but she was probably sponsored by cochlear geneering corporations.

Tana was staring open-mouthed at the main residential area of the suite. My entire apartment wasn't as big as the sitting room, and the furnishings would have cost me a year's salary on the High-Rig, including triple-A hazard pay.

"What are we doing here, Ballen? This is insane."

"We need to get to Rohloff. We can't walk in and ask for his room without alerting him. They have restricted access—only guests and staff can get through the lobby into the residential areas."

"How can anyone afford to live like this?" Tana folded her arms. "It's obscene."

I didn't know the answer to that. But I wondered how much I was going to owe Dollie by the time this was over. At this rate, I'd be in indentured servitude for the rest of my life.

"Now what?" Tana asked.

"We need some outside help." I picked up the hotel phone and tapped in a number. The screen lit up, and Charlie's hangdog face filled the screen.

"Buntin Cabs—how can I... Joe?" Charlie glanced around. "What the hell's going on? We've heard some really bad things about you. The news was full of it."

"I haven't got time to explain, Charlie, but you were right. The Fundies are getting set to make some big moves."

"See, what did I tell you?" Charlie's face cracked with a huge toothless grin. "Everyone said I was mad. They thought I was a crazy old fool. But I'm not eh, Joe?"

I felt bad about tricking Charlie, but it seemed the best way to get his help without having to explain everything. It was too complicated, and he probably wouldn't believe me if I tried. Playing on his weakness was a lot easier, and I hoped he'd forgive me when he found out I'd lied.

"If you're crazy, that makes two of us." Given the circumstances that was probably true. "Look, I need some help. One of their top people is at the *Hilton*, and I need to find out what room he's in. Could you pretend he called a cab? You should be able to worm the room number out of the desk."

"*Hilton*? Room number?" Charlie hesitated, as he tried to push the idea into his head. "Sure, I think... I mean probably. But, is this okay? The cops were here..."

"The cops will be more than happy when they get their hands on this guy." I tried not to sound desperate. He was smart enough to tell if something was wrong, and I needed him to do what I asked, no questions. "The man you're looking for is Devan Rohloff."

"Rohloff? Okay, got it." Charlie scratched his cheek. "Say... the spaceship guy?"

"That's him."

"Well, I'll be. Those Fundie bastards are everywhere." Charlie winked flamboyantly. "Leave it to me, Joe. I'll winkle him out for ya."

"I owe you one. Listen," I tried to sound casual. "Has Dollie been around?"

Charlie jumped. "The boss? No. I mean why should I... that is, well, she ain't in. Not for a couple of days. I ain't seen her or nothing."

His reaction made me suspicious. I don't think Charlie really understood Dollie's hermaphroditism, and I knew he was scared of her. Yet, he was acting like she was unimportant. If she hadn't been in for a few days, I'd expect him to be happy not to have her around.

"Okay, Charlie. Rohloff will be leaving here in the morning, so don't leave it too long. Call me as soon as you have his room number. I'm in the *Hammett* Suite."

Charlie's eyes bulged. "*The Hammett*?"

I hung up and slumped in a barrel-sized armchair, the sumptuous upholstery almost swallowing me whole. Charlie was lying to me about something, and I couldn't figure out what or why. I was worried about Dollie too. I'd expected her to head for the office. That was the most obvious choice. It would be difficult for Gabriella to make a move against her in such a well-traveled and public place—safer there than going back to her apartment for sure.

"How do we do this?" Tana said.

She'd interrupted my thoughts, and it took me a few seconds to refocus on the immediate problem. "Let's see how Charlie does. If he doesn't come through, we'll have to figure something else out."

A licensed taxi driver looking for someone at a hotel isn't exactly suspicious, so no problem there. But Charlie himself was the weakness. I hoped he didn't flake out on me and could get the job done. Strangely, Tana reminded me of him in a lot of ways—both lacked any connection with the real world.

Charlie called back in under an hour—pretty good considering the travel time. I hoped he hadn't got a ticket. I already felt bad enough about involving him.

"He's in seven-two-one." Charlie was watching traffic, not looking at the phone pickup. "Watch yourself, Joe. Those Fundies can be nasty, and they're tricky bastards."

Five minutes later we were outside Rohloff's room. Tana knocked lightly on the door when I nodded, and after a pause, we heard his voice through the speaker.

"Who is it?" he said sharply.

Rohloff probably wasn't in the mood for unannounced visitors after being roused over a taxi he hadn't ordered, but his mood was going to get a lot worse if I had anything to do with it.

"Room service." Tana smiled into the door pickup, holding the bottle high while I stood out of sight. "Champagne, compliments of Minister Sarnelli."

The lock rattled, and the door swung open. Rohloff was in a dark blue *Hilton* robe, clutching a large Scroll full of mathematical symbols and formulas. He was smiling, but the smile vanished when I pointed the pistol at his face.

He took a half-step backwards. "What's the meaning of this?"

"Inside. Now." I gestured with the gun as we pushed into the room. "Do what I say, and you won't get hurt."

Rohloff shuffled back, only stopping when his legs hit a small couch. He glanced behind him then dropped down awkwardly.

His room was smaller than our grand apartment and crowded with the typical mess of hotel furniture. Tana put down the champagne and moved to his left.

"Who *are* you people? This is—" He looked from his Scroll to us and back, as if wondering where we fit in among the formulas.

I smiled broadly. "We're the people you're trying to have killed, Professor."

I knew I had to keep him off balance. With his academic background, I hoped hard accusations would confuse him. If he had time to think he'd quickly realize how little we actually had.

"What are you talking about?" Rohloff's eyes burned, and he reached out. "I'm calling the police."

"We know about you and Doctor Ganz' murder." I pressed his hand down with the barrel of the gun.

"This is insane." Rohloff pulled his hand back as if bitten. "I've n-never even heard of a Doctor Ganz." He glanced at Tana. "You're not going to hurt me. This is some kind of wild scheme. I don't have any money."

All I had were hunches, and it looked like I was batting zero. I hesitated, trying to think of another approach. We needed to rattle him.

"I suppose you've never heard of Doctor Ganz' work on analyzing quantum fluctuations either." Tana stepped in as soon as I faltered. "If you don't remember, I have copies of the conversations between you and Ganz from GARNET—we can always turn them over to the police."

The effect on Rohloff was immediate. He froze for so long I wondered if he'd had a seizure. He tried desperately to produce another smile, but failed completely.

"I'm sure we can clear up whatever m-misunderstanding there is." Rohloff wiped his forehead and edged back on the couch. "And you realize unauthorized accessing of a GARNET account is a crime."

Tana shrugged in dismissal. "I was Doctor Ganz' assistant, fully authorized."

"I didn't mean to imply… That is, I didn't know he was dead." The Scroll he was holding clattered to the floor next to him. "A sad loss to s-science. My involvement w-w-with him was very slight."

His work verified some of my calculations for the Jump field generator."

Tana leaned over. "So you plagiarized his work?"

"What kind of man do you think I am?" Rohloff whispered. "I used his work to check my calculations for the zero-point energy field used by *Ananta*. Ganz' data is fully attributed in my research."

"Did you hire the killers, or did you leave it to your friend, Sarnelli?" I threw the question at him to keep him confused.

"K-killers?" Rohloff frowned, the dark lines on his forehead almost black. "The Minister is in charge of the *Ananta* project—his job is to clear up p-problems."

"And Ganz was a problem," I shouted. "Like we are."

"N-no. Doctor Ganz made some speculations. If they got out, they could have caused questions. Slowed the project down." Rohloff stood and walked towards the bedroom. "I must get dressed. I can't hold a conversation like this."

Tana followed him, not letting up. "Ganz was a problem. His work was a problem. You had him killed."

"No," Rohloff gasped. "I asked Minister Sarnelli to stop him publishing. We couldn't take further delays."

I closed in. "Ganz was thrown from the top of a building. He certainly wasn't going to publish after that."

"I thought... No, he fell. It was suicide." Rohloff rubbed his forehead.

"His body hit the ground so hard, it left marks in the concrete." The memory of Ganz splattered on the sidewalk flashed through my mind. "They had to scrape up what was left of him."

"No," Rohloff half-whimpered. "I'm a scientist..."

"*You* killed him." Tana slapped Rohloff repeatedly. "You! Even if you didn't actually push him."

"Get away from me... Harmon was behind—" Rohloff clamped his mouth shut.

"Who's Harmon?" I pulled Tana back a little. "Were you working with him too?"

Rohloff looked sick. His lips fluttered as though he were trying to smile, but missed by several kilometers. "I'm not... I mean... I don't understand."

"You said *Harmon* was behind something." Tana had brought herself under control again. "Did they kill Hubert?"

Rohloff pressed back against the bedroom door, as though hoping he could sink through it. "Doctor Harmon died in 2137. Check the records."

"Screw that." I slammed my fist into the door next to his ear, and Rohloff jumped. "We saw you talking to Professor Idell earlier. You called us your *little problem* and asked for us to be assassinated."

"A project the size of *Ananta* has many little problems. If you knew anything about GEO space engineering and construction, perhaps you'd understand that."

His dig about space construction hit me as deep as a laser drill stuck in my side. "Listen, you windbag, I've worked on more High-Rig projects than you—"

Tana spoke over me. "So, who was Harmon?"

"Doctor Harmon worked for *me*. He did some minor research in the early days of developing the *Ananta* systems. His role was mostly of a technical nature, hardly vital."

"So what was he behind? Something you'd worked on together? Something he'd worked on with Ganz?" I asked. Tana had picked up Rohloff's Scroll and was searching for something.

"H-he is... *was* a minor contributor." Rohloff seemed to relax the more he talked. "Every project is built on a series of small successes, but I had to push most of the work through. No one believed my dream could work."

Tana jumped back in. "Do you remember a paper entitled *Preliminary Analysis of Quantum Fluctuations and their connection with Zero-Point Energy Fields?*"

"I'm... not sure. It sounds familiar." Rohloff staggered, and I grabbed his arm to steady him.

"It was co-authored by you and the late Doctor Harmon. I would have thought you'd remember something like that."

"I've authored over five hundred publications, young lady. And that was a long time ago."

"Interestingly, Doctor Harmon is listed first—you are given second priority. That's not usual for a *minor contributor* or someone who only had a *technical* role, is it?"

Rohloff's face darkened. "What can I say? I was generous in those days. Before so many of my ideas were stolen."

"That does sound very unselfish." I leaned closer. "Amazingly so, considering the contribution you say he made."

Rohloff made a play of drawing himself up, but it didn't ring true. "My record speaks for itself. I see no benefit in standing here while my bona fides are questioned at gunpoint."

Tana was working on the Scroll even as she spoke. "How about *Warp Drive Theory and Zero-Point Energy Fields: Practicality, Effectiveness and Applicability*? Do you recall that one? That was authored by Doctor Harmon alone."

"I... that is..."

Tana tossed the Scroll onto the couch. "Do you want to tell us the truth about your relationship with Harmon and Ganz, or do *we* call the police?"

Rohloff wobbled to the other side of the room and poured a glass of *Old Alamo* from the drinks trolley. The smell of the sweet whiskey filled the room as he swallowed half of it. "Harmon was my partner in the beginning. We shared a vision to help humanity reach the stars once more. Our future, our children and grandchildren, all of that amounts to nothing if we're trapped on this decaying ball of rock. We need to escape. We've seen what the Atolls are capable of. Do you want to hand the future to them?"

Rohloff wiped his forehead. "He had the knowledge of zero-point energy, I had the engineering background with ship design and materials science. We made a good team, until..."

As interesting as this was, it wasn't the reason we'd come. Although Tana still wanted to find out who killed Ganz, we had much bigger issues to deal with.

I stepped towards him. "Why did you try to have us killed?"

Rohloff took another big swallow of whiskey. "Why do you keep saying that?"

"You talked about getting rid of us." Tana was back in his face once more. "With Idell and Sarnelli."

Rohloff stared at her blankly. "Ganz was working independently. His interest in quantum fluctuations was tangential to our work. But he stumbled onto something and started to spread wild conjectures. He put the entire project at risk and we couldn't allow that."

"So you had him killed." Tana spat the words like daggers.

"Don't be ridiculous. We tried talking to him, but he wouldn't listen. He was intent on publication once he finished his analysis. Then he died. An accident. Or suicide. Who knows?" Rohloff looked from Tana to me and back almost pleading. "But his work would still be damaging if it came out. Sarnelli has been a key supporter of the project inside the government. He offered to help. All I wanted was for publication to be delayed until after *Ananta* launched—after I'd proven my theories were correct."

I broke in before Tana could say any more. "He did much more than delay it. Everyone who worked with Ganz is dead, and they're trying to kill us too."

"That's... that can't be." Rohloff slumped on to the couch, massaging his temples with stiff fingers. "We only needed a delay, that was all. It's been thirty years. Thirty years of my life. So many failures... so many setbacks... I couldn't risk another."

"Black, Acevedo, Ganz." The names came from my mouth like bullets. "All dead, thanks to you. What was so important? What had Ganz discovered?"

"Nothing!" Rohloff's head snapped up. "Nothing. It was wild speculation, below any threshold of significance."

"But enough to have people murdered." I grabbed his collar. "It's time you told all of this to the First Minister. You can explain how insignificant everything was."

"The First Minister? I can't. He'll stop the project. I can't let it end now. Not after all this work. I'm going to call Minister Sarnelli, this minute."

"That's probably not a good idea, *Professor*." Tana looked at him as if he was some kind of diseased bacterial growth. "Sarnelli doesn't think the project needs you anymore. You're marked, just like we are."

Rohloff reached for the hotel phone. "I must make... some calls. Would you excuse me, please?"

I put the gun on the phone and left it there. I didn't care who he wanted to call, the only place we were going was to see the First Minister. All I needed was for Logan to tell us it was arranged. "The police let you make one call, but I'm not that generous."

Tana grabbed him by the arm. "I really think you'll be better off coming with us. It's probably your best chance of staying alive."

Rohloff's eyes jerked wildly, and sweat broke out on his cheeks and forehead. "It's Harmon, isn't it? He's behind this. He can't stand the thought of me finishing the project without him. That the *Ananta* is going to be a success. *My* success, not his."

He squirmed harder, and Tana's grip tightened on his elbow as she pulled him towards the door. She might want revenge, but was going along with my plan, at least for now. Rohloff was helpless against her strength and almost in a trance as she marched him forward.

"But you're with Ganz. He mustn't publish his work. His files must be held. *Ananta* must launch—don't you see that? You must see that. We need to save..." Rohloff hesitated, finishing in a whisper. "...the world."

"Let's get him out of here, Ballen."

Twenty-Eight

Before I could open the door, a knock sounded. My hand tightened on the pistol, and I grabbed Rohloff's arm. "Expecting someone?"

He seemed dazed, as if he didn't really know where he was or what was happening.

"See who it is and get rid of them." I lifted the gun. "I still have this."

I edged back into the room with Tana until we were out of a direct line of sight. It was probably a harmless visitor, but I was tired of being a target for anyone with a gun.

"Who... who's there?" Rohloff called out.

"USP Security," a deep voice called through the thin door. "Minister Sarnelli sent us to ensure your safety with the rioting."

"Sarnelli? Security?" Rohloff fumbled with the lock in his eagerness.

"Wait," I hissed. "It might—"

He swung the door open, and it disintegrated into a cloud of splinters. A deadly hail of gunfire mixed with energy weapons, forming a cone of destruction that reached all the way to the opposite wall. I jumped back, pushing Tana behind me.

The security system triggered. Whether a stray round had struck a sensor, or the energy weapons had triggered it, I wasn't sure. What was left of the door started to close, trapping Rohloff's blood-soaked corpse and temporarily blocking the entrance.

The gunmen might not realize we were there, but they would as soon as they walked in. I pointed my gun around the corner of the entrance and fired a volley of badly aimed shots. I doubted I'd

239

hit anyone, but maybe I could slow them down.

I looked around. There was no other visible exit. I yanked the drapes open. There was a small balcony outside, but the window was sealed. Despite that, it was our only possible chance of escape. I shot a couple of rounds into it, and it exploded in a cloud of twinkling glass pellets.

"Come on."

I pulled Tana through the shattered window, slipping dangerously on the pile of glass shards. The balcony was empty and so small it barely held us both. In a Solido thriller, we'd be able to jump to the next balcony or climb to a different level, but the reality was very different—the nearest balcony was almost fifteen meters away.

"I know you're in there, Ballen."

Gabriella's sweet voice and refined accent were easily recognizable.

"If you come out with your hands up, I promise we won't kill you."

I didn't hesitate. "Okay, we're coming out. Keep your guys in check."

"No, wait. We can't—" Tana hissed. "What are you doing?"

I knew Gabriella's promise meant nothing, but it might gain us a minute or two. I leaned over the balcony to see if there was any way out. The only option was to jump to our deaths—which would save us from Gabriella's tender mercies, but I'd have preferred something that offered long-term survival.

Gabriella's men waited longer than I thought they would. I wondered why they didn't storm the room. It didn't seem likely they were worried about hurting us. I lifted the gun, pointing it towards the doorway. If I was a real hero and there was no way out, shouldn't I try to take some of them with us? It seemed like a stupid idea, even as I thought it.

A heavy whine filled the air, growing louder by the second. At first I thought it was from inside the hotel, but then I realized it was above us. I turned in time to see a cab float down, hovering next to the balcony.

The rear door slid open, offering a tantalizing glimpse of

possible sanctuary. I didn't know who was in the cab, but we didn't have any other options. I grabbed Tana and pushed her to the edge. "Jump!"

She clambered onto the low wall, effortlessly balancing despite the height, then catapulted headlong into the back seat of the cab.

"Last chance, Ballen!" Gabriella yelled behind us.

The cab bucked when Tana landed, the door spinning away from the balcony. The driver steadied the car expertly, and the rear end drifted back towards me. I stood on the wall, hoping my legs would have enough strength to push me across the one-meter gap.

There were shouts behind me, and a heavy pop as a bullet tore into the rear of the cab. I leaned forward, pushing as hard as I could and managed a clumsy half flop that almost sent me tumbling to the pavement eighty meters below. I flailed and caught hold of the seat, my legs hanging outside pathetically. I felt myself slipping and clawed at the upholstery.

More bullets slammed into the sides of the cab, and we lifted, my grip slipping even more. Then a pair of strong hands grabbed me, pulling me inside. The door closed as we climbed, but it was several minutes before I got my breath back and checked who was driving.

"Charlie?"

Charlie didn't look back and banked the car around the hotel and between several other tall buildings. He might be bumbling and confused at times, but he knew how to fly a cab. His movements were light and defined, speaking of years of flying Aeros as efficiently as possible.

"I told you to watch out for those Fundies." He was grinning like his numbers had come up on InstaMillions. "Good job I hung around, eh, Joe?"

I couldn't argue with him, but despite that I felt slightly resentful. After a lifetime of avoiding those kinds of commitments, I was sure racking up debts. Soon I'd be buying Christmas cards from the bulk store.

Charlie piloted the cab low over the rolling hills, heading toward the downtown area. I turned to Tana. "Are you okay?"

"Yes, despite getting shot at on a regular basis."

I felt my anger boil at the touch of truculence in her voice. It wasn't my fault a pack of bloodthirsty killers was chasing us across the city. All I'd done was give someone a cab ride that I'd never been paid for. Then I remembered how she'd pulled me inside the cab and my anger died, leaving me feeling foolish and awkward.

"Thanks for saving me back there," I said.

Tana nodded briefly. Her eyes met mine before she turned toward the window. "So, what now?"

It was a good question, and I wasn't sure myself. "Where are we headed, Charlie?"

Charlie's hands were firm on the controls, but he glanced back momentarily. "That's up to you Joe. I was headed back to Base, but I'll take you anywhere."

The Base was no good. Gabriella and her men were sure to check there. Once again we were animals scrambling for another bolt-hole, with our options dwindling all the time. Not only that, Rohloff's death would undoubtedly land on our doorstep, and we still had no evidence of our innocence.

"Charlie, can you lend me your Scroll?"

"Sure, Joe." He scrabbled one-handed through the pile of receipts and candy wrappers that polluted the center console and finally held out a large plastic rectangle.

It was a miracle of construction. The miracle being that it was still working. The design had to be at least fifteen years old and resembled a modern Scroll the same way clay blocks resembled electronic paper. The screen was a rigid pad—no roll-out dynamic stiffening surface here. The whole thing had to be over a centimeter thick and weighed probably half a kilo. It was faded and discolored through years of use, and the edges were chewed as if it had been the plaything of something with sharp teeth.

I handed it to Tana who raised her eyebrows. "Rohloff didn't want Ganz' files releasing. I know you looked before, but double check. There *has* to be something there."

Tana took the Scroll, balancing it on her knees as if reluctant to touch it. "I'm not sure I know how to use this... *thing*."

"Hey, that's a good Scroll," Charlie called from the pilot seat. "Don't let her talk about it like that, Joe. Why's she being so nasty when I'm trying to help?"

The cab buffeted as a cross wind hit us. "She's upset, Charlie. We've had a rough time."

"Well, she should be more grateful. Just saying, that's all."

Tana lifted her hands in frustration, and I pointed at the slab-like Scroll. "Please try."

Using only the tip of her finger, Tana navigated through the options on the Scroll, tutting softly. "This is so slow and ancient. It's going to take a while, even once I work out how to use it."

Despite its age, she got it working fairly quickly, and her movements became more assured as her familiarity increased.

I turned back to Charlie. "We need somewhere to hide out. Until we can figure out what the hell to do next. Everyone who helps us ends up dead in pretty short order."

"Those Fundies sure are nasty." Charlie whistled a death march. "Nasty, Joe. *Real* nasty."

"We need somewhere off-grid, Charlie. They've been tracking us with Argus. If we're spotted, they'll be back on us like a bad rash."

"Off-grid? Gee, I don't know... I mean that's a tough call these days."

Charlie's home was off-grid, and I knew it. Maybe he didn't want to get involved, but I had the feeling there was more to it than that. I'd been to his place a few times and he'd always made me welcome before.

"Charlie?"

I didn't ask directly. I couldn't. Call it independent pride, or dumb stubbornness. It was the way I'd been since back at the orphanage—either something was given freely, or you didn't take it. Sometimes principles come with an exceptionally high cost—if Charlie had misgivings, I wasn't about to persuade him otherwise.

Charlie was silent for several minutes, so long in fact that I wondered if he'd heard me. When he did answer, he showed no obvious trace of reluctance, despite the wait. "Sure, Joe. You can stay at my place. I got plenty of room, you know that."

"Thanks, Charlie. That's another one I owe you."

Charlie eased the car around and lifted us into the highest speed level. His place was north of Westminster, about a dozen treed acres inside the old Pennsylvania/Maryland border. An old farm from an earlier, gentler time—before we'd screwed up the planet with the insatiable desire to "make a profit" regardless of the actual cost. The land had been in his family for at least two hundred years, he'd told me. Originally the property had been bigger, and his great grandfather had been an honest-to-god farmer—before the corporates sold the world on the idea that it was "better" to buy our crops from the starving.

Tana hunched over the archaic Scroll, peering at its dismal screen. "Find anything?" I asked.

"Nothing since the last time I looked. Did you expect something new to magically appear?"

"I thought..." I took a deep breath. "Maybe you missed something. We *were* kind of rushed at the University."

"Don't project your weaknesses onto me."

I was going to respond. After all, it wasn't as if she was infallible. There was recent, direct evidence to the contrary. But I decided it wasn't worth the argument.

"A file has been deleted," Tana hissed. "I was checking the inventory list. One second it was there, then it wasn't."

"Who could do that?"

"No one. The system of priority would break down if files could simply be deleted from someone's GARNET account. A rival could remove all evidence of your research."

Tana seemed to think that the scientific world was purer and less screwed up than the one the rest of us lived in, but I didn't see it. I was sure access wouldn't be a problem if someone had the right combination of money, power, or both.

"We still have copies of the files."

Tana was jabbing at the controls. "I told you. Those are useless. The only accepted evidence of Hubert's work is the GARNET files. Someone's destroying his legacy."

The cab bucked as we crossed a thermal. I looked out. The skies were darkening as a storm front closed in.

"Can you stop it, Tana?"

"How do you stop something that's impossible?" Tana's nails clicked on the screen. "Another is gone. How are they doing this?"

I could see the files vanishing one by one on the Scroll. "You know this system better than anyone here. There must be *something* you can do."

If we didn't stop it quickly, there'd be nothing left and we'd be even deeper in the mire. Tana gasped and stabbed at the screen.

"Of course! The system has controlled file access. When someone tries to delete a file I'm editing I'll get a message saying who it is."

"How does that help?" A flash of lightning flooded the skies, closely followed by a rumble of thunder.

"I don't know." Tana nervously tapped the edge of the Scroll, thin layers of brittle plastic flaking off as she did. "It's all I can think of."

"I'm going to have to switch to a lower skyway, Joe," Charlie said. "That storm looks bad."

I ignored him, keeping my eyes on the Scroll in Tana's hands. A few seconds later a message popped open. "What does it say?"

She didn't answer me. Reaching into her pocket, she pulled out the Scroll she'd used outside Sigurd's, tossing Charlie's to one side.

"What are you doing, Paresh?" Tana screamed when the call connected. "Stop this madness."

I couldn't hear the other side of the conversation, but I could well imagine Paresh's reaction. I picked up Charlie's Scroll—it showed an access request by Hubert Ganz, followed by a network identification.

"You know what I'm talking about." Tana's words were harsh. "How did you get Dr. Ganz' access? You can't erase his life's work. What gives you the right?"

"How I got access is not your business." Paresh's supercilious voice grated through the speaker. "He was a senile fool more interested in having sex with his students than doing quality research. His work is nothing."

"I'll bring charges against you with the Ethics Committee," Tana sobbed. "I'll make you pay for this."

"Do you *really* think the committee would be interested in bringing charges against a foreign student?" I sensed his smug grin, even without seeing him. "That wouldn't help their international profile, would it? Besides, I have friends."

The list of files was now about half what it had been. Paresh wasn't giving into Tana's demands, no matter what she said, and I wished she'd punched him harder.

"Your *friends* have already looked there. You've looked. I've looked. There's nothing in his files." Tana's was pleading. "This is pure spite."

"Call it what you want, *chinaal*." Paresh spat the last word. "But my friends could still help you. I'd be happy to put in a word for you."

Tana sniffed. "In exchange for certain *considerations*, no doubt."

Paresh's laugh was loud. "There is a price for everything, Tana."

There was only one file left and I realized it must be the one Tana had opened. It would probably stay there until she released it. I gestured at her to mute the phone. "If you close the file it's gone?"

Tana nodded.

"Is there anything else you can do with it?"

"I can copy the contents to a file of my own, but that wouldn't help. The traceability to Ganz would be lost." Tana pointed at the screen. "It isn't even an important file, just a list of Hubert's teaching duties."

"That's all?" I was bewildered.

"I didn't specifically choose it." She looked furious. "It was the first one there."

"Then that's what we have. Anything else?"

"What is it, Tana? Afraid to speak?" Paresh's voice crackled from the speaker. "No, of course not. How stupid of me—what game are you playing now?"

Tana unmuted the Scroll. "Do you think Sarnelli will protect you? He's only using you to do his dirty work."

"You are concerned for me? I'm flattered." Paresh scoffed. "But I think you have bigger problems."

Tana swiped over Charlie's Scroll, and a new display appeared. A few gestures and she closed all the windows, then the screen updated and the file list was empty. Any vital information Ganz might have had was gone—other than valueless copies.

"Make sure you clean the archives, Paresh. It wouldn't do for someone to dig around and find all those missing files." Tana looked away, unsuccessfully blinking back tears.

"It's all under control." Paresh hesitated. "If you want me to help you, come to my rooms. You will have to be *very* convincing though."

Tana trembled. "Not if I were dead."

"That may very well be the result," Paresh said grimly. "You know where to find me."

The phone went silent.

"That was hard on you." Tana flinched when I touched her arm. I hated to push her at that moment. "Did you get anything?"

Her shoulders dropped, and when she spoke her voice quivered. "I don't think so. All I could do was copy the file and its properties. That was all I could think of, but it's routine information. They may not be able to get at the archives—access is more restricted than on the working file system—but they seem to have thought of that too."

Despair dropped over me like a lead-lined radiation suit. The storm seemed to be passing us as we flew on, but the clouds inside me weren't so easy to clear. Yet another sliver of opportunity had evaporated even as we watched, powerless to fight. I stared at the space between my feet for a long time.

The cab lurched slightly as we touched down and a second later the doors slid open. "Everybody out," Charlie announced cheerily.

The storm was a dark patch hovering in the distance over the city, and we stepped out into a rain washed freshness. But even the sunshine couldn't lift the black mood that wrapped around me and tied my thoughts into useless knots. To put it in purely scientific terminology, we were completely fucked.

Twenty-Nine

Charlie bustled around like a mother hen, guiding us inside the rustic log-faced home that was nestled in a stand of cedar trees. At this time of year, the landscape was bare and wintry even though we no longer got any snow. Inside it looked, well, like a junkyard and even worse than the last time I'd visited. At one time it had been a clean, efficient interior, modern by twenty-first century standards, but piles of assorted tubing, boxes, and electronics formed a scattered mess that covered almost every inch of flooring. In many ways, it was the perfect example of bachelor living and probably explained why he lived alone.

"Wait!" Tana stopped, her hands clenching. "Why didn't I think of that before?" She turned to me, a triumphant look on her face. "Acevado said *It's in the files.*"

"Yeah, the customary death-bed revelation." The reality was that she'd probably only been thinking some variation of *Oh shit… I'm dying!* Whatever it was, we'd never know. "You've checked Ganz' files and found nothing."

"I need to keep this." Tana pointed to Charlie's Scroll.

He shrugged, his stick-like shoulders wriggling inside his baggy shirt. "Feller can't rely on things like that, makes him too dependent. In fact, I think I have another one around here just like it."

Charlie started to dig through one of the mounds of trash, almost vanishing in an eruption of dust and random shreds of paper. There was a musty smell that grew stronger the more he dug.

I tapped him on the arm. "It's okay, Charlie. She only needs this one."

"You sure? Cuz I know I got another one somewhere."

"I'm sure." I helped him away from the pile. "Do you need anything else, Tana?"

"A quiet place to sit while I work."

Charlie dumped a pile of magazines off an armchair. I tried to remember when the last for-real paper-printed magazine had come out. It must have been over seventy years ago. You never saw them anymore, outside of a museum. Sure we had electronic flimsies that were similar, but nothing with pages you actually had to turn.

Charlie smacked the chair several times, raising an even bigger cloud of dust. "Is that okay?"

Tana was coughing, but she pulled the chair over by the already glowing fireplace and curled up on it. She immediately started swiping at the Scroll's surface. It must be a blessing to shut everything out and concentrate on a single problem like that. I felt as needed as a spare leg.

Charlie disappeared into the kitchen. He returned with two giant beer steins and handed one to me. Each one must have held at least a liter, and my arm muscles strained at the unaccustomed weight. I took a drink, and my taste buds seemed to melt. It was as smooth as it was golden, the hops brewed to a mellow taste like liquid honey and chilled to a thirst-quenching level that made you want to guzzle it forever.

"I make that from my own water. Got a drill-hole. Goes down seventy meters, right into the rock."

He offered the second stein to Tana, who didn't even look up to shake her head. Charlie shrugged and took a long draft himself, smacking his lips noisily when he lowered the mug.

We wandered outside to the porch and sat on a weathered bench, the gray wood worn smooth through age and long use. The air was sweet despite being cold, and I looked out appreciatively at the rolling countryside as I swallowed another mouthful of the heavenly beer.

The last time I'd visited had been summer, and Charlie's place had been noisy with the buzz of everything from insects to frogs, but right now it was still and only a few degrees above freezing. Despite that, it would be good to have a place like this. Being able to escape the bustle and grime of the city whenever you wanted and shut everything out would be paradise. It wouldn't happen on my pay though—driving a cab brings in more of a survival income than anything. Without my small medical pension, I'd have been struggling. Not that Dollie was stingy—she paid higher rates than were usual—but there's only so much you can pay someone and remain competitive.

I wondered what it would cost to buy a place like this new. It was probably a few million credits at least. I raised my glass to Charlie. "If you're looking to add anyone to your will, keep me in mind."

"It's sure nice out here. Do you ever think about things, Joe? Life and so on. Remember how it used to be before we screwed everything up?"

I'd never thought about it for the simple reason that I'd never seen it. By the time I slid into the world, the human race had already messed up the planet. The world's leaders had collectively ignored the problem of climate change. All too busy *fiddling* with the interests of mega-corporations, while *Rome* sank rather than burned. What rising sea levels couldn't reach, the human disasters of greed and resource maldistribution did—and the ensuing riots destroyed much of the polluted mess left behind.

I remembered sitting around a campfire at Logan's family ranch as the embers darkened, his grandfather reciting a story that drifted around the clearing like woodsmoke. The story told how an ancient tribe settled around a beautiful lake. The ground was fertile and grew anything planted, game was abundant and easy to trap or hunt. Children were raised to respect the lake as the source of all their wealth, with mothers admonishing the young, "Don't pee in the lake."

The population grew, consuming more and more of the bounty. After a while the younger ones started to ignore the advice of their elders, thinking it was the out-of-date whining of old curmudgeons. As more people peed in the lake, it became increasingly polluted until it was impossible to drink or bathe in it. People were forced to look further and further for clean water, but it was too late. Eventually, the water turned to sterile acid in which nothing could survive. The animals left or died, the fields turned brown, and nothing would grow. Finally, the people gave up, leaving behind the dead lake in search of another paradise.

Now we'd used up all the "lakes." I felt angry. The people who could have avoided this had wiped their hands, taking no responsibility for *their* actions and cheerfully handed the mess down to their descendants. All so they could live in happy oblivion.

"If it was all like this"—I waved my stein toward the horizon and took a big swallow of beer—"it must have been fantastic."

"We did terrible things, Joe. Terrible. Even worse was what we didn't do." Charlie shook his head. "We lied. Told ourselves nothing mattered. And we could fix *anything*. But we couldn't fix nothing, and it did matter. Now all we got left is wreckage. It's all just wreckage."

I thought I heard Charlie sob but wasn't sure. He stood and took my stein. "I'll refill these."

Poor Charlie. I couldn't imagine what it must have been like to live as part of the *culture of selfish waste*, then see the results of it unfurl before your eyes. I leaned against a post, watching the sun as it chased past the horizon. The leafless trees clawed at the burning red skies--it looked like the whole world was on fire. Maybe it was, maybe we really were on our last legs and deserved it.

I lowered my head, unable to face the sunset anymore. I imagined humanity being viewed by an alien race. We'd look like a pathetic self-destructive mass of ants grubbing through the decaying remnants of a world we'd already destroyed. Right then, I felt as old and worn out as the Earth. Was anything left for us? The Atolls barred us from space, and more of the world disintegrated around us each day. The old corporations still controlled most of the wealth, only now mostly from orbit—far away from the destruction they'd created.

I hated what we'd become, while at the same time dreaming of all that we might have achieved. It wasn't self-hatred, it was far beyond that. A frozen numbness. At that moment I couldn't drag up even the slightest emotion or care for anything. It didn't seem to matter if I lived or died. Or whether humanity did either. I heard a noise behind me and reached back, expecting another beer. "Thanks, Charlie."

"I love watching a grown man wallow in self-pity."

I jumped up. Dollie was standing in the doorway. She looked pale, as though she'd been crying and was wearing a long gray *something* that covered her like a sack—not the kind of thing I'd ever expect to see her dressed in. Her eyes were deep fiery pools as the sunset reflected in them.

"Are you chasing me?" Her words trembled. "I thought you had what you wanted."

"I didn't know you were here."

Dollie ignored me. "You made your choice. Where is *she*?"

"We... I... needed evidence to clear me... us. What's wrong with that?"

The muscles in my chest tightened. Although Tana was difficult sometimes, there was something about her that connected with me. I wasn't sure what that connection meant exactly. It might have been an attraction or maybe my damned sense of obligation kicking in. Hell, it could actually be a genuine sympathy for another human being.

"You're a grown up, Joe. You can figure it out by yourself."

I spotted Charlie in the shadows of the doorway and warned him off with a small shake of my head. He scuttled into the depths of the house, not wanting any part of us.

"Dollie, I like you a lot. You've helped me in so many ways that I can't begin to express my gratitude to you. And I respect you too. You're my boss, but more than that, you're my friend." I stepped closer. "You've made a life that most people wouldn't dare think of, let alone do, *and* you've made a success of it. But even with all that, you don't own me."

Dollie looked sad. "Who'd want to own your broken down carcass?"

"Medical researchers?"

"Even they're not that desperate." She took several deep breaths. "I can't do it. I can't stay mad at you, no matter how much I want to."

I bowed dramatically. "Must be the Irish charm in me."

"The only Irish inside you is whiskey."

"True enough. Sadly, all I have is beer right now." I held out my hand. "Friends?"

Dollie looked at my hand for a few moments, then her arms locked around me so tightly I could hardly breathe. Her hair tickled my chin, and my nostrils filled with the aroma of wild strawberries. "Be careful with her, Joe. You could break someone's heart pretty easily."

I held her for several minutes before pulling away. Dollie's eyes were wet, and I didn't know what to say. Any words I could think of seemed callous, trivial, or both.

"I've found it!" called Tana from inside the house.

Dollie got to the door first, but only because I was reluctant to trample her underfoot. I followed her into the living room where Tana was jumping up and down like she'd unlocked the chemical composition of Unobtainium.

Charlie was clapping his hands and stamping his foot as if he was at a barn dance. "She's crazy, Joe. I like her."

"This is tagged as collaborative work between Hubert and Dr. Acevado." Tana swiped through several pages on the Scroll. "It must be what they've been looking for."

I peered at the screen, but it was meaningless. The scrawl of indecipherable symbols could have contained the secrets of the Universe or the recipe for Ganz' favorite breakfast cereal. "What does it say?"

"This isn't really my field." She bit her lip. "It's an analysis of low-level quantum state probability."

"And this was in Ganz' files?" Dollie tried to get a closer look at the pad.

"What? No. It would have been found immediately. This is *Acevado's* GARNET account."

I looked from Tana to Dollie. "It was in *her* files?"

"There for everyone to see." Tana was still scrolling through the data. "They were so focused on Hubert, they didn't think to look."

Dollie looked grim. "You might want to take copies of those files."

I half expected Tana to give Dollie the sermon on why copies were useless, but instead, she nodded. Her fingers danced on the Scroll. "These numbers are strange."

I wanted to tear the Scroll out of her hands. This might be the key to what was going on, and the delay as she worked through the data was maddening. I stuffed my hands in my pockets, knowing there was no point—I'd probably have trouble understanding even the title.

"Strange how?" Dollie asked.

"If I'm reading this correctly," said Tana, "the kaon decay rates are asymmetric. That might be caused by a shift variance of quantum fluctuations in space-time. Hubert and the others were analyzing the results. I was too, though I didn't realize it."

People often accuse engineers of descending into the abstruse, but for my money, scientists beat us hands down. I had a rough idea of what kaons were, but that was all. I noticed Dollie's face cloud over and spoke up before she did.

"What does that mean, in simple terms?"

"Kaons are subatomic particles created and destroyed continuously in the chaos of quantum foam all around us. They decay in known ways and at known rates that never change."

That seemed clear enough—I could follow it at least, but there must be more to it for Tana to get so excited.

Tana frowned. "The rate of decay is determined by a quantum property known as *strangeness*. If the rates change, it has to be because of fluctuations in the quantum world. Does that make sense?"

I thought I understood what she was saying but still didn't see the significance. Random events can always produce variances— that's what *random* means.

"But the randomness isn't as random as it should be?" Dollie seemed to catch on to what Tana was saying, but sounded doubtful.

"Exactly. The randomness should—over time—produce predictable results. As the quantum particles flash in and out of existence, the end result should be zero. What Hubert and Acevado found was that the results didn't average out properly."

"Okay. That's... interesting..." I was struggling here. Interesting to a physicist maybe, but not exactly a neon sign saying *here's the real killer*. I'd hoped for something that would give us the motive for the murders, something substantial enough that we could take to the First Minister.

"You don't see." Tana's grip tightened on the Scroll. "The randomness fluctuated. The analysis shows there are patterns to the variances."

What was it with Tana? Here we were with the police and a pack of killers trailing us and she was getting excited about some minor quirk in experimental data? I was about to say so, but Charlie spoke up.

"That can't happen. There ain't no patterns to natural random events. Any fool knows that."

Tana nodded and looked at me. Suddenly it clicked. "The variances had structure? So they're not natural. It was *communication?* From where?"

"Hubert thought it was from another Universe, co-existent with ours, but occupying different dimensions."

The idea of parallel universes had been kicking around the fringes for a couple of centuries at least, but no one had ever shown they were real. They were a possibility allowed for in multi-dimensional space-time, but being possible didn't mean they existed—nothing prevented the world from being destroyed by the monsters in your closet, but that didn't make them real either.

"Did they decipher any of what they detected?" Dollie asked.

"Not that I can see. That's what Acevado was working on." Tana walked to the half-shuttered window, peered out momentarily then turned back to face us. "One more thing. The fluctuations changed periodically. Intensifying in line with the tests on the *Ananta's* space drive."

That seemed ridiculous. Even if these minor variances had a pattern that could mean they were a form of communication. *And* that they could be *interpreted* as being from another Universe. What connection could they have to the *Ananta?* It didn't make sense, unless—

"*Ananta's* space drive is powered by zero-point energy fields." I remembered the briefings from when I'd been putting together the crew to work on her construction. "Energy from nowhere, we always called it. Stealing energy from the quantum froth. An almost inexhaustible power supply, *if* it could be made to work."

"Hubert went further. He believed that the field effects of the space drive spilled into the other Universe." Tana blinked rapidly. "Quantum effects in our Universe are indescribably tiny, but would that be the same in an alternate Universe? Warped through different dimensions, who knows what scale they operate on. What are quantum fluctuations here could destroy whole worlds, star systems, or galaxies. Operating that ship might cause extinction-level events in another universe. The notes show they discussed this possibility."

"We don't know that though." My mouth was dry. "Did he have any evidence?

"Nothing to show they'd confirmed anything. Hubert strongly believed it though." Tana rubbed her eyes, tears suddenly spilling down her cheeks. "I remember picking up his concerns about the ship when we..."

Tana glanced over at Dollie, her words stabbing out between gritted teeth. "When we stimmed. I never understood why he felt that way. Now I do."

"That don't matter none. People don't care about those things now. Maybe they used to, but not now." Charlie burrowed his nose in the heaped froth on top of his beer. When he lifted back up, the suds matted his mustache into a bushy white line.

"You listen. That ship ain't nothing but a testing ground. If they make it work there, we'd have power for anything. Nothing could stop us. Power from nothing. The Fundies, Pan-Asia, the Atolls— we'd beat all of 'em."

Charlie was right. If it worked, the USP would have the upper hand. Success is derived from the control of power. Whatever the problem, just about anything can be solved if you have enough of it. That was what tripped up the generations during the *denial decades*. They acted as if they had inexhaustible power, but in reality, their resources were all too limited.

"They'll make all the same mistakes." Charlie's voice cracked. "They'd kill what's left of the world even quicker."

"Never mind that." Dollie clenched her fist. "What would happen if it got out that this *free energy* killed intelligent beings in another Universe?"

Tana spoke first. "There'd be a complete investigation. And while that was happening the project would be frozen."

"And anyone with a vested interest would do almost anything to hide that," Dollie said.

I edged over to the peaked set of cathedral windows that stretched up two floors to the vaulted ceiling. Most of the glass was boarded up now, but some of the bottom panes were still functional. I watched the last red sliver of the sinking sun, trying to imagine how the world would look with infinite power. "All we have is speculation on very marginal data. It's supposition—not proof."

"It was enough to get all the people working on it killed." Dollie pointed to each of us. "And nearly get us killed by being tangentially involved. As Chaos said, no one could stop the USP with all that power. Sarnelli is betting on that to make him the First Minister, and it'll probably work too. He'd stop at nothing for that kind of political advantage."

"This can't be." Tana was still working on the Scroll and looked up. "Ballen, this is impossible."

"You've found something else?"

"I was checking the access logs from the file I copied from Hubert's account. Rohloff said Dr. Harmon used to work with him, but died. I've verified that." Tana held up the pad showing a grainy picture of a gaunt man with a scruffy beard. This is his obituary—he died of incurable cancer thirty years ago. I thought perhaps Rohloff was lying. Hiding the fact that he'd stolen Harmon's work."

"Is this significant?" Dollie asked.

"I don't know." Tana spoke quietly but deliberately. "But there's a record of someone using Harmon's ID to access Hubert's files last week."

I felt a tingle run down my spine. "Could someone have stolen Harmon's identity?"

Tana tapped on the Scroll. "It's possible, but something that also bothers me is the signal location. It came from the former Brookhaven National Laboratory. Harmon was working there at the Sustainable Energy Department when he died."

"Former?" I asked in unison with Dollie.

"It was part of the old US Research network before the USP was formed and was closed down when Long Island seceded."

Charlie looked around slack-jawed. "If it's on *The Island* it's as good as nowhere."

Tana nodded, and Dollie let out a low whistle.

Thirty

I was sitting on Charlie's porch, buried in the depths of a big Adirondack chair. The windows were shuttered, and the only light came from the fat gibbous moon hanging close to the horizon. My breath frosted in the cold night, and I'd wrapped up in a couple of heavy blankets purloined from Charlie's seemingly bottomless supplies.

I heard a creak and glanced round as Dollie slipped into the seat next to me. She handed me a steaming mug of coffee and sipped from one of her own. For several minutes we sat there watching the speckled glow of the stars above us.

It's impossible to really appreciate the stars in the city. The lights and haze spoil the view, to the point that even the great Milky Way fades into obscurity. Even in space, you didn't usually see that—spaceships and windows aren't ideal partners. About the only time you could really see it was on a space-walk, and only when shadowed from the fierce brightness of the sun.

"It must be nice up there, away from all this," Dollie murmured.

"The High-Rig's mostly a working town, but Luna Free State can be fun. Would you like to go?"

"Is that a proposition?" Dollie's voice was quiet, as if not wanting to intrude on the peaceful night, but still held a hint of challenge.

"What if it's true?" I said. "What if Tana's right? What if Ganz was right?"

An owl hooted in the moonlight, as though deriding our conversation. Dollie looked more serious than I'd ever seen her. "You mean if there are aliens in another universe and the starship is screwing with it?"

I nodded. "We wouldn't know any more about them than we do about microscopic life here on Earth. Sure, it's there. If we look hard enough we can find it, but on a day-to-day basis, we're not even aware of it. How many species have we killed off in the past? How many are we still killing? Just walking around we step on God knows how many insects."

"Not only insects," Dollie said. "By breathing in and out, don't we kill thousands of bacteria and viruses? It can't be helped, Joe. It's life."

"We're not talking about microscopic life though. It's intelligent. It's trying to communicate."

Dollie shrugged. "We have a long history of killing without thought. For food, for sport, for profit, and countless other reasons. Life is one long death struggle."

"You sure make it sound like fun." I smiled briefly. "That doesn't make it right though."

Dollie sighed. I thought it was exasperation, but then I realized it was actually sadness. "What's *right*, Joe? Do you know? Right isn't universal. What's right for Earth isn't what's right for the Atolls. What's right for humanity isn't right for other species, even if we care about them and maybe need them. There are microbes inside us that help us live, but many die in the process. Should we nobly sacrifice our own existence for theirs?"

"That's different." I knew what she meant, but it wasn't the same. "We're talking about much more complex life forms versus simple ones. We deserve life more than them."

"I'm sure they'd say the same if they could argue their case."

I lifted my coffee cup, but stopped. "It doesn't bother you?"

"In an abstract sense maybe. Look, Joe, we're pragmatists. Let's say it's all true, and there are human analogs in another dimension who die every time that starship flies. What then?"

That was the big question. What should we do, if anything? "We should stop the launch, at least until they can investigate further. Don't you think?"

"Maybe. Turn it around. Say there were some beings in another dimension that were doing things that affected our universe. Would you want them to stop?"

I sipped my coffee. "That would depend on what the effects were."

"Think big. Let's say they're causing stars to go boom." She made an explosive gesture with her hands. "Destroying entire planets. Wiping out entire species."

I couldn't remember us ever having a conversation like this. Maybe some of Tana was rubbing off on us. "Well, of course, I wou—" I stopped. Stars already went nova so it could be happening even as we talked.

"The complex elements in our Universe were created in stellar explosions. Without them, nothing around us would even exist. Including us. Isn't that so?"

She had a point. Everything we know, including us, is made of elements created in nova from the early days of the universe. If those explosions hadn't happened, we wouldn't exist.

I frowned. "We don't know that's what's happening here."

"We also don't know if it *is* what's happening." Dollie paused. "People used to think there were no consequences to their actions and look what happened—they nearly destroyed the world and each other."

She sighed. "I don't believe in hurting things unnecessarily, but surely there have to be limits? No one can take infinite responsibility. There has to be a cut-off point, otherwise wouldn't life simply stagnate from inaction? And we've been stagnating under the Atolls for a long time."

I slapped my coffee down on the flat arm of the chair, the loud crack obliterating the night silence. Something scrabbled away at the noise, probably a rodent. They didn't hibernate the way they used to. "Damn it, we've lived under the Atolls for too long. I want *Ananta* to succeed. It's time we moved out from Earth."

"Then we're going to have to tread on some toes." Dollie took a deep breath. "We're a rough and tumble bunch. I don't think that will ever change."

I looked up at the sky. The latest animated message appeared on the OpenSkyBoard high above us, sending a special greeting to someone down here on Earth. I still remembered the commotion the board caused at the time it went live, even though I'd only been a kid. "You think we should let it launch?"

"That's your call, Joe."

"Well, what about Long Island?"

"You make your own decisions, remember?"

I looked out across the monochromatic fields, baleful moonlit shadows waving all around us. The night was with us in all its frightening darkness, and morning seemed like a distant dream. The future is a scary place—it always is until you get there.

We'd gone back inside as the temperatures dropped to a point where it was too chilly even with blankets. Tana and Charlie huddled around the stone chimney that formed a centerpiece of the living room, the fire radiating cozy warmth in all directions. The fire wasn't real, of course—but Charlie had modified a super-efficient infra-red unit to sit neatly where logs would have once burned.

"There's no way in." Dollie squatted on her haunches next to the fireplace, looking like a cat waiting to pounce. "You can't simply drive up to the gate and say *Please let me in, I'm looking for a dead scientist.*"

She was right. Originally Long Island's perimeter wall was a way to stop the rising water—that it was equally effective at keeping out "undesirables" was an unforeseen bonus. After the initial construction, it had been extended and independent traffic control enforced. No one entered without the requisite permits and authority.

Depending on your viewpoint, Long Island is the last bastion of "free commerce," a fortress to protect the undeserving rich or a symbolic expression of everything money can buy. After being almost wiped out several times, super-storm Sumner finally dealt the death-blow. Queens was flattened, and the Bronx left swimming under a few meters of water. That's when the evacuations started, and once the poor were excluded, not letting them back was easy.

"That would be true if we used a regular car." I saluted Charlie with my refilled stein. "But there's another option."

Charlie's eyes widened, and he slid back in his chair, putting his beer down so heavily that the straw-colored liquid slopped over the table. "I can't let you have her, Joe. She's my pride and joy. No way. You're going to have to find another ride. 'Sides, I'm the only one who can handle her."

Charlie's reaction surprised me, and I tried to catch his eye, but he focused on the flames dancing in the fireplace. After a short silence, I spoke up. "We don't have a chance without it."

"What are you two talking about?" Tana looked up from the Scroll. She'd carried on working on it, digging for more on Harmon. "You're not making sense."

"Chaos has an old Broadsword. A military transport from about thirty years ago. No way that pile of junk will fly." Dollie shook her head. "It's not traffic-controlled—needs a qualified pilot. Preferably one with a brain."

I ignored Dollie's barb. "I can fly anything. All I need is thirty minutes to get familiar with it."

"I think Charlie's more worried about getting his car back in one piece." Dollie snorted. "With the way you destroy cabs, I'm not surprised."

I sighed. "Stop making him nervous. I haven't had a single accident."

"Uh huh… What's the total so far this week?"

I glared at her. "That's different."

"Not from where I'm sitting."

I wasn't sure whether to take Dollie seriously. Sometimes she's harder to read than maintenance reports. "Pay no attention to her, Charlie. You know I'm a good pilot."

Charlie looked away. "Sure, Joe. I know that."

Usually, I'd have backed off as soon as I sensed Charlie's reluctance, but I was stuck. Without the Broadsword there was no way to get to Long Island to investigate further. I stood and walked closer to the fire, the heat from the burning logs prickling my skin.

At the time of the disaster, Long Island's population contained around seventy percent of the wealth on this side of the continent. Now it's what economists call a *pure consumption-based society*. The only thing the residents make is money and lots of it. Their day-to-day needs get brought in through the wall, along with hordes of the unwashed, to do the work those rich, delicate hands wouldn't care to touch.

"Charlie? I'd really appreciate it."

He didn't say anything, but he still didn't make eye contact. He took a long draft from his stein, the beer froth sticking to his grizzled mustache, making him look like a rabid old bloodhound. He stood and wiped his mouth with the back of his hand. "Sorry, Joe. Can't help you."

He turned and shuffled into the depths of the house, vanishing into the shadows.

Dollie looked at me and shrugged. "I'll talk to him." She hopped up from her place by the fire effortlessly. "Don't worry."

I wasn't worried. I'd been living on borrowed time since Ganz did his terminal swan dive, and my stress fuses were pretty much burned out. All I really felt was numb. "Leave him, Dollie. Everyone has the right to make their own choices."

She gave me a strange look, her eyes locking with mine for several seconds. I wondered what she was thinking right then. The moment vanished in an instant, and she left. "And then there were two." I chased down the last of the beer.

"It's definitely language. I'm sure of it."

Tana's eyes looked like molten metal as the reflected light from the fireplace combined with the glow from the Scroll. She was so still, you could almost imagine her atoms freezing in position.

"You've lost me." I tried to force my brain cells to reignite, but they resisted.

"The signals Ganz found. There's a lot of analysis, much of it Paresh's." She sounded almost awestruck and for once said his name without a trace of venom. "He specializes in Optimality theory, a way of universally analyzing language structures. His work shows almost categorically that intelligent beings from another dimension are trying to communicate."

"What? Are you sure?"

"The evidence is right there." Tana tapped the Scroll. "It's at least two, probably three-sigma."

I dredged up the remnants of half-forgotten statistics classes from over fifteen years ago. Three-sigma wasn't enough to be classed as formal *proof*, but it meant the probability of it being accidental was less than one percent.

"But even if that gets confirmed, we're still helpless."

"They have to stop the *Ananta* launch. Until there's further analysis of the readings, they can't possibly go ahead."

I tried not to sigh and failed. The world didn't work like that. To a politician, probability only translates to fact if it gets them elected. "They won't believe it. They'll dismiss it as the ravings of a lunatic."

"I thought you wanted to stop this?" Tana waved the Scroll in the air. "Isn't that what we're trying to do?"

I sat down heavily. "Right now, all I want is for people to stop shooting at me long enough to let me die of old age."

"Are you really that selfish? I suppose I shouldn't have expected any more though. You're just like the others." Tana took a deep breath. "We *have* to stop that ship."

I stood up again, the chair grating against the bare wooden floorboards. "No. We *have* to prove we weren't involved in the deaths of Ganz and the others."

Tana glowered at me. "How do you suggest we do that? We're stuck aren't we?"

"Not necessarily. If we can find whoever's impersonating Harmon, maybe that'll be enough." It was the only strand we had left. We had to pull it and hope it didn't break, like the others had. "Whoever's doing that knows what's going on and can prove everything. They can testify against the lot of them—Sarnelli, Rohloff, and Idell."

Tana jumped out of the chair and marched to her room. I felt a cool draft against my skin.

"Sorry to be such a disappointment." I gulped the last of my beer. "And then there were none..."

Thirty-One

I have a special talent for winding people up, and it seemed like this was one of those magic nights when it was operating at full strength. I thought of checking if Charlie had any whiskey, but decided I should face the morning with a vaguely clear head. The inside of the cabin seemed claustrophobic, so I grabbed my jacket and headed outside.

The moon had risen higher, covering the fields around the house with a pearly light that shadowed everything. I shuffled around the building, following the outside walls. I hoped if I walked for a while it might lift the mawkish feeling.

Twenty meters from the back of the house was a barn. The main beams were crooked, and the roof line dipped like a bowl. It looked like it had last been used some time before the last ice age. I realized I'd not seen the Broadsword anywhere, so unless Charlie kept it off site, the barn was the likeliest place. Okay, sue me, I was feeling nosy.

I wandered over, picking my footing carefully in the muddy ruts only partially visible in the pale light. The door hung slightly open on the remnants of one rusty hinge, so I slipped through. There was a very faint light from somewhere, but it took a couple of minutes for my eyes to adjust to the gloom. In the middle of the dirt floor was a large shape covered by a tarp. That had to be the car.

I pushed the cover back, peering at the squared off armored paneling. It was bigger than I'd imagined, about the same size as a limo and maybe a bit wider. And ugly wasn't the word. From the jutting nose to the oversize engine covers and awkwardly cut-off tail, it screamed a triumph of function over form. My engineer's eye told me the design was solid enough, but aesthetically it looked like a bulldog that had been in a fight with an excavation drone.

A noise from the other side of the car startled me. I tiptoed around, and there was Charlie next to the Broadsword, holding a large calibration wrench over his head, ready to beat my brains out.

"Hey, Charlie," I said quietly. "It's me."

"Joe? What the hell? You spooked me good. Thought maybe it was one of those goons been chasing you. How come you're creeping about out here and not with the women?"

"You know how it goes." I shrugged. "Sometimes everything you say is right—sometimes everything's wrong. There's no reason to it."

Charlie fished around in the darkness, and a moment later several dusty light-strips lit up the inside of the barn, casting long shadows on the gray wooden walls and a stack of auxiliary rocket boosters. The paint on the boosters was eaten away with a combination of rust and old fuel stains. They looked about as stable as a crate of twenty-year-old mining charges.

The Broadsword looked smaller in the light, but only by a few microns here and there. Charlie pulled the rest of the tarp off, revealing the full extent of the deep blue-black paint. The car came with built-in stealth field generators. The fact that someone had taken the time to polish the skin spoke about the care lavished on it.

I sauntered around the car. It looked tough enough to drive you to hell and out the other side without taking so much as a scratch. I'd held out the secret hope that Charlie might change his mind and allow us to use it, but seeing its pristine condition made me doubt that. "You sure dropped lucky on this one, Charlie."

He blinked several times, and for a moment I thought he was going to cry. "It doesn't work. The damned thing just doesn't work, Joe."

"Huh? But you said it was running smoothly."

Charlie shook his head vigorously—the loose skin on his neck flapping from side to side so he resembled a cartoon turkey. "It *was* running when I got it. But it needed a rebuild. Old Bruerge never looks after anything. So I started working on her."

"And?" Without the car, we had no chance. Any clues on Long Island might as well be orbiting the moon for all the good they'd do us.

"Now it doesn't."

"Why didn't you say?"

"I didn't want *her* to know. I mean, if she thought I was no good anymore..." Charlie trailed off, his mouth trembling a little. "It's not the same for me, Joe. She likes you. If she got the idea I couldn't handle things no more, I'd be gone."

"That's not true. She likes you too."

He shook his head. "She thinks I'm getting senile. An old dog ready to be put out of its misery. The cars at work, they're a lot simpler than this. All I do is make sure the filters are clean, and the fluids topped up, and that's it. Anything else, I follow the diagnostics and order the components. It ain't like that with this."

"You can always ask me for help. Don't you know that?"

Charlie tutted. "You're too close to *her*, maybe. And then, you've had your own problems this little while."

"How about we take a look together?"

Charlie thought for several minutes. So long that I wondered if he'd heard what I said.

"You wouldn't tell on me? Not on old Charlie? It's between you and me, right?"

I patted his shoulder, feeling the bony limb underneath the padded jacket. "You don't even need to ask."

"Cross your heart and hope to die?"

I gestured appropriately. "Cross my heart."

I hit the starter, but there was nothing except the click of some of the power relays activating. Then I opened up the right-hand access panel, and Charlie brought up a bright work-light so we could see better. Everything looked to be in place at first glance. Engines essentially come down to three things, and you need all of them to make one work: fuel, air, and power. If you've got all three, you should be good.

I opened the primary chambers and operated the injectors by

hand. Though I could see them actuating, nothing else happened. I should have got an immediate cloud of aerated fuel, but I didn't see so much as a droplet.

Unlocking the injector housing on the closest I popped out the injector and grimaced. The polished surface was literally spotless, but it had been installed one hundred eighty degrees out—it was in backwards.

I blew on it for Charlie's benefit and pulled the next in sequence. Thirty minutes later I had "cleaned" them all and surreptitiously flipped each one.

I worried what else might be wrong. Charlie certainly had the experience to work on a vehicle like this, but it looked like he'd reached the point where he was making basic mistakes. Newer AeroMobiles like the taxis weren't the same challenge—they were designed to be as idiot-proof as possible. The Broadsword was different.

I went through the main systems one by one. The main and secondary control modules had been swapped around, coil packs were installed in the wrong sequence, and the flight stabilization module had no power. It was no wonder it didn't work. The thing couldn't have flown a meter without cracking up, even if the engines had fired.

I ran through all this as if doing a systems check, routine maintenance that you'd carry out for any flight. Finally, I was convinced I'd got everything.

"Hey Charlie, look at that." I pointed to the fuel safety cut-off that I'd surreptitiously switched off earlier. "Did you...?"

Charlie turned pink. "No way. Are you saying..."

I reached over and deliberately moved the cut-off to the on-position. "Try her now."

Charlie clambered into the cockpit and flipped the flight switches. He hesitated, licked his lips, then hit the ignition. Sure enough, the thrusters lit up, and the Broadsword rose until it was floating thirty centimeters in the air.

"How could I make such a simple mistake, jeez. Thanks for checking my work, Joe. You know, I was starting to wonder if I was losing it."

I stretched my arms, wiggling my shoulders to get the kinks

out of my muscles after being squashed up and bent into the access panels. My leg was starting to throb from the unaccustomed contusions, and it was so late all I wanted was to lie down.

"We should get some sleep."

"You can take her, Joe." He slapped the armored side of the Broadsword. "Fly her to Long Island or the Moon, for all I care."

As much as I needed the Broadsword, I didn't want Charlie to give it to me out of gratitude. "You don't have to do that."

"Sure I do! Hell, I'd have let you have her right away if she'd been working." He shook his head and laughed. "Can you imagine... forgetting to switch the fuel on. You must think I'm a senile old fool."

"It's a mistake anyone could have made, Charlie. Sometimes I even forget my own name."

Charlie scrambled down, holding out the actuator fob. "She's all yours, Joe."

The hairs on my arms stood up like I'd stuck my fingers in an electrical outlet. Partly because of the trust Charlie had in me, but also because of the potential danger involved. His generosity might give us the chance to finally get out of this mess.

Or it might kill us.

The Broadsword was as crowded as *Madame ZaZa's Gentlemen's Boutique* the night after a pay-day bonus, but smelled incomparably better. Seating was nominally for four, but that was for soldiers going into combat—plenty of elbow room was probably not at the top of their minds.

Charlie was wearing full-out combat armor circa forty years ago. Where he'd found it, I had no idea. It made him look like a robotic gorilla with a tyrannosaurus' maw and the legs and shoulders of Hercules. He had the blast visor up, so at least we could see his face. His eyes were gleaming brightly, like a kid on the way to the fairground.

"We're gonna kick some serious Fundie butt, eh, Joe? Those guys ain't gonna know what hit 'em. Time for some payback!"

I smiled and did my best to make it look friendly, rather than the belly laugh I was holding back. With his bald head poking out of the combat helmet, Charlie did a good impersonation of a giant bipedal tortoise.

Judging by Tana's red eyes, I guessed she'd spent most of the night working on the Scroll, though she'd shared nothing new with us. Was there really nothing to share, or was she holding back again?

I didn't feel fresh either. The late night with Charlie, combined with the stresses of the last few days, had finally caught up with me, and I felt like I could play the "before" part in one of those ads that start "Not feeling like the man you used to be...?"

Dollie was the only one who looked bright. Her eyes were green today and flashed in the morning light with what seemed to be a hint of malice. She was wearing black fatigues that were almost painted on and had a pink utility belt around her waist.

"Looks like some of us had a late night." Dollie smiled, but there was no warmth in it as she looked from Tana to me and back.

"I was working on Hubert's research notes. What he and the others were doing was fascinating." Tana glanced up briefly. "Their analysis shows a high correlation with language. Although they didn't get to ascribe meaning with high confidence, there's a strong implication that the messages contain a warning of some kind."

"Really? That *is* fascinating." Dollie purred. "How about you, Soldier? Were you *correlating* too?"

I didn't like Dollie's tone, but I couldn't say anything without giving away Charlie's secret. "Couldn't sleep. I was thinking about what we'll find over there."

Dollie let out a scornful laugh. "I never took you for a *thinker*. You always impressed more as a man of action."

"Stop picking on Joe. He's a good guy—you should know that."

I'd never heard Charlie speak up against Dollie before and it was nice that he was trying to defend me, even if there was no need.

I banked the Broadsword to starboard, hugging the coastline tightly. I didn't know how far out the LI sensor screen came, and I had no intention of finding out if I could help it. Flying close to the ground gave us our best chance of not being picked up. Once we got to the wall, it was different. We'd have to hop over it, but I was hoping the ship's stealth capabilities would hide us.

Although we were flying in weak sunlight, doom-laden clouds were massed off the shore in the Atlantic. We'd decided on a daytime crossing despite the fact that it made us more visible. The Broadsword was electronically camouflaged, and with luck, the LI security forces would be pre-occupied with the mass of commercial traffic passing through the Manhattan gateways.

Dollie was sitting directly behind me and leaned over, the low bulkhead creaking as she leaned on it. "I came to visit you last night. After everyone was asleep." She spoke quietly so no one else could hear. "Funny thing—you weren't in your room."

I deliberately jerked the Broadsword up and down—following the terrain far closer than necessary. The buffeting from the ground-effect bounced her and everyone else around heavily, despite being locked into full safety-harnesses.

"Must have been visiting the little boys' room."

"More likely the little girl's room..." Dollie hissed.

As I let the Broadsword arc over the trees, a rocky outcrop appeared in front of us and forced me to yank on the controls, kicking the car into the next valley. I heard a grunt from Charlie, and Tana squeaked. They were undoubtedly impressed by my flight skills.

"I wasn't with Tana." I spoke quietly from the side of my mouth. "If that's what you're insinuating."

"Really?" Dollie's breath was warm against my ear. "Are you telling me Charlie is more your type?"

I brought the Broadsword down to tree-clipping height once more. "There's more to life than sex."

"Are you sure?" Dollie's anger seemed to fizzle. "Is it me, Joe? Because of who I am? *How* I am? Does it bother you *that* much?"

I tried to come up with an answer, but couldn't. We were on our way to invade Long Island in the hope that some guy who'd been dead for decades might provide a clue to why people were trying to kill us. Did any of it make sense anymore? Especially the idea that Dollie would get so upset about an imagined assignation between me and Tana.

"I could change it. I don't have to be both ways. I'd change that for you, Joe... If you wanted me to."

I turned to look at her. What Dollie was suggesting was both amazing and terrifying. I wasn't sure if I should be incredibly flattered or scared out of my pants.

My passengers knew. At least their screams told me they were scared out of *their* pants. I snapped my head forward. A forest of densely packed red maples was lined up with the nose of the car. I twisted the controls, and we came around, missing the main trunks, but slicing off some minor vegetation. I whispered back to Dollie, "You sure as hell pick your moments."

The roiling gray water of the Atlantic opened up ahead of us as the coastline swept away to the west. This was the riskiest part of the journey, where we crossed the open channel, and I needed every bit of concentration.

"Get ready. This is going to be a wild ride."

I switched the Broadsword's thruster profile over to contour mapping. That would give us maximum maneuverability, but slow our forward velocity. The stub delta wings reconfigured themselves into an extended concave shape to maximize ground-effects in the turbulent boundary between water and sky. Theoretically, we should skim over the waves like a bubble, but I wasn't leaving it to chance and gripped the controls with both hands.

The port wingtip dipped several inches into the crest of a wave, tugging hard at the car and I compensated with the thrusters, twisting the controls to maintain course. The rough gray composite panels inside were squeaking as the car twisted.

"Joe?" Charlie's voice shook a little. "You sure we need to be this low?"

I was going to answer, but Dollie got there first. "Shut up, you old fool. He doesn't need you distracting him."

There was no need for that, but as I jerked and twisted the controls in almost every direction at once, fighting to keep the car between the swells, I appreciated the lack of interference.

Two waves came together directly on us, giving me no time to bank either way. I hit the vertical thrusters, and the Broadsword kicked up. The water curled around the wing tips, trying to suck us down as the engines strained to pull us up. An acrid smell of fuel flooded the cockpit, and for a second I thought we were stuck. Then we popped up, and I reduced power, letting us drop safely into the noise of the waves.

The gray concrete wall loomed directly out of the water. The engineers had locked the structure directly to the bedrock to stabilize against future circumstances, no matter what the impacts of climate change might be. The rising waters made the island look more like a medieval fortress from an old fantasy than a natural piece of land.

I held the Broadsword brushing the waves until the very last second, then flipped on the ShimmerField control while jamming the control stick hard back. Stained concrete slab filled the front window, and out of the corner of my eye, I saw Charlie's knuckles whiten as he gripped his restraint.

"Joe..." Charlie shouted over the tortured whine of the turbines.

I relaxed the stick, the car shooting up almost vertically like a rocket. The stall warning alarm sounded and the engines whined in protest as they choked. The nose dropped, and I feathered the stick, making our climb angle shallower to maintain control. It worked, but brought us even closer to the concrete.

As the engines started to splutter, the wall slid out of sight, and I flipped the nose down. The engines coughed, despite our now downward trajectory, and the ground rushed upwards as the car buffeted in the updraft on the other side of the wall.

Throttle steady, let her fly herself, I thought. Let. The. Air. Stream. Feed. The. Engines.

"Joe!"

I don't know who screamed. Then the turbines reignited, drowning out the remainder of the shout. I pulled back again, my chest tightening as the tangled treetops rushed up to meet us. We started to lift again, and the trees flashed by, missing the car by centimeters.

We twisted through the tree canopy, ducking through the valleys and hills like we had the waves minutes before, and I dropped the throttle to a respectable level until the Broadsword settled into a stable flight. I hoped we'd appear safely boring if anyone saw us and they wouldn't look too closely—the Broadsword was armored like a rhino, and there was no way it could be mistaken for civilian traffic.

Being caught without the proper service identification would mean a direct and unpleasant trip back across the border at the very least. Depending how annoyed the constabulary was, we ran the risk of possible incarceration and all kinds of *interesting* interrogations. LI Police were essentially mercenaries, not renowned for their warm and fuzzy skills.

Thirty-Two

"They've attacked Mars." Tana held out Charlie's Scroll like a tombstone. "Those idiots have attacked Mars."

Mars doesn't have more than a few dozen hardened prospectors on it at any one time because of the dangers from the Martian regolith. The planet's main population consisted of remote-operated mining platforms, service bots, and ore launchers that fed the stream of rare metals and minerals space-ward from the surface. I flipped the controls and transferred the news feeds to the display screen in the center console so everyone could see, while I let the autopilot keep us steady. The plastic-faced presenter appeared mid-stream.

"…attacking the relay stations orbiting Deimos. These stations were responsible for packing mineral loads from the surface and launching them on high-efficiency trajectories to the orbital catchers near Earth and the Atolls. Up to now, the operations have been largely unaffected by the ongoing embargo, because the Atolls benefit from the resources. This depraved attack has resulted in over six hundred casualties, and the subsequent loss of vital mineral supplies will have a severe impact on Earth's economy."

The woman's face was replaced by a 3V "actual reconstruction" of the attack, showing two Atoll ships firing on the bulky unarmed relay stations.

"Estimates put the cost of lost manufacturing in the billions. Not including rebuilding the relay station. An unofficial source from the Trans-Ares Corporation said that full liability rests with Earth."

"Bastards." Charlie was barely audible. "Bastards!"

It was the kind of insanity that only humanity could come up with. Sure the Atolls controlled most of the technology for space exploration, but they were far too comfortable in their artificial homes to be driven to the rigors of further expansion. That was why most of the people on the relay stations were from Earth—our constant population pressure meant there'd always be people like me who'd risk everything to go into space. A war between Earth and the Atolls was like two castaways clinging to a piece of wood and fighting over who got the biggest share.

The *Ananta*, as the only potential interstellar technology, should have been a triumph to share, but instead, the Atolls treated us like imbeciles—sub-human creatures to be corralled and herded. About a third of Mars' mineral production had been directed to the *Ananta*'s construction, though at this late stage the destruction would have little effect. It was a symbolic attack more than a practical one, but that didn't reduce the human cost.

"Charlie? Are you okay?" Dollie asked quietly.

I looked around. Charlie was hunched over, his shoulders jerking repeatedly, making the PlaSteel plates of his combat armor squeak sympathetically with his movement. Haggard intakes of breath came from him like the last gasps of a dying man.

"Charlie..." I put my hand on his arm, the worn armor scraping roughly against my skin. I don't know if he felt anything through the protective layers, but he jolted upright, his black eyes filled with tears.

"My brother worked on Deimos Station..."

Charlie's voice was rough but otherwise devoid of any intonation. I'd never heard him speak like that before, and it somehow reflected death much more than if he'd been emotional.

"I didn't—" I started, but Charlie cut me off.

"Twins." Tears formed silver trails, dancing in and out of the lines on his cheeks. "Danny was three minutes younger."

I glanced around for some help, but Dollie looked down when I caught her eye, and Tana was staring fixedly at the scene through the window.

"He was always the happy one. Things were tough back then, but he never stopped smiling. He went into space, and I stayed here."

I reached out and squeezed his arm ineffectually through the armor.

"Forty years ago." Charlie's body trembled like a flower in an earthquake. "Never saw him again, except on 3V calls. He loved it out there, never wanted to come back."

I'd never had any family, so I didn't really know how Charlie felt, but it didn't take world class empathy skills to guess. Something like that would tear you apart. From what I'd heard the bond between twins was much closer, so it was probably like Charlie had lost part of himself.

"I'm sorry, Charlie." The words sounded empty even as I said them.

He twisted away from me and faced the window, his armored back filling the gulf between us more effectively than the wall we'd crossed.

I'd have liked to put the Broadsword down so we could give Charlie some privacy, but the island is split into fixed sized lots with every square meter owned by someone very rich. This made it a dangerous place to be. If we landed we'd inevitably get someone's back up, and that could be the end of our journey.

I looked at Tana. "Where should I be heading?"

"The last papers I can find show Harmon was located at CRAIT, the Center for Research on Artificial Intelligence Theory." Tana tapped the Scroll. "It used to be part of the Brookhaven National Laboratory, but the facility was shut down when the Islanders carried out the purge. Here are the coordinates."

I fed the details into the navcon. The Broadsword's autopilot was rudimentary, but at least I could set the bearing and distance on the simple map view. We'd come across the wall near Oakdale, after passing over Fire Island. The "island" was visible, but looked more like a reef instead of inhabitable as it appeared on the Broadsword's outdated maps.

I turned east and set the throttle. We were barely fifty kilometers from our destination, and I wondered if we'd find anything to help us. It seemed unlikely after so many years, but it was time to find out.

*

"There!" Dollie pointed over my shoulder to the left.

I followed her gesture. The scars of the giant circular accelerator were visible despite more than seventy years of overgrowth. The ring was over a kilometer across and from our position, the complex looked remarkably intact. Off to the right, a bunch of irregular support buildings and a smaller circular structure looked almost pristine in their platinum-gray concrete.

But as I moved us closer, reality quickly set in—what must have been impressive structures at one time were crumbling to dust. Weeds and bushes were eating through the concrete, producing a patchy green fur that made the buildings look diseased. Whoever owned the land now evidently had no interest in preserving it. That was surprising—rich people are extremely vain, and it was strange that they'd leave things in such a mess.

"What happened here?" Dollie gestured out of the window.

"They couldn't keep up," said Tana. "Funding was cut repeatedly and better facilities were built in India and China at a fraction of the cost. There were also some scandals about nuclear material leakage. By the time the island declared independence there wasn't much left here to fight for." She sighed. "It's not an uncommon situation."

Dollie shuffled behind me in her seat. "This place is *hot*?"

"Not enough to cause a problem." Tana fiddled with the Pad and then passed it over. "According to the records, Harmon's office was at the Quantum Technology Research Center."

The map she'd found was hard to follow against the overgrown bushes taking over the landscape, but it was enough. The Research Center was one of the better-looking buildings, and I set the Broadsword down in an old ground-vehicle parking lot next to the large cross-shaped structure.

The building had a shell of glass cladding that must have been arresting in its day but was now mostly smashed and crumbling. One corner of the "cross" had collapsed, merging the two upper-most floors together. The main entrance was still accessible, but looked like a gaping maw designed to swallow people whole.

I put the turbines on idle, unlatched the door and grabbed a couple of flashlights from the Broadsword's auxiliary equipment supplies. "This doesn't look hopeful. Me and Tana will go and look around. You two stay here in case we need to get out fast. Okay?"

My choices weren't random—though the logic might not be the kind you could design a circuit from. I wanted Charlie where he couldn't cause trouble and Dollie out of harm's way. On the other hand, Tana's scientific knowledge might be useful.

"Got it, Joe." Charlie reached into the back of the Broadsword and pulled out the QuenchGun we'd liberated from Gabriella's men. He looked ready to guard the gates of hell and unlocked a side-panel with a snap, drawing back the charging slide until the gun crackled into life with a blue glow.

"If you think I'm staying with Chaos, then you better think again. This trigger-happy ass is as likely to shoot me as anyone. Try and keep up." Dollie jumped out through the door and started to march towards the building, followed more slowly by Tana.

I glanced at Charlie and shook my head. Dollie had no problem pissing people off when it suited her. "Don't worry, Charlie. She doesn't mean anything. We still need someone reliable guarding our escape."

"Sure she means it. She's one hundred percent bi—"

"Ballen! Stop jerking off and get over here." Dollie's abnormal larynx projected her voice like a loudspeaker.

I shrugged. "Watch our backs, okay?"

Charlie nodded, and I scrambled after the others feeling like a kid caught dragging his feet. I caught up in time to walk into the main entrance with them, but my hopes plunged. The area was littered with flakes of concrete, glass shards, and other rubble. In several places, the internal walls had crumbled. They were obviously partitions and not load-bearing, but I couldn't stop myself from wondering when the next collapse might be.

I fingered the pistol in my belt, suddenly feeling self-conscious.

Dollie spotted my reaction. "What're you going to do, Soldier? Shoot the building as it falls on our heads? It must be shaking in fear at the thought."

I gave her a sheepish smile and shoved the gun tighter into my pants. She was right. There was nothing here a gun could help with.

"Any ideas?" I looked at Tana. From what I could see we were wasting our time.

She hesitated. "There are three floors and three of us. One each? If someone finds something they can call the others."

I couldn't think of any arguments against it, even though I didn't like the thought of us separating. In a 3V thriller, this would be the perfect opportunity to pick us off one at a time. But the more rational part of my brain said there was more danger of having the ceiling coming down on our heads, or plunging feet first through the broken flooring.

"Okay. I'll take the top." That looked the worst part of the building, and I felt I should be the one to check it out, despite the climb. "You two decide the others between you. Let's make it quick. I don't think we're going to find anything, but be careful."

"I'll take the second," Dollie said and followed me up the stairs. "You know there's nothing here, don't you?"

We were at the landing of the second level, and I peered into the gloom of the corridor. "You're probably right, but I'm not giving up that easily."

Dollie sniffed loudly and tramped away, the rubble crunching under her boots. I edged up the final flight, wondering what we'd do if we didn't find anything. We'd battled to uncover the clues and follow them but might still end up with the fat end of a giant zero.

I reached the top floor. It was definitely more broken up than the others. The collapsed end opened to the air in a dangerous looking ledge of rubble that I didn't want to get too close to. I looked out across the rest of the broken down buildings. This was stupid. Then a flicker caught my attention, and I squinted as my eyes watered in the buffeting wind.

A scream shattered the air. I ran to the stairwell and raced down, my feet slipping dangerously on the rubble. Dollie barreled out of the second floor as I got there and we ran down the final flight together, almost piling into Tana at the bottom. She was shaking, her breath coming in ragged bursts.

"Rats..." She looked away. "There were rats. I think."

"Rats?" Dollie stared at me coldly, her mouth tight enough to bare her pristine teeth.

I knew she was about to unleash a barrage in Tana's direction, but I shook my head. It was pointless, there was nothing here. "Let's get back to the car."

"But..." Tana hesitated. She seemed like she might cry but drew in a deep breath instead. "There must be something. We can't have come all this way, gone through all this... for nothing."

"This place is a tomb." I pointed across to the distant buildings I'd seen from the upper floor. "But we might want to check over there."

"You're not serious, Ballen?" said Dollie. "We could be surrounded by uniformed thugs at any minute."

I started back towards the Broadsword. "Maybe. But we should at least investigate why there's a light shining over there, don't you think?"

Thirty-Three

Charlie took the controls and we hopped about a kilometer eastwards to the ring-shaped structure where I'd spotted the light. It was a long shot, but if it still had power, maybe there was something else. No one spoke on the short flight. The inside of the Broadsword seemed even more cramped than it had on the journey out.

Surrounded by thick stands of spiky maples, the building didn't look in much better shape than the place we'd last visited. As we dropped down, I spotted the light again, shining over an entrance-way. I hadn't imagined it then.

We left Charlie guarding the car while we went to investigate. Maybe it was an unnecessary precaution, but the irrational part of my mind said there was something alive here that shouldn't be.

The inside of this building was relatively free from debris, though it didn't make it much cleaner or look any less abandoned. The foyer had that overly dramatic architecture that was designed to impress prospective supporters, but ultimately was a waste of space. Now it was a wide hall that smelt of age and decay. Some of the vaulted glass panels were broken, and I could see the remains of birds' nests tucked under the corner of the roof and walls.

I peered around the darkened lobby. "I'd love to be smart and say *this way*, but it would be a guess. Anyone got any ideas?"

Tana shook her head briefly. Maybe she was still feeling self-conscious about her earlier panic. "According to the maps, this was the Synchrotron Lab Office building. Nothing I've found connects this with Harmon."

"Why would there still be power here?" Dollie looked around. "There doesn't seem to be any reason."

We worked through the three-story building, wandering through the ancient facilities in silence. Even our footsteps were muffled by the gray dust that choked the floors and walkways. I decided it was probably better to stay together this time, but after working our way back down from the top floor, I was ready to call it a day. My legs were aching, and the rest of me was sore from the abuse I'd taken recently.

I kicked a potentially malicious cardboard box out of the way, and it crumbled into flakes in submission. "We could head back to Charlie's. Maybe there's more from Logan."

Tana's shoulders dropped. She looked as defeated as I felt at such a futile ending.

Dollie pointed off to the right. "Is that another light, down there?"

I looked down the corridor, and sure enough there it was—dim in the distance, but the glow was unmistakable.

"Did we miss that when we came in?" I asked, not really believing it.

Tana shook her head. "I don't see how."

"Let's get the hell out of here, Joe." Dollie clasped my wrist lightly. "I don't like it."

Dollie's usually pretty fearless, so I was surprised. If only she hadn't pointed out the light. I'd been ready to leave, but now I couldn't. "We'll check it out, then go. Only take a couple more minutes."

I hoped I sounded more confident than I felt. If I didn't, Tana and Dollie were polite enough not to say anything, and we edged along the curved corridor, picking our way through the wash of debris.

"What are you hoping for, Ballen? What do you think you'll find here?"

Dollie had a good point. The facility hadn't been in use for over a hundred years. Even if something had been there, it was almost certainly gone by now. I'd imagined we might find papers or records that would help, but looking around I knew anything like that would be dust.

"I traced the file access *here*." Tana tapped the Pad. "There has to be something."

"Maybe it's a relay," Dollie said. "Could someone use that to make us think it's coming from here?"

We were almost whispering as we approached the light, as if we were worried it could somehow hear us. A relay *could* explain things and might provide another clue, even if it wasn't the answer we needed.

I looked at Tana. "Could you trace the source?"

"Possibly... If it's a single relay there'd be a chance, but a generalized router would be difficult unless we monitored and analyzed specific transmissions. But that would take hours, maybe days."

The light turned out to be an industrial fixture over a heavy closed door and could easily have been on automatic. I nudged the door open, trying to be quiet, but the rusty hinges groaned loudly. Inside was a metal staircase twisting down into darkness, the steps and handrail pitted and tarnished with age.

"'Will you walk into my parlor?' said the Spider to the Fly; 'Tis the prettiest little parlor that ever you did spy,'" Dollie whispered as I shone a light down the stairwell.

Something deep in my primordial mind told me to run away—a primitive cave dwelling fear that gibbered when faced with darkness. But unless we abandoned our plans we didn't have much choice. I started down the stairs, placing my feet carefully to try and muffle the sound of my footsteps. I pulled out the gun. This time no one objected.

The stairs didn't screech halfway down or any of that nonsense. At the bottom was another door. It opened silently on well-lubricated hinges. Unlike the stairs, the corridor inside was illuminated by dim emergency lights running along the bottom of the curved walls. The passage was lined with an array of blackened metal conduits and ducting that contrasted against the gray concrete. Something else was different too.

"It's clean." I pointed to the floor. There was none of the rubble we'd seen everywhere else.

"You think the rats are better housekeepers here?" Dollie hissed.

I ignored her and crept forward. There was another door about fifty meters along. It looked as solid and forbidding as the previous one, and I paused next to it, listening for several seconds. I thought I heard a faint hum, but it could have been my imagination.

My mouth was dry, and I swallowed painfully. Sweat ran down my spine and puddled into the small of my back like ice water. Holding the gun high, I pulled the door open and stepped through. The room was abuzz with softly flickering lights. At the far end, a globe around two meters in diameter pulsed in a shifting kaleidoscope of colors. I took a step forward and felt the cold metal of a gun barrel press against my temple. A figure stepped out of the shadows ahead of me.

"If you'd be so kind as to drop the gun, Joe. I'd appreciate not having to kill you quite yet."

I recognized the charmingly cold voice of Gabriella, even without being able to see her face in the dim light. I let my pistol drop, and it clattered to the concrete floor. I sensed a quick movement as someone next to me kicked it into the darkness. He moved closer, pushing me forward with the muzzle of his own gun.

I heard rather than saw Dollie and Tana moving up behind me, no doubt suffering the same "encouragement." When all three of us were lined up in front of Gabriella, she smiled as though she were royalty receiving guests.

She waved a large pistol at us. "I think it would be safer for everyone if you all got down on your knees."

"If you want to execute us, do it." Dollie's voice was sharp. "Don't play games."

I heard a soggy thud of something hard hitting flesh, followed by a gasp. I jerked reflexively and started to turn, only to feel the gun grind into my neck, pushing me down until I dropped to the floor.

"If I'd wanted you dead you would have been a long time ago. Do you really think I couldn't get to you while you were at the Geneium or that simpleton's ranch?" Gabriella paused. "You must think me very incompetent to let you slip away that easily."

"I suppose Sarnelli told you to leave us alone to make us think we'd lost you." The barrel of the gun was painful behind my ear. "That way you could lure us out here and get rid of us where it wouldn't be such a political embarrassment."

Gabriella laughed, the sound musical over the hum of the equipment surrounding us. "Good guess, Joe, but completely wrong." She leaned over to stage whisper to me. "Let's say the Junior Minister won't receive his anticipated promotion and that I have a new employer.

"Loose ends are so unprofessional, don't you think?" She stood back upright. "The headlines will tell a tragic story of a promising politician, his friend Professor Idell, and the detective investigating the case, all murdered by the fugitive cab driver who's been on a scientist killing spree."

The concrete was biting into my knees, and my head was starting to swim from the pain, but I knew Gabriella was shoveling it. "If that had happened we'd have heard. We've been watching the newsfeeds."

Gabriella glanced at her Scroll. "How silly of me. It *will* happen in around seventeen minutes."

There was something in the tone of her voice that told me she was serious. I didn't doubt her ability to do something like that—she was certainly bloodthirsty enough—but I found it hard to believe she'd changed sides. She worked for money—who could pay better than the government?

"You're the one who's been masquerading as Dr. Harmon?" Tana spoke quietly. "I don't believe it, you're not—"

"Before you decide how you're going to insult me, why don't I introduce you to my new employer." Gabriella moved to one side and the globe I'd seen earlier flickered, the patterns of light on the surface becoming more intricate and intense.

"Dr. Harmon, I presume?" The words tumbled out almost without thought.

"Very perceptive, Mr. Ballen. Welcome to my little hideaway. It's certainly been a long time since I had so many... *guests*. If only the circumstances were a little more pleasant."

The voice boomed in the confines of the room as though it came from all directions simultaneously. It sounded older than time, as if we were talking to Odin or Zeus. Or maybe Satan.

"You'd probably like an explanation. Normally I'd find that tiresome, but with such a large audience I find the idea somewhat... intoxicating. Yes, intoxicating indeed." The lights on the sphere flickered rapidly.

My brain shuddered. Who or what was I talking to? A machine? A person? Was the flickering ball Harmon? Whatever it was, we'd probably only last as long as it wanted us to, so if it wanted to "speak" why not let it? "Dr. Harmon died over thirty years ago. What are you exactly? Some kind of machine fakery?"

"You're right. I did *die*, as you put it, except it was only my physical self that ended. I'd been working on the quantum modeling of cerebral systems alongside my other research for several years. When I was diagnosed as terminal, it was only natural to use my talent to preserve my brilliance."

"And the scientists you worked with agreed to this?" Tana sounded incredulous.

Harmon hesitated almost imperceptibly. "Not exactly. I told them I was building an experimental artificial intelligence and had the influence, and cunning, to convince them. They thought it was the final vanity of a dying man."

Even a "mechanic" like me knows it's one thing to build a computer, but a thinking machine was a whole different problem. That's why AI research never really panned out—how can you create intelligence when you don't know what it is or how to recognize it? They'd only ever succeeded in creating very fast dumb boxes.

"I invented a way to impress my thought engrams onto a quantum matrix. After that, it was simply a question of transferring my memories across. It was interesting even before the end result."

"I can only imagine." I kneeled upright despite the hands pressing on my shoulders. "Must be fun spending time as a giant Christmas decoration."

Harmon ignored me. "After transferring forty percent of the major structural elements of my mind, I found I could 'think' in two places simultaneously and transfer ideas, thoughts, and memories between the two at will."

"Telepathy? That's impossible," Tana said. "What proof do you have?"

She wasn't buying what Harmon was saying, but if we were lucky, the scientific criticism might distract him and keep him talking.

"I don't make that claim," Harmon said. "I simply observed it. Whatever you call it, it greatly improved the transfer time, and I was ready long before my body gave out. That gave me the chance to take over this facility and ensure its preservation when the Long Islanders removed the academic staff.

"Rich people are so stupid. They track their wealth through intricate computer systems and believe the numbers they see are real. Once embedded in the network, I had the wealth of the world at my fingertips. No one ever thinks the machines might lie, do they?

"I found an ancient brain wave pattern of a pathetically egotistical businessman stored in the dusty corner of a company storage system. It was a fad many decades ago, allowing rich people to supposedly ensure their survival after death, though the systems were more like primitive games."

"Maybe you should have stuck to playing games." One of the men jammed his gun into my spine, making me squirm in pain.

Harmon laughed, the lights oscillating over the surface. "Despite that, the brain pattern held a great deal of information on financial and business manipulation. I'm now the single richest entity on Earth, tied into every financial institution. I can, quite literally, print money."

Gabriella laughed. "You have to be smart enough to choose the right side, Joe."

"I realized many years ago that this world is too small for intelligence such as mine." Harmon's lights flickered faster. "Do you know the real problem with infinity? Loneliness. My brain runs a thousand times faster than when I was alive. I have access to every information feed in the world and can correlate discoveries ordinary humans would never dream of, but I have to slow my mind massively to communicate with you. Communicating is so painful."

"You manipulated Rohloff to your own ends?" I said.

"Rohloff was nothing before I found him, an ant with delusions of grandeur. I tickled and prodded him, gave him the means to dream bigger. His invention and insight were mine, fed to him in trickles so even he believed it was his own work."

"You're a real genius, Harmon." I was tired of his lecturing, despite the danger involved in provoking him. "You must be a riot at parties."

"The *Ananta* is mine—I built it." Harmon's voice rumbled as if accompanied by a distant peal of thunder. "I provided the design. I kept it funded when short-sighted minds pulled out. I controlled every aspect of its development. Rohloff never questioned why the ship's computer system was so advanced. He simply built it to the specifications I supplied."

I shifted my weight, trying to ease the pain in my knees. "Where did Ganz fit into all this?"

"My monitoring systems alerted me to his research. I offered to help him. He was eager, just like Rohloff. I can access so much data, scientists can't resist. They'll trade *anything*." The flashing lights rippled back and forth on the sphere. "I pushed him away from critical information, but somehow he guessed what was happening and insisted he was going to publish his findings. Can you imagine the effect? I could have been trapped here for even more years. Of course, I couldn't allow that."

"So *Ananta* is your escape vehicle? Is that it?" I grunted the words—pain tearing along every nerve in my legs. "Pretty selfish hijacking Earth's last chance, just so you can escape."

"Selfish? I invented the Casimir generators and the Jump drive. I brought it to fruition. I paid for it. After I leave, the plans will still be here for anyone to use. Rohloff insisted they were stored in GARNET and nothing would persuade him otherwise. The only difference is that after I leave, they'll have to pay for it themselves, if the idiots even understand the work."

"You invented nothing," Tana hissed. "You leeched everything possible from the rest of the world. You're no scientist. Just a digital parasite, sucking the lifeblood of its host."

I enjoyed the image but was surprised when Harmon didn't interrupt.

"And your so-called *intelligence*? You stole that from the rest of us," she continued. "The money you embezzled by manipulating the financial markets. You rode roughshod over people you despise and dismiss as idiots. You had the power to improve the world for everyone, but you chose to steal instead. You're a thief, through and through. And now you boast of how wonderful you are?"

I heard Tana whimper and guessed Gabriella's men were trying to shut her up, but she was on a roll.

"Your precious spaceship has a flaw. It produces quantum eddies that send shock-waves through universes in other dimensions. *That* was what Hubert discovered, and that was why you killed him. Launching the *Ananta* will cause devastation on an unimaginable scale."

Harmon's voice grew louder. "Would those life forms worry about us if the tables were turned? Of course not."

Tana almost seemed to be pleading. "You *can't* launch the ship. Not until the impact can be fully assessed."

"The Atolls have forced the decision." Harmon's lights coalesced in rapid waves. "Those cretins will stop Earth's space program again. Once they completely dominate the local volume, nothing will escape Earth orbit without their permission. Do you think they'd allow me to escape?"

"Couldn't you subvert their systems too?" I goaded. "Wouldn't that be child's play for someone like you?"

"Your game is entirely transparent. You won't keep me talking a single moment longer than I want to, and it wouldn't do you any good if I did. No one is coming to your rescue."

I laughed. "So you couldn't get inside their systems then?"

"You've been an irritant far too long, Mr. Ballen." Harmon paused. "I had to stop you all those years ago when you started poking around the *Ananta*. There was too great a chance you'd discover what was being built didn't match the specifications."

My hands clenched, and my pulse thudded inside my temples over and over. "You?"

"Space Pod safety controls are so easy to unlock by remote. I dissected you like a bug. Unfortunately, you survived, and now you're annoying me again. You won't be so fortunate this time, I assure you."

I wanted to slam my fists into the flashing globe and rip out the circuits with my bare hands, but Gabriella's men held me even as I strained against them. This *thing* had taken my arm and legs. Taken away my life. All I wanted was the pleasure of smashing it to pieces. Perhaps before the accident I might have struggled free, but not now. "You goddamn bastard!" My scream was raw.

Harmon chuckled. "Penetrating the Atoll systems would prove

no challenge. But why wait? *Ananta* is ready. I'm ready. There's no reason to delay the equivalent of another ten lifetimes to become embroiled in this petty skirmish of yours. Enough of this. Bring the girl forward."

I heard a man yelp, and then the recognizable slap of flesh against flesh. Two of Gabriella's team dragged Tana forward, one of them sporting a bloody nose.

"What do you want?" Tana was rubbing a dark swelling on her face.

"You have such a deliciously libidinous mind. You'll make a wonderful companion for my journey. We can share all those salacious thoughts you hide deep inside."

"What are you talking about?" Tana's eyes widened.

"Don't play the innocent. I've already *tasted* you." Harmon paused momentarily. "The good Doctor let me sit in on many of your encounters."

"You're lying, Hubert would never—"

"Ganz was the same as Rohloff. I told you, scientists will do anything for knowledge. *Anything*." The lights on Harmon's brain were flickering more quickly now. "Even down to killing himself when I asked him to. He was such a wretch. Had to *see the world* one last time, poke his head into all those places he'd never been interested in before."

"You killed him." I heard Tana sob, small pathetic gasps wet with tears.

"Not at all. I explained how much attention his death would gain for his cause and how he'd lose nothing if he joined with me. He didn't even know of my connection to the *Ananta*." Harmon's lights rippled. "He was worried about you at first, but I soon persuaded him that it was a worthwhile sacrifice, especially to avoid the danger of his relationship with one of his students becoming public. When the time came, he was a more than willing accomplice."

Of all the low things one human can do to another, *StimJacking* is probably the lowest—when someone breaks into, or in this case, is invited into a Stim session without the knowledge or consent of the others involved. I couldn't believe Ganz had let Harmon do that.

Harmon laughed again. "And while he was running around

town, what were you doing my little Tana?"

Tana's head dropped as she seemed to collapse in on herself. "That's right. You were Stimming. But not with Ganz. We'd already transferred his persona across to link with mine. You didn't notice, did you? But you responded deliciously to my thoughts."

"No." Tana's whisper was barely audible.

"Would you like to share the experience with your friends? I could replay it on my displays. It's quite stimulating."

Tana dropped to the concrete floor, shaking her head.

"Imagine how much better it will be when we're one mind. We can share everything. As a scientist, think how much we will see and discover, roaming the galaxy at will."

"Hubert..."

"He's here too, don't worry. I keep him confined for the most part, but I might be willing to let him play with you from time to time. That might be amusing too."

"Take the women to the *Ananta*. Kill him. I'll transfer myself to the ship. This meddling has changed my schedule. I'll have to do it all at once now."

I wrenched against the hands holding me. "Wait! You can't—"

Dollie sprang up from nowhere, using her enhanced strength to barrel through the men holding her. In front of me, I heard a sharp crack and realized Tana had also broken free. I don't know if they'd somehow planned it, but the two of them acted in unison and took out several of the men in seconds.

I dived at Gabriella and was almost on her when she side-stepped. Her knee came up into my chest. A fraction later her elbow slammed into the back of my neck, and my vision turned red. I wasn't going to last. I scrabbled painfully on the ground and looked up into the barrel of her unnecessarily large gun.

"Goodbye, Joe. Sorry it has to end like this. I was hoping we might have some fun before we got to this part."

Her finger squeezed. I saw a blur of movement to the left. Pain exploded in my upper chest, then everything went away.

Thirty-Four

I felt myself floating when I opened my eyes. For a split-second, I wondered if I'd died and gone to heaven, except I don't believe in it, and even if it was real, I was sure I'd be heading in the opposite direction. My doubts were confirmed when a grizzled jowly MedTech leaned over to examine me—looking nothing at all like a cherub.

I tried to sit up, but the straps on the hover-gurney held me back. My left shoulder and arm felt like they were embedded in concrete.

"Your shoulder is full of repair goo," the MedTech growled. "You won't be able to use your arm much while the 'mites are working. You're lucky we got here before you bled to death."

I stopped struggling. "Could be worse. I knew it was a mistake to try arm-wrestling my girlfriend."

"Don't be so sure. The LIPD don't seem pleased about you being here." He checked the diagnostics at the head of the gurney. "That's going to hurt like hell, but apparently you'll live."

"Yeah, I'm a tough SOB." I spotted a Long Island MedTech badge on his sleeve.

The MedTech shrugged and pushed the gurney with a light touch of his hand. "What happened here?"

I glanced around. We were already outside the University buildings, and I heard a heavy motor in the distance. "I'm part of a mainland invasion force, spearheading a mission to retake Long Island."

"Looks like you lost." He didn't even glance down. "All we found

299

was you and the old guy."

"Charlie?" I'd forgotten about him. "Where is he?"

The MedTech stopped, but still didn't look at me. "He didn't make it. I'm sorry. He was wearing some freaky old armor, but something still punched a hole through his chest."

I was suddenly angry. At everyone, including myself. For all his quirks and paranoia, Charlie was completely harmless. He might not turn his back to a Fundie, but he wouldn't be inhospitable. I thought of how upset he'd been when he heard the news about Deimos—but he'd outlived his brother by less than a day. I tugged at the gurney straps.

"Before you do something stupid, there's someone who wants to talk to you." The MedTech handed over a Scroll and walked off to a waiting ambulance. The screen showed Logan's wide-jawed face.

"You look worse every time I see you, Joe."

"Thanks." I tried to smile and failed. "You're not exactly improving with age either."

"I had some friends contact the LIPD." Logan raised a finger to his lips. "We told them you were on SecOps business. They weren't happy but agreed not to prosecute."

"Thanks." I wondered how much one person could owe another. "Again."

"Tell me you found something?" Logan's eyes narrowed. "I'm running out of favors."

My head was spinning—partly from the drugs and partly from thinking about Charlie. "Yeah. We found some *thing*."

Logan nodded. "I hope it's good. I've got a line to the First Minister, but he'll lose interest if I don't give him something soon."

"I need to go." I tugged at the restraints.

"People died there. Don't be stupid, Joe." He leaned closer to the pickup. "It's time to leave it to the professionals."

"Any clue who they are?"

I ended the call. Using my good hand, I unhooked the restraints and slid off the gurney. My legs almost collapsed beneath me, and I held on until I felt stable.

"Hey, wait a minute." The MedTech spun around, dropping the handset he was holding. "There are some people who—"

"There always are."

My head was pounding as I dragged myself to the Broadsword and slid in awkwardly. The medical straps on my shoulder made it almost impossible, but with more determination than strength I hauled myself into the seat. There were dark red-brown stains on the outer hull marking Charlie's last stand, and they fueled my anger even more.

I began the turbine start-up sequence and a few minutes later pulled back on the controls. The Broadsword lifted into the cloudy gray skies, and I turned west, no longer worrying if I was seen. I needed to get back to the mainland and fast.

I hadn't felt any responsibility for the other deaths, not even Acevado. They were killed because they were already involved, but Charlie was different. He was there because I'd brought him into this mess. Whether you called it revenge or justice, he deserved *something*, and I was the one who had to do it.

The rocket boosters at Charlie's place were almost impossible to move on my own. I worked through the pain from the frozen shoulder and finally mounted them in the racks on the Broadsword's hull. After that, it was simply a case of launching and flying up to the High-Rig. It sounds easy, but the Broadsword bucked wildly every time I triggered a booster and jarred heavily when the burnt out shells were ejected. It was like getting shot from a cannon, landing in a tree, and going back for more.

A little over four hours later, I was coasting outside the outer navigation point for the High-Rig. The domed inner cylindrical section and radially mounted habitation units were starkly shadowed by the Sun's undiluted might. The station looked as huge and impressive as ever, seeming to float impossibly while tied to the Earth by a gossamer-thin tether—the carbon lines anchoring it through a heavy skeleton of tapering rings and stanchions on its underbelly.

Almost hidden by a bulk ore carrier on one side was the sword-like shape of the *Ananta*—the large Casimir generators forming the hilt and the cylindrical Jump drive representing the handle. It looked finished compared to when I'd last seen it, and I had to fight the urge to accelerate, or I'd overshoot. Back then it had only been a framework. Now it glittered like a jeweled Excalibur.

Using the maneuvering thrusters, I guided the Broadsword towards one of the smaller maintenance bays. I was hoping to get on board without drawing too much attention. The authorities might be expecting me. I waited impatiently while the airlock pressurized, then slid out of the car when the atmosphere light turned green and hurried to the inner door controls.

"What were you using for brains today?" Logan's broad frame filled the doorway. "I knew you'd have to try some crazy-ass scheme."

"It's good to see you too."

Even if Logan had guessed I'd head to the High-Rig, that didn't explain how he knew where I'd dock. Hell, I'd only decided at the last minute. He had no information on my launch point, my flight capabilities or trajectory, but despite that he was waiting for me. "How did you know?"

His face gave nothing away. "Would you believe me if I said the Great Spirit told me where to find you?"

"Only if you mean you've been drinking."

Logan slapped me on the shoulder. "We do have a fully working radar grid."

I rubbed my shoulder, wincing as I tried to get sensation back into it. As always, Logan's dark eyes missed nothing.

"How long have you been on the go?"

I tried to think. I'd slept for a couple of hours at Charlie's and before that it felt like half a lifetime ago. "A few days maybe. If you've come to collect the fifty I owe you, I've got some bad news."

"Me too." Logan's voice deepened. "Several people arrived ten minutes ago. One of them was your boss."

Gabriella had set off much earlier than I did, but coming up the Elevator was a slow process. I'd hoped to get there before her. With Logan's help, I might have had a chance of laying some kind of ambush as they arrived. Now they'd be more dangerous to deal with. "Any idea if they're armed?"

Theoretically, everyone going up the Elevator had to pass through security, but there were ways around that. Harmon and Gabriella would know every trick.

"Someone arranged for them to travel as a Special Tactical Unit. And there's something else." Logan looked grim. "There's an Atoll ship coming. And I don't think they're looking for a social dance."

"Then they better stay out of my way."

Logan gestured at the gun in my belt. "Is that thing safe up here?"

I pulled the QuenchGun out and checked the capacity. Charlie hadn't got off a single shot. I dialed the power setting to throw the needles at the lowest velocity—enough to do damage, but not punch through the walls. "I'm set. You?"

Logan produced two Shock-Wands and flicked them in tight arcs through the air. "The armories are locked down, so this is it. After Deimos, no one wants to hang around to see what the Atoll forces have planned."

I nodded. "How long?"

Logan shrugged. "Maybe an hour."

I strode onto the open promenade that followed the perimeter of the inner hub. It was brightly lit and dotted with seating and commercial booths at regular intervals designed to snag any wandering tourists. Van Der Waal's carpeting made it easy to maintain grip, but allowed experienced people like us to cover ground quickly in a series of long skating hops. People were milling in all directions, almost in a blind panic as they looked for a way off the Rig or a place to hide.

"Something strange is going on."

"Stranger than this?" Logan bounced alongside me like a mountain lion.

"After I was shot, they stuck one of those medical 'mite packs on the wound. It healed the wound okay, but I think it's done more." I hopped again and almost didn't catch Logan's questioning look. "I think it's healed the replacement legs and arm too. They don't feel the same."

"Seems you're pretty tough for a *cripple*," Logan said. "Don't know many who could have gone through what you have in the last few days."

We were getting close to the *Ananta* airlock, and I slowed down. The crowds had gone, leaving the wide avenue empty. "Maybe... but *something* has to be different."

"The change is here, Joe." Logan tapped the side of his head. "There was never anything wrong with the new body parts. It was the connections in your head that were broken."

It didn't seem like it could be that simple, but what did I know? Limb replacement is complicated. Whatever had happened, the weakness wasn't as debilitating and even though I'd been shot, my replacement arm and legs seemed better than they'd felt since the accident.

We'd reached the service corridor to the *Ananta* when the plastic wall next to my head vaporized. A long blast of needles ripped the laminated surface open, sending a cloud of painful slivers burning into my cheek. I jumped behind a thick pillar and crouched low, snatching a glance around the corner.

"I can see three, Logan. You?"

He didn't answer. I looked across to see him dive like a rocket, straight at the gunmen. The Shock-Wands flailed as he passed over their heads, catching two of them heavily. They both screamed, then collapsed as the neural disruption fried their brains temporarily.

I brought up the QuenchGun and sent a spray of needles into two more of them. One had been aiming at Logan's back, but both collapsed to the floor, the bloody stains evidence enough that they wouldn't cause anymore trouble.

"That's enough, gentlemen."

Gabriella stepped out from behind a support, pushing Dollie and Tana ahead of her. Her last two men stood just behind them, guns pressed against the women's heads.

"Stop following me, Joe. I know you care about at least one of these ladies." Gabriella flashed her perfect smile. "I think you know me well enough by now to understand I'll happily kill them both."

"Let them go, and I'll let *you* go," I called from behind the pillar.

"My employer wouldn't approve, and I do *so* like to get paid." Gabriella released her hold on Dollie and pulled out her gun. "Perhaps you need something to occupy your time."

"Wait!" I froze.

Without warning Logan launched himself at Gabriella, the whips flailing again. Gabriella fired, and he jerked repeatedly in mid-air as the needles buried themselves in his thick torso. Dollie spun, burying her knee in Gabriella's gut. It should have been a knock-out blow, but her inexperience with low-grav made the impact less than perfect. Gabriella brought her gun round, and the blast caught Dollie full-on.

Far too late, I fired. The needles missed Gabriella, but caught the man holding Tana in the face, and he fell. Gabriella locked her arm around Tana's throat, pressing her gun into Tana's side.

"Deal with him," she ordered the last of her men, keeping herself shielded as she dragged Tana backwards into the corridor.

The pillar I was behind disintegrated as a stream of needles tore across the surface. I'd be shredded if I moved even a centimeter. The barrage stopped, and I guessed the guy was reloading for another assault. It was a slim chance—maybe my only one.

I tensed ready to jump. Red warning lights flashed all around us and a klaxon blared. Someone had sounded the collision alarm, presumably in response to the approaching Atoll ship. I ignored it and shoved forward.

Gabriella's remaining thug was distracted by the alarm and didn't spot me immediately. Then he brought his gun up and fired wildly. His feet came away from the floor, and the recoil sent him twirling helplessly through the air. I braced myself against the roof and traced his path with the QuenchGun, sending a long stream of needles into him until almost his entire body was oozing red.

All I could think of was Dollie. Not even bothering to check if the guy was dead, I jumped over to her. My eyes were stinging as I fought back tears and eased her over. Her stomach was a mess. The bitter smell of blood caught in the back of my throat. It seemed impossible she'd survived. I cradled her to me, her head in my lap, then she looked at me and grimaced. "Damn that bitch. It hurts."

Tears were pooling in my eyes, and I wiped them away with my sleeve. "I thought you were dead."

"Armor implants. Courtesy of Sigurd." Dollie winced. "She's paranoid, but sometimes it pays off."

I checked her stomach more closely. The skin was badly torn, and I could see the white material of the implants poking through in various places, but other than that she seemed okay. "Why didn't you tell me?"

Dollie coughed. "No point in a secret defense if it's not secret." She had a point. "I'm glad you're not dead."

"That makes two of us." Dollie produced a small tube of MediSkin from her belt and sprayed it on her stomach. "How's your friend?"

In my concern over Dollie, I'd forgotten Logan. I helped her up and supported her with my arm as we limped over to him. He was curled up next to one of the couches, the station alarm controls in his hand. He looked in a bad way, but as I checked him his eyes opened, shining like obsidian gems.

"I thought that might be useful," Logan said, waving the alarm control like a magic wand. He smiled, and a trickle of blood floated from between his lips. "You haven't had the chance to be a warrior for a while, Joe. I think that's about to change."

My heart locked in my chest like a granite boulder. "Take it easy. We'll get you patched up in no time."

"The Great Spirit watches over me." Logan coughed, creating a crimson cloud around us. "Take care of your girl. I like her, Joe, she has spirit."

I looked over at Dollie. "Can you help him?"

"I'll try." Dollie pulled out the MediSkin she'd used earlier and started covering the small puncture wounds, a strong antiseptic cloud drifting up as she applied it. "You can't let them take Tana. You know that, don't you?"

Part of me wanted to say it was too late. All I wanted at that moment was for Gabriella, Tana, Harmon and everyone else to disappear and leave me to hold Dollie, but even as I thought it I knew I couldn't. On 3V shows the hero saves everyone, the bad guys get what's coming to them, and everyone walks, rides, hops, or flies into a metaphorical sunset. But the real world doesn't work that way, and I didn't feel like much of a hero. I scrambled to my feet to follow Gabriella nevertheless.

Dollie grabbed my hand. "Make sure you come back. Saving Tana isn't worth losing you."

"I'm not cut out to be a martyr."

"Me neither." Dollie looked up at me. "And Joe, I look terrible in black."

"That's a lie if ever I heard one—you couldn't look terrible in anything."

Dollie's smile flashed briefly. "Sometimes you say the sweetest things. Now move before I bawl all over you."

I started to turn, but Dollie pulled me back. Her lips were hot and sweet against mine, and my arms slipped around her almost on their own. She seemed liquid and boneless as I held her. Several centuries must have passed before she let go, and we both gasped to get our breath back.

"Dollie, I—"

"Tell me later."

I nodded and steadied myself to push off again. My heart was thumping for a different reason than earlier, and my ears roared as if I was surrounded by an ocean. I pushed off the couch, jumping down the tunnel towards the *Ananta*.

It was time to see if Logan was right.

Thirty-Five

I checked myself against a side-wall halfway down the corridor. I hadn't seen any sign of Gabriella and guessed she was heading straight for the ship. With the Atolls on the way, her window for delivering Tana was closing rapidly. I suspected Harmon wouldn't wait if he felt threatened. I couldn't simply blunder forward and hope nothing happened though. She could hole-up at any point to ambush me.

I edged towards the *Ananta's* 'lock in smaller jumps, trying to make use of what little cover there was in the access tunnel. I thought at one point I heard something ahead of me, but it wasn't clear. It could have been the airlock cycling or the tunnel shifting.

I pressed my ear to the 'lock and listened for several seconds. I couldn't sense any vibration through the door, but it was an obvious choke point and a good place to stage an attack. I cycled the door, working the controls from the side so I'd be out of any possible firing line. I counted to fifteen before glancing around the doorway. There was nothing in sight, and I snaked inside, my gun pointed ahead.

The inside of the *Ananta* bothered me, and it took me a while to understand why. Most structures are built to accommodate people, but here the design was purely functional—providing access for engineers and technicians, but without any of the usual concessions to comfort. Although the *Ananta* was designed to take a crew, it was currently set up as a test vehicle. So amenities would have been pointless. It also seemed like some of the work had been rushed—I spotted several panels roughly glued in place, and a couple of sealant guns floated past me as I edged inside.

The corridor branched. One tunnel led towards the stern of the ship, and the other turned towards the center. The main computer systems would be central. The other direction would be access for the engines and field generators. I turned right and used the handholds that dotted the walls to pull myself deeper into the ship.

I reached a large doorway, a faint aura of light coming through it, and hesitated. Before I could think too much, I stepped into the wide room. A glowing sphere similar to the one I'd seen on Long Island stood at the far end, but this was larger and surrounded by a ring of antennas of some kind. A knot of cables thicker than my arm ran from the cradle of the sphere back into the wall. I was guessing, but it seemed likely Harmon had tied his power supply into the main generators—his brain pattern would live as long as the ship did.

"Ahhh. Mister Ballen. I see. I see you've come to bid. Bid us farewell."

Harmon's voice clicked several times, stopping and starting as if the circuits weren't fully connected. I lifted my gun and placed the barrel a few centimeters from the sphere. "Where's Tana?"

"Mista. Balleballen. Don't be hasty. Hasty." The lights on the sphere pulsed slowly. "Tana. Tana. Ballen. Primary systems check—green. Initial charging sequence online. Maneuvering thrusters—check. Disconnect umbilicals and couplings in six minutes. Ballen, you're a very minor annoyance. You're too late to interfere with my plans. Leave before I lose my patience. Patience. Leave."

I wondered if Harmon's transfer had gone wrong. Maybe his brain was stuck half way between here and Earth. I sure hoped so. I heard the soft ripping noise of someone moving on the carpeting behind me.

"I'm afraid I'm not so generous."

I spun around. Gabriella pushed Tana ahead of her through the doorway, her gun pressing hard against Tana's spine.

"You okay, Tana?"

Tana was shaking, and her brown eyes pooled with tears, but she nodded silently.

"Let her go, Gabriella." I dialed the QuenchGun up to

maximum and pointed it at the flashing sphere. "There's no way you can kill me before I empty my gun through your boss's brain. He probably wouldn't be in much of a condition to pay you after that."

Gabriella laughed. "That won't stop me killing your little friend."

"Maybe, but what good would it do you?" I pressed the QuenchGun directly against the flashing ball. "I'd still kill you. Either way, you don't get paid."

"Gab. Gab. Ri. Ella. I want the girl. I want her. I want. Alive." Harmon's voice filled the room.

I tasted blood and realized I'd bitten my tongue at some point. "You better do as he says."

"Your logic is impeccable." Her face lit up with one of her incredible smiles. "Unfortunately for you, I don't always operate on logic."

Gabriella lifted her gun and started to squeeze the trigger. As she did, Tana squirmed out of her grip, sending them both tumbling as they lost traction against the carpet. Gabriella recovered first, pointed her gun at me and pulled the trigger.

Tana screamed. "No!"

Before I could react, she dived across Gabriella, blocking the stream of needles aimed at me. She spasmed as she absorbed the full impact of the shot, her body crumpling as she hit the wall.

"Tana!"

Harmon's bellow was so loud I thought my eardrums would burst. One of the antennas I'd noticed earlier crackled, and a blue beam flashed from the tip to strike Gabriella. She convulsed, screaming briefly before being hurled into the corridor.

I rushed to Tana and turned her over. She groaned. The needles had penetrated in several places, and at least one had entered directly over her heart.

"Thank you, Joe." Her voice was so low I almost couldn't hear her. "For trying to protect me. No one has ever done anything like that before."

"Ballen? Can you..."

Harmon's voice had changed, but I recognized it all too well. "Ganz?"

There was no reply for several minutes, but finally, he spoke again. "Yes, I'm Ganz." He paused. "It's hard keeping Harmon inside. Can you save her?"

Bright red arterial blood was soaking through Tana's shirt. It might be possible—if I could get her to a full emergency unit immediately, but I doubted it even then. "Harmon?"

"He made a mistake. I wasn't strong enough to fight him when he was in full control, but he moved me here first. I managed to block him as he was transferring. Gained control." Ganz hesitated. "But not soon enough."

"I'm sorry."

"I'm sorry too," Tana said softly. I wasn't sure if it was meant for me or Ganz.

A long panel opened on the far wall, and a wire-mesh cup slid out. "That's a neural interface. I can save her mind, Ballen. Help me do that."

That seemed impossible, but what did I know? I was already dealing with two virtual dead people. Was a third any more improbable? "I'm not sure she'd want to be with you. Harmon told us about the StimJacking."

Tana squeezed my hand weakly. "It's okay, Joe. That was Harmon. Hubert would never hurt me."

Spending eternity with someone who'd sold you over seemed more like a version of hell than a last minute reprieve. I thought I'd prefer to be dead. Despite that, I maneuvered her close to the interface, settling her as best as I could in the ZeeGee.

"Will it hurt, Hubert?" Tana whispered.

"Only briefly." The lights on the sphere danced. "Then you'll never feel pain again. I promise."

She gripped my hand with surprising strength. "Do it, Joe. Please."

I arranged the mesh on her head, adjusting it snugly with Ganz directing me. The sphere flashed in wild patterns almost too fast to see, filling the room with a dancing light that hurt my eyes.

Tana gasped lightly. "Goodbye, Joe."

I kissed her forehead. "Goodbye."

The lights flared, and I shielded my eyes from the glare. Then the globe went completely dark before settling into a more regular pattern of changes.

"Tana? Ganz?"

"I'm here, Joe." It sounded like Tana but not quite. In the background, there was a faint whispering with the voice of both Tana and Ganz saying "We're here."

I looked down at Tana's body and stood up clumsily. "You're okay?"

"Everything is fine. It feels funny." A laugh tinkled out from the speaker. "It feels warm too. Like Stimming, but closer."

"Ballen?" Ganz' voice seemed to become more prominent. "I can't stop the launch sequence. It's automatic. There are barely three minutes left."

I edged towards the doorway. "I'm not ready to be the world's first human Jump experiment."

The mixed Ganz/Tana voice sounded again, the lights flashing wildly. "The Atoll ship will be in range before we can Jump."

I stopped. The Atolls would never let *Ananta* get away. The starship represented Earth's dreams and hopes. Even if the Jump failed, her launch would be a huge victory for the people of Earth and a massive thumb in the eye to the Atolls. "Isn't that what you want? To stop the ship? You know, all that stuff about destroying life in other dimensions?"

There was a pause that seemed to last for hours, but in reality could have only been a few seconds. When the voice spoke again, it seemed hesitant.

"It feels like I've been inside here such a long time," Ganz said. "There's so much I don't know, so much I'm unsure of. The analysis I did earlier... "

I remembered what Harmon had said about the rate of time and how slow it was communicating at human speeds. "If you're going to tell me you were wrong—I might dismantle you myself."

"Harmon had access to data he didn't let me see. Far more than I could ever have known. There are correlations in the research I was unaware of that are suggestive of a different model."

"A lot of people died for your idea—including Tana."

"I know." The voice was small and quiet. "Believe me, I know."

"Override the launch sequence—postpone it until we're sure." It was Tana's voice that came through more strongly.

"What do you think I've been trying to do?" Ganz sounded

desperate. "You don't understand what it takes to keep Harmon in check. He's fighting. I have to focus on holding him down, or he'll take over again."

"If you launch, the Atolls will fire on you." I glanced toward the doorway. Time must be getting tight.

"Help I/we/us, Ballen." Ganz' words came out as a tortured cry, then seemed to meld with Tana's. "I/we/us can't take responsibility for this."

Were Ganz and Tana human anymore? Would they act in the best way for humanity or what was best for their co-joined electronic mind-meld? I remembered what Dollie had said the night we'd talked outside Charlie's. *No one can take infinite responsibility.* She was right, but she was right in another way too. I couldn't expect a couple of academics to make this choice. Both of them had lived the better part of their lives in isolation, cocooned from the turmoil of the real world, and now they were entirely disconnected from it. This had become *my* decision, whether I wanted it or not.

Earth needed *Ananta* to succeed. *I* needed it to succeed. We couldn't stagnate any longer. If that made the Atolls unhappy, then they'd have to learn to live with it. They'd put Earth through far worse. I also couldn't help but think of Tana and what she'd gone through. What life would she have if they stayed? "Here you're a circus attraction," I finally said out loud. "I think Tana deserves better than that. Launch. I'll take care of the Atoll ship."

The lights rippled, and the strange combined voice sounded again. "Less than one minute."

I nodded, not even sure if they could see me. "Look after each other."

I hauled myself down the corridor and turned towards the exit. Gabriella had disappeared, but I didn't have time to be cautious. Left at the next corner and then a long dive down to the airlock. I sealed it and hit the controls to disconnect the access corridor. As I did, I sensed movement behind me and whirled around.

Dollie was holding her side with one hand, and in the other, one of Logan's Shock-Wands.

"Logan?" I asked.

She stepped closer. "I'm not sure. I did what I could."

I wished I had the time to sit down and talk things through with Dollie, preferably over several whiskeys—but I turned to head toward the ore carrier I'd spotted earlier.

Dollie grabbed my arm. "Where are you going?"

"Ganz and Tana need help. The Atoll ship is nearly here. They'll blow them out of the sky if they can."

Dollie lifted a perfectly defined eyebrow. "*Ganz* and Tana?"

"Long story and I'm short on time."

"Okay. What's the plan?" Dollie looked me straight in the eye. "You don't have one, do you?"

"Not exactly."

"Don't think you're getting away from me now, Soldier. When I get my nails into a guy he's mine till I say otherwise."

With that, she dived down the corridor ahead of me. A few minutes later we were at the airlock of the ore carrier and swinging inside.

I stopped her at the 'lock. "You don't have to do this."

"Neither do you." Dollie pulled away, heading for the flight deck.

The control room was as cramped as any I'd been in, but I didn't stop to complain. Some comedian had glued a glass box containing an old-fashioned can opener onto the bulkhead over the controls with the instructions, "In Emergency, Break Glass." I wriggled into the pilot's chair, pulling the straps tight around me. This was going to get ugly, and I didn't want to end up as jelly on the first hard maneuver. Dollie slid painfully into the co-pilot's seat and did the same.

"What now?" she asked breathlessly.

I tried to ignore the quiver in her voice. The armor implants had saved her life, but she was still hurting and what I had in mind wasn't going to help her. "You know how to run block? That's what we're going to do. Hopefully, we'll come out the other side intact."

"I've dated football players," Dollie grunted as she activated her view screens and switched them to the RearView pickups. "And you're not the only pilot here."

I checked the sensors. The *Ananta* had undocked from the

High-Rig and was accelerating away from us. We were already falling behind. I hit the controls to unlock the docking clamps and punched in a burn to move us away from the station too. "Where's the Atoll ship?"

"Aft and thirty degrees high. We need to gain at least three degrees."

I brought the thrusters up to one hundred percent. The ore ship responded like an asteroid and even using full power, I was barely keeping pace between the *Ananta* and the Atoll ship. I checked the loading screen and cursed. There was a full cargo of ore on board, but even empty I wasn't sure we'd have done much better.

"Multiple heat signatures from the Atoll ship. At least four missiles." The bulkheads rattled until every bolt and rivet seemed to be screaming. Dollie had to shout to make herself heard.

I triggered another burst on the thrusters to push us upwards, hoping to lift the ore carrier in front of the missiles. "Where?"

Dollie glanced at her screens. "Roll fourteen degrees port."

I maneuvered the ship, and seconds later the missiles slammed into us. The ship lurched drunkenly, but the warheads pounded into the ore containers rather than the superstructure. I leveled our flight, trying to cover the *Ananta* as much as possible.

"Another launch," she gasped. "Pitch seventy degrees and roll nine degrees starboard on my mark."

The wait was so long I started to wonder if I'd lost Dollie, then she called out. The ship bucked as I triggered the move, the superstructure groaning as it fought against the maneuvers. The ship kicked immediately as the missiles detonated against us.

I checked my screens. "We're losing the cargo. We won't survive another hit."

"They're not breaking off." Dollie looked over at me. "We're done, Joe."

I punched the comms button, signaling *Ananta*. "You have a couple of minutes. That's it."

There was a delay, then I heard the combined Ganz/Tana voice. "Jump sequence ninety percent. We need more—"

A banshee scream of tearing metal deafened us. The cargo containers were breaking free. Dollie shouted over the sound of twisting metal.

"Eight missiles launched." She smashed her fist into the controls in front of her. "We're screwed, Joe."

I knew she was right but couldn't give in. "Bearing? Distance?"

"Coming in hot. Roll seventeen, pitch fifty-three. Mark!"

Ananta glowed on the viewscreen. They'd reached critical velocity, and the Jump drive had activated. Its outline started to shimmer, the Jump only seconds away. The ore carrier staggered, and the ship snapped as the backbone superstructure tore apart. The control room pitched down, and I saw two of the missiles streak towards the *Ananta*.

"Joe?" Dollie lifted her hand to her mouth.

"Nothing we can do."

The ore ship tumbled down and down, the motion making me nauseous despite my experience. Then *Ananta* vanished. Nothing but a retinal blur of a phantom ship left behind. That ship...I'd helped to build it... gone. The ship that had cost me half my body and almost my life. It worked! I felt a confusion of triumph and victory, mixed with the screams of a billion dead alien worlds and the voice of Ganz and Tana... we're here, Joe... The missiles vanished into the distance without exploding.

"Tell me this thing has lifeboats," I shouted, the ore carrier lurching heavily as another explosion rattled through the superstructure.

Dollie didn't answer. I unfastened my seat harness and hauled myself over to her, tearing open her straps and dragging her out of the control room. The corridor was thick with smoke, and the acidic smell of burning metal scoured my airways. The first lifeboat bay was empty. I scurried to the next, pulling her through the narrow hatch.

After fastening Dollie into an acceleration chair, I jumped into the second one, punching the big red button as I strapped myself in. The launch sequence triggered, and the chair kicked me in the ribs. I blacked out momentarily with the explosive thrust, then Earth appeared as a swollen globe ahead of us. A series of bright flares erupted around the lifeboat as debris from the ship impacted the upper levels of the atmosphere, forming momentary dazzling fireballs.

"What's going to happen to us now?" Dollie said, between choked coughs.

We'd aided in the loss of the Jumpship and destroyed a freighter, not to mention shooting up the High-Rig and probably starting a war. I had no idea what the penalty for all that might be, but it wasn't going to be pretty. "With my luck, they'll lock me up in prison for space piracy and forget where they put me."

"Poor thing. I'll buy you an eye patch and visit every month."

The tenuous gases tugged violently at the lifeboat's nose. I grabbed the controls to compensate and keep us stable. Dollie reached out and wrapped her hands around mine on the control stick.

"Hang on," I said. "This is going to be a wild ride"

Dollie's eyes locked with mine, and I melted into her smile.

"That's just how I like it, Joe."

Also available

PERIMETER - Deceit has no boundaries

Joe Ballen's working on a new ore-processing platform in the harsh environment around Mercury. When a savage Atoll attack decimates his crew, Joe is injured and must return to Earth to recover. While it's a setback for the project, at least it means he can rebuild his relationship with his wife after nearly a year away.

But then the security forces come calling. Vital starship engineering files are missing, and without them Earth has no hope of escaping Atoll domination. Someone has to locate the files, and Ballen is bulldozed into the not-so-choice assignment.

But he's not the only one in the hunt. As Joe struggles to find the data, he becomes tangled up in a high-stakes game of cat and mouse. It's a journey that will take him to the perilous depths of space, where no one is quite what they seem. Can old enemies ever make good allies? And can Joe trust even the people closest to him?

Ballen's back in another action-packed sci-fi noir thriller, guaranteed to keep you turning the pages.

TRANSFORMATION PROTOCOL - Change can be deadly

With his life crumbling around him, Joe Ballen is close to going out in a blaze, fueled by cheap alcohol and self-hatred. But when something "out there" starts destroying spaceships and stations, the only Jump-Ship available to investigate is the Shokasta—locked away by Joe in an attempt to get justice for his family.

But when an old friend offers him the chance to return to space in the hunt for a missing ship, it proves more complicated than either of them imagined. With all sides of the political spectrum looking to grab a piece of the newly explored star systems, Joe soon realizes that some people will go to any lengths to get what they want, and are willing to sacrifice anyone in the process.

And when Joe's past catches up with him in a way he couldn't have seen coming, he must battle enemies new and old as well as his own inner demons.

The Joe Ballen series is a near future, sci-fi noir thriller series, featuring a smart-mouthed space engineer, engaging characters, cynical humor, and plausible science.

Acknowledgements

Thank you for reading. I hope you enjoyed this novel. This book would not have been possible without the help and support of my family, friends, and other members of the writing community. I'd like to thank them all. I would especially like to thank my wife, Hilary, for her constant love, support and patience. A special mention goes to my editor, Michelle Dunbar, who went above and beyond the call of duty in helping thrash the kinks out of my (very!) messy draft and transform it into something I feel proud of.

The best way to help any writer, especially an indie like myself, is by word-of-mouth. Please consider leaving a review on Amazon. Even if it's only a line or two, it's very much appreciated. Also, please look out for other independent authors. There are a lot of us out there who work hard to bring you stories that you would never see through commercial publishers.

For a complete list of my fiction, please visit my website (davidmkelly.net) and consider signing up for my free update newsletter. I won't share your information with anyone for any reason and won't bombard your mailbox either. I only send updates when I have a new book or special deal for my readers to know about.

Thanks again.

David M. Kelly

About The Author

David M. Kelly writes fast-paced, near future sci-fi thrillers with engaging characters, cynical humor, and plausible science. He is the author of the Joe Ballen series and the short story collection Dead Reckoning And Other Stories. He has been published in Canadian SF magazine Neo-opsis.

Originally from the wild and woolly region of Yorkshire, England, David now lives in wild and rocky Northern Ontario, Canada, with his patient and long-suffering wife, Hilary. He is passionate about science, especially astronomy and physics, and is a rabid science news follower. When he's not writing, you can find him driving his Corvette or exploring the local hiking trails.

Find out more at davidmkelly.net

To sign up for the mailing list, go to davidmkelly.net/subscribe/

You can also follow David through the following channels:

Goodreads: www.goodreads.com/DavidMKelly

Twitter: www.twitter.com/David_Kelly_SF

Facebook http://www.facebook.com/David.Kelly.SF